To Claire
You are amazing.

MW00986940

DARK CITY OMEGA

BEASTS OF GATAMORA

ELIZABETH STEPHENS

Elizabeth Stephens

Cover Design by Regina Wamba (reginawamba.com)
Cover and Character Illustrations by Lu Tenorio (@lhunatica)
Maps of Gatamora by Lu Tenorio (@lhunatica)
Edited by Happy Ever Author (www.happyeverauthor.com)

THE BEASTS OF GATAMORA

Dark City Omega

Shadowlands Omega

Gang Mountain Omega

Fallen Omega

Glass Flats Omega

www.booksbyelizabeth.com

To the Dark City Omega Alpha
and Beta readers who waited over a year for this...

...and to baby Fiona, flower of my heart,
who inspired the delay.

Gatamora
The Rookery
Prayersville
Glass Flats
The Guild
Dark City
Emerald Plains
Town of Teeth
Trash City
Gang Mountain
Paradise
Ruby City
Mirage City
Sea of Zaoul
Cliffs of Oblivion
Shadowlands
Gold City
Hjiel
N
W
E
S

North Island
The Rookery
Prayersville
Glass Flats
The Guild
Dark City
Trash City
Gang Mountain
Paradise River
Ruby City
N
Mirage City
Sea of Zaoul
E
S
Cliffs of Oblivion

ECHO
TRASH CITY

I'VE NEVER BEEN SO AFRAID.

I've never been so afraid…and I know all about fear. No, not fear — Fear. That irreverent yet loyal madame. She's been my only unfailing companion these twenty-eight long years. When I'm wide awake in the deepest parts of the night, listening to the sounds of larger creatures tearing smaller ones apart, she's there.

When I ascended as an Omega and was exiled from the Beta compound I'd been living in for over a decade and tossed into Paradise Hole she was there, waiting with arms outstretched, fangs flashing, wicked claws reaching, reaching, reaching out to welcome me back into her embrace. And I ran to her, because I knew that from this bitch, there was no escape.

Escape what? There'd never been any hope for that as a Beta and there sure as hell wasn't any hope for that after I woke with my body on fire, soaking wet with that painful arousal that Betas are blissfully immune to. That was six weeks ago, now. Six weeks since November, Lima, Antonio, Maven, Victor, Romeo, João, Hannah, Yankee, Jesus, and the other Betas I dared to call family cast me out of our shared home and shoved me through Prayersville's gates, high and imposing, all shiny and chrome.

I didn't expect them to try to protect or hide me, but what hurt most was that they didn't need to physically push me down the road. I would have gone on my own.

They didn't even give me time to grab my stuff or any supplies. I think maybe, they didn't expect me to make it very long — certainly not six weeks and counting. I don't think *I* expected to make it this long, either. But I did — I have — and now, as I scramble hand over foot up the mountain of trash, trying to get to Trash City where I might be able to hide my scent, it occurs to me that six weeks might be all I get.

I can hear them on the wind.

Different Alphas from different cities have different preferred methods of travel. Glass City Alphas use carriages, Dark City ride motorcycles, Gold City use camels, Shadowlands and Mirage City use horses, Ruby City are conniving enough not to bother with land travel at all and are content to steal Betas trying to cross the Sea of Zaoul by boat…

Judging by the cacophony of sounds, I count no less than *six* different Alpha gangs converging dangerously close to where I'm at and if they catch me… No. I have no intention of being caught —

— *alive.* I won't be caught *alive.*

My foot punches through a cardboard box and sinks into whatever was once inside of it. Wet and squishy, whatever it was, it reeks. A rabbit must have burrowed its way into the box and couldn't get back out. Its corpse is fresh, covered in maggots. My throat muscles work, vomit rushing into my mouth, but I know what I need to do. A scent like this might just be strong enough to save me.

Pushing aside the wet cardboard flap, I reach into the rabbit's open stomach. I dip my fingers in the black, rancid blood and smear it across my chest, around my neck and around both my wrists. Behind my ears, too.

I wrap a torn bandana around my nose and concentrate on just breathing out of my mouth as I climb the trash heap, collecting stenches as I go. By the time I slide down the other side, my arms and legs are shaking, my eyes are burning and bile is prairie-dogging up and down the back of my throat. I stagger into the center of the small clearing where trash is packed down and covered by large slabs of discarded metal, making a sort of floor.

It pops and bends underneath my feet and I hold out my arms for balance, like I'm on a boat. I remember being on a boat, but only once. I'd liked it. I'd been young, on a boat of orphans bound for Ruby City. That was the first time I met November. She'd been eighteen and one of the rebels who helped steal us off of the Ruby City Berserker's ships. I'd been six and thought she was a queen. Even though her fist was tightest on my collar when she shoved me out the Prayersville Beta compound, I still think she is.

She saved me once and I knew that, when she tossed me out of Prayersville, it was to save the other Betas who lived there. There is no doubt Alphas would have ransacked Prayersville if they knew the compound was keeping an Omega from them. It's happened before. And she couldn't have killed me, either. If they found out what she'd done, it would have been worse than if she'd tried to keep me.

No, as much as it hurts, what she did was right. What was necessary.

Wind picks up, like it senses the battle at my back and is ratcheting up tension to set the scene. The sky is already dark — it's always dark in Paradise Hole, which is anywhere in the outer lands that isn't an Alpha city. Dark and grey. Not a light grey either, but a dark, oppressive grey-blue-purple that makes me think I'm stuck in a world that's getting perpetually smaller and smaller around me, shrinking until one day I won't be able to escape.

It wasn't always like this. There was a time before Paradise Hole when the entirety of Gatamora was rich and abundant. A time before cities. A time before someone gave names to the different pheremones that distinguish Alpha from Beta from Omega. That's all it is. Just a scent — an instinct. A telling premonition of something that could be. Everyone is born a Beta, though just over half of Betas ascend as Alphas, if you're lucky. An even luckier few ascend as Berserkers. An even unluckier few ascend as Omegas.

Omegas, whose scents appeal so strongly to Alphas and whose extraordinary gifts make them precious, were fought over during the Alpha Wars. Cities were built and walled and resources were preciously reaped and hoarded within them — Omegas included. Berserkers, too strong to be challenged, took control. Alphas fell in line beneath them and occasionally challenged and took down ruling Berserkers by forming packs. Betas, rejected from the Cities — or enslaved within them — fled and retreated to compounds in the swamps and deserts only to return if they ascend as Alphas… or are enslaved by Alphas as Omegas.

During the Wars, once fertile, paradisical lands, over time, became this grey, muddy, murky tomb that stretches miles and miles — all the way to the sea of Zaoul and across it — that we no longer call Paradise but Paradise Hole, where sunshine and salvation have become things of a history long past. Where the best hope for salvation for a runaway Omega like me is a compound made out of trash.

I slip over the pocked metal floor and arrive in front of a small door that you wouldn't be able to spot if you didn't know it was there. Built directly into the trash pile, it's just a flap of jumbled pieces of metal strung together by rope. Any Alpha would be able to tear through it with a slash of their claws. The rebels of Trash City built the place on the fundamental creed all of us non-Alphas live by: Hide to survive. Resistance is futile.

I knock on one of the metal slats paneling the door and a shiver racks my body even though I'm dressed in most of my clothes. Last time I traded with Trash City, the entrance opened quickly, but not today.

The roar of two horses and an engine screeches through the cold fangs of the wind. *The Alphas are converging.* I duck my chin lower into my hoodie and knock again.

The door swings open. Bright blue light hits me and even though it hurts, I blink my eyes open and let them search my pupils for the signs. There's no red or gold tint to my irises. My pupils don't refract light.

The light dims as it parts around a shadow. A gruff, muffled voice says, "What do you have to trade?"

Not much. I'm low on supplies. I'll have to give them everything I've got to hide here for the night. "I have a jar of lavender oil, a jar of pesto and the dried meat off of three rabbits."

"You pressed the oil yourself?"

I nod sharply.

She doesn't answer and I can feel a question floating in the weighted air. A motorcycle engine backfires in the distance. "I'm good with plants."

"Hm." She considers.

I lean forward onto the tips of my toes. I hand over the jars and watch her open one then the other. She nods and pockets both.

"Lemme see the rabbits." I hand the meat over. "You got the skins?"

Fuck. "I've got one skin." I traded one and used the other already.

"Good stuff, but that's not enough," the woman says. "If you're good with plants, you could work here for a month as payment. Otherwise, no dice." She snorts as she reads the expression on my face. "Yeah, I didn't think so. Anyway, good luck. Thanks for the oil." She takes a step back and starts to close the door.

Ordinarily, I wouldn't be this bold, but this is a desperate day. I shove my hand against the door, blocking it from slapping shut. The cardboard scrap against my hand is dry this time, making me think mad thoughts about lotion. *Six weeks without lotion is a death sentence. If I don't survive today, please send me to a heaven where there's tubs of lotion big enough to bathe in.*

"You can have my boots."

She jerks back, recoiling like I punched her in the chin. "Your boots?"

"Yes."

She pokes her head outside and glances around, like this is a trap. And it is. But I don't tell her that.

Outside where the harsh, fluorescent blue light can't quite reach, I can see her a little more clearly. She's bundled in rags, most of which are black. A mask shields the bottom half of her face and she's got on goggles — likely for the blue light — that stick out of her head like bulbous eyeballs. Tufts of short, ragged white-blonde hair shoot out of her headband that looks almost…clean? But most surprising? She's got a gun slung across her chest and she points it around at me and at the trash surrounding me.

I flinch and don't manage to stifle my gasp. I've seen two guns in my whole life and both were in the hands of Alphas. I've never seen a Beta scavenger with a gun before and immediately, my mind fires with questions. No, just one question… Where'd she get it? It's on the tip of my tongue to ask, but at the last moment, I manage to restrain myself. It won't get me anywhere, asking her about that gun and, more likely than not, I don't want to know the answer.

She lifts her goggles. Under her dirt-streaked face, she's white. She has green eyes and right now, they're ringed in red prints from her goggles. They make her look funny, but I don't laugh. "What are you?"

"Just a Beta on my own."

"The fuck you are." She reaches out and grabs me by the jaw, pulling my facemask down. She tilts my chin up to the blue light and inspects me for the longest moments of my life because, in the background, I can hear sounds…new sounds…sounds that I know aren't a motorcycle backfiring, even though I tell myself again and again that's all they are… *gunshots. The Alphas have converged. The fight to find me has begun…*

"Shit. You reek," she hisses.

I rip my chin out of her grip. "I've been scavenging."

The woman looks at me more closely, leans in and sniffs. "You've been doing more than that." She pushes me back and takes a step away from me, pointing the tip of her gun at my chest. "Can't get a good scent on you underneath all that *perfume* you're wearing, but you're pretty underneath all them rags. Too pretty. And not damn near skinny enough to be a scavenger."

"I'm a good hunter." I am. It's how I've survived at all. "And a better gatherer. I know what plants to eat and what not to eat. I could teach…"

"That don't explain the way you look. Brown skin, dark freckles like you've been lying out in the sun."

"What sun?" I sneer. Everyone knows there's only sunshine in the cities and sometimes, not even then. Never in Dark City, which is the closest one.

She ignores me. "And that red hair? Nah." She shakes her head. "If you were serious about convincing me you were a scavenger, you'd have cut it off. You stand out like a damn tulip in all this trash."

I clench, but try not to show it. I keep breathing in and out through my mouth, itching to pull my mask back into place — both because I don't like the way she's looking at me and also because of the smell. I've never smelled so horrible. And she's right. I *should* have cut off my hair. Should have tried to darken it somehow. The startling red color is a weird combination with my light brown skin tone — at least that's what November and other folks at the compound used to say. But I never had much, and I like my hair, as red and as puffy and matted and tangled as it is. It's *mine*…and if she takes my trade, it'll be one of the only things I have left.

The woman grunts and shoves me back. "You should get outta here. They might mistake you for…"

"I'm not," I tell her, but my voice catches.

When she smirks, my heart performs a circus inside my chest to an audience of organs. They all feel too small, shrunken and desiccated, like the rest of me. But they keep working. They keep fighting.

She shakes her head. "Clever, but not clever enough."

She cocks her chin to dismiss me just as a violent roar fills the air. Her hand flinches on her gun, startling me, and that's when it comes to me. A final act of desperation, so much bolder than I knew myself capable of.

"I'm not leaving. You're going to have to shoot me."

"Don't think I won't…"

"I'm counting on it. But you think they won't hear the shot? I heard at least six different transports — horses and engines with them. You might not be an Omega, but I am," I hiss that terrifying truth. I watch her face change, first into melting wax before it rapidly solidifies into a horrified grimace. "What do you think's gonna happen if you shoot one of the last Omegas left? What do you think they'll do to you when they find the body?"

The body. Not *my* body. Because I'm not willing to die just yet. Willing might be a stretch, but *ready*. I'm not ready to give up, not unless they catch me. I know what happens if I'm caught though, the kind of life that awaits me. *Trapped.* If it comes down to it, I'll be ready if they catch me.

"Fuck. Come in quick. But don't you tell anybody and you get out as soon as the war party clears. And don't even think about scavenging the bodies — those are ours. You got me?"

"Yeah, I got you," I say, shoving inside and pulling my mask back up to cover my nose. I wouldn't go near an Alpha with a thousand-foot pole, not even a corpse, no matter how good the loot might be.

She closes the door behind me, leaving the two of us caged together in a small room awash in blinding blue light. A ramp — also made out of metal-plated trash — descends into the bowels of Trash City where roads and roads of trash form the dirty Beta underworld, forgotten by Alphas in their towering cities.

We wind through streets made of tin and cardboard and compressed plastic, passing marketplaces with stalls selling all kinds of junk that I'd kill to barter for, but can't. I spy rags that pass for clothing, the occasional fur, all kinds of herbal concoctions their sellers boast contain medicinal, if not magical, properties, food — even *bread* — and…is that soap? *Fuuuuuuuck.* My feet stutter before the tip of my guide's gun presses against my spine.

"Keep moving, *beautiful,*" she sneers the insult.

I wish it didn't hurt, but it does. It's just a reminder of my place here and how short my lifespan's likely going to be all because of some stupid genetic marker. "Fuck you."

"Ha." She lunges forward and snatches up a swatch of my hair. She holds me still and leans forward, her cheek brushing mine… "You'd like that, wouldn't you?"

"Your breath stinks worse than I do," I snap back.

She shoves me forward and I fall, tripping into a group of people haggling over what look like towels — actual towels — who shove me back upright with hisses and angry grunts. Turning from them, I follow the path down, down, down, turning left at a place that'd be a stretch to call a bar and then right again when the dormitories start.

The dormitories are actually just plastic and trash-cobbled walls. There aren't any doors, but that doesn't matter. The fact that there are walls at all is more privacy than anyone living in a compound would get. She guides me to an empty stall and I stand in the center of it. There's nothing on the floor that I could cobble together into a bed, but that's okay. It's clean. For trash.

"You gonna watch me all night? I promise, I don't make for a good show."

She snorts. "Nah. I'm waiting for those boots."

I tense and think about begging, but don't. Instead, I sit down, pull out the last of the rabbit I got and yank off my boots. She whistles when I toss them up to her one at a time. "Damn. These are actually good boots. Scuffed to shit, but the soles are still attached to the leather." She smells them. "Shit smells real, too. Where'd you get 'em?"

I hesitate, then tell her, "Prayersville."

Her smug smile falls just a little and she looks at the rabbit skin I pass up to her. "How long ago?"

"Six weeks. Take or leave a week or two."

"Fuck. That long ago?"

I nod. "Yeah."

"And you've made it this far?"

I nod again.

"Shit."

"Yeah. Here. Take it." I thrust the rabbit up at her again.

"Nah." She shakes her head and shoves her goggles up onto her forehead. "Keep it." She hesitates, fidgeting with the shoes she's got looped over one shoulder. I try not to look at them. The loss already stings. I flex my toes in my thick socks, grateful for them now more than ever.

"Sorry," she offers with a shrug, but it sounds like *I'm sorry for your loss.* And that loss? My own life. I just haven't realized it yet.

I don't say anything. Just keep rifling through my bag, trying to find my space blanket. A high-value item, I had to trade six rabbits for it and I'm sure it'll be the next thing that goes.

"I'm Merlin."

I nod, unsure of what to say… My gut instinct is just to keep quiet and tell her to shove off, but it's been so long since the last time I introduced myself to anyone, I'm compelled to tell her, "Echo."

"Echo. You kept your Beta name, huh?" Most Betas are given names from the military alphabet and most change them when they get to be fifteen or seventeen or so, after it's sure they won't ascend as an Omega or an Alpha. I didn't.

I nod.

"I uhh…" She crouches down just outside of my open-door cage and rubs her chin. She glances around quickly and, with the coast clear, she leans in. "So what's it like? Being an Omega?"

I shake my head and shrug. "Uninteresting." It's not true, but I don't bother telling her about the life of a scavenger. She already lives it.

"You don't have any secret powers or anything?"

I shake my head and spread my blanket out on the floor.

"No mind reading?"

Head shake.

"No telekinesis?"

Head shake.

"Can't change into a bird?"

Head shake.

"Can't even change your eye color?"

My lips twitch at that. Woah. Was that a smile? Not quite, but close. It's been a while.

"Shit. You got the short end of the stick, beautiful. You're an Alpha magnet with no extra powers to protect you," she says bluntly, as if this wasn't something I already knew. And then more quietly, "And you still made it six weeks." She whistles between the gap in her front teeth.

The sound chills me. I don't like it. Because while sounding impressed, she makes me think that I've already outlived my timeline.

"Alright, fine then. Keep your rabbit outsides and your rabbit insides, too. I'd give you back the boots, but you know I can't. Got a city to run here."

"It's not a city, it's a compound."

She smirks. "For now."

I give her a funny look.

"Want the rabbits back or not? I won't ask a third time." She shakes the pelt and sack of dried meat in front of me and I reach up and take the bundles gladly. Getting back the dried, salted rabbit is a gift. One I don't take lightly. I squirrel it away into my pack before she reconsiders, along with the rabbit fur I'll have to make shoes out of later.

"But Echo?"

I look up at her.

She offers me something perhaps even more rare than rabbit. Even more rare than boots. A smile full enough to show all of her teeth — the ones that are left. "You're gonna die soon, but until then, I'm rootin' for you."

I snort.

"Need to be out by morning." She turns to walk away, beat up sneakers squeaking on the patchwork metal flooring. From around the corner I hear her say, "And thanks for the boots."

ECHO

GANG MOUNTAIN

MY TOES ARE COLD. SCRATCH THAT. MY TOES ARE fucking freezing in my rabbit skin shoes — if you can even call them that. It's colder today, more miserable. There's a sticky fog that lingers in the air like icicles suspended from the stars. Every time I move, it's like those imagined icicles stab deeper into my clothes. I shiver. And then I shiver some more.

Fear is present again today, though I don't know why. She just stands in the woods waving at me every once in a while. Pain's lurking behind her, even further back, just waiting to pounce on my feet anytime I move them. She's my other friend. My only other friend, besides Fear. Pain likes me quite a bit, too.

My heart stings and I rub the thin skin over it as I kneel at the edge of the river — well, the *water*, as pitiful as it is. My space blanket's under me, stopping the mud from seeping through the knees of my pants, but not the cold as I try my best to rinse the nasty dead rabbit stench out my clothes. It's slow going in the shallow, muddy pool.

I was able to trade some dried rabbit for a hunk of soap before I left Trash City early that morning. The vendor took pity on me. Well, his wife did. She took one whiff of me and tossed a scrap of soap my way. I only offered her the dried rabbit Merlin let me keep and that her husband had not so politely declined afterward. Even as small a chunk as it is, it's a gift. I haven't had access to soap in a long time. Much longer than six weeks…

A twig snaps in the forest behind me and I freeze, fully prepared to abandon everything in my possession and run… but it's nothing. There's nothing there. Nothing…but Fear. I release the frozen air in my lungs and go back to scrubbing and, as I do, I remind myself what Merlin told me. The Alphas battling yesterday had moved further west — those that survived, anyway, and it didn't look like many had according to her. Even for a Beta, she seemed way too excited by that fact.

I didn't ask follow ups. I just formed a plan to head south to the Way Station. An informal Beta trading post just north of the Mirage City ports, it's my best shot at stocking up on supplies. I plan to hunt as many animals as I can on my way down, press more oil, gather more herbs, berries — whatever the frick I need to in order to be able to barter. I need hardware — tools, better knives, another fire starter. *But I* want *bread. Fuck, I want bread.* No. Bread's a luxury I can't afford.

After I stock up on stuff I actually need, I'll come up with a new plan. Maybe, I'll go east and try to make it past the trolls over Paradise River, around Dark City to the plains. Even though they still call it Paradise Hole and say it's just as dangerous and inhospitable as this swampy forest or the marshlands furth south or the brutal ice world north of Glass City, at least it'll be warm. Dry and warm. I'm sick of the wet and the cold.

A shiver racks my body at the thought and I glance up, my shoulders slumping against the barely there breeze. I look up, past the spindly black trees reaching endlessly for a forgotten sun. Their branches are all gnarled, like the fingers of the dead clawing out of their graves. If you manage to survive the climb past them, you can reach dry land up the mountain, but only the desperate or idiots are that brave.

Alpha gangs live up there, those who reject city life or were exiled and formed dangerous marauding communities of their own. Passing around the base of Gang Mountain is dangerous enough. The only thing more dangerous would have been heading for the Ganjor mountains up north with the lack of supplies I have, or east directly into Dark City. I hear the young Berserker there is dying for an Omega. Any Omega'll do. Just one that will cement his power after he killed the last Berserker of Dark City and took over rule.

It won't be me, though.

As clean as they'll ever be, I get up and hang yesterday's clothes on a few low branches above the small fire crackling in my metal fire pit. I drag my muddy space blanket over to it too, sit down and hold my feet up towards the flames.

Worry has me gnawing on my lower lip. My rabbit-skin shoes aren't holding up in the damp soil and they'll hold up even worse in the marshes, the closer I get to Paradise River. I glance up Gang Mountain at the sound of a faraway scream carried on the wind…or maybe it was just the wind. I shiver.

Yeah. Just the wind. I return my focus to my shoes but as I tip my chin down, a flash of light pulls my attention to the dark forest to my left. I twist my upper body to look and meet the enormous eyes of a beast.

I sit and watch it in stunned disbelief. Time passes. Enough time that my heart starts to thump like boots on a gangplank, slow…but heavy. Inevitably doomed. I don't look away from its eyes and it doesn't look away from me as it just sits there, watching. A goddamn beast.

No, a goddamn Berserker.

The creature is massive, larger than a rhino, nearing the size of an elephant. He's got huge back legs and even more massive front legs with weighted fists the size of my backpack — when it's full, which it hasn't been for a while — dripping off of the ends of each. He's got claws. I can't see them now, buried as they are in the mud on the other side of the piddly little river, but I know they're there.

His head is the size of a big ugly boulder and his eyes are each the size of my fists. Small compared to the rest of him, I can still see those eyes in the dark by their gleam. Their shiny centers are surrounded by liquid gold that shimmers in the firelight. He has a flat snout and beneath it, his enormous mouth hangs open. Silver venom drips from all of his knife-like teeth.

I take him in, all of him, as I sit there and wonder how in the universe he found me. I was told the Alphas had dispersed. Nobody mentioned any Berserkers. Why would they have? Berserkers are lords who sit high and mighty in their glass castles. They send other Alphas to do their dirty work. I know I would if I had that option. I'd *never* come into

Paradise Hole. Not for anything. No matter how valuable and I'm nothing valuable except for a symbol of status he can show off at parties. I don't have an ounce of magic in me.

My gaze darts away from him quickly, just long enough to be able to make sure he's alone. He is. I don't let that rattle me. The fact that he must have killed all the other Alphas who'd come hunting for me means nothing. Yeah…nothing at all.

I grab the edge of my bag and the Berserker, from so far away, flares his nostrils. I jump, but don't let that deter me. Instead, I focus on my waterproof bag. I pull it onto my lap and reach into it blindly, knowing exactly where everything is without sight.

I locate the handle of my knife and grab onto it. I'm going to have to be fast because yes, Merlin was right — I *am* going to die soon — but it's not going to be in some Alpha City dungeon or chained to a Berserker's bed. I promised myself a long time ago, I'd never let it get that far.

I take in a deep breath and the Berserker beast shifts. His eyes flare, the gold darkening to deep brown or black. That darkness bleeds across the gold like ink swirling through water. And then he shakes his massive head. A low growl tumbles out of his throat and his Mohawk's brown and blonde fur ripples. I get the sense he's condemning me already, but it doesn't matter. As of now, I don't have to obey. *But if he bites me, all that changes…*

"An Omega is nothing but a toy." That's what November said to me right after she threw me out of the compound.

"I won't be."

"You won't have a choice. It's biology. Once the first Alpha scents you, he'll bite you, bond you, and you'll be done. You won't be you. You'll be his."

"Then I'll die."

"Yes. You will either way."

My body is pulsing in a way it only has once before, right when my Omega instinct first flared. Then, it was hot and bright and painful enough to pull me out of sleep and off of my bed, but it only lasted a few minutes. Just long enough for me to know it was there. But now it lingers underneath my skin, making it feel too thin, like I'm not full of butterflies, but full of maggots, already halfway to the grave.

The Berserker drops his head. My hand firms around the hilt of my knife and his shimmery fur ripples again as his forearm muscles engage. He slinks forward, splashing into the water with a sense of finality that has me tensing my abs and holding my breath.

The Berserker moves at the same time I do. He's already in motion, charging me as quickly as a lightning strike, but he's not going to be fast enough. I have the knife out of my bag and take a deep breath. I ignore the horrible way my skin sizzles and the way my pulse pounds through me to the beat of his steps, shaking the whole damn world. My Omega instinct are kicking, demanding submission.

Never.

I roll my left thigh out, feel for my pulsing artery through my three layers of pants. He's almost on me… He takes a flying leap. I stab straight down in a motion I've practiced many, many times. I don't even close my eyes and the shock of it — seeing the blade sinking into my skin so easily —

makes me slow to react when he lands on the ground next to my frozen feet.

My good buddy Pain doesn't even have time to comfort me before the Berserker's huge paw slams down on my shin. I expect to feel the slash of claws and Pain soon after, but as he touches me, his paw transforms seamlessly into a man's meaty fist. Tan, white fingers dig into my calf as he wrenches my body towards him. The space blanket crinkles angrily underneath me while he continues his transformation, becoming fully Alpha by the time my torso flies back leaving me sprawling over the dirt.

I grunt as I try to peel my body off of the ground to reach the knife — I need to pull it out so that I'll bleed out faster — but he presses his hand, another huge five-fingered hand — against my sternum and pushes. I hit the ground hard enough to knock the breath out of me and, when I blink, Pain smiles at me from the trees. Fear is right beside her. And then both rappel down and claim me with delight.

The Alpha grabs the knife hilt before I can and rips it out of me roughly, but sweet serenity remains elusive because as soon as the blade is free, he arches over me and bites. The fangs slicing into me are too large to be Alpha fangs, but not fully Berserker and each one causes Pain to squeal in delight.

I immolate.

I scream bloody murder.

Venom floods my body in the form of pure liquid agony — agony and *desire.* My mouth opens wide and my back arches. My heels dig into the wet ground and I sob as tears prick the edges of my eyes. Even my tears *hurt* like dainty fingers plucking out all my eyelashes.

My eyelids flutter open and I see the top of his head. Brown hair everywhere, streaked blond in places, as if from the sun. A bushy beard covers the bottom half of his face that's now pressed against my wounded thigh, *biting*. No, not biting, *bonding*. Renewed anger fills my muscles with strength — and courage. My fingers slam into the ground and luck leads me to my knife.

I lurch up, knife in hand and stab — not for me this time, but for him — anywhere that I can. I catch him in the shoulder, blade plunging true. He wrenches up, fangs elongated and jutting out of his mouth like four daggers, the ones on the top twice as long as the ones on the bottom though they're all sharp and glistening red and a shimmery silver that's also spattered on the torn leg of my outer layer — sweatpants too big for me, now they're shredded through.

Pain. Fear. Desire. My pussy clenches up and his nostrils flare. He opens his mouth and I know that the moment he gives me that first command, it'll be the end. I won't survive if I obey him. *I'm more than this. I'm more than a pathetic Omega...*

Pain. Fear. Desire. Rage. *Resistance.*

The earth beneath my ass rumbles and groans and, above it, a vine moves like a loosed arrow. It rips from the ground and circles his neck like a whip. Shock makes me jump. He snarls and rips a clawed hand through the vine, severing it.

The venom is pushing through me faster now, making my whole body feel warm, charging it like a battery rebooting and releasing the only other thing an Omega is good for... *power...* Powers. *But...I thought I didn't have any.*

The Berserker seems to have caught onto what's happening faster than I have, because he doesn't wait to defend himself and instead launches his next attack. He tackles me to the ground, rolling me onto my side. A heavy weight slams across my chest between my breasts and a hard, heavy hand moves to cradle my head, pulling warmth of a different kind through me. I clench my teeth and fight against it, my legs squirming, kicking wildly as they try to find purchase in anything. My fists clench just as uselessly.

And then I feel the prick of fangs against my throat and I'm beat over the head by Pain again when his fangs sink into the muscle between my shoulder and neck. More vines whip down onto him when I froth at the mouth, *screaming*. The ground rumbles louder. I kick my legs into the mud and fight harder. The vines wrench him off of me and he breaks them but not as easily as he did the first time.

He pins me again while my muscles strain and my lungs ache from how fast and hard I'm breathing. He rears up and bites down, his fangs sinking into the soft front of my shoulder and my shoulder blade this time, while his hands reach around my body to cage both of my wrists.

The tangled mass of what was once my hip-length red hair has been captured by his other hand, making Merlin right, yet again. I should have cut the shit off, I think as he forces my head back, back until I can't breathe. Until I strain too much to feel, to see. I can't hear anything but my pulse rattling.

More vines slap down onto his back, this time so violently that they draw blood. I can *smell* it, more coppery and rich than my own. He twitches behind me and withdraws his fangs long enough to wrench me tighter against his hard body. I'm crushed.

"Still," he says.

"No!"

"Still — that's an order."

"No," I scream like a psycho, fighting with everything I have against the command he's given me — a command I know my Omega instinct will have to obey without question. Fear stomps on my chest proudly but when I open my eyes and see the sky, stillness settles over me. Still, like his command. But to use my Omega powers, I don't need motion.

I close my eyes and settle my breath and the Berserker releases a menacing roar as the earth suddenly opens up below us, pitching our bodies with sudden violence. The Berserker barks out an inhuman sound as our bodies fly, caught in a mudslide of my own making.

My arms windmill as I reach for something — anything — to anchor myself. My back collides with hard soil and fresh, wet clumps of dirt splattering my face. *Get up. Get up get up get up.* I try to push my arms beneath me, but the Berserker is there — he's freaking everywhere! — and grabs the back of my sweatshirt. He yanks me over the mud, revolves our bodies so that I'm on the ground and he's hovering over me, body planking above mine.

The Berserker tosses his head back and shouts up at the sky, "What the fuck?" It's such a *human* exclamation, it pulls my eyes to him, but I can't see him clearly because the mud rain is coming down harder and thicker. He covers my head with his arms and ducks his own and, separated by so little now, I try to avoid the disaster of looking directly into his gaze, but I don't manage.

At first, it's all I can see — gold, so much fucking gold it makes me wonder if he's the Berserker of Gold City — until more colors flash into my peripheries. His skin is white, but deeply tanned and his hair is forest brown spliced through with honey. A thick dirty blond or maybe brown beard covers the bottom half of his face and is tangled and matted. He looks like a wild, untamed creature. Almost as wild as me.

"Stop this," he says to me and it doesn't even occur to me until this exact moment that I am the one who started it. But I am. I don't feel it, I just know it. Because there's no tingling, no rush of power. There's nothing to indicate that this is an act that I took, except for that *knowing*. Like gently throwing a ball and watching it come down. By the time your arm has dropped, you can't feel any effects of your effort. But the ball is still where it landed, forced there by actions all your own.

That he knew before I did astounds me.

"Now!" he shouts, wet mud chunks dripping around his body and into my eyes as the earth pitches even more violently, threatening to swallow us whole. I gasp and on my breath comes stillness.

My abdomen twists and so do my arms. I grab at his beard and yank on it as hard as I can. He releases a muted grunt and tries to pin me down, but the mud is thick and slippery and he struggles to grab hold of me. We grapple over the ground, I press my heels into the wet, wet earth underneath me and lift my hips, trying to flip us, but it's fucking pointless. He's heavier than a tree trunk. I shake my head wildly and release a shriek in frustration, wondering if maybe I can't blow his eardrums.

He grabs my jaw and stares penetratingly into my eyes in a way I can't escape. "Lie still and the bonding'll hurt less," he snarls in a thick Dark City accent. It makes his words sound more like *lae still and the bahn'in' ll heart less.* "Don't, and you'll be presentin' right here for me so I can fuck the disobedience out a you. Don't test me."

"Fuck you, Berserker!"

"*Order* you to lie still."

And there it is. I whimper pitifully, my entire chest shuddering with the sound. His face twists into a strange expression, not one I know. His eyebrows draw together and the muscles in the hard edges of his jaw all twitch. My eyelashes flutter uncontrollably and every muscle in my body is tense and straining and on fucking fire from the effort. His fingers are hot and rough and painful as they dig into my cheeks.

I want to resist. *But he says to lie still and Omegas have to obey the Alphas that bond them.* "No..." I choke, coughing while my chest shudders and shivers, being torn in half by the desire to do everything that he says and the even greater desire to not do any of it.

His big, clawed hand releases my jaw and smooths over my forehead in a touch that's as gentle as the last was brutal. "Shh," he coos, voice a low purr. The muscles in his body ease. His chest starts to make this strange rumbling sound, like thunder only twice as frightening because I don't know what it means, or what it precipitates.

At the thought, lightning flashes in the sky, refracting off of the dagger's hilt still sticking out of his shoulder. I want to grab it, but the knowledge that he wants me still stays the motion of my hand and I *hate* that. More tears swim in my vision, making me momentarily blind. I shake my head rapidly, furiously, but he holds me down in the mud until I'm forced to either look up into his eyes or close mine. I opt for the latter.

"Understand this transition is difficult for you." Fucking rich. "But you don't need to fear me." What a joke. "Not here to hurt you." Too late for that.

His huge hand slides through my hair to the side of my face and his thumb roughly strokes the tears underneath my right eye. I shriek between my teeth and try to rip away. "Not here to command you. I'll release you from the commands, for *now*, but I'm askin' you to stay calm. Promise I'm not gonna hurt you."

Was that permission? It sounded like fuckin' permission and I don't hesitate. My fingers claw into the earth. Vines rustle…and then comes a tearing from beneath our bodies and the sound of something huge ripping, cracking…falling.

A shadow moves at the edge of my vision and the Berserker curses and shifts so fast, it's like he's pulling on an outer coat, instead of a second skin. He lunges to cover my body with his huge, furry, beastly form and, before I can so much as think to move, his hand — the size of my entire torso — maneuvers around my back. His claws sink into my sweatshirt and pain digs several grooves into my body when he throws me to the side.

I roll over the ground, skating over twigs and rocks and wet soil. A roar sounds behind me. There's more crackling too, more wet mud sailing through the air, moss and water and bark, too. I look up just as the second tree falls — the first already has him pinned to the spot where I was lying just a second ago. The second comes to cover the first, two trunks cracking against one another that must weigh several tons between them. Still, he's lifting up against them, refusing to give up.

I blink and the earth rattles and roars, dislodging three more trees from where their roots had kept them grounded for decades, centuries — until I came along. They fall and fall until he's completely buried. The wind swirls. I hold my breath. He must be unconscious — stuck, at the very least. *I should help him.* The thought comes and goes and I feel panic and guilt and shame and pride roll themselves all into one and try to shove themselves down my throat. But I don't let them stall me. Instead, I turn and grab the outstretched hands of my two best friends — Pain and Fear — and I run.

ECHO
PARADISE RIVER

I COLLAPSE ONTO THE RIVERBANK AND, FOR AS LONG as I can stomach not moving, I don't. My chest rises and falls in waves that never crest. I can't catch my breath. I can't even begin to describe the agony I'm in, what with Pain and Fear tap dancing across every inch of my flesh. I ache. I'd do anything to be free of this fresh Hell. *Maybe, a life of servitude isn't so bad. The Berserker smelled nice, at least.* Anything but that.

I moan out loud, unable to help the liquid that spills out of the corners of my eyes. I try to think of something else other than the agony, but my thoughts all return to last night and all of them confuse the shit out of me. I remember bringing the trees, bringing the vines, the rain, the thunder, the storm. I remember that he felt like a storm. The way he came so fast and hard and with such violence. Why did he bite me like that? Why did he try to talk to me afterward? I'm not sure which I hated more.

Or maybe…maybe I'm remembering it all wrong. It was coincidence, the storm, the lightning, the wet ground and the vines of the forest responding to my wants. There was no Omega power. His bite *didn't* act as some kind of trigger, giving me access to dormant powers…because something like that has never been known to happen before.

I prop my feet up on the rocks just below me and am just about to start the arduous and singularly painful task of peeling the wet rabbit skins from the blocks of swollen ice I now call feet when I hear the crackle of twigs directly across the river.

This can't be fucking happening.

The Berserker hasn't caught up to me, but along the way, it looks like six other Alphas did.

"No fucking way," the Alpha closest to me with a Dark City Slayers tee shirt says, parroting my thoughts. My gaze drops to his clothing, confused. It looks like a band tee and it's *clean,* suggesting these young Alphas aren't part of a Gang Mountain gang, or any other. But Alphas don't prowl outside of their cities unless they've got a really good fucking reason to… *Like an Omega on the loose.*

His face twists into a horrible grin as he plunges into the freezing cold river up to his thighs. Paradise River is deep, rapid and wide. He's a fool to try to cross it. But…he is trying. I scrabble backwards, crab-walking up the muddy slope to the best of my ability, mostly dragging my injured leg. It oozes blood and my back stings where wounds crisscross over it. With fresh bites, I can't move my head at all. I'm swollen and sick, not yet feverish, but barreling towards infection. I'm gonna die soon. I shoulda probably died a long time ago.

"You were right, Victor." He takes another step.

The guy with the skin like mine — brown and freckled — whistles loudly and walks into the river alongside his friend. "I fucking told you I smelled Omega pussy out here." He shoves the first guy in the chest as he struts past him, water sloshing around his feet, and then his thighs and then his waist… He wobbles and tumbles in — *yes!* — only to resurface a moment later. His friends all laugh and Victor curses them as he finds his footing. *Frick!* His confidence gives the others confidence and slowly, they all begin to wade in after him.

I'm so badly injured I don't have it in me to panic. I should be dead. How I'm not is as much a mystery as the powers I exhibited last night. I know I can't outrun the young Alphas, so I concentrate hard on the water instead, wondering if I could somehow freeze it, or maybe turn the muddy river bottom to quicksand and swallow the Alphas all up.

I think about doing it, focus on it with every ounce of fleeting determination left in me, but nothing happens. My Omega power — a power that I don't understand at all but that was so bountiful the night before — dries up. Maybe, it never was.

"What would you know about Omega pussy?" A third guy says, this one wearing a white tee shirt painted over with a giant smiley face whose eyes are red Xs.

"I'm about to find out," Victor says.

"I can't believe the intel we got from Mirage City was actually right." The first one — Slayer tee — laughs. "Though the letter didn't say she'd look like this."

"No shit. We coulda done a lot better for an Omega," Smiley tee adds. "She looks fucking wrecked. We'll have to be careful when we fuck her so we all get a chance."

"I'm going first," Slayer tee says.

"No fuckin' way."

"Why don't we bond her?"

"No!" Victor and Slayer tee shout together. Victor says, "We'll leave that shit to the Dark City Berserker. He'll give us a fat reward for her."

"If we bonded her," Slayer tee continues, "Berserker Dragnovic would challenge us for her and I'm not tryna die over some worthless Omega. Just wanna sample one."

"She could have strong powers. We could use 'em."

"We won't know until we bond her and give her a command. You willin' to risk it?"

The Alphas argue for another bated breath and the air sizzles with their aggression. They turn from me to face off against each other and I'm confused…I thought Omegas were supposed to *respond* to displays of dominance with submission, but I don't. Right now, I still just want to run, and this is likely the only chance I'll get.

I reach back for my faithful companions, Pain and Fear, but my hands find fur instead. *My day just gets better and better, doesn't it?* I think as I glance up at the creature while his massive shadow falls over my body. The smell of wet fur and metal radiates from him now and heat flares off of his enormity. The wet ground squishes around his massive paws as he prowls up beside me, gaze focused on the Alphas in the river. His head hangs low and his jowls drip silver venom.

He lets out a low growl and I look up to see the young Alphas staring at the Berserker in complete stunned silence. And horror. "Ber…Ber…Berserker Dragnovic. I mean… uhmm…we didn't know you'd claimed this Omega already…" says one of the idiots.

"We were just going to bring her to you," Victor tries.

Smiley tee is one step ahead. "Run!"

The Berserker above me attacks without warning and has already bitten through the head of Slayer tee before he's got one foot off the ground. Slayer tee's friends seemingly realize that they don't stand a chance running on their own and, as Slayer tee's body disappears down the river in a flurry of hungry waves, one of them screams, "We have to fight!" He's not wrong, but it's a bravery from this group that I didn't expect.

In the middle of the river, with water raging around them, the young Alphas roar out battle anthems of their own and launch themselves at the Berserker, jumping onto his back and clawing at his fur. One of them produces a knife from somewhere and drives it down through the Berserker's right shoulder close to where I stabbed him.

The Berserker flings the Alpha on his back onto the opposite riverbank and pounces, landing one paw in the center of the Alpha's chest and tearing meat and flesh and bone out when he retracts it. At the sight of the carnage, I remember that I have feet and hands that still work and *move.*

I edge up the bank another half a foot, still crawling backwards, when the first flare of gunfire bursts through my eardrums. I jolt and cover my head with my arms, only daring a peek. The river is alight with spray from bullets as the Alphas take hit after hit delivered by a new enemy approaching from behind me.

More gunfire explodes as whoever it is draws closer, boxing me in between the gun-toting lunatics and the river, leaving me nowhere to go. I clap my hand over my ears as I take in the sight of smallish people dressed in rags holding guns… *Betas.* They're freaking Betas and they're *advancing* on the fucking Alphas. Betas are *attacking* Alphas! What the fuck are they thinking? What is happening!

I'm too panicked and freaked the fuck out to do anything but sit there for the next beat…long enough for another spray of bullet fire to hail down on the river…and for one of those bullets to tag me.

I gasp, the breath knocked out of my lungs when my left arm shatters like porcelain dipped in glass. I'm hit. I'm fucking hit! A roar shakes the foundations of the earth and a shadow moves over me while my thoughts move in and out of this plane of existence into one much nicer. *Big fluffy pillows. Warm, dry sheets. Rain hitting glass windows. A fire crackling softly in the hearth. A bed of flowers surrounding me…*

Reality jerks against my consciousness and I feel the warm press of a body on top of mine as I'm cocooned by fur and smushed further into the cold, wet ground below. The smells are inundating, nauseating and arousing all at the same time. Blood. So, so much blood. And venom that smells like mint and cinnamon. Water that smells like a storm. Fur that smells like the animals of the forest I've hunted before.

Bullets continue to spray and spray and spray. I can hear the sounds they make leaving their weapons and I can hear the sounds they make as they meet flesh and I can feel every time the Berserker above me jolts in pain when he's hit again and again and again. His weight sinks even further onto me. He's dying. *Thank the god of small mercies.* And then the bullets stop and he collapses on top of me entirely.

His weight is smothering and I cough and choke. I kick my heels into the wet soil and grit my teeth and use every muscle in my body to try to push myself out from under him. He rumbles, releases steam from his nostrils and lifts up on one shaking right leg…just enough for me to be able to maneuver out from beneath his weight.

I kick back onto the bank and lie there, staring up at the sky, trying to breathe while my good friend Pain does her best to skin me alive. Through the agony of so many competing wounds, I hear the plod of soft footsteps followed by a much louder voice.

"Shit, Echo. What the hell happened to you?" I know that voice and try to open my eyes. It's hard work when each eyelid weighs a respective ton. "You look like you need some medical assistance." A tuft of blonde hair flops down over dark goggles.

I just grunt, surprised to see her…but not that surprised. If any Beta has the stones to hunt Alphas in Paradise Hole, it's this one.

She pulls down her black mask and, when another burst of gunshots flare and the Berserker emits another pained grunt, she looks back over her shoulder and snaps, "Hold your fire. Are you blind? This is a fucking Berserker!"

"I thought they wanted all the bodies, especially Berserkers…" someone answers from further away, confusing the shit out of me. Someone wants Berserker *bodies*?

"Yeah, no shit, but use your head for two seconds, Erwin, we've got an *Omega* here."

I don't know what the fuck she's talking about, but the dead-not-yet-dead Berserker seems to and growls.

"Easy, Berserker." Merlin swings her gun around, presumably at him, though I can't see him from this angle without lifting my head, and if my eyelids are too heavy to move then my head is a nonstarter. I need medicine. And I can't pay. Anybody else might have taken pity on me, but not Merlin. Not a Beta who hunts Alphas.

"Merlin," I croak.

She glances down at me and lifts her goggles. Her grin is wide — way too wide — and I flinch. She sees and smirks, "Echo, you look like hell. Want us to take you back to Trash City for some much-needed medical attention?"

"Your gifts, Omega — bring the river," the Berserker's low brogue commands.

I gasp, too distracted by the command he just gave me to turn Merlin's words over for a second and third and thirtieth consideration. I grip the soil beneath me with my left hand, squeezing the fingers of my right limp arm into a fist against my chest. My eyelids flutter. I feel a cool wind cover my body that carries the cries of dying Alphas on its wings.

"Holy fuck! There's a *wave*!" *A wave? How lovely. I wish I could see it…*

Iterations of the same thing rise up, but Merlin's voice cuts through them. "You lied to me, Echo!" Merlin shouts. "You *do* have Omega gifts."

I'm prepared to fucking rail at her given the day I've had — the night, the past six weeks — but am cut short. She swings her gun around, leaving me looking straight up the barrel. She shifts just a little and then, without warning, pulls the trigger.

"No!" The Berserker roars.

I choke on my tongue when the bullet pierces my already injured right shoulder, triggering thoughts of suicide and of homicide in tandem. I've never wanted to hurt a Beta before but right now, I'd like nothing more than five minutes alone with Merlin. And a machete.

I scream through clenched teeth while, above me, she cocks her handgun's hammer and trains the killing end on my forehead like murdering me in the cold open here, right now, might not faze her at all. Then she confirms it when she says, "Next one is through her skull, Berserker. Now tell her to quit it with the river and the rest of her powers."

"Omega, stop. Do what she says," he says, though it sounds like Pain might have made a new friend in him, too. Still, he might be her new friend, but I'm her *best* friend. Right now, she's dug a trench just for me and she's filled it with all kinds of sharp and cutting things…and I've hit every one on my way to the bottom.

I exhale and my back settles against the ground, sinking into the wetness. I can feel mud against my wounds. Merlin's smiling down at me, shaking her head softly, but at least she's got her gun trained on my forehead instead of any other part of me that will actually hurt to get hit.

"You ready to come back to Trash City, Echo? This time, I promise we'll give you the deluxe suite."

"Do it," I whisper, glancing at the gun, "just end it."

The Berserker roars and my vision fades. I try not to give him the satisfaction of hearing how fucking badly he's beaten me, so I bite through it…and black out again. When I come to, Merlin's face is covered in her mask and her goggles and she's crouching down at my side.

"You know, I think your Berserker might *actually* be into you." The Berserker snarls in the background, voice sounding somewhere between animal and man. Merlin grins wider. "That's bad news for you. And that's *really* bad news for him."

ECHO
TRASH CITY

MY CHAINS RATTLE AGAINST THE WALL WHEN I PULL on them with my one good arm. They rattle against the floor when I kick with my one good foot. I've been in this room for what feels like a week, long enough for my adrenaline to crash and the sleep deprivation and freezing chill from trudging all night through the woods to crash with it.

I'm shaking violently now and, even though only one of my hands is bound, I can't use the other to get away. It's swollen beyond recognition, hanging like an angry stump against my chest, weighing me down.

Pain needles at the edges of my eyes, pricking at them with her sharpened talons, wanting me to cry, delighting in my slow capitulation. My arm hurts so fucking bad and I know that if the door doesn't open soon, I'm going to die here, sitting on a mattress on the floor in a room made of trash, chained to a wall made of trash, all alone in Trash City.

I'd been prepared to off myself earlier, but I don't want to die now. Then, dying felt like it was on my terms. Now, dying's on theirs — the Berserker's and Merlin's. It's also going to *hurt.* Fire and brimstone and all that dark, delirious shit. A nightmare of pain from which I won't ever wake.

Red fever and black dreams dig into my brain, find my ability to reason, and sever it. I'm wavering back and forth, pulling at my restraints until my skin chafes raw, incapable of giving up even though it's only making Pain giggle louder from her position in the corner.

Maybe, if I pull hard enough, I'll break my remaining arm. Maybe, if I break it, the bone will stab through and I'll bleed out. I pull with my entire bodyweight and even though it hurts like a mother, I can't…I just can't hurt myself anymore. Not even to end it. Not without the *guarantee* of ending it.

I make a sound that's somewhere between a groan and a screech as I sink down against the mattress. There's no pillow so my neck is cricked up against the wall, some piece of hard plastic jutting out like a fist and digging into the back of my head. I feel like throwing up. I think I might feel better if I throw up, but I can't do that either. Seems like the only thing that isn't soggy wet in this room right now is my throat, and that's bone dry.

"Merrrlinnn," I croak at the top of my lungs. I need water. I'd give my left tit for a glass of water. I'd give a lot more than that for some pain killers. "Merlin!"

The door explodes open and ricochets against the wall, loosing a few pieces of trash and sending them dribbling pitifully to the floor in a pile of charred plastic and cardboard. He's there. Here. In the small room with me.

And he's not in chains. And that can only mean one thing.

"Merlin, you bitch!" I jerk harder against my restraints and his stoic face floods with color. His lips bristle and he storms forward, and I notice that somehow, by some magical fucking feat, he's acquired a pair of black cargo pants that don't even have any holes in them *and* the bastard has boots on his giant feet.

He drops down onto one knee beside me and rips the chain out of the wall. He has no problem touching me freely and his hands immediately drop to my waist and the back of my head. He pulls me fully onto the mattress so that I'm out of my awkward crick-necked position and lying flat.

He looks over his shoulder, dirty tendrils of his hair sticking to his chest. He's still wet and sweaty and covered in blood but *completely* healed from all of his injuries. I hate his guts. I hate all their guts.

"The medics," Merlin's voice says, followed by the banging of feet against trash. They bang closer to me and I hate them, too.

"Merlin, you bitch," I shriek again. "Did you make a deal with the Berserker?" Rage clubs Pain in the head, knocking her out of the way for the moment. I thrash wildly against the mattress, fury unraveling me to my essence.

The Berserker holds me down by the shoulders and I fight as hard as I can against him, hard enough I feel bruises light up under his palms. A young woman and a slightly older Beta man crouch down on the side of the mattress opposite the Berserker. The man takes the lead, touching my face, my neck. His fingers come back bloody.

"Don't do that," he says to the Berserker.

The Berserker's got his mouth open and four ivory white fangs poised towards me. Like he's gonna bite me again. I'm dying — why the hell wouldn't he? Get one nice little snack in before I don't have anything left? He growls low and deep in his throat. His eyes darken before settling back to gold.

The man doctor gestures to my throat and makes a disgusted face that I don't entirely expect or want to see from the dude who's supposed to be saving my life. "She won't survive another bite, if you want her to survive, anyway. If not, then you should tell us now so we don't waste all these meds. She's going to entirely deplete our supply."

His words are morose, but his hands are still helping the woman doctor prepare several vials filled with clear liquid. He hooks an IV bag onto the trash wall behind me. An IV bag. I haven't seen one of those in years. How the heck do they have one in Trash City?

"Angel, do you wanna start making space?"

"I would, but he's hovering."

"Alpha, would you stop hovering?" the man doctor says.

"Berserker," the Berserker corrects.

"Berserker, would you stop hovering?"

The Berserker continues to glare at the medics while I continue to rage against his grip. I kick my feet harder and wonder if there are any important arteries in your feet worth breaking or if I'm just inviting Pain back. How I've missed her in these precious seconds.

"My venom will heal her," he says, voice full of authority and, if I'm not entirely mistaken, just a *hint* of uncertainty.

The man doctor's lips flubber as he laughs a dry, throaty laugh. He shakes his head. "I don't think so. *If* that was your goal before, it makes you marginally more sympathetic, but only marginally. The blood on her neck is still wet. If that's from your bite, then it did not heal well. Not in the slightest."

He whistles as he flicks a syringe. I'm slowing down. My lips are so dry. I try to look anywhere but at the Berserker looming above me, staring at the doctor with narrowed, bloodthirsty eyes.

"Not possible," the Berserker says, irritating the shit out of me because not only does he speak in an incomprehensible accent, he also never speaks in full sentences. It annoys me unnecessarily in this moment.

"If you'd back up, Angel will show you. Angel?"

Angel moves in as the Berserker reluctantly releases my shoulders. I'm not really fighting anymore, if I ever was. I'm so tired. So, so tired. When Angel comes close to me brandishing a pair of sharp-looking scissors, I sink into the mattress, wondering inanely what it's stuffed with. It's lumpy as shit. Probably trash.

"What's in the bed? Dead cats?" I murmur raggedly.

Angel snorts and lifts the edge of my sweatshirt. She skims the scissors all the way up the fabric and I choke at the loss. My lower lip quivers against my will. I'm trying everything humanly possible not to sob and give these assholes the satisfaction, but a few tears escape, the Traitors.

From the foot of the bed, Merlin's voice manages to sound annoyingly empathetic. "Aww come on now, Echo. You didn't cry when I took your boots. Your sweatshirt's gone anyway."

"Fuck you, Merlin." I sniffle hard and jerk when I feel cool air touch my bare stomach and both my tits. I jerk harder at the press of warm, callused knuckles on my cheek. The

Berserker's looking down at me, his lips pressed together so hard he could spit diamonds. His gaze is one hundred percent black and focused on my eyes. We share a bleak and horrible moment before Angel tries to take my injured arm in her hand.

I scream wildly, "Stop it!"

"Easy," the man doctor says, holding up a hand. "Insert the IV first, Angel. No — in her *other* arm."

He shakes his head and Angel has the decency to look mildly sheepish as she gets up and moves around the mattress to kneel next to the Berserker. "Um…may I?"

He pulls his hand off of my cheek and I shiver at the absence of his heat. He moves to stand at the foot of the bed, Merlin a few feet behind him. His eyes flare when they move over my body, lingering around my neck where things feel most gruesome. I can feel the slippery blood pouring out of me. I don't want to see it though. Not ever. I hope I never again come in contact with a mirror.

"Damn," Merlin says, and her cheeks are pink. She breaks my gaze quickly. "I thought when an Alpha bonded an Omega, the venom was supposed to heal her up."

"You useful here?" the Berserker barks and he doesn't wait for her answer. "No? Then get the fuck out." He spins, grabs her by the front of her shirt and throws her so hard against the wall she leaves an indent in it before falling to her knees.

Just out of my vision, she hisses, "I'm not the one who butchered her, so don't get mad at me…"

He releases a carnal roar that makes my insides melt and my Omega instincts writhe in pleasure. *Submit.* I'm so weak in the head, I might have if I weren't so weak in the body. My fingertips tingle and energy zings through my bones. Air that smells like darkness and the woods and metal spirals up my nostrils.

I'm grateful when Angel finally gets my sweatshirt cut off my half-functional arm and gets the IV drip set up because whatever's in it dulls the sizzling burning sensation licking all my wounds. It dulls everything. My good friend Pain slinks to her seat in the corner and weeps.

The Berserker starts to pace back and forth across the small room. His eyes never leave me. It's disconcerting. With the fresh drugs obliterating my senses, Angel's able to get my swollen, shattered arm out of my clothes while the man doctor starts rinsing off my bloody neck.

Tossing my mutilated sweatshirt aside, I shiver harder at the wet noise it makes when it falls. "We'll get you a blanket," the man doctor reassures. "Angel, get a move on and take off her pants. She's freezing. We don't want to lose any more toes than we need to."

"Need to?" I croak. "Do we need to?"

Angel is the only one who reacts to me at all. She gives me a small smile that I don't find remotely encouraging, but she does what he says, cutting up each pant leg, removing my sweats and my jeans next until I'm down to my last layer. There, she stops.

"Holy shit. Lou…" Angel's voice trails off. Her fingers delicately peel apart my leggings, tags of flesh getting mixed in with the material. I can feel the prickly sensation of my skin being pulled in directions it's not supposed to be and vomit bubbles in my throat. Tears spill down my cheeks.

"Blankets," I croak. I look up at the Berserker pacing across the room. His face is white as a sheet. He's not pacing anymore, he's just staring at my legs.

"Oof. That doesn't look good," Lou quips, not sounding at all like he gives even the littlest fuck about this situation. "Blanket's out then. Here, we can use this to cover your breasts, but we don't have any sheets clean enough to cover the rest of you. I didn't realize how open your wounds were. It's bad enough you've got cuts on your back pressed against the mattress. For the record, it's stuffed with trash." As I suspected. "Let's not make it worse." He makes a face that makes me wonder just how many people have died on this bed listening to him make piss-poor small talk.

He lays a towel over my boobs and then carries on washing out the bullet holes studding my shoulder and arm. The towel doesn't help. My nipples are still hard enough to cut diamonds and my feet are ice. My left foot is shaking so much I can feel it all the way up to my hip on that side, but I can't feel my right foot at all except for the burn. It sizzles every time I move it and is so bloody painful.

"Fucking fr...freezing..." My clenched teeth have started to bang against one another.

The Berserker moves suddenly, making my whole body jerk and pangs, dulled by the drugs, throb all over me. He kneels on the mattress and takes my right foot in between both of his huge hands.

"Fuck!" My head thrashes at the violent heat, but man doc, *Lou* I think Angel said, holds me steady.

"I'm going to start stitching you now. We need to do deep stitches, too. He tore apart some muscle here. I'm surprised you're able to move. The venom must be holding some parts of you together somewhere, or it's your Omega gift doing that, because you should be dead. You should be dead three times over…"

He's talking to himself, which is good because I don't have any answers. My right foot has gone from nothing to numb to throbbing. More unwilling tears dribble down my cheeks. Pain makes a jerky approach, but after a few moments, disappears again. I miss her when she's gone because what's left is unknown and confusing as the throbbing in my foot eventually turns to a dreary warmth. I shudder and flex the toes of my left foot and the Berserker's hands move from my right foot to cover them.

"Knock me out," I croak, hating the Berserker's pitiful attempts at *kindness*.

"Hm?" Lou says, distracted.

"She wants you to knock her unconscious, I think," Angel supplies.

As the Berserker rumbles deep in his chest I can feel the vibrations through the mattress. I think they're meant to soothe, but I don't like them. I don't like *him*. And I like him even less when he says, "No. No sleep. You sleep and you might not wake up and I didn't come all this way for a corpse."

"Not for lack of trying," I grit, kicking out with my left foot and, now that hazy sensation has returned, hating the way I can feel the cold chain still burning against my ankle.

"Venom shoulda healed you…"

"It didn't."

"Not fucking blind."

"No? Then why, after the first bite, did you keep biting?"

"Don't tempt me, Echo." *Echo*. The word hits me like Merlin's bullet did and hurts just as much. He must have overheard her using my name and I hate that. *Hate* that.

"Stop it!" Angel shouts. "Her pulse goes up, she'll bleed more and we don't have any Omega blood to donate. If your venom didn't work, the Beta or Alpha blood we have on reserve might make her sick."

"Alpha blood?" the Berserker hisses. "From where?"

My eyes are closed now, so I don't see Angel's reaction even though I'm curious about it — I've been wondering about these supplies, too, and where they came from — but I hear her voice warble when she says, "From…from our last shipment."

"Shipment from where?"

Lou cuts in. "Alpha, do you want your Omega to live?"

"Berserker."

"Berserker."

"She dies, Trash City burns."

"That's what I thought. I need your help. Start washing out the wound on her shoulder. Her arm needs a full surgery. One of the bullets hit bone and shattered it. I'm going to have to cut her open, reset the bone, and insert a plate. When you get back to Dark City, you can have your docs remove it."

"I'm not going to Dark City…" I whisper, but Lou is already fiddling with the IV and reality is sprinting away from me at a brutal pace. There's no way I'll be able to catch it.

My good fingers curl into the sheets and a large, warm hand covers my forehead and presses my head down onto the lumpy mattress.

"Y'are," he says, his accent thick with that Dark City trademark.

"Over my dead body." His hands touch my neck gently and I strain my face away from him as far as I can get. I don't want him touching me. I don't want him anywhere near me. Not even to save my life.

"Alive and breathing," he counters.

"Not if I can help it."

His heat crashes into me and when he speaks, I can feel the brush of his lips against my cheek. His breath smells like blood and river water as it fans over me. "I give one command, and you will."

Fury makes me choke, "So, why don't you?"

"Told you already," he says after a moment, "don't want a corpse. Don't have any need for one."

His hands resume their work as he uses a turkey baster and a towel to rinse out the inside of my bonding wounds that should have but definitely did not heal up. The drugs running through my veins are my new friend now, and they don't let anything hurt me. Doesn't mean I can't still hear the awful sounds of water spraying against my neck, or the Alpha's frustrated grunts.

Sorry — *Berserker.*

He must be having the same thoughts I am because he says, "Isn't fuckin' right. You defective somehow?"

I laugh — *laugh* — though I don't know if the sound can be identified as such. "What? You want to return me *now*? After you've gone and bitten the shit out of me?"

His hand slashes out and grabs my chin. He tilts my face towards his. The strange, out-of-character gentleness he showed to my foot is gone now, that anomaly successfully placed in his rearview like a hit-and-run. "I *bonded* you to protect and heal you after you fuckin' *stabbed* yourself in the leg."

I laugh a little more and his grip tightens to the point that I can feel it through the druggy veil.

"Ahem," Lou says, "if you want to make more work for us, then please proceed. But if you'd like for there to be enough drugs left for us to keep Trash City running until you hold up your end of the bargain and provide us with the supplies you promised, then please loosen your hold on the Omega."

"With her injuries after the bonding, are we even sure she's an Omega?" Angel has the stones to ask.

"She's an Omega," both Lou and the Berserker say at the same time.

I look up into the Berserker's eyes. Now that he's fully in his Alpha form, no beast to be found, they're brown, not gold and not black either. The color of burned sugar. His pupils are fully blown in the center though, much larger than I think they should be, making the color hard to see. He blinks and I jolt.

"Omega, I'm going to cut open your arm now to reset the bone," Lou says.

I shake my head frantically, which is difficult, since the bastard I'm trying to get away from still has a solid hold of me. He's everywhere. His eyes refuse to leave mine, like the residue underneath a stubborn sticker. It's just stuck there forever.

"Don't let him," I huff, totally crazed. I'm giving an order to a Berserker. Hah. What a day.

His left eye twitches microscopically. I don't win more of a reaction from him than that. Looking into my eyes, he says to the doc, "Alright. Knock her out."

I feel the dull edge of the knife press into my skin and a moment later, waves of euphoria blanket my bloody, freezing, sticky body and I know that everything is going to be much, much worse when I wake up. But at least for now, Pain has left the building. All that's left are burned sugar-colored irises, and then nothing.

ECHO
TRASH CITY

"DON'T MOVE OR I'LL GUT HIM LIKE A FISH."

The Berserker glares at me like I've just insulted his mother. "Whether he dies or not makes no difference to me. You're leavin' here with me or not at all."

"The fuck I am." My voice, like my arm, is shaking. "You don't own me." I plaster my back against the wall, dragging doc Lou with me as I move. I refuse to get closer to the ramp that leads top side. I refuse.

"Not true. Bonded ya. Paid these fuckers for your life." He crosses his arms over his broad, thermal-covered chest and plants his booted feet hip-width apart. His tangled brown hair is long and falls around his pecs. His brown beard tilts slightly to the right, still disheveled from when he woke up this morning, not that I saw that happen. He's always awake before I am and sleeps after I fall asleep. For all I know, he might not even sleep. I've just gotta assume he does.

It's been eight days. At least, that's what they tell me. I don't know what the Berserker bartered to get us a stay in

Trash City for *eight* fucking days, but it must have been a lot more than a pair of boots.

I've gotten medical care each of those days and food, too. I even got a bucket of allegedly *distilled* water to drink and a bucket of rainwater to wash up in one-handedly along with a third bucket that I pissed and shit into.

My left arm's a goner, held together by metal plates underneath my skin and thread pulling that skin together. It's bandaged to my chest like a newborn infant. My left leg is doing better than the arm on the same side, but only marginally. Angel has offered to help me with some basic tasks, but I don't let her. I don't like to be touched and, these past days, I've been touched, mauled and mangled aplenty.

For the last eight days, the Berserker and I have shared that shitty trash room. We don't talk. We both make active effort not to look at each other, especially when we're washing up. Anytime he needs to shit or piss or I do, the other leaves the room and waits outside. I've learned nothing about him, why he came for me, why he bit me, or what he thinks will happen next. But what I have learned is far, far more interesting.

I might not have learned what he traded them, but I learned what he *didn't*. He *didn't* trade them guns. *They have enough guns*. I overheard Lou say as much. That was right before I stole his scalpel and started threatening to cut his throat with it if they didn't clear the way to the south entrance, provide me with a gun and promise to give me a head-start.

"With what your Berserker is trading us to keep you alive, you can kill Lou. We'll recover." Merlin's tone is a thousand times harder than any she's used with me before and it makes me sweat. Literally. It also kinda makes me want to cry.

"You," I accuse, wanting to throw the dagger at Merlin's nose, but I've only got one hand, so I keep it to Lou's throat. "You said you were rooting for me…"

"I am rooting for you. But like I told you already, I have to keep all of this alive, too." She gestures around her at the trash in the walls.

Fury and regret hit me. "You stole my boots and then you *traded* me."

"Don't you remember what else I said? I said I thought you were gonna die soon. I still kinda do. Not worth sacrificing for a corpse. Well, not your corpse, anyway." She shrugs, like what she's saying is the most logical thing in the world. It is, but that doesn't mean I have to be on board with it.

"Not gonna die, Echo." His voice cracks like a fist through an old brick, threatening to crumble me just as easily. I hate the cavalier way he uses my name, like he has every right to it. I never gave it to him.

He stands on the gangplank leading up to the light. It touches his right shoulder in shades of white, while everything that hits his left side is doused in the red fluorescents overhead. Red, not blue, because this is the East entrance, closest to Paradise River and Dark City across it. I'm not going with him there.

"You're right, I'm not. You're going to get out of my way and I'm going to keep doing what I've successfully been doing the past six weeks until you came into my life. Staying unharmed and alive."

His face does something dramatic then, eyebrows pulling together, grimace cracking into a frown, nostrils flaring. Muscles in his neck bounce and a pulse across his forehead throbs. But he doesn't answer. He just looks at Merlin and then at my feet where I've only got on socks. Sometime in my sleep somebody tossed everything I owned and gave me replacements.

"Give her back the boots."

Merlin hesitates, but does what she's told. She tosses the boots across the crowded walkway so that they land in a jumble between my feet and Lou's. Trouble is, to put them on, I'm going to have to let him go.

I flash a hateful gaze to the asshole responsible for all of this, but his face hasn't changed out of that confused, kinda tortured expression. I turn my hateful gaze to Merlin then, but she's just standing there looking annoyed.

"Look, we've got stuff to do. We don't have all day. Everybody here knows you're not going to kill Lou. You've just got that kinda face."

"What kind?"

"The good kind."

I frown, tears bubbling to the surface of my eyes that I don't want anyone to see. I have a sudden, momentary tantrum all to myself and I decide that I hate everything. I push Lou away from me and ignore his loud squawk when he stumbles into Angel amidst a cluster of scavengers gathered to Merlin's right.

I drop down onto my knees and start fussing with my shoes, but it's pretty hard to put boots on with only one hand without any practice. The fingers of my other hand keep flinching, desperate to complete the actions they know by heart, but can't. It doesn't help that I'm bundled in more layers than I've ever owned and all of them are soft and warm and jack up my impulse to cry.

I don't want to go back outside. I don't want to be wet anymore. I don't want to be cold. I'm tired of my best friends, Pain and Fear. I want new friends. And I don't want those friends to be Alphas of any kind, least of all Berserkers.

Palms cover mine and are so large that they completely dwarf my hand and shoe beneath their surprisingly light touch. I flinch. Silently, he pulls the boot out of my hand and slides it onto my foot, like in some fucked up fairy tale. Efficiency wins out over gentleness as he laces it up quickly, and after, asks me if it's tight enough. I just grunt. The backs of his hands have scars that gleam like eels swimming through dark, rough waters. I focus on them instead of on his face.

"Too tight?"

"No," I say, but my voice breaks, giving me away. *This* is why I hate talking.

His hands still, the loops of a neat bow strung between them. "You cryin'?"

I refuse to meet his gaze just like I refuse to answer. I inhale a shuddering breath and wipe with my one good hand at both of my cheeks. I push back against the wall of plastic behind me, cringing away from him while knobs of long-discarded things dig into my spine through my many layers. "No."

“Don’t lie to me, Echo.” His hand slashes out and grabs my chin, forcing my face up. I close my eyes. A small rebellion. “Will you look at me?”

I growl.

“Echo, look at me.” The order sends *feeling* cascading through my entire body, but especially through my crotch. It’s uncomfortable, my core filled with a sudden maddening pressure, my mind hallucinating thoughts of turning around and presenting for the Berserker. I hate it. I hate me. I hate Merlin with her pragmatic underhandedness. I hate Lou for his casual flippancy over my life and his affable certainty about my death. I hate Angel for the small, maddening way she smiles. I hate *him* most of all.

I open my eyes and his smug expression makes me feel like nothing. Less than nothing. I jerk away, pushing his callused fingers off of my cheeks and quickly rubbing my nose with the back of my sleeve.

His expression slips, but I’m not looking at him so I don’t have a chance to fully assess it. His heat warms my front. He smells like the forest, clean and masculine though I don’t know how that’s possible. He got the same bucket of dirty water I did.

“Watched you get shot twice and shatter your arm and you didn’t cry. Why you cryin’ now?”

I don’t want to go back into Paradise Hole. I don’t want to go anywhere with you. I hope he can read the words I don’t feel like saying out loud through my expression alone. When his hard face hardens more, I know that he can.

“Want me to compel you to tell me? You know as well as I do that you can’t deny your Berserker.”

"You're not my *anything* except the monster who fang raped me and almost killed me." My voice comes out hot and mean. Something moves against my palm, the one rooted on the ground, and when I look down, a vine is crawling over my skin, having grown up from between two crushed pieces of tin packed into the floor below. The vine crisscrosses over my palm before breaking off when I lift my fist, so that I wear a vine wrapped around my fingers like brass knuckles.

We both stare at it. Somewhere, in a land far, far away, I hear Merlin say, "Shit."

"Do it. You'd have every right." He brutally cinches my shoelace and presents his left cheek.

"It's not gonna hurt you, but when you hit me back, I might not survive it."

His arm snakes out again, this time reaching for my injured neck. The display of dominance is something my inner Omega preens at, but I still wince wildly, afraid of Pain. Even through the painkillers, my neck still hurts. But he doesn't touch me. I blink and see him flexing his hand outstretched hand before curling it into a fist. He opens his mouth, tongue pressing against the backs of his teeth, before exhaling suddenly.

"Other foot."

I don't reply, just stare at him waiting for violence.

Heat radiates from the Berserker even though he's only wearing a faded green thermal shirt and the same black cargo pants he's been wearing all week. I feel branded by his touch when he taps the side of my left ankle firmly. "Other foot."

Numbly, I slide my left ankle forward and let him shove on my old boot. His hands work deftly and efficiently.

"Too tight?"

I sniffle again, this time for the last time. "No."

"Good. Then move."

"No."

He exhales and rakes a hand down his face. His beard has grown longer since we've been here. It's burly and makes it hard to tell what his face looks like underneath. "Not givin' you that option, Echo."

"Stop calling me that," I hiss, not liking the way everyone in this hall is so damn silent because they're all clearly listening to our conversation.

His fury pulses hotter, brighter. "What d'you want me to call you? Omega?"

No. Not that. Definitely not that. I nod and sniffle — okay, this time is the last time. "Yes."

"*Omega*, get up. Tryin' not to order you here, but I will if you make me wait any longer. Sick of bein' in this fucking dump. Wanna get back."

I shiver and he sees. He sees everything. He edges closer to me and I flinch. He grimaces, not liking my aversion to him, and he proceeds forward with a little more reserve, making sure to keep a little bit of distance between us. It's a generosity of the most meager kind, but I still don't expect it from him. Monsters don't know kindness.

Behind him, Merlin barks, "Echo, get the fuck up and get out. I wouldn't let you stay here even if the Berserker let you go."

I'm about to tell her to fuck off, but the Berserker beats me to it. He whips around and holds up his hand, middle finger and thumb pressing together, his other three fingers lifting up.

It's not a gesture I'm familiar with, but it seems to scream shut the fuck up more than any other hand gesture I've seen could.

"Quiet. If she needs another eternity here, you'll give it to her. If she needs the shirt off your back, you'll fucking give it to her. No one commands my Omega but me, you fuckin' got that, scavenger?"

Merlin snarls, but her face still turns pink. She lowers her goggles from her forehead to cover her eyes and turns back to the other Betas. "I don't have time for this," she grumbles. "Get back to work, all of you. We have a shipment to fulfill."

"Shipment?" the Berserker and I say simultaneously. We share a glare before turning our attentions back to Merlin.

She snorts, literally tilting her nose up at us. "I don't answer to you." And before the Berserker can bite her head off, she twirls her right pointer finger in the air and whistles between the gap in her front teeth. "Alright, scavengers, to rendezvous point G. We'll leave the Omega here to her pity party."

I want to cuss at her, rage and roar, but my chin is quivering too bad to say anything at all, which just makes me feel like a pussy. My left arm and leg don't hurt so much as throb and the stitching in the right side of my neck has already started to itch. It feels bruised down deep, not sliced open anymore, but that's only thanks to the pocketful of drugs I've got handy. I try not to think about how they'll run out eventually.

"Bye, Echo. I hope you feel better," fuckin' Angel has the gall to say.

"Fuck you, Angel," I say and my sniffling is worse now. This is the last time, dammit, I swear!

The Berserker is glaring at me again, his irritation at Trash City transforming as effortlessly as he can into irritation with me. "Wanna stay here?" he says, voice incredulous and disgusted, even more so when I nod. "You'd rather stay in a pile of garbage than come to Dark City with me?"

So he *is* the Dark City Berserker.

...

Fuck. I *knew* that, but hearing him confirm it...just...fuck.

My chin wobbles even more.

He grabs it, physically stopping the wobbling with his fist. His eyes narrow. His expression turns feral. He whips his head and hand back and snarls, "Don't wanna corpse, told you that already. I'm not gonna abuse you. I fang fucked you once, but that's because I thought I was helping you. I was wrong. Won't make the same fucking mistake again. We get to Dark City, you don't even have to talk to me if you don't want. You'll live good. You won't want for shit. Sit pretty and come to a few events. That's it."

I don't believe a word he fucking says and that doesn't matter. It doesn't matter. Because I don't want to go back into Paradise Hole. With or without him. And even if I did, I still wouldn't want to make it to Dark City to live the rest of my days as a prop. I want *more*. I don't know what it is, *if* there even is, but I want it. And if there's not, then I want to spend my whole life searching until I know for sure.

He leans in again, even closer now. So close his mangy beard brushes my jaw. "You're braver than this. I've seen it."

I slap him. I don't know where it comes from, and I know it doesn't hurt, but it still leaves a splotch of red on his cheek and the neon sign in his eyes flashing murder. "I don't wanna go back into Paradise Hole," I squeeze out in a single puff of air.

His reaction is horrifying. His face transforms, eyes widening, caramel lashes parting wide, eyebrows lifting, mouth softening, diamond cheeks relaxing. He moves one hand onto my forehead, the other onto my knee. I don't like it and tense up. It doesn't draw anger out of him though, not like it has in the past. Instead, his hands do that awful flinching thing again and he lets go of my leg and combs my hair behind my right ear.

I bat his hand away, the slapping sound echoing, but he still doesn't get mad. Instead, he says in a low, lethal voice, "I'm not going to let anything bad happen to you up there."

And I lose my mind. "You *are* the bad thing that happened to me up there."

And whatever grace he's given me ends. He fists my hair at the nape of my neck and drags me up to standing. He pushes me towards the ramp leading up to daylight and tosses me out into cold, wet air.

DARK CITY BERSERKER
PARADISE HOLE

"FUCK." NOTHING ABOUT THIS IS GOING AS PLANNED.

She has the fuckin' audacity to snort at the predicament we're in. I kick my motorcycle, my fucking baby reduced to ripped metal and rubble, and toss aside one of the cracked propulsion canisters I'd mounted to it myself. It's empty now, having spent the last of its gas on blowing up the scavengers who tore her apart. Three of 'em lie dead around my motorcycle now, but clearly, others got away and they stripped 'er a *everything*. Every. fucking. thing. Down to 'er worthless plastic coating, down to the bolts.

"Is this where you fought the other Alphas?" Her voice startles me. I don't hear it very often and I never hear it unless it's warped by anger. Now, it's tinged by curiosity. Her gaze sweeps the glade speckled with bits of my motorcycle and other metal parts of the bikes and trucks the other Alphas brought with them. There's blood on the soil, marking the battle that was fought.

I nod. "Yeah."

"Did you eat them?"

"The fuck?" I stare at her, blinking while she just watches me with those large, brown eyes that are impossible to fuckin' read. The only time I can is when she's a little bit vulnerable. I fucking ache for that vulnerability. Makes every instinct in my body come alive with a desire to tear the world down around her and lay it at her feet.

I shake my head when she doesn't say more. "No."

She frowns and glances around again and it takes me until that moment to realize what was wrong. What she noticed from the start, while I was lamenting the loss of my bike. "Trash City took the bodies?"

She gives me a look — an indecipherable one — before shrugging and turning her back on me. Rage and concern and a fleeting desire to go back on my word and tear Trash City to pieces distract me from the loss of my bike and the knowledge of what that means for my return journey.

Our return journey.

Meanwhile, my Omega starts stompin' her ass off like she's got better places to be. Her earlier vulnerability completely slaughtered, she's back to the cold, hard casing she had when we shared that trash room together. No better than the warped plastic the scavengers built their city with.

What the fuck was I thinking, letting the Fates guide me here when I should have gutted them? I force off thoughts of my childhood, the prophecy, the Fates I should have murdered, the shit fucking brewin' in my gut telling me that something about those damn scavengers was off. They do me no fuckin' good now. Now, I need to be focused solely on keepin' Echo — the Omega — safe from Alphas that'd bond her…

Because I haven't. At least, I haven't bonded her *correctly*. She got her gifts and she seems to respond a *little* to the commands I give 'er, but watchin' her limp off like that makes my bones hurt. *Why didn't I heal her?* It also makes me surprisingly and shamefully proud. *I did this to her and I'm proud she survived it.*

Not for the first time, it occurs to me that I'm not fucking ready for her, for this, just like I've been too fucking weak for every other thing that came to me. Without those fucking Fates whispering in my ear all those years ago, I'd be nothing. I am nothing. Can't even keep Echo safe from me.

"Where you goin', Echo?"

She doesn't answer, just trudges up the next incline and eventually disappears into the trees. I kick my bike again, fucking flabbergasted by the audacity of Merlin and her Trash City scum. Sacrifice their own to strip a lethal motorcycle? I wouldn't even do that to my lowest deputies.

If it was dangerous, she shoulda come out here herself — that's what a leader does. That's why I came for Echo while so many other Berserkers sent packs of their Alphas. It felt so fuckin' good tearing those others apart — or sending them scattering with their tails tucked. And then I caught up to Echo in the woods, no idea that was when the *real* battle would begin.

Now, I'm not sure if comin' after her myself was a good idea or the worst one I ever had.

I catch up to her and move in front of her, cutting her off. "Need to rest. It's been eight hours since we left the garbage dump and you need food and water." I start to remove my pack, but she laughs — not a real laugh, but her mouth opens and a grating sound comes out that makes me want to shred something. Not her, but I'd take a solid oak as proxy.

She shakes her head and continues trudging past me.

"It's a six-day walk to Dark City," she spits, "twice that if you're as injured as I am and that's only if you don't get stopped."

"Aware a that, Echo." As I look her body over, I know even sixteen days is a longshot.

Her face twitches and she pushes her hair out of her face with her good hand, an involuntary gesture, one she's made almost every time I've called her by her first name. I hate that she doesn't like bein' called by her name. Nah, that she doesn't like *me* callin' her by it. That, in her mind, I'm not fuckin' worthy. *I'm not. The Fates knew it. That's what they told me.*

"You even know where you're goin'?"

She nods. She doesn't talk to me unless she absolutely fuckin' has to. She just nods.

"That were true, you'd know you're heading north. We need to go east."

She shakes her head and rolls her eyes, like I'm a goddamn imbecile.

"What?"

She shakes her head again.

"Talk to me, Echo."

Her mouth twitches so damn bad it nearly brings a smile to mine. When I edge her further and further in an easterly direction and she tries to resist, she finally comes to a stop. Better to stop than to touch me. *I didn't think having an Omega of my own would be like this.* And then I remember, she isn't mine. I haven't bonded her. I failed, just like I failed at…

"It's too dangerous to stop here." She refuses to look at me, continuously looking away when I move to intercept her gaze. I want her eyes on me. I like her eyes on me. Even if I don't like anything else about her. She's stubborn and rude with tears in her clothes and tears in her eyes. The only thing illustrious about her at all is her stare. She has black gemstones for eyes and they are excoriating. Given my upbringing, it's no wonder I like the pain.

"Did you forget who you were traveling with?"

She gives me a look that makes me feel about two feet tall. I should punish her. I should force her to bend to my will... But I don't want to. That doesn't sound like anything I want. I just need answers.

"Echo, tell me what you're thinking. That's an order."

She staggers and it fuckin' guts me. She falls against a pine sapling and braces her unbroken forearm against it, then presses her forehead against that. She breathes heavily, uneasily, and just as I'm about to rescind the order, she shouts, "Gang Mountain." She seethes through her teeth, fighting tooth and nail against the command I've given her. "Gang Mountain owns the river crossing east of Trash City. Everybody knows that from Trash City you have to go either north or south to one of the troll bridges if you want to cross."

She doesn't want to say more, she doesn't want to confide in me. Why would she? Still, I'm impressed by her rebellion and resistance. Maybe, more than just her eyes have me interested. Maybe, both of those things make me want to slice her tongue out of her mouth. Maybe, if we're stuck in Paradise Hole together for the next sixteen days, one of us won't make it out. Wanna strangle her and I can sense that the feeling is more than mutual.

"Travelin' with a Berserker. Don't need to go the long way."

She snorts, "You're nothing against the Alphas of Gang Mountain." I stagger at the force of her insult, and then stagger again when she lobs the next. "And I don't feel like getting ripped apart for the second time."

I roar. It just…bellows out of me. I've always had a short temper, but this is more than I can handle. This Omega called Echo might be what finally short-circuits me. Unravels me. Fucking annihilates me. I want to kill every Alpha on Gang Mountain just to prove her wrong and I stop in my tracks. I glance up at the mountain rising in the distance and inhale deeply once, twice, a third time — a technique I learned in my youth, though I ordinarily would count all the way up to ten. Not this time. Don't have the patience for it. Returning my gaze to her, I fight to decide how to proceed — break her, or prove her wrong?

I take a step towards her, tree roots bending and snapping underneath my boots, and she flinches.

She fucking flinches.

The fight drains out of me, but only by half. Still, it's enough for me to see straight. Enough for me to be able to read her terror. It pisses me the fuck off and I don't know how to fix it.

"Not gonna let any Alphas rip into you."

"Oh right. That honor's just for you, huh?"

Rage ripples and bends and breaks, just like the roots under my feet, as I plod forward past her, following the longer route she's taking north, away from the mountain, away from Dark City. *One, two… Fuck it.* "Didn't let the Alphas touch you back at the river."

She doesn't answer and that pisses me off worse than her insults. And I'm still pissed about it, even as she follows me north, marching in line behind me silently as the day fades to night and we make camp in the middle of a wet fucking swamp.

We have enough rations to last us two weeks comfortably, three if we push it, but she hoards hers like she's tryna make 'em last months. I know what she's doing, can see it in her eyes every time we stop. Three silent nights pass before I bring it up.

"No point in savin' your rations, Echo." I lay out a space blanket and unfurl a ratty blanket over it. Smells like wet human hair and I'm not desperate enough to crawl beneath it. I run hot and, if things get bad, can just let my Beast form sleep through the nights for me. He's never cold underneath all that fur. Same can't be said for Echo.

She's got a sleeping bag, but at night I can still hear her shiverin'. It's her teeth. They clench and occasionally clack when a hard gale clips us. I make us a fire the second night, but the third, it's too damn wet. Nothin' to light. And with as little as she's eaten, it's no wonder she's hurtin'. And my venom doesn't fuckin' work. Unease trickles through me.

"Why's that?" she asks. She's goading me. She doesn't talk to me unless it's to provoke, to throw up more walls between us. And right now she's doin' a damn good job. The wall between us is six feet deep, topped in barbed wire and surrounded by a flaming moat. No gettin' through that. Don't know why I'm fuckin' botherin'. Should just leave her alone. Do what I said I'd do. Take care of her and tuck her away someplace in Dark City where she can live in isolation. All she is to me is a prize. A way for me to prove that I deserve my seat, that I deserve to have ascended a Berserker.

I open my mouth to tell her that there's no point in savin' her rations because she's not gonna get away from me. Instead, I surprise myself when I tell her, "You're hurtin'. Can't heal if you don't eat."

She doesn't answer — and she doesn't eat. Pisses me the fuck off. I want to cross the ten feet of space that separates her mat from mine, rip her pack open at the seams, take the dried deer meat out and ram it down her fucking throat.

"Fine. Suit yourself." And just like that, I've sunk to her fuckin' level again.

She turns her back to me and it makes my fingers clench and curl. I don't know why, but it's hard for me to stay in my place — on my side of the packs that take the place of a firepit between us. Every instinct in my goddamn body is fightin' me to get the fuck up and wrap my whole body around her.

Wanna get in that sleeping bag next to her, cram myself in that thing that's too small for me and definitely too small for two people and keep her warm all night. Even if she hates me. Especially because she hates me. Even if she keeps tryna hoard rations so that when I let my guard down, she can try to run. Or maybe she won't run. She's too smart for that. She knows I'd hunt her down. She's going to have to kill me. Or herself.

The thought makes me feel urgent and paranoid. I glance at her pack, hatin' it like it's the one that's made the threat. I went through it while she slept in the trash pile, clearing it of all weapons, but she's crafty. There's a chance she's sourced more in the meantime or stolen from me in the minutes I've slept.

"You tryna starve yourself?"

No response.

"Slow way to die."

No response.

Sparks ignite at the base of my spine. "Echo, you can't die. Won't allow it. You belong to me, you're my responsibility, I'm your Berserker and it's my responsibility to ensure your wellbeing."

"You're doing a great job."

I'm gonna fuckin' kill her. "If you're waitin' for a fuckin' apology, you'll be waitin' til you die of fuckin' starvation." My pitch has dropped. I roll onto my side to face her. My chest is fallin' and risin' more heavily than it was. "Was tryna save your life after you stabbed yourself, heal you from that and bond you quick so other Alphas wouldn't…"

"You *bit* me, you didn't *bond* me. You failed at that, too." *Failure. Failure. Failure.* The word rings in my head on repeat along with another word, one she didn't need to say but only because her body language screams it. *Unworthy. Unworthy. Unworthy.*

I sneer, "That makes two of us, doesn't it? After I killed the Alphas who came for you from the cities, it took me one fuckin' day to find you. For all your power and all your confidence it only took me one day to sniff you out…"

"Fuck you." *There.* There's the button I can push… *Fuck* pushing, I want to rip the damn thing out.

Spinning back around to face me, her eyes blaze with hurt and anger. "I was out in Paradise Hole for six weeks on my own. You have no idea what I've done to survive. You're just Berserker royalty, dumber than a box of hair and so used to your little luxuries you wouldn't last a day in my shoes…"

Even though I'm fucking alarmed to hear she's been out here six weeks on her own, I'm so startled by her first impression of me that laughter cuts out of my chest. Hard and hacking, it grates, nearly hurts, but I can't help it. Shit's fuckin' hilarious.

"Think you know me, Omega?" For all her talk and all her bravery, she flinches when I call her that. I roll onto one knee and sweep my hand at her and at the miserable suck hole of a world surrounding us. "You think I somehow wasn't born a Beta, too? You think I'm special? You think you've got a fuckin' clue what I've been through? What I've had to do to survive? To fuckin' claw and climb the tower to the Dark City throne and take it?"

I laugh again. "Think you're better than me because you've slept on the streets, but baby, that's only because you've never slept in *dungeons*. You're mad about bein' wet but that's only because you've never lived in a swamp, hidden out in it usin' a fuckin' straw to breathe through while the mud presses down on you and you hope to fuckin' god that they don't find you because when they do, they won't take just you, they'll take…" Fuck. I choke, realizing what I was about to say and cursing myself for it.

I shake my head once, neck snapping to the left as I peg her with my gaze, refocusing on her and her mirrored rage. "You ever been strung up by your heels, had your nails pulled out with pliers? They don't regrow until your transformation. Fangs don't grow back either…"

Her face is getting redder and redder and when she shouts, her voice breaks. "You can't intimidate me, Berserker, or try to freak me out with tales of violence." She doesn't even believe me, and that's fine. That shit happened to another Beta in another life. "You have no idea what it's like to be an Omega and lose your free will. To know that if you get caught you'll be used like a fucking doll by whatever Alpha takes you…"

"Well, you better get used to it, because if you don't change your fuckin' tune, that's exactly how you'll be used and it won't be by me. You're too much of a coward to bother keeping."

"Oughph," she releases a garbled yell and grabs her chest. The ground beneath her feet starts to rumble and I don't even bother to morph into my Beast. I need a fight. I'm ready.

"You think *you* can intimidate me? I'm *your* Berserker."

"You don't command me!" The ground shivers, roots flying up to spray mud into the air like fireworks before slamming back down, aiming for me. But I learned from the last time when she leveled me with entire fucking trees. This time, I react in time to grab the roots as they fly and sever them with the downward strike of my boot. Another root I rip out of the ground with so much force it topples the tree that belongs to it.

"You think you can fucking destroy me? They call me the Destroyer for a reason, Omega, and I will break you by any means necessary. Compared to the enemies I've fought, you are nothing."

She shrieks, thunder rumbles above, the ground shakes below. A violent jolt sends me to my knees, but I surge up, grab two more roots, rip one mangrove tree from the ground and use it to shatter the trunks of two others.

I surge across the space between us as the wind picks up, carrying fat droplets of rain. They splatter her cheeks when I grab her by the hair and tilt her head back so that her face shines up at me. Her lips are pressed so hard against her teeth they're white. She smells like mud and like something died.

I know she's got some dead thing in her pack that she refuses to get rid of, but I didn't come all this way to be deterred by that because the musk of her cunt is too strong beneath it. It's a fuckin' beacon and, if I can't figure out how to bond her, it's gonna attract a lot more than a few scavengers and Alpha boys from Dark City.

Another fuckin' problem. I recognized one of those kids and he was Alpha royalty. *What the fuck were they doin' out here? So far from home?* When I approached in my beast form, I heard one of 'em talkin' about a letter. Somebody wrote 'em a letter? About Echo? Doesn't make any fuckin' sense and is just another headache to sort out when I get back home with my Omega.

"Omega," I whisper against her taut, cracked lips, "I command you to still your gifts."

She screams and it's a tortured, horrible sound that sends branches and debris and half our fuckin' shit scattering in the small tornado that crescendos in its wake. Everything comes crashing down a moment later, settling to stillness that isn't *still* so much as it's *waiting*. Her breaths are ragged and raw and she's clutching her chest in a way that makes my hands wanna do somethin', but I know she doesn't want that just like I know she doesn't fuckin' want me. *Unworthy.*

I shove her back, releasin' her and flexing my hands, tryna ignore the way her heat scars and scalds my fingertips. "That's right. Just a fuckin' doll. Coulda been more, but I'll treat you like one if that's what you wanna be."

She grunts and is so slow to move, I anticipate her before she's even got one boot securely planted on the ground beneath her. Still, I let her come at me. I let her throw her full weight against my chest and am unmoved by the blow. I just grab her by the unbandaged wrist and let her twist and kick and stomp and yell.

"Let go of me!"

I do and she flies back, landing on her good shoulder — thank fuck. Still, she isn't able to get up right away, or she chooses not to. She just lies there in the mud for a beat longer than a breath — a beat that drags an unfamiliar and unpleasant sensation across my shoulders like a string of shattered Christmas lights — before eventually rolling onto her stomach, and then propping her arm underneath her body and lurching up.

She manages to stumble onto her feet and stagger away from me, but I know she won't go far. She doesn't have any supplies and there are things here she'll need if she wants to live more than a couple hours — things she'd need if she wanted to end it and live less than that, too. So I don't follow.

I just sneer at her retreating form, unable to get my own breath and heartbeat under control, wondering who the fuck I am and how she made me this…this fucking wretched thing. I didn't used to be like this. Three weeks ago, I was a calm, confident Berserker with a closed box of memories of my life as a Beta and the darkness that brought me to Dark City.

Now, I'm just a wound that she's ripping leeches off of, letting it fester and rot, filling us both with poison. My Berserker energy has never been more tangible, nor more distant. I don't feel like retreating to it. And it doesn't feel like surfacing. I feel like going to her and touching her in soothing ways with my Alpha hands. I feel like cradling her and sheltering her from all the bad shit that goes down out here in Paradise Hole. I feel like telling her kind things and doing her kindnesses…

"Don't think those gifts even belong to you — do they, Omega? Nah, from where I'm standin', they belong to me. And without 'em, y'aren't worth the boots on your fuckin' feet."

A tree she stomps past breaks for no reason, literally exploding through its core. I'm startled by it — by her defiance to my commands — even though she doesn't seem to register the significance. *An Omega shouldn't be able to defy a Berserker like this.* She doesn't look back at it or at me. She just hunches her shoulders around her wet, mud-soaked body and keeps walking.

And that flaming moat?

Turns into a goddamn ocean.

7 ECHO
TROLL BRIDGE

THE BRIDGE IS A BAD IDEA, IS WHAT I WOULD HAVE said out loud if I hadn't recognized it as a potential opportunity.

"What are you waiting for? Trolls?" I ask, aiming to goad him.

He gives me a suspicious look and I glance away quickly, not wanting him to mistake my impatience for excitement — even though it is. "Trolls aren't real," he mutters turning back to face the stone bridge that looks like it's seen better days. I wonder absently who built it and how long ago, but I don't ask him. I don't want him to think I'm making polite chit-chat — or worse, engaging him in meaningful conversation. We're not in this together.

He steps up to the muddy bank and looks down at the river before plodding over to the foot of the bridge. He takes a step onto it and presses down with his foot, as if he thinks the stone might give.

I scoff, “That Tr…” I was going to call it a Troll bridge — whoops. “That *bridge* has been there longer than we’ve been alive and it’ll be there long after we’re corpses. It’s not going to buckle to one single Berserker.”

He looks back at me and doesn’t say anything for a second, then grunts, “Stay close.”

I purse my lips and I know he can read the words I don’t say because he glowers more hatefully in my direction.

“Don’t want you close to me either, you smell like shit, but I don’t want you tryna jump or get up to any other funny business. Not when we’re close.”

And that’s the pain of it, isn’t it? We are close. Less than three days out and he hasn’t given me an opportunity to run yet. He’s been on me like wet on a swamp. My feet hesitate and it costs me. He lunges for me, grabs me by the strap on my right shoulder and yanks me forward roughly. His meaty hand goes to the back of my neck and his claws — short in this form — pinch my pressure points. His hands are so damn big, those short, sharp claws overlap at the front of my throat. I can hear the little sounds they make brushing over each other every time I fucking swallow. Every second, I’m just a full belly breath away from decapitation.

I try to shrug him off but he just squeezes harder. Well, at least it’s not an order. I’d rather be pushed around than ordered. If he knew that, he’d probably order me around all the time. It seems like, ever since our last fight, he’s been pushing me further and further away. Not that I’m complaining.

But he was a Beta too, once.

Hiding out in swamps just like this one — worse than this one — his life might have started harder than most Betas did… Fuck no. I shake my head, refusing to think about what he said before. He's a *Berserker*. The rest is moot.

We're halfway across the bridge when the Berserker comes to a stop. He curses. "Knew this was gonna happen, didn' ya?"

I don't actually know what he means because, so far, what I thought was going to happen hasn't happened at all, but I shrug, not wanting him to know that. He curses again. A moment later, the forest in front of us starts to stir. More lush than the wet mangrove forest behind us, the forests to the east have pine and oak trees with heavy branches whose shadows are dense enough to conceal a small army…up until they choose to step out into the light.

I freeze in the Berserker's grip, blood running cold, flight instincts kicking in all at once. I lurch for the edge of the bridge, fully intending to jump, but the Berserker keeps me plastered to his side. "Don't even think about it."

I thrash harder, whimpering as I do. Pain isn't gone, she's just muted for the time being. Fear, however, makes a surprise appearance. Huh. It's been…a few days since I thought about her.

I see her clearly now as I look toward the Alpha leading the pack and then quickly take stock of the dozen other Alphas with him. I don't know if they're from Gang Mountain or are from some other marauding Alpha pack, all I know is that they are *not* the trolls I'd been hoping for. These Alphas don't look anything like the Dark City kids who attacked us, either. Those kids looked green and dumb. These guys look rough.

Wearing pants made out of animals of the forest and carrying weapons made of its wood, they have tattoos and braids in their hair, feathers and beads, too. There's something feral about them, *and oddly beautiful*, like they're at home here in Paradise Hole in ways I've never been and never will be, no matter how many weeks I spend mucking through the mud. These men look…less *hardened* by Paradise Hole and more like they're *born* of it. It hits me that maybe they are and that scares me for some reason. I understand the motives of stupid city Alphas and their Berserkers and I understand the motives of compound Betas and I understand the motives of the exiled, the trapped, the caged, the lonely…

But I don't understand the motives of the *free*.

I gulp in a breath that gets trapped in my throat and surge again, forgetting entirely about the Berserker until he tugs me back again, this time by the collar. I land against his side, engulfed in his heat. He fists the back of my coat and sweatshirt.

Under his breath, he says to me, "Don't insult me. Killed at least this many to claim you before. No problem doin' it again."

Pitching his voice loud enough to carry through the damp, stale air, the leader calls out to the Berserker beside me, speaking to him like I'm not even here. "We don't want trouble, Berserker, we just want the Omega."

The leader's bare-chested and his freckle-free skin is two shades of brown darker than mine. His hair is dark brown, maybe black, long and straight to his shoulders. He has a long, straight nose and hawkish eyes that are as dark as pitch and remind me of coal forming embers.

"No," the Berserker responds.

I'm still frozen stiff, eyeing the crumbling edge of the bridge. So focused on it, I can't figure out why the Berserker holding me shifts so that he's standing parallel to the edges of the bridge, not facing the Alpha…at *first*. But then I hear the squish of feet through mud and glance back the direction we came from and spy a dozen more Alphas crowding us from behind.

"What d'you say now, Berserker?" I hiss, hoping the other Alphas can't hear me over the raging river below. "Still think you can take 'em all?"

"Nah, but *we* can take 'em." His breath is cool against my cheek and smells like roasted chestnuts. I don't know how or why, but it smells so damn good. Makes me want to turn towards him. Makes me want to run for my life.

I don't bother trying to run away, but I do reach to my hips, feeling my belt for weapons that aren't there. He stole them all. "I'm not your tool, Berserker."

He sighs, sounding exasperated. "Fine. I'll do it myself. Stay behind me and don't fuckin' jump." He pushes me behind him, against the stone rail of the bridge. It…surprises me. I don't expect him to let go of me at all, and again instincts flare telling me to jump into the river, only…it looks turbulent…and wet…and choppy, and I only have the use of one arm. Maybe, it's a bad idea. Maybe, he really can beat them.

Uncertainty eclipses my capacity for reason and I watch as the two Alpha war parties converge on the lone Berserker. I can't decide what's the worse option, or what I should do next. Should I intervene? Can I even? Should I jump and leave the Alphas to kill one another? And what the hell is that scraping sound? Duller than a blade against a whetstone, the sound grates and comes at irregular intervals. It doesn't seem to be coming from either of the approaching groups, either. The Alphas, meanwhile, haven't noticed and continue closing in…

"She killed one of our hunting parties," the Alpha leader says and my gaze flicks to him. He glances at me only fleetingly before returning his gaze to the Berserker. "She needs to atone for her crimes."

Flabbergasted by the accusation, I shout, "No, I didn't."

The Berserker shoots me an annoyed look over his shoulder and says in a firm tone that doesn't broker argument, "You blind, Alpha? My Omega is badly injured, can barely fuckin' walk, has the use of only one arm and has been making her way through this fuckin' wasteland from Trash City with me for the past twelve days. You think she somehow managed to take down a pack of Alphas on her own, you're outta your fuckin' mind."

The Alpha has the decency to look disgruntled. He looks me over again and then looks back at the Berserker. One of his Alpha pack mates steps up to him and whispers something in his ear. His resolution refocuses. "Her gifts are strong. I can smell it. She's the one we're after."

"Callin' me a liar, then?"

"She's the witch of the woods."

"Don't know any witches. Don't know any liars, which means you must be mistaken, friend." My Berserker steps forward, towards the Alpha leading this horde. It's just a microscopic shift, but it feels as if he's moved mountains.

The other Alphas get agitated, shifting their weight, snarling low under their breaths… I get nervous and glance back and forth, waiting for the violence to begin…but there's that damn scraping again.

I look over the railing, its cold stone lip pressing into my lower back, but there's just river water. *Cold* water. Not a great idea if I want to survive the night. I might not be able to start a fire. I could die of hypothermia. Fuck. Somehow the thought of being cold and wet is worse than the thought of spending another night with this Berserker. Nope, guess I'll watch him fight to the death — maybe let him get near it before intervening, if I have that kind of control…

And before I can even finish the thought, the Berserker's fist grabs me by the front of my coat.

I jolt, look up into the Berserker's eyes and see the way they spell murder. "Don't," he hisses. I shove him off with my right arm. I'd just decided not to, but he doesn't need to know that.

The Alpha on the bridge says, "My hunting party was killed six days ago. The bodies have Omega scent all over them."

"Hers?"

The Alpha hesitates. "Similar."

I step forward, pushing against the Berserker's outstretched arm. "How were they killed?" I ask.

The Alphas start to twitch even more ravenously at the sound of my voice. One of them calls me a bitch under his breath. I roll my eyes. How original. "They were ripped apart by bears."

"Bears?" I balk.

The Berserker glances at me and we exchange a look identical to the one we shared when we realized that Trash City was exchanging *something* with *someone* powerful enough to have access to guns — a lot of them. *What's going on here?*

"I don't..." I don't even know how to say this, it sounds so fucking stupid. "I'm not a bear."

A few of the Alphas chuckle darkly, but the leader narrows his already narrow eyes. "It's not a question of what you are now, but what you can become."

"She isn't the Omega you're looking for. Her gifts don't extend that far."

"Are you sure?" the Alpha says. More scraping. I ignore it, so confused am I by the conversation at hand.

"Yes, he's fucking sure. I can do stuff with plants." I'm gesturing with my good hand and, unconsciously, I pull my gift out of my sleeve like a damn clown at a children's party.

Vines grow out of my fucking lifeline, small and slender, they spiral up into the air and freak the shit out of me. I jump and shake my hand off and they fall to the stone ground. When I look down, I see something odd...something beautiful. Was that a...a *flower* in the vines? I think it might have been purple, but I don't get a fair look. *I've never seen a flower before...*

The scraping is back, louder now, and coming from underneath my feet. My gaze is wrenched away from the sight of what was probably just a weed by the memory of what November told me once. *Trolls. They hide* under *bridges.*

"Shit. Berserker, I think..."

One of the stones in the center of the bridge suddenly disappears and three plastic balls come flying out. The Alpha gang leader is the first to react. "Cover!" he roars.

The Berserker doesn't hesitate, but grabs me by my outstretched arm, shoves me down where the stone bridge meets the stone railing and morphs into his Berserker form. As he explodes his clothes and morphs into a beast, he shreds through his clothing and the straps of his pack in the process.

I curse as the pack is lost to the river below but I'm not left long to lament its loss when a huge, furry weight settles over me and three explosions go off, one right after the other. The beast above me jolts, then releases a low hiss. The world settles to silence. What the fuck just happened?

His beast form ripples across his skin, taking fur with it, until the Berserker's left draped half over the rail, looking like a man half dead — a naked man...a naked corpse. Seriously, what the hell just happened?

I stand shakily and glance around. The bridge and surrounding area are covered in slumped over Alphas. Even those that were carrying large wooden shields were hit. Some are trying to crawl away, but most are already passed out. *Darts.*

They've all got darts sticking out of their backs and faces and chests and legs and arms. Plastic shrapnel is all that's left of the bombs. *Dart* bombs. Since November first told me about trolls — Betas who live in Paradise Hole and attack anybody daring to cross one of *their* bridges that traverse Paradise River — it's clear they've updated their methods. *They just took down an entire gang of Alphas.*

This is the second time I've seen Betas take on Alphas in just as many weeks. I don't know whether to be proud or terrified. Right now, I'm definitely feeling more the latter than the former. Because I might have made it past the first stage of their offensive, thanks to the naked Berserker slumped over beneath me, but they're starting to swarm the ends of the bridge and soon, they'll be coming to collect their bounty.

I've only got seconds before they see me and shoot me with one of their darts and I'm down for the count, passed out — or dead — like the rest of these Alphas. A bold move to try to take on so many, but these trolls clearly have practice and must think that the reward will be greater than the risk. I'm not sure. Aside from what's in my pack, the Alphas don't seem to be carrying much on their persons. From what I can see, they carry smallish leather packs and hand-hewn metal and wooden weapons. And given that I've got the biggest pack on the bridge — and am an Omega, besides — that makes *me* the most valuable thing left on the bridge at the moment, just ripe and ready for their culling.

I lurch left, prepared to run back the way we came, but there are three trolls there, climbing out from under the bridge in so many layers of clothing, they look more like shadow-wrapped monsters than humans. I turn right, and there are six. Fuck me.

I glance at the river and slam my teeth together, trying to use the pain of it to think. I'm terrified. The spray from the river water is *freezing* and I only have the use of one leg and one arm. And this isn't an easy river. There are *rapids*.

I glance over my shoulder and the trolls, with their soot-covered faces, are looking at me. The whites of their eyes are flashing and they're discussing something amongst one another, but in voices too low to hear. I'm not going to wait around for them to come to a decision, though, draw their dart guns and blast me in the face. I'm going to *have* to jump. *And see what fucking happens…if I live at all, or if I die in agony.*

I step up onto the railing, right next to where the Berserker is draped over the stone edge, only to be shocked when he grunts, pushes himself onto one side and strokes my ankle above my boot.

He blinks up at me and a momentary thread of something terrible pierces my heart, tethering bits of it together that were adrift. "Jump," he croaks, sounding on the brink of collapse. "Won't let you drown."

Thwump! A dart hits my pack and the Alpha's hand on my ankle steels and wrenches. He drags me off of the rail and I yelp as I go tumbling down towards the icy river. I'm vaguely aware of him tumbling down right after me…and then *splash!*

No. Oh no nonononononononoonoooonno.

As the river water and I collide, my soul leaves its rickety frame then smashes back down in icy thunder. My body seizes up. I can't do this. This was a bad, bad idea. I blame the Berserker. I should have gone with the Alpha gang and let them kill me for crimes I didn't commit. It would have been more pleasurable than this.

My limbs can't move, even the ones that work. Waves crash over the top of my head and rocks bang against my boots. They're heavy, those boots. Boots the Berserker got back for me. I blame him for that, too. They're weighing me down.

A gut-wrenching moan sobs out of my mouth as I collide with a river rock, my injured arm taking the brunt of it right before a heavy weight slams into my left side. Hot and hard as a brand, it coils around my chest, holding me awkwardly against an even greater weight.

I break the surface of the waves a minute later and the Berserker's voice is in my ear. "Get us out of here, Echo. That's an order."

I don't know what he means and gasp, pulling in more water than air.

"Breathe, Echo," he orders and I do. I mean, I try. I'm still choking as he spits, "Now, get us out of here. Use your gifts to push us…onto…the riverbank." He sounds like he's in as much pain as I am, his words coming slower with every second that goes by.

I open my mouth to tell him he can't order me around like this, but I can't taste anything but ice and minerals, can't even feel my tongue. But I can feel his arm, hot as an ember, and his body lining my back. He jumped into the river. Why? He was already drugged, his risk was even greater than mine. It still is. Unless I do something.

Over the frothy tips of the rapids, I see two friends I'd have rather not. Fear and Pain are with me now, waving wildly from atop their canoes as they navigate the rapids with a gravity-defying grace that I don't have. Or maybe…I do… Because the Berserker ordered me to, which means *I can do this.*

"Augh!" I roar and I close my eyes and I repeat his command again and again in my thoughts. *The Berserker wants me to move us onto the riverbank. I can do this*. The fact that the river bends beneath the command *he* gave frustrates and elates me in the same breath. But I don't dwell on the whys or even the hows, I just *do it*.

Energy pulses out of me like a wave. I black out, but I can feel the water working beneath me, pushing me up, giving my bottom a boost and tossing me onto the muddy shore.

Right next to him.

Wrapped and trapped in his arms.

"Good Omega. You did good, baby." His voice is really close and I can feel hot breath on my forehead. I preen, my back arching, my fingers reaching for him through the veil of my hatred. My instinct to please is too strong. His smell is too strong. The cold is too strong. Everything is too much. Everything except the encroaching darkness… Darkness is so inviting…

"No, Echo. No. You did so good. Stay with me." His voice is lazy and slow and I hate its encouraging tenor. It's a tone I haven't heard him use before. Must mean bad things are coming.

I shiver and it hurts. My skin prickles and my palm…my good palm is against something harder than the Berserker is…hard and cold. I blink once, but the world is harsh so I close my eyes. I'm up high on some rocks out of the grip of the icy water and its hungry current. It doesn't seem to matter, though. I'm not going to make it.

"Cold," I try to say, but my teeth clack so hard, the word gets separated into fourteen syllables. "C-c-c-c-c-c-oh-oh-oh-el-el-el-duh."

I cough up another lungful of liquid and my chest rattles. It doesn't feel good. I don't feel good. I'm going to die here unless I can get warm. I've got a dry sleeping bag in my pack, but that's it. That's all that would fit in the waterproof bag. Maybe, I can find refuge tonight, hunker down, stay dry and warm and my clothes will dry by the morning. Or maybe, my own body heat won't be enough to survive the night.

And then his voice crashes into my thoughts, reminding me of something quite odd: I'm not alone — anymore.

I'm not alone *anymore.*

"Nah, baby." His slur is worse and sounds further away, but I know that can't be right when I feel that brand up against my chest and then circling around me, covering my every inch. "Gonna be okay." His voice turns into a growl and suddenly, I'm being dragged over the ground, further away from the river, higher up onto the embankment where the mud turns to grass. "Gotta be okay."

I don't know how he's still awake with darts covering him. Nor do I know how he expects either of us to survive this. But he doesn't stop. He doesn't give up. And as he continues to drag himself up away from the water — and me with him — I recognize that if this stupid Berserker can keep going after dropping into the same river I did and getting shot a million times, I can, too. He's not better than me in anything, least of all surviving, no matter what his Beta upbringing looked like.

Claws ripped out of his fingers. Fangs ripped out of his head.

I blink and see blood and wince. I open my eyes again and as my gaze slowly comes into focus, I realize I'm staring at the wall of his chest and the darts studding it. I glance up, my eyeballs straining, my neck, too. His strong neck is bulging and his face is bright red. He's got his arm stretched up overhead and I watch, fucking flabbergasted, as he punches the claws of his right hand into the soil and climbs.

His left arm remains firmly coiled around me. He doesn't let me go. He just drags us forward, ever forward, until we near the first of the trees and it's here, finally, that he starts slowing down.

His jaw clenches and he looks down at me. Our eyes connect and his expression changes, becoming more neutral, as he looks at me trying to free my good arm from between us and reach up to employ the same tactic he has by jamming my fingers into the ground and dragging us to drier ground.

I rip out a fistful of grass and chuck it aside, and when I try again, I rip out another, even bigger tuft of grass. The Berserker makes a sound, but when I look up at his face, he's not watching me anymore. Instead, he's back to dragging. *He's smiling though.*

I start clawing at the ground with renewed determination and find that the exertion helps warm me up and bring me back to life.

"Berr-berr-serker?" I whisper, rolling to face him as we hit the first copse of trees. He's not pulling anymore and I can't pull the both of us together. I try kicking with my feet, but my legs are two meat popsicles and he's a goddamn ton. We don't move at all.

We. I said we. *Fuck.*

"Berrrrrrsssserk-k-k-ker." His eyes are closed, his mouth is relaxed in sleep. I glance over his chest, intending to pound on it, but there are too many darts still sticking out of him and nowhere that isn't bloody.

My too-many-layers of soaking wet clothing are heavy as shit and I struggle to move in them. "B-b-berserker." I whack instead on an unaffected part of his arm.

In a move that startles me, that arm snakes out and catches my wrist. "Omega."

I jolt. "D-d-d-don't fall asleep. And d-d-d-d-don't c-c-call me Oh-oh-ohmeggga."

"Can't call you Echo. Havena earned it, Omega," he sighs in a rumbling breath. I hate it. I hate how it moves me. It moves me to action.

His eyelids twitch, but he stays asleep as I manage to roll onto my injured shoulder and use my right arm to pluck the darts out of his chest, neck, shoulder and the bits of his back that I can reach. I need him alive. I need his heat.

"Ber-ber-serker? Berser-k-ker, hey! D-d-don't sleep. If you don't sssssleep…if you st-stay awake, you c-c-c-can call me Eck-eck-eck…" I can't even choke the word out. "Echo. Berserker?"

I yank a dart out of his neck and he groans and rolls onto his back, wincing in pain when he does. I shiver uncontrollably, out from under the umbrella of his warmth and somehow, some way, I manage to shove my good arm under his enormous, heavy-as-shit body and search for darts. I pluck out the remaining three.

When I look up at his face, his eyes are slitted, but he sees me. He's got a drunk little smile strung between his lips that I don't like at all. "Good Omega."

"F-f-f-fuck you," I whisper, but my heart picks up its pace and I feel stronger than I did just a second before. "Are yyyyyou on d-d-d-drugs?"

He snickers at that and he's so lazy and docile he almost looks…sweet. It's revolting. What the fuck is going on? What the hell is in those darts and can I get some? And what happened to my savage Berserker? I liked the monster. I understand monsters.

"Still cold?" I nod emphatically and he chuckles. "Come." He opens up his arms and I don't have any other choice but to roll into his chest.

Well, I might have had choices, but somewhere in between him opening his arms and telling me how good I did, I lost the list.

He hisses the moment I get in close and starts to pull and push at the strap of the pack still slicing through my shoulder. "Naked," he says, but his hands are big and clumsy and he's not making any progress.

"N-n-n-n-nnnoooo. I'm not g-g-getting naked."

"Cold," he breathes, voice tight, but nowhere near as choppy as mine, which only pisses me off more. "Not gonna make it like this, Echo."

A shiver breaks through my restraint at the absolute worst moment.

"Naked," he says again, only this time, his arms are both in motion, pulling my sweatshirt off.

"Not-not ev-ev-ev-ev-everythi…" Cold air caresses my bare back and I lose consciousness for a critical second.

"Echo." My eyes open and I'm instantly aware that all of the layers that once covered my torso are gone. "Pants," he says next and I hiss when I realize where I am and what's happening and the warmth…dear fuck, the warmth…it feels heavenly.

His chest is pressed right up against my chest, my small boobs mashed against his pecs. He's looking down, but his eyelids are closed tight over his eyes as he fights so damn hard for control. His hand is on my button, pushing and prodding. My injured arm is cradled carefully between us, naked of the bindings that once covered it and frighteningly exposed. But it doesn't feel that way against the cage of his body. It feels… okay here.

"Gonna have to help me, Echo. Don't got a lotta time. Gonna have to protect us while I'm out. Can you do that, baby?"

I shiver at the contact of his fingers on my lower abdomen. He's got the button free and his fingers are moving down, inside… I suck in a breath and nod real tight. I brace my good palm against his abdomen and manage to lift my hips and shuck off my boots, socks, pants and panties.

Just as naked as he is, I look up at his face to see him looking down at my body. He meets my gaze and his cheeks redden. Mine respond with an equal heat. I start to try to cover my boobs, but before I can so much as lift my arm, he revolves our bodies, rolling us over so that I'm trapped between him and the trunks of two large trees. Pines. Not mangroves.

I tip my forehead forward until it touches the center of his chest. He bends his arm and wedges his bicep underneath my head, and pillows his own head with his hand of the same arm. I don't like it. I don't like that it feels *thoughtful*. But that doesn't stop me from lining his meaty thighs with mine and curling my shaking hands into fists and coddling them desperately between us.

His other arm wraps around my back and pulls me against him, and as my consciousness flickers in and out for a few more moments, I register three final sensations:

The rumbling of his chest that flares before dying out to deeper, more peaceful inhalations…

His cock, for the love of all that's wretched, somehow partly erect and flaming hot and pushing at my belly…

And moss-wrapped vines coiling around us, shifting our bodies subtly, so that we're no longer touching the wet ground.

Before I can figure out what nefarious plan those vines are concocting, his rumbling chest rocks me to sleep and I'm lost to the sound.

ECHO
PARADISE RIVER

I BLINK AND THEN SHAKE MY HEAD AND BLINK AGAIN, trying to make sense of this…this shaking. A dull quake, it follows a certain pattern. I inhale, try to focus my gaze, but it's my ears that find understanding first. He's rumbling. He's rumbling for *me*.

I don't know where the idea comes from, but now that it's arrived, I can't shake it. *He's rumbling for me. He's a Berserker trying to soothe his Omega.*

Alphas, like Berserkers, can purr for their mates — it's one of the only remarkable differences between Alphas and Betas, other than their slightly larger sizes, and is often used as the marker to distinguish them when the gleam of their eyes cannot. But Berserkers? Berserkers don't just purr, they *roar*. The sound is unlike anything I've ever felt before. It makes me feel like I'm not lonely — like I've never been lonely. Like I'm worthy.

I tilt my face up like a flower reaching for sunlight, but there is no light. At least, not enough to make out any more than the fact that we're trapped inside of something and it's...porous somehow, while still being firm and soft around me. *Vines.* And moss, too. They're layered on top of one another, creating a shelter for us that's less tree house and more sarcophagus.

I expect a quiver at the thought — some sort of negative reaction — but I've never been claustrophobic, and I never want to leave this. It's not *dry* in here, but it's almost dry and, above all else, it's *warm,* almost heavenly.

I try to move my right leg but there is nowhere to move it. The cocoon that surrounds us leaves no quarter. I grunt when my toe hits the shell around us and his hand darts out of nowhere, palming the side of my face. I gasp. He rumbles louder. His fingers dig into the back of my head *hard* and my good hand slaps down onto his chest. I rub my fingers across it, distracted by the feel of his scars.

There's one over his heart that stands out the most. Raised from his skin, it feels like a giant X. I lean forward and he lets me go where I want until I breathe against it. He rubs his thumb beneath my eye and I stop moving, then lean further into his touch. He purrs even louder, roaring quietly for his Omega, drowning out my thoughts, erasing them. My breathing is a little panicked and rough and spots fill my vision, purple and yellow blooms exploding in time with my pulse.

I'm grateful for the hazy lens I'm seeing him through. Helps me keep my distance from the fact that he smells like snow and metal, like two Berserker warlords of old battling to the death in the dead calm of a winter's night. He smells like war itself. And I like the scent. I inhale it deeply and know that I should have let him drown in the river. In saving him, I doomed myself.

I close my eyes when I feel the press of his hot mouth at the point where my hairline meets my forehead, just right of center. His kiss is wet and hungry and there's a tingling in my nipples that I feel mirrored on the tops of my thighs. I don't know what to do with either.

He presses his mouth more forcefully against me, bruisingly, and my thighs squeeze together — they try, but the left one is half-healed mess of scabs trying to scar. The pain intensifies when a cramp hits my lower abdomen that's so out of place — I haven't had a period since coming out into the woods. A little spotting, but I haven't gone into heat yet. It can't be happening now. *Shouldn't* be.

But the cramp twists harder and I moan. He freezes. The rumbling gets more intense, shaking my whole body. It… somehow releases the pain from the cramps without releasing me from them completely. No, the twisting has become a dull pressure and I stifle a whimper by biting my bottom lip.

He rumbles louder and I can't take it. I gasp, "*Present.*" I say the word because that's what I want to do. That's all I can think about. "Present to my Berserker." My fingers count his abs twice before my palm flattens and slides down. *I want to feel it.* I'm warm and dry. No. I can't. I can't possibly want… Maybe this is a dream. *It has to be a dream. It has to.* Anything can happen in a dream. There are no consequences here that will translate to real life. I whimper as my gut cramps harder.

His kiss turns hungry then, moving across my forehead like he's trying to blanket my dirty skin in his scent, before moving down the bridge of my nose. He kisses the tip and he does it so tenderly, I wonder if this isn't a different male than the Berserker I know, one I've never met before. And then he grabs my jaw so hard it hurts and it rips a smile out of me. *It's him, alright.*

My fingers find his erection, that hot length of silk-wrapped steel. It's dry and smooth and too huge to fit anywhere it's supposed to and my cramping intensifies, wanting to try anyway — in *all* the ways. *I need him inside of me.* The thought comes like a slap to the face — like a knife to the neck — and I gasp desperately, words mumbled and indistinct. My healing arm spasms. Desperation cuts me down. I mewl wildly and fist the head of his cock, and his reaction is pure violence.

His hips buck into my grip so hard my entire body slams against the mossy wall caging us. Pain splinters down my spine, erasing the pain in my gut. He doesn't give a shit because the startled *ooph* that punches out of me is captured immediately by his mouth.

He doesn't just taste me, he fucking *impales* me. He's fangs and tongue, fire and brimstone, a demon trying to resurrect itself through my taste. I fight back, matching his violence with a violence of my own. I bite his upper lip and he hisses. His purr becomes a rumble again, more like the call he'd make before going into battle, full of rage and foreboding. It fills the air with an aggression I can taste and want to sing to.

My jaw clenches and I scratch my chipped nails across his chest and the rumbling turns wild. He jerks, like he's gonna come back and kiss me, but he's too late because I'm on the attack as I surge against his mouth, hurting my injured arm in the process. I cry out and my aim goes wild and I end up shoving my mouth against his jaw and getting a mouthful of beard. It's rough and tastes feral but if he wanted me to, I'd suck it clean. *I am his Omega. He is my Berserker. And I will present for him. I'll do anything he wants.* No. No… *Yes.*

Just this once.

"Omega, watch your fuckin' arm," he hisses, giving my head a punishing shake which I don't feel because all I can feel is that angry rattling in his chest getting louder. It's so loud it drowns out reason as he rolls our bodies over into the only other position this tiny shell of a thing will allow…

He's on top of me. I scratch his neck, wanting to draw blood and pull him forward at the same time. He doesn't react to me taking my cracked fingernails to his skin. He just moves my injured arm to the center of my chest and is careful not to put any weight on my torso even as his knees slide between my knees and his hips press forward until his pubic hair is crushed against my pubic hair and his cock is crushed against my cunt.

My sanity starts to unravel. I moan and grab for him, reaching for anything and finding beard. I yank him down to meet my mouth and I lose myself to the taste of him.

I lick his bottom lip, I bite his beard hair and yank, pulling strands free. I wipe my mouth off on his shoulder, leaving trails of spit. I bite his throat. I plant feverish kisses across his shoulder and over his heavy collarbone until I reach the V at the base of his neck. I flatten my tongue to his trachea and lave it, licking away the salty tang of his sweat. Tears come to my eyes. I *need.* I need so badly. His taste…his taste is magical. His taste is safety.

I pant, on the verge of shaking apart or maybe blacking out. I'm so overwhelmed. "You taste like snow," I tell him, voice cracking.

"You taste like sin." His palm comes around the front of my neck and he pushes my head back, back until it rests against the surprisingly squishy floor. He's moving so slowly, my eyes get hot, my hips buck, but he just holds me down and plants lingering, languid kisses on both of my cheeks before sliding his tongue deep into my mouth, like he's trying to suck the bitch out of me, moan by moan.

Good thing, because I'm also trying to bleed the bastard out of him drop by drop. "Mhmm…" My anger peaks and, when he kisses me softly the next time, I bite his upper lip again, tasting blood.

He doesn't mind. He doesn't slow or stop. He kisses me more deeply, more slowly, and I wrap myself around him, and by that I mean I just desperately arch my back and heave my chest up off of the ground while he holds me down, carefully pressing on my throat with what feels like very little effort on his part.

His lips move to my ear and suckle the lobe. The scrape of his fangs against my cheek makes me tense, but softly, so softly, in the darkness he whispers, "Won't bite ya, Echo. Never again. Promise on my fuckin' heart."

I start to breathe harder, my chest shuddering, gut cramping, things getting choppy as a foreign sensation makes its way into my crotch and bursts. I feel like I'm gonna have explosive diarrhea. *Nah, I'm gonna have an orgasm.* There isn't enough though…not enough. I need…to fuck…something. *No. I need to fuck my Berserker.*

I reach for his dick again and fumble trying to find it. I'm so lost. I hope I stay lost forever because I know already I won't forgive myself when I wake from this. I find his cock wedged between our lower abdomens just as he licks a line from my ear across my jaw and back to my mouth.

He shoves my head to the right with his own and kisses me harder, his head angling to the left so he can gain better access, moving deeper. His lips move in careful motions, even hungry as they are, nipping and biting something feverish, and it suddenly occurs to me that he might be…teaching me what to do. Does he know I haven't kissed many boys? Does he know I've kissed even fewer men? Is it that obvious?

I jerk, trying to break the contact as some of the cramping in my stomach hollows out into embarassment, but that must piss him off because he reaches between us abruptly and shoves my hand off his cock. Am I doing that wrong, too? My mortification is high, but not so high as my need as he lines himself up with my pussy and presses the bloated head of his cock against my wetness. My pussy quivers and I squeeze my eyes shut tight.

I clumsily search for his mouth, missing it for the second time. I find his neck now and bite. He moves his hand from my neck to my hair and wrenches me back down onto the floor. I can't move and am left pinned and immobile underneath him. I blink and see a gleam, but maybe it's just a hallucination. The inside of this coffin is pure darkness. It's not real.

It's not real. I'm not about to fuck the Berserker who owns me.

He pushes forward a little, but it's enough for a jagged moan to tear out of my whole body. I must be moving because the next thing I know, he's carefully pressing his fingers against my chest, holding me down carefully.

"Fuck," he cusses and he starts to draw back.

I squeeze my shaking thighs around his hips in a total panic. "No."

"Baby, gonna hurt yourself. Can't have it."

"Please." My eyes burn with fresh tears all over again. I can't stop them.

"Nearin' heat. Could send me into rut. Could fuckin' kill you, Echo."

"You won't," I gasp, and an uncomfortable warmth slides across my chest, making me doubt — not him, but myself. Because he's the Berserker I fucking hate, but there's still truth in what I said.

His rumble drops to a deep purr again and it fans the flames in my heart and in my crotch simultaneously. "Can't know that..." His voice jerks. "You fuckin' cryin'?"

Yes. "No." *This isn't a dream.*

He starts to pull back and I clamp my legs around his hips as tight as I can. It sends pain radiating through my left leg, but a pain that dull by comparison to the need crashing through my glass bones like a sledgehammer. *Smash, smash, smash.*

"Please. I just want...something. Need it, Berserker. Please. Please, Berserker." I've never begged anything of anyone before and I just begged him. *Him.* I hate myself. *No. Let the dream live for now. I'll hate myself in the morning.*

He flattens his body to mine, but leaves a hollow between our chests where my injured left wrist lies. His mouth comes against my ear. He suckles the lobe again before swirling his tongue inside. His growl rolls through me until my eyes roll back and I start to pant.

"Gonna fuck you, Echo, but…" I whimper at his words, trying to tilt my pelvis up, but I can't move at all. He's fully in control of my body, so I sit taut, waiting impatiently for his demand. "…you gotta call me Adam."

I can't breathe. My thoughts turn to fire. The coffin is actually a crucible. I roast alive, immolating from within. I can't breathe suddenly, but I can feel *everything* and it's moving. It comes alive. I feel flutterings next to my face and I can hear Adam curse in confusion right before he whispers, "Flowers."

His voice sounds like it's coming at me from the bottom of that icy river. I don't want to hear it, don't need to hear it. I just need his body, that connection. I didn't want his name, but I need it to force his hand, to quench my thirst.

My hips piston up, but he pushes them down, retreating.

I start to sweat, head tossing to the side, trying to reach his lips — anything — but he's a cruel master and holds firm in his denial.

"Please," I beg the Berserker. "*Adam*, please…"

His hips surge forward and he splits me down the middle like an axe through wood. There's no gentleness here. No slow edging forward. There's just one brutal fucking concrete thrust that sends all however many inches of him into my body. I break apart and utter his name on a scream.

"Adam!"

"Fuck me." His grip on my hair is hard and so is his dick. He's so hard, massaging my core on every thrust, every retreat, I'm so fucking full as he fucks the need out of me. I'm wet enough to take it. Thank god. Because he moves in brutal jerks for a while before he slows down and grinds against me, moving his hips in a figure-eight motion so that his pubic bone and the hairs dusting it smash against my clit. It's pure nirvana.

I didn't think it would be like this — so punishing, like a reprimand for ever thinking I could escape him.

"Oh god…Adam…" I can't take it. I can't take any part of this.

"Don't you fuckin' go into heat, Omega."

My synapses fire, but I don't know what he means or how to stop it. "H…heat?" I've never gone into heat before. I don't even know what he's talking about.

"Fuck…augh." He groans in pain and fever grips me and his lips are the only things that anchor me to the planet. My soul is trying to rejoin the earth it came from. My memories are unwrapping themselves to reveal the happy little girl beneath, the one who once had hopes and dreams and wanted things and spoke of sunshine like it was something she might actually one day see.

"Didno," he says, though his voice has dropped and is so deep and scratchy that I can't really understand him. I also don't need words from him now. "Prouda you, baby. Pleasin' your Berserker so fuckin' good right now."

I drag air deep into my lungs but somehow still can't catch my breath. My thoughts spiral and my gut pulls into a knot and my arousal pools between my legs and fires. The pressure against my clit is too much, and whatever's happening on the inside is too deep. He's reaching past all my organs and grabbing hold of my heart in a vise and it doesn't belong to him. But I don't want him to let go, either.

The orgasm slams over me and I buck and collapse. I hold onto his shoulder with my right hand, my nails biting into his skin as my arm shakes all the way up past my stitches to my ear. Coming down, there's wetness on my face and also heat, and it takes me a moment to realize that I'm crying and he's lapping up each tear, catching them on the tip of his tongue. It only makes me cry harder. My bones are brittle and old and so is my soul. I'm tired of being tired and I'm afraid of being afraid. Pain is my only friend and she fucking sucks.

But this…this is *amazing.* The stultifying pressure between my legs, his cock entering my body, massaging my channel, until it's in all the way in, wedged deep, even the knots in my belly which his dick seems to release…it all feels incredible.

Adam moves slowly above me and, wherever my hand travels across his skin, muscles ripple and bend beneath it. Makes me feel like I'm in control of some great and powerful ocean. I slide my palm down the length of his back and try to reach his ass, but can't. I knead his side roughly and reach up and do the same to his neck.

He exhales on my lips and kisses me too tenderly for me not to hate him for it. Of all the things he's ever done to me, I hate him for that the most.

I wrench him down until his forehead is touching mine and my mouth opens and I try not to sob as his groin massages my clit like waves on rocks and my thighs start to tremble all over again. He doesn't say anything and continues to move in a wonderful figure-eight motion that has me pounding on his back and making every small movement I can to show him that I like this and that I don't want him to stop.

"Please me so good, Omega," he purrs.

I open my mouth, and a small, strange sound comes out that makes him curse. Softness touches my cheeks and lingers there and I don't understand what it is until he brushes it away and says, "*Flowers*. That's it, baby. Come for your Berserker, now."

He keeps thrusting even and smooth until stars appear behind my eyes. My entire body tenses up, but he's there, surrounding me, guiding me through the wilderness as my second orgasm lights up the night.

I feel it from the soles of my feet to the tips of my hair, all the way down my ribcage, through my throbbing arm and wildly shaking injured leg. Everything hurts, but in the best possible way. Tears stream down my cheeks inconsiderately and he continues to patiently wipe them away with his tongue, alternating between that and plucking at my mouth with his lips. His scent slaughters me. I am his shield-maiden.

And he's just a Berserker warlord who doesn't have any idea what he's done.

The orgasm shakes me to the roots of my hair, but he holds firm, unaffected except for a small tensing of his body. He also holds his breath. He keeps moving, keeps swiveling his hips in that horrible pattern that makes me want to scream. I do.

"Don't go." I sob.

"Won't."

"I'm scared of Paradise Hole."

"Know it."

"I'm scared of being alone."

"Not alone, Echo," he says, or it's what I think he says because in that moment, the rumbling of his chest is so loud and the force of my orgasm is so powerful that they drown out reality.

A terrible serenity cuts through me like a blade, leaving space enough for the monstrous Berserker to shove his hands into the wound and leave small flakes of himself inside. As my eyes roll back and he holds me carefully, cradling my arm between us, I know that when the dream fades and morning dawns, I'm going to regret everything.

I also know that I'm going to want to regret everything a second time.

He grunts and his labored breathing picks up as the pressure between my legs finally releases in one liquid gush. I'm sloppy and wet down there. I can hear it. My whole body goes limp and so do my legs, but I can hear the wet, sloppy sound of him swiveling in and out of me, moving in that erotic pattern that never breaks, not even when I come all over him and my inner walls tremble and squeeze. It makes me feel momentarily self-conscious, or it would have, had I not been so shattered by this. Had he not released me from the prison of my need.

I sniffle and hold onto his shoulders, waiting for him to erupt just like I did. Instead, he kisses my swollen lips almost *sweetly*, before slowing down. "You finish?"

I nod until I remember he can't see me. "Yeah."

His rumbling flares. He whispers, "Good, Omega." Slowly, *painfully*, he starts to withdraw his erection from my fluttering core. He's still stiff as a board.

I try to clench my thighs around him, not wanting the heat to go away, not wanting to break the connection, wanting to use him to anchor me to something that isn't cold or wet or painful, but *almost* sweet, definitely rough, and unrepentantly glorious.

But he's stronger than I am and I'm a boneless fish. I have no strength at all to stop him from pulling out of me, his hot, still very erect cock slapping the inside of my thigh. He carefully rolls the both of us over and I let him, too confused, too stunned. *Why didn't he come?* He pulls my body on top of his, using me as a blanket. *But why didn't he come?*

I close my eyes and my arms flop out to either side. He holds the good one up and curses, then rotates us further so that I'm on my back beside him, both of us unable to fit on the floor part of this cocoon together, leaving us each curled up against the walls. I hear vines tearing and then his hands start working my bad arm upright.

Finished, he settles against the curve of the cocoon. I can't move my left arm at all. I can't see him, but he seems to be able to. He rigged my arm up with what feels like vines and now my arm hangs suspended above my body so that my fingers point to the missing sky. I know what he's done and why he's done it — *to take down the swelling* — and both the action and the reason behind it make me sniffle harder.

"Good, Omega." His rumble soothes. He presses a kiss to my left temple. He wraps one arm around me and I close my eyes and I forget that I hate him and that I'll still need to try to escape and that he's only after me because of my gifts and that he didn't come in me even though I came so hard all over him, and instead, I breathe in the scent of a battlefield and I cry myself into the deepest, most peaceful sleep I've had in this long, listless thing I call a life.

Turning my head to the side, I breathe in his battle-brewed scent and exhale over the X carved above his heart.

ADAM
MOMENTS EARLIER

THE OMEGA IS NEARING HER HEAT.

The Omega wants to fuck.

Those two truths slam into me, waking me slowly and painfully, making me feel feverish and insane. I wake to the smell of her body. I've trained myself on how to wake up captive in the dark, how to move my mind into boxes and use those boxes to bag up feelins a pain, a bein' tortured. I trained for this over and over…but here? Now? In the dark where threats could be imminent, all I can sense is her. All I can smell is her need. Her arousal.

My Omega needs her Berserker. Simple as that. Nothin' else matters.

So I take my training and abandon all of it.

It's that damn smell. My Berserker is ravenous for that scent. Like something concocted, brewed just for it. For *me*. She smells like a goddess should smell. Like every flower all at once. She smells like fresh-cut grass and green leaves. It's a delicate, clean scent that doesn't belong to the foul-mouthed survivalist who wears her hate like a cloak that she tries so desperately to hide beneath. But underneath that hate, there's more. Just like, underneath her pack that she's filled with the pelts of dead and rotten things, I can smell that distant forest. Paradise, before Paradise Hole was born. A bruised perfection that exists, just like her gifts, constantly trying to break free.

She thinks she's bein' hunted by us Alphas, when the truth is that she could lay claim to any Alphas she wants to. Between her broken softness, her vulnerability, that maddenin' fuckin' scent, the vines she wields, ropin' outta her, flingin' at us poor, unsuspectin' Alphas...we don't stand a chance and I don't give a shit. I'll kill anybody who ever tries to break the chains that she's already laid on me. *Or die tryin'.* I think of the Fates, what they told me. Then I force those thoughts aside. Right now, my Omega needs me.

A split second of sobriety reminds me that she's injured and that I should try to put space between my dick and her hips but fuck knows I won't.

I inhale even deeper, letting her smell suffocate me, and when my lungs are full to bursting, I take in just a little more, wanting to be sure that I don't survive the onslaught. I don't. Because when I exhale, every fury I've ever carried with me bleeds out into the world and my chest does somethin' terrible, somethin' incredible, somethin' it's never done before. The warning rattle morphs, changing, becoming both deeper and softer — something that comes from my belly, not from my lungs or from my throat.

I release a rumbling Berserker *purr,* a mating call.

I purr for my Omega. I didn't…I didn't think I was even capable of it. *I'm done for.*

I wrap my arms around her. I slide one hand underneath her back and feel my way along her shoulder blades to her spine, up to her neck. I press my fingers into her skin too hard, I know, but with her, I struggle for gentleness. She can take it. She's a fucking savage.

The sound that comes out of her mouth has me clenching my teeth together and tightening my thighs. She starts to shift, her hips lifting into the air. The fuck is she doing? Where the fuck *are* we?

Images flash into my consciousness, spliced with the fever dreams that make it hard for me to distinguish reality from fantasy. Because this is a fantasy. I've dreamed this dream every single night since I saw her holding that knife, since she stabbed herself in the thigh. Fucking savage. Fuckin' warrior.

Mine.

My aggression spikes and my chest goes back to rattlin' out a hard melody while my hips piston into whatever warmth they can find. She tilts her face up to me and her hips shift up again. "Pre…present…" she says, still half-asleep, eyes closed, tone way, way too soft to belong to an Omega scavenger who held a knife to the throat of a Trash City doc, that sanctimonious prick.

"What?" I rumble back, voice too thick for her to understand.

She whispers something too low to make out, but when I press my fingers into her lower back, somehow having enough awareness not to cut her with my claws, she mewls, "Present to my Berserker…"

"Fuck."

I drop my mouth from her forehead to her lips and exhale a harsh breath over her chin. I wanna taste everything, wanna leave behind my scent for any other Alpha to sense and know that I'll rip the skin from their flesh if they don't respect the edict that she's mine.

She reaches down and grabs my cock and my hips buck. I react wildly, my hips slamming into her body and throwing her against the wall of the thing encasing us. My thoughts scatter and swarm.

The dart bomb. Ducking over Echo. The fucking scavengers wearing all that bloody clothing crawling out from under the bridge like cockroaches. Pushing her off of the damn bridge and using every last drop of energy I had to follow. Fighting against the drugs. Fighting onto the riverbank. Fighting to keep her close.

Close…but I want closer.

I shove my tongue down her throat and pull the next breath out of her mouth, and it tastes fucking godly, like the forest around us, like her sweet, hungry cunt, like the blood she just drew from my lip. *Savage. She's nearing heat. She needs me.* I fucking need her. Desperately.

She keeps trying to arch her back and shove her tits against me, but somewhere in the back of my fuckin' brain, I remember that her arm is hurt to shit and I manage to get it into a safe space between us.

"Omega, watch your fuckin' arm." I grab her hair and give her head a shake, wantin' her to hear me in this.

She gasps and my fever triples and erupts in a loud rattle. I roll us over, maneuvering her onto her back. My thoughts are wrecked, my restraint more so. The little creatures responsible for relaying commands between my mind and my body have thrown all the directives up into the air and set fire to everything.

Gonna fuck her now. My Omega needs her Berserker.

I settle between her thighs and I shove her knees apart with mine. She moans and sighs and scrapes her nails across my chest and tries to reach for me with her mouth, but fumbles clumsily because she can't see in the dark. Or maybe, she's just fumblin'.

She ever kissed anybody before? She kisses without finesse, with pure, concentrated passion, her lips and tongue moving hurriedly over mine. She pulls my tongue into her mouth and when I want deeper, she arches and makes space for me before divin' for my neck, my beard, my damn jaw — anything she can sink her fangs into and, unlike me, she's got no fangs at all.

"You taste like snow." Her voice hits me like a punch in the dark. She's breathing hard, her whole body shaking with the movement. Her broken words make me damn near lose my mind. The rattling in my chest intensifies and my fist in her hair is suddenly not tight enough. I want her still, I want her complacent. I want her to submit to me fully because I want to submit to her fully and mark her with my cock in my venom's absence.

It's her vulnerability. It wounds me. It makes me feel like I matter, but only because she needs me to make sure she's always alright. "You taste like sin," I lie, because she doesn't. She tastes like *redemption*.

I grab her by the throat. She starts to shiver, but not from the cold. Her hips are pushing up against mine and mine are pinning hers down hard. She wants this. I can smell it in the air. *I* want this. But when my lips find her throat and she winces, I'm reminded that I don't deserve this.

I can feel her stitches against my lips and roughly remind her that I won't bite her, never again. It's a promise I vow to keep, even if it means I have to work ten times as hard to protect her from the other males who'd try to bond her in the same fucked way I did.

"Won't bite ya, Echo. Never again. Promise on my fuckin' heart." Don't know if she hears me. She doesn't reply. Instead, her clumsy hand is reachin' for my cock again, beggin' me to fuck 'er, but I just kiss her slow…so damn slow, tryna stay her movements so she doesn't hurt herself, go into heat, trigger my…fuck. It's comin'. *I can't fuckin' rut.* Not now. Not here.

I shove her hand off my junk. I can't think. My thoughts are in flames, my resistance in shambles, because when I kiss her harder, deeper, tiltin' her head to the side so I can control every damn movement she makes, I crumble.

Every part of me crumbles. I…was built the strongest of my kind, but against her need, her clumsy movements, her kiss, her cocoon protectin' us, I'm nothin'. My stomach clenches and I hear a…crinkling in the space around us. Don't know what it is, but it doesn't sound threatening, so I don't bother rootin' it out. Instead, I line myself up with her entrance and prod the bloated head of my cock forward, pressin' it into the brand of her heat. She's so fuckin' wet for me.

A rough sound breaks free of her lips and her chest lifts. Can't have it. "Fuck."

"No." She feebly tries to hold me to her with her thighs, but her grip is weak and a good reminder why this is a bad fuckin' plan.

"Baby, gonna hurt yourself. Can't have it."

"Please."

"Nearin' heat. Could send me into rut. Could fuckin' *kill* you, Echo." I'd snap my dick off first, but I need her to know how precarious this situation is between us.

And then she does somethin' unfuckin'fair. "You won't," she says on a watery gasp, with puffy red lips.

"Can't know that..." I look down and my rattle immediately warps into somethin' less aggressive, returnin' to that purr again. Because she's cryin' in my arms, the perfect, savage thing that she is. "You fuckin' cryin'?"

Though she denies it, she sniffles again and I'm done. Fuckin' ruined. "Please. I just want something. Need it, Berserker. Please. Please, Berserker."

Fuck me.

I remember the Fates. I remember what they told me. That in Paradise Hole I'd find her. And that there'd be no mistakin' who she was when I met her. I'd know I met my wife.

I know.

She's nothin' I expected and everythin' I want. I'd expected an Omega who was meek and beautiful, grateful and obedient. Instead, I got rage dipped in honey, dragged through shards of glass. An Omega who'd rather kill herself than be mine, and right now she's beggin' me.

Damn Echo. I've never begged anybody for anythin' and I only dare because I know she hasn't either. But I'm not gonna let her use what I am as distance between us anymore. I want her to see me. For once, I want her to see me. So, while she begs me for *somethin'*, I'll beg her for that.

"Gonna fuck you, Echo, but you gotta call me *Adam*."

She cries out, the sound soft and sad and full of surprise. It's loud, but it isn't so loud that I miss the sound of that crinkling again. I open my eyes and, above her head, I see them for the first time. "Flowers."

My eyeballs strain in disbelief as I take in the sight of so many vines. We're wrapped in them, cocooned by thick, brown vines laced with dead leaves and moss, but newly studded among them are vines that are much thinner and more delicate than the violent, thorny limbs she's grown before. Green vines. Delicate curls. Not meant for rage or decimation or protection. Just…beautiful and covered in dozens of tiny flowers. Either white or yellow, I can't tell which, the flowers all carry her scent. They smell incredible, stifling, cloying, captivating…broken perfection.

My eyes get fuckin' hot and I close them, praying to the fuckin' suns she can't see in the dark like I can. I've never seen flowers before. *Too good for me. Unworthy.*

I release a shuddering breath and am about to fuckin' crawl off of her beautiful, damaged body when she says, "Please. Adam, please."

I moan and collapse onto her further, my grip on her hair too hard, but I can't control it. I can't control anything. My cock, which has been idling at the entrance of her hot, sweet cunt, pushes inside of her, meeting no resistance.

Her pussy is wet and open for me, ready and eager. Hungry. I rotate my hips against hers, moving slow and in a way I can tell surprises her, and that she doesn't like. Why would she? She expected hard and fast, but I don't want that. I don't want…I don't want her to think I'm here just for this. I'm not. I didn't come here for this.

She's panting so hard, her body wild and shaking against me. I hold her down, careful as fuck with her arm. It takes her moments to come and she does with a scream that nearly breaks the rigid hold I have on my composure.

Gotta use chains and guns, pure, unyielding determination to keep myself from fallin' into rut. And she isn't helpin'.

"Adam!" She screams my name. Not Berserker, not a fuckin' insult, but my name. The one I chose because I liked it. The only thing I had that was mine for years…decades. Now, it's hers, too.

"Fuck me." I let her come all over me and I want to release and come all over her and inside her body, but when she whispers sad, tortured words into my ear, I know I can't. If she's this close to heat, she could get pregnant by me and I'm not puttin' a fuckin' kid in her out here in Paradise Hole. It's a nasty fuckin' place and, somethin' happens to me, I'm not gonna let her walk this world with my kid, alone. She's got enough to worry about without that burden.

She curses and I tighten my grip on her body, my will and my restraint. "Don't you fuckin' go into heat, Omega."

"Heat?" she stutters.

No fuckin' way. Fuck. "Fuck!" Her vulnerability hits me like a battering ram. I fight the hardest battle of my life not to give in to it. Instead, I kiss her face. Kiss her deep. "Didn't know." Didn't know that she didn't know.

From what I know of Omegas, their heat is triggered only in the presence of an Alpha. That she's never gone into heat before doesn't surprise me. That she doesn't know what her heat *is* terrifies me. I'm going to need to be even more careful with her.

Fuck me, what have I been doin'? I've been tryna break down a savage named Echo but, as a Berserker, I haven't been carin' for my Omega at all. I've completely abandoned her.

"Prouda you, baby." I am. "Pleasin' your Berserker so fuckin' good right now." She is.

She gasps and her body spasms in my arms. I hold her still, tryna be careful with her arm. I wait for her to ride out her orgasm and I squeeze my eyes shut tight and lick the tears from her cheeks. I wonder if she knows that some of that salty wetness is mine. Not cryin' of course. Not findin' her vulnerability, her naivety, her *trust* and her goddamn flowers a beautiful thing. Nah. A Berserker doesn't cry. *But Adam. What about Adam?* Haven't cried since…haven't cried since the last time I was in Paradise Hole, and only once, only for a minute. And then the pain started.

I'm used to pain as I prepare to pull out of her, unspent, refusin' to fall into rut, refusin' to breed her, refusin' to hurt her, refusin' to let my first time with her be like this. Who ever said I wasn't a fuckin' romantic?

"Please me so good, Omega," I tell her, but only because I can hear a small sound underneath my rumblin' chest, an uneven, lurching sound, a quiet beat that sounds like a stray tabby learnin' affection for the very first time. She's purrin' for me. Not quite, but she's tryin'.

"So fuckin' beautiful, Echo." Around her face, like a halo, a ring of white and pink flowers grows. "Flowers..." Beautiful. "That's it, baby. Come for your Berserker, now."

And she does.

I move my thoughts into boxes, separating the pleasure from the pain of not finishing inside of her. I focus only on her. Her taste, her mouth, her flowers, her scent. I have to distance myself from the pressure of her pussy ripplin' around my dick and think about it like somebody watchin' the scene unfold, but not experiencin' it for himself. And I hold. I kiss her and I hold.

She's cryin' harder, her defenses are down. She's an exposed heartbeat. "Don't go," she says to me and she breaks every piece of my fuckin' heart. *Bam, bam, bam.*

"Won't," I vow and it's an easy vow to make.

"I'm scared of Paradise Hole."

"Know it."

"I'm scared of being alone."

"Not alone, Echo." I slow down, stop poundin' into her, kiss her hot, wet, salt-stained lips. "You finish?"

She sniffles and goes entirely limp in my arms. "Yeah."

"Good, Omega," I say once, and as I pull out of her, I repeat it.

I move our bodies around and tie her arm up against the ceiling, hopin' that the swelling goes down. When it's all done, I tuck her weepy body against my chest and make her promises in the quiet dark, promises I know she doesn't believe I'll keep.

She cries herself to sleep, her vulnerability tearing me to fuckin' shreds, while my chest heaves and I hold her tight and curse the Fates. So far, they've been right about everything, but I hope to fuck they're wrong about what they said will happen next.

ADAM
PARADISE RIVER

I WAKE BEFORE ECHO DOES AND ANY OTHER DAY, I mighta railed at her for oversleeping, but not today. I want her to sleep longer, gather her strength. I use the time to pluck some holes in the vines encasing us and, as I do, I admire her handiwork. Fuckin' beautiful. We're gonna have to figure out how she's doin' this.

Vines, like ropes, drop from the oblique cocoon — shaped like something from outer space and borne of the earth at the same time. The inner layer is composed of moss and flowers, most of which died off in the night. It makes me sad lookin' at the dried-up shells of flowers that once were. Makes me try to think of the last time I saw flowers but, if there was a time, I can't remember it.

I pull the moss away, noting its dry and crisp texture under my rough hands. No wonder we're so warm. The moss is thick, and my heat does most of the work. It frightens me how Echo's skin gets goosebumps the minute I get even the smallest hole carved in the vines above us. *We won't be able to move today. Her clothes are likely still wet from…* Wait.

Careful as I can be, I tear a hole in the outer shell of our safety, cutting through the tougher vines with my claws. I have to decimate more of Echo's work than I wanted to in order to be able to fit my shoulders through. The minute I'm out, I go for her pack, open it and find a ziplock pouch inside that has a disgusting blanket shoved into it. It pisses me the hell off.

I unfurl it anyway and return to the cocoon, shocked by the way it looks in the light. It's creepy as shit, clearly not intended to be here, yet blending in with its surroundings like camouflage. I brace against a gust of wind and drop the blanket inside the cocoon, covering Echo with it entirely, all except her suspended arm.

Her fingertips'll turn blue if I don't move fast, so I do, ripping free a few of the tougher vines carefully so as not to break them, then twisting them together, forming a huge loop that I judge'll be the right size and fixin' it with a thick knot. I do this twice more, until I've stripped the cocoon of most of the thick vines, leaving behind a shell that'll disintegrate over time.

I reach in and pull Echo out. I stuff all her wet shit into her pack and tie it to the vines. Then I pull Echo onto my back, keepin' the blanket over her, and lie flat in the middle of the vines, making sure they go over her back and under my stomach.

We look fuckin' stupid, of that I'm sure, but when I change into my Berserker form, things work out right. Takes me three tries a' changin' to get it so that the vines are tight enough around her to hold her in place on my back and not so tight they're suffocatin' her. But once we're set, we're set. She still hasn't woken, and I'd be worried if she didn't hiss at me every so often, issuin' sleepy words of protest. The sound of her cursin' at me like she is makes me do somethin' I never thought I'd do in Paradise Hole — smile.

And with my Omega strapped safely to my back, I take off into the grim, muted daylight.

ECHO
PARADISE HOLE

THE RUMBLING HELPS ME SLEEP, BUT IT DOESN'T KEEP me there. I wake with a start and find that I'm not... uncomfortable, or cold, but I'm sure as shit not warm and dry like I was before. I open my mouth and taste fur. I open my eyes and see fur. A broad expanse of it. It's dark brown and, in patches, glistens a lighter honey. The fingers of my bad hand are curled into it to the best of their ability, though I can't see much of the arm they belong to. I'm covered with a blanket. Swaddled by it, really.

A shuddering sigh releases beneath me, like a train engine announcing its arrival at the next station. The fur beneath me fades away like grass growing in reverse and soon, my palms are pressed against the flat expanse of a bare, muscled back. Together, we lower to the ground.

What I didn't realize were low tree branches hanging at my eye level soon become tree trunks, and then roots. I start to slide, too stunned to stop myself from hitting the ground. I release a premeditated "ooph," but the jolt I expect to feel as I slam against leaves and dirt and mud never lands.

Crouched on the ground like a superhero falling from the stars, he pivots on the balls of his feet and catches me mid air. His right hand slides under the mess of my hair and his left hand catches my injured left arm. He gently lowers me onto my back with a smile on his face while I stare up at him like I've never seen the dude before in my life.

A dude I fucked.

Oh my god.

He made me come.

If there was any doubt in my mind that last night was a dream, the tender — and dare I say, wickedly smug — smile on his face erases it. I came for him. I came on his cock. I came and he didn't. I came on his cock but he didn't come for me. He didn't want to. He didn't want me.

My Omega instinct breaks apart inside of my chest, threatening to tear the castle down. Fighting it, fighting the surge of defeated misery that skips across the moat and ransacks the gates, I look anywhere but at him. Heat blisters my cheeks and I quickly gather my senses — and the blanket. I hug it to my chest and squeeze my legs together.

His gaze flicks down my body and he snorts, "Don't gotta worry, Echo. Not gonna fuck you."

"Why?" Wait, *what?* Why did I say that? What is *wrong* with me?

His eyes crinkle at the corners in a way that's not chill. "Didn't get enough?" Not chill at all.

"No…I mean yes. Back up, Berserker. Please." My voice cracks.

The humor in his gaze is gone. He hardens and I shiver a little, recognizing that I've made him angry…or something…and not liking it. My pussy lips clench open and closed, knowing how to make it right, but then I consider that he didn't want me in the dark. Why would he want me in the daylight?

I close my eyes and look anywhere but at his naked body kneeling in front of me, the huge weight of his uh…junk just hanging out there, like it's got nothing better to do in this shitty weather than get hard.

Don't look don't look don't look.

The harder I think the words, the harder it becomes to obey them. Hard. Why do I keep thinking the damn word? I shiver and my gaze rakes down his blazing hot, naked form, skipping over a lifetime of scars and settling on short pubes the same color as his beard, maybe a little darker, that don't do damn near enough to cover his package. *That thing was inside me. I begged for it. I came. I came but he didn't.*

I swallow hard — *there it is again, fuck!* — my gaze moving over thighs the size of my waist, a waist the size of my torso, and a chest four times larger than mine. His neck is as thick as my thigh and his head is a big stump of a thing that makes me feel small. I'm not, but that's how I feel as I sit on the cold, damp ground underneath him in nothing more than a blanket.

"Where…" I clear my throat, wishing that my voice didn't come off so pathetic as I finally croak, "Where's my stuff?"

"Wet. Found new stuff. Get up and you can help me scavenge some of it."

He's got scars on his chest, one big one in the shape of an X, just off-center from his heart. *I touched it last night. Stroked it. Clawed at it.* But in the cold light of day, I don't see any claw marks. I shouldn't. I shouldn't see any scars either. Berserkers don't scar. Their venom heals them. Their venom should heal the Omegas that bond to them, too. But it didn't heal me. It didn't heal him, either. Maybe, there's something wrong with him. Yeah. He must be defective.

No. This happened to him when he was a Beta, because he was a Beta too, once.

Somebody hurt him. Or took something from him. Isn't that what he said? Did he come for me to replace someone he lost? The thought needles me in ways it shouldn't and I panic when I look up and see him watching me with a steady expression that betrays concern and something ugly.

"Take off the blanket."

I clutch it tighter to me and shake my head.

He grunts, "We been traveling since sunrise. Didn't get a good look at you then. Wanna see what I'm workin' with. You got bruises around your eyes and on your jaw."

"I bruise easy. It's fine. I'm fine."

"I hurt you last night?" His expression does something horrible then. It softens. He rakes a big stupid hand down his stupid dirt-smudged face. "Fuck, please tell me I didn't hurt you. Tried hard not to, but it was dark. Couldn't see how weak you looked. Could only feel how strong you felt in my arms."

"Please, stop." I can't hear anymore. I don't want to hear anything about last night. "Berserker…"

"Omega, pull the blanket back. Let me see. Not gonna fuck you…"

"Adam." My voice is loud. It wobbles.

The Berserker stiffens and meets my gaze, his eyes betraying little.

I glance around, a rabbit caged. I hunt for explanations even though I shouldn't — they don't belong to him. Nothing about me does. *Except for my pleasure. He had that last night.* I latch onto the first thing I can think of and the words blast out of me in terror, "I've always got bruises. There's nothing I can do about my bruises out here. I just need my…my shoes." I sniffle. I hate that I do that.

"Why d'you bruise so easy?"

I scoff, all wet and ragged. "It's Paradise Hole."

He sits back on his heels and waits for more.

"Everybody's sick in Paradise Hole. I'm not special."

"Disagree."

Frustrated, I comb my hand through my hair — it gets stuck in knots and tangles — then I pull it free and gesture wildly. "My shoes, Berserker…"

"Don't need shoes. I got you."

"I *need* them."

His shoulders are rigid blocks of wood for another several long, still moments. Then they sink down his back and he sighs, rubbing a hand roughly over his face one more time. He scratches his bearded cheek. *I remember tugging on his beard last night…with my teeth.* Today, it looks even more matted. I *like* the way he looks like pure wilderness.

I glance at his lips. I liked the wilderness of his beard against my face last night. My chin and the area around my mouth feel a little raw because of it. He's a good kisser. *Fuck. Don't think that, especially because I don't think he'd think the same about me.* I tear the thought apart with my blunt teeth because that's all that I have left to defend myself with.

I quickly bite my lips inside my mouth until Pain taps me on the shoulder and helps me refocus on what I need. And I don't need kisses. I don't need anything from him. Just the damn boots.

"My boots," I bite out.

He mutters under his breath and stomps away, returning a couple moments later carrying two huge backpacks. He drops them at my feet. "Start goin' through these. See if there's anything to wear. Your boots are soaked and so is all your shit. Can't put 'em back on yet."

I glance around, not wanting to make any more conversation than absolutely necessary with him, and try to figure out what the hell happened. How did I get here? How am I even still alive? I rub my eyes while Adam —*fuck* — the Berserker turns his back to me and moves through what looks like the vestiges of an abandoned campsite. Where the hell are we and what happened here? I glance around, taking it all in and not liking any of it.

We're on the fringes of Dark City now, at the border where Paradise Hole's murky greyness begins to transform and where the leaves sprouting off of the trees are actually green in places and their trunks have faintly greenish moss.

The sky overhead is dark, but that's nothing new — the only thing that isn't. Because scattered around us now are clustered fires — at least three — clearly abandoned in a hurry. Packs were left open, their contents scattered, and whatever Alphas they belonged to — or wily Betas — were well-equipped.

Spilling out of half-opened packs are canvas sacks of rice and half-eaten bags of dried meat. The Berserker drops one in front of me, a sack of raisins and peanuts alongside it that look virtually untouched. "Looks like enough for you for tonight. Want you to eat all of it."

"If I eat all of it, what are you gonna eat?" Why did I ask that? I don't care. Stupid stupid stupid.

"Beast caught a deer. Gonna skin it now. Then, I'll get a fire going."

"Are you sure we should linger here?" I glance around, skin prickling with awareness and unease.

"I circled the area. Not an Alpha or a Beta for miles. Whoever came here left fast and they're not comin' back anytime soon, if they're even still alive."

I shiver as a surge of wind spirals down through the trees and gives my cheeks a loving caress. My neck strains when I twist towards the packs and start to go through them with my good hand. Augh. The stitching. I try not to scratch at it, but it itches.

"Don't scratch it," he grumbles.

"I'm not." I am.

He gives me a withering look, but I scrunch my face up and refuse to back down. He shakes his head and saunters off with a swagger I definitely don't like. *His butt is so muscular.* Gah.

I ignore him to the best of my ability, which doesn't count for shit. So, I watch him out of the corner of my eye as he continues to rummage and collect stuff in the light of the fire he created. The sky darkens. He skins a deer and I watch him handle the carcass, shaking my head. He makes a mess of the thing. It's clear he's not used to this. His Berserker's beast probably just swallows the animals whole. And in Dark City, he probably eats off of porcelain plates.

I snort at the thought and his gaze flicks up to mine. One corner of his mouth lifts and it does terrible things to me — not the half smile, but the half smile coupled with the blood splattered across his cheek and mouth, and the droplets that have made their way down his neck and onto his chest. *Fuck.*

"Like your outfit." His gaze flicks down to the long-sleeved shirt and hideous pants I've pulled on.

I grunt. "Better than yours."

The Berserker's cargo pants fit him like leggings, so tight every seam looks exhausted from trying not to explode apart. Cutting the knees out of them helped in the sense that he can now bend his knees at least, but the way they strain around his thighs is frankly ridiculous. Hilarious. I don't laugh, though. *Fight it. Fight it!*

He looks down and stretches one leg out fully. When he bends it again, he winces and the knee tears halfway up the thigh and halfway down the shin. "No disputin' that."

A sharp, loud sound bursts out of me and keeps bursting. The hand I throw over my mouth is too weak to stop or smother it. The Berserker jerks and whirls to face me. His eyes are huge fists in his face and his lips are slightly parted. *His eyes…* No! Look away look away look away! His expression is surprised at first, but then his stare becomes absolutely ravenous, the caramel color of his gaze brightening to a fire-tarnished gold.

I laughed. I laughed for him.

No, I laughed *at* him. At him. Yeah. That's it.

I yank down on the sleeves of my gigantic flannel. It's hot underneath and that heat intensifies as my face and neck flood with embarrassment. "At least yours doesn't smell like some other Alpha's BO."

He doesn't answer. It makes me uncomfortable. I get more uncomfortable the more time passes and it doesn't help that I don't have anything to do with my hands. I've already disassembled the four packs placed in front of me, consolidated all of the equipment, and reorganized everything into the largest two packs once, twice, and then, when I got bored, once again.

I shove my hand in the nut sack — I mean, the sack of peanuts, the bag of peanuts and raisins, *fuck* — grab a fistful, and carefully examine each peanut before tossing it back. I choke on peanut dust so hard that my eyes water and I don't hear the sound of the Berserker coming over to me until he's already there, squatting down, making his other pant leg rip to match the first.

I start to laugh at the sight and choke more on peanuts. A metal cup is thrust under my nose and I recognize the smell of it. Mangrove root tea. It's a good antiseptic. I'm surprised he'd know that until I remember…*he was a Beta too, once.*

I drink the tea down, coughing a little when I take in a root on accident. I spit it back into the cup, which the Berserker takes and refills. He brings it back, root-free this time, and as I sip at its dirt and sort of spicy tang more gingerly this time, he watches me. I don't look up, but I can feel it.

"What?"

"Finished up with the deer. Wanted to give you this." Against the size of his palm, the dagger he holds looks normal-sized. It's got a sharp-looking blade, too, but I still don't understand.

"What?" I tilt my head and push the bushel of my hair back over my shoulder.

"For you. Take it."

I'm deeply uncomfortable as I stare at the knife and its blackened handle and its even darker blade. It's just a straight shot of knife, no crossbar or whatever that thing is that separates the hilt from the sharp part. It's not a quality dagger for sure and it's too big for me, but I still feel like a rich city Alpha who's just been offered her choice of fine jewelry.

"Don't want it?" I glance at his face. I shouldn't've. The light refracts off of the strands of his hair, illuminating their bloody tips. I want to run my fingers through those locks. I want to stroke my hands down his chest. I want him to force my head down and pop my hips up, kneel down behind me and…

"I…" I look between his hand and his face and scoot back. It…doesn't seem to piss him off as much as it did a week ago, or even yesterday. In fact, the corner of his mouth twitches, like he might want to say something *not* mean to me…and then he just has to go and friggin' say it.

"Merlin showed me the oils you traded her when you were in Trash City before and told me about the skins she let you keep. Based on what she said, my bet is that you're better at this than me." He cocks his chin back toward the fire and the deer he attempted to skin laid out beside it. "Should do the next one for us, after you get back the use of both hands."

My stomach does this tightening thing that I don't like and my left eye twitches. I rub it, crossing my right arm over my chest to be able to reach it. I'm hoping the whole display and the time it takes me to make such insignificant gestures will exasperate him and he'll give up waiting for an answer...but he doesn't.

He just kneels there holding the knife out to me like he really expects me to take it. I fiddle with the strap of the pack resting in front of my crossed legs and ignore the way they clench, remembering how they clenched around him in the dark, begging him to stay. So fucking humiliating. Makes me want to cry. Why do I always want to cry around Adam? The pain in my injured arm is still constant and making my head hurt. Maybe that's why I want to cry. Maybe that's why I can't figure out his game, or what changed between us last night. He hates me, wants to use me, disgusts me, repulses me...

But he was a Beta too, once.

"Saw you watchin' me skin the deer just now. Know you know it's true."

"What's the catch?"

He makes this rumbling sound in his chest that somehow manages to have intonation. Last night it turned me on, but now it makes me ravenous with the urge to please him. He's displeased with me now, somehow, by what I've said. "No catch, Echo."

Echo. Echo and Adam. I open my mouth to tell him to call me something else, but I...change my mind. "Hm."

I extend my hand toward it slowly and, just as I reach it, he pulls it slightly out of my grasp. "You're right. There is a catch."

I knew it. I purse my lips and wait.

"Use it to gut me if you want, but don't turn the pointy end on yourself." He places the hilt in my open hand and his eyes flash. "Please."

Please. That single word terrifies me and my whole face melts with heat and emotion. I grab the knife and quickly shove it in the oversized, overstuffed backpack, making sure to memorize its position in case I need it on short notice.

Feeling like I need to do something with my now empty hand, especially with him staring at it, I bring it up to my hair and try to…I don't know, pat it in place.

His lips twitch again, this time on both sides. "When we get back to Dark City, think you'll be needin' a comb, first thing."

Shock. He's insulting me. I open my mouth to retaliate until I register the laughter in his eyes. I can see it in the way their corners crinkle. My throat tightens unexpectedly and I have a hard time maintaining eye contact. The heat in my face flares down my neck and chest and makes my tits feel heavier than they were a moment ago. I look anywhere else — up, at his hair!

"You too." My voice is blocky and hard, but it doesn't seem to matter. Because as soon as the words are out, the worst thing ever happens. He *smiles*. Not wide enough to show all of his teeth, but wide enough for me to see that they're white and straight and square except for the canines, which are a little longer than the rest and sharpened to deadly points. But I know how fast that grin can transform to a mouthful of knives, ready to bite. *But he thought it was a bond.* It doesn't matter. *Maybe it does.*

I look away, knowing that if I stare for too much longer, the strength of my determination that keeps me from crying or gutting him or turning around, stripping and presenting will be denuded to dust. His smile is…I swallow…*nice*. Yeah, nice.

"Probably right about that. Could use a shave, too." He scratches his mangy beard.

I snort, "Yeah."

"And a new pair of pants." He stretches his right knee up, and another seam pops free along the outer leg.

This time *my* mouth is the one to twitch. I pivot away from him, unsure whether to keep sitting there or just…I don't know what. Make conversation? "You were lucky they had any pants at all," I offer and I realize as I say it that it's the longest sentence I've ever said to him that wasn't shouted, screamed or sobbed.

He must realize the same thing I do, because he pauses before answering and when he does answer, his voice is rougher than it was before. "Don't know if I got lucky or they got unlucky."

"What do you mean?"

"Mean that it seems kinda suspicious that a gang of Alphas woulda left good shit here."

"Trash City?" I offer.

"Too far. They're bold, but they're not bold enough to cross the river. We're too close to Dark City."

My throat works. I fight to stay quiet, but I can't. "They're bold enough to have guns."

He gives me a long, penetrating look and scratches the underside of his chin. His beard is matted to hell and makes him look feral and insane. It also sparks something inside of me that my Omega preens at and I ignore purposefully. He's a Berserker and an Alpha but he's a beast no matter which form he takes.

"Don't know and I don't like it. I plan to look into it when we get back to Dark City. I'll need your help."

I stare at him blankly, waiting for the other shoe to drop. I'm horrified. *Horrified* at the offer. Horrified by the idea that he doesn't plan to shackle me to a wall and invite his Alpha guests to use my body or my gifts for a small fee. *That's* the fate I was expecting. Not going with him and helping him solve a mystery.

His stare turns concerned. He wipes his palm down his chest in an absent gesture, smearing mud and blood across it. We're both filthy. I inhale a sharp breath. *Filthy filthy filthy.* I want to present. The urge comes on strong and sudden and a traitorous whimper slips out from between my teeth.

His eyes flare and he straightens up, then the bastard has to go and take a step away from me. Because he doesn't want me. He proved that last night. "Echo?"

Another desperately swallowed moan wheezes out of me and I quickly cross my shins over one another even tighter. I rub the space between my eyes, closing them, trying to reorient myself and think. He's a Berserker. *He was a Beta too, once.* He owns me. He hurt me. *He was trying to save me.* He's a bastard. He commands me. *He helps me use my gifts.* He's the Berserker. *He's Adam.*

"You want me to help you investigate Trash City?"

"That a problem?"

"Just out of pity though, right? To give me something to do?"

"Got knowledge of Paradise Hole I don't. Got gifts I don't. Already thought I could do this without you once and look how that turned out." His gaze travels from my hair down my face to land on my injured arm, and then my injured leg. "Saved us out here more than once, Echo."

"You did, too. And I…I can't even use these Omega powers or whatever they are without you telling me to." What is *wrong* with me? The orgasm must have rearranged my fucking insides. I can't *think!*

His eyebrows are pulled so far together they nearly fuse over the bridge of his nose. "Nah. You got your gifts when I bonded you, even if the bondin' didn't go…quite right." He clears his throat and red suffuses his cheeks. "Just need time with 'em. You'll learn control," he finishes quickly.

"How do you know?"

"Seen it before. With my sister. Though she got her gifts before an Alpha ever crossed her. Didn't need to be bonded. Made her special."

The blow of his words hits me sideways and I open my mouth…and immediately start to choke on my own spit. He starts to crouch back down again, but I hold up my hand. "I'm good. Good. All good…" Cough cough. Choke choke. "I'm fine."

I straighten up and immediately scramble to my feet and put another six feet of space between us. I move to the other side of the fire, giving him a wide, wide berth. Kneeling before it, I feed a couple more dried twigs into the flames and nod jerkily. Distance, yes. Distance is good. *He was a Beta too, once. And he had a sister… Had, being the operative word.*

"You ever thought about practicin'?"

"Wh-what?" I say, still coughing a little bit — choking at the direction this conversation has taken.

Crouching down so that we're at eye level, he rolls forward onto a knee and plucks something out of the open pack beside him. He shows it to me, but I'm too far and the flames are too bright for me to be able to make it out easily. I shake my head.

"Flower." *Flowers*. I remember the way that single rumbling word slaughtered me last night. "You made this. A flower's not far from a fruit. You think you could make us somethin' to eat? A nice little Omega dessert?" He winks and I shake my head vigorously.

Distance! I need distance, goddammit! Distance from his indulgence, distance from the idea that he wants to *help me*, distance from the lascivious way he's talking to me now and his even more lecherous looks.

And then he sighs, "Echo, think about it. You can grow a flower, you can grow food. Gotta try."

"Is that an order?"

He rolls his eyes and tosses the flower over his shoulder. It's lost to the dark. "You want it to be?"

I hesitate, but that small hesitation is enough for my mind to fill with the vision of one single gigantic, perfect peach. I haven't ever actually *eaten* one, but I saw one once. I was a small Beta kid living in Grasslands and an old man had pulled this somewhat desiccated-looking thing out of his pocket. He'd slipped it into the pocket of the old woman standing beside him and she'd looked at him, shocked, then she'd kissed him and I'd known that whatever he'd given her was something special. Precious.

"Maybe?"

He looks surprised, but he doesn't hesitate. He's not a dumb brute, I'll give him that. Had he hesitated, I'd have taken the request back. "Omega, I command you to raise a —What kind of fruit do you want?"

"Peach," I tell him.

He gives me a funny look, almost a sad look, before he tips his head down. "Omega, I command you to raise a peach tree."

I'm looking into his eyes when I feel the earth beneath my fingertips react, and I keep looking at him as vines move over the soil...only, they're not vines, are they? They're *roots*. They twist together, spiraling up and out of the ground, wrapping around each other as they move. But, instead of standing tough and firm, they're bending and swaying, never forming a trunk, not turning green.

I fall back onto my butt when they suddenly twist towards me. Freaked out by my own abominable creation, I close my eyes and hold up my good hand to ward off the impending attack but, when it doesn't land, I see that they've stopped. Now, they just...wilt back to the ground, their knobby heads making them look like dead rose bushes.

Adam — the *Berserker,* goddammit — is covering his mouth with his hand, pretending like he's rubbing his jaw, but that smile is too wide to hide. "Are you laughing at me?"

A warm gust of laughter, like a gale of ocean wind fresh off of the sea, hits me square in the forehead. Feels so…so *good.* "Never."

The ease between us freaks me out even more than the root formation before me. It's ugly, for sure, like some sort of ill-formed stalactite — stalagmite, whichever one comes up — but when I reach out to touch it, it breaks. "It's dead."

"Practice," he says. He doesn't sound disappointed at all. No. On the contrary. The Berserker kneeling across the fire is looking at me like he's *proud of me.* No one's ever been proud of me before.

"I…um…yeah, that's uh…" I swallow and start over. "I'll help you investigate Trash City."

"Because you like to please me, don't you, Omega?"

"Are you making fun of me? For what happened last night?" Fuck. There. I said it.

And his response? Calm. Cool. Collected. "No."

He stands and spears the end of a large stick into the ground and then does the same thing with four other sticks. Across the top, beneath a part of the fire that's only embers, he spreads an actual metal grill that was left behind in the mess and tosses strips of the deer on top of it. The sizzle and the smell make my mouth water even though I'm far from hungry. With all the other stuff left behind, there's enough food to feed ten of me for days. Strange that he hasn't eaten much of it.

"Aren't you hungry?" I ask at the same time that he says, "So where do you think they got the weapons? And no. Wanna see you eat, though."

"Oh. Um. They must have traded an Alpha." I swallow hard, responding to the former half of his sentence and not the latter. "No Beta compounds have weapons like that."

Successfully distracted, he rubs his matted beard again and stares at me from across the flames. "You sure?"

"Positive. I mean, when you were a Beta, did you ever see guns like that?" When he was a Beta.

He gives me another lingering look that's a little...raw, a little afraid. He breaks the line of our eyes first but in a different way than he does when he's frustrated with me. *Because he's not frustrated with me now, he's nervous.* "No, I didn't. But that was a long time ago. Things mighta changed."

"No." I wrinkle my nose and rub it roughly with the back of my hand as I realize what I've done — the parallel lines I've drawn connecting us. "Things don't change for Betas." I turn to face him and there's a crease between his eyebrows and his lips are turned down at the corners. "It's not a bad thing. It's a gift, in some ways. In others, it's purgatory. And purgatory is better than hell."

He nods, considering for a moment, then says, "You're right." *I'm what now?* "Must be an Alpha tradin' with 'em. I just can't think of any Alpha who'd be so stupid. Can't be a Berserker. Even Shadowlands isn't that crazy." He pegs me with his gaze. "Got any other theories, Omega?" Omega. I flinch at that so imperceptibly I hope he doesn't notice. But he does. Immediately after, he says in a voice that's softer than the echo of a heartbeat, "Got any theories, Echo?"

He moves to stand over me, but I get up a beat later and grab my newly formed pack. I drag it closer to the fire and pull my space blanket out of it. I try to fan it out, but it's hard with one arm…until the Berserker intervenes. He spreads two of the corners easily and lays the blanket on the ground that's not so much wet as it is a little dewy.

I look up at the him, twisting my neck to look at him from the side. His stare gets very concerned and he stops playing with his beard. His hand strokes down his chest and I focus on the shape of him, thinking back to Trash City, thinking hard.

"Did you see what Trash City did with the Alpha bodies?"

"What bodies?"

"The guy with the Dark City Slayers tee shirt."

His frown gets gruesome then and his eyes get distant. "Don't know. Don't care. Hope they burned 'em."

"I don't know who's giving them guns."

"Why'd you ask about the bodies?"

I shake my head again. *I think they're connected.* "I don't know."

"Thinkin' whatever happened to those bodies happened to these?"

"I don't know. Even the trolls' behavior was weird. They'd normally never go for targets that big. Alphas? An Alpha *gang*, probably from Gang Mountain? A Berserker? Pshh. No way. Not unless they had something to gain that would make it worth it and none of us were carrying much. I don't think those Gang Mountain Alphas were carrying anything…"

"Fuckin' nuts, those Betas. Remember the battleground, where I took on those other Alphas? Where I parked my bike? You think those parts of my bike were worth it?" He makes a disgusted sound in the back of his throat. "Your Trash City friends sacrificed three of their own for motorcycle parts."

"Did they look like my friends?"

The temperature of the air is getting hotter and his chest is getting fuller with each breath. He looks angry again, and I feel angry again. And I'm ready for us to fight. Almost relieved that that's where we're headed… But then the Berserker has to ruin it. He cracks his knuckles and shakes out his mud-locked hair. He gestures at my pack and gruffly says, "Lemme help you with your sleeping bag."

"I…what? You don't want…"

"Want what?"

"To fight?"

He barks out a laugh that startles me so much, I jump. When I stop hallucinating and come back to the present, he's not laughing anymore, but he is shaking his head and smiling at me with that damn toothy grin that's hard not to get lost in. "Gimme your damn pack."

As we spread out my sleeping bag over the space blanket, I can't shake this strange thought. It goes all the way back to the beginning, when I first met Merlin. She said that I wasn't allowed to go back to scavenge the Alpha bodies — bodies that this Berserker killed in order to lay claim to me. I thought she meant that I wasn't allowed to go scavenge the bodies and take their shit…but maybe she meant that I wasn't allowed to scavenge *the bodies*.

Is she…stealing them?

"What you thinkin', Echo?"

"Nothing good."

"Wanna hear it."

"You don't get everything you want," I snark, hoping to get a rise out of him only to be wildly disappointed when he snorts and says, "Don't I fuckin' know it."

"What's that supposed to mean?"

He just smiles at me. "Sit. Meat's almost ready."

We eat in silence on opposite sides of the fire, me on my sleeping bag, him on a discarded bundle of damp, smelly blankets. It's quiet, yeah, but it's not…unpleasant. And before I know what I'm doing, *I'm* the one initiating conversation.

"Could it be someone in Dark City?"

"Echo," he says threateningly, lowering the bone he's gnawing on.

I shrug with my one good shoulder. "Dark City's closest. And given that the only way to get that many guns anywhere is by the Highway Lines, there's no way your people wouldn't have noticed. Unless your patrols aren't that strong…"

"Echo."

"…or they somehow sneak the guns past you through Paradise Hole."

"Omega."

"Maybe it's someone who works for you. An Alpha sheriff or something. Could be that Dark City is involved and you're being kept in the dark."

"That a punny joke or you really think I'd let shit like that happen out of Dark City? *My* city?"

"You can't control everything."

His teeth clench in a way that spells doom, but I watch as he takes several deep breaths. His eyelids flutter and I get the crazy idea that he might be counting to himself. "Ain't that the fuckin' truth." His eyes open and bore holes into me. When he speaks next, he's calmer than he was before and I… can't help but shrink beneath him. I can see very clearly now how this brute rules a city. "But I'm sure about this. Trades aren't comin' outta Dark City. It'd be easier for Trash City to get hold of weapons any other direction but east — crossin' Paradise River ain't a fuckin' walk in the park, as we've seen.

"And even if they got past Gang Mountain scouts and past the damn trolls and their stupid fuckin' bridges, they still wouldn't trade with Dark City. I'm a walled city, not like Shadowlands down south. Gettin' in and out ain't easy.

"Weapons manufacture is also somethin' I keep an eye on personally. I know exactly how many guns go missin' every year and I track down the ones responsible. Not into anarchy. Not into mutiny. And the numbers a' guns that do go missin' aren't anywhere near enough to supply what Trash City was armed with. They didn't just have a couple'a missin' guns, Echo. They were an *armed* fuckin' militia. What I wanna know is what they've got that's valuable enough for someone to wanna stock 'em. You got any ideas on that?"

"I do," I say quietly, turning his words over and recognizing the likelihood that he isn't talking shit. "I don't think you're gonna like them."

"Tell me."

"The bodies," I blurt.

"What?"

I take one last lick of my already polished bone before tossing it into the fire. Embers and ash spiral up into the air.

"I'm stuck on the bodies. I feel like they're doing something with the bodies."

"Sellin' 'em? For guns?" I don't answer and he balks, "The fuck good would that do anybody?"

I shake my head roughly and scratch my scalp, which feels…gross. I make a face at the grit and dirt and head oil that's come off under my fingernails and quickly wipe them off on my pants, which are…just as filthy. "I don't know, but back in the beginning, when I first met Merlin, she was pissed at me because she thought I'd try to scavenge the Alpha bodies. But I don't think she meant the stuff. I think she meant the corpses themselves."

"Pshh," he grunts and even though it sounds like he's dismissing me, the crease between his bunched eyebrows hasn't dissolved. He's also rubbing his gnarly beard again and I'm distracted by it. *I want to see what he looks like underneath that matted beard.*

I wonder…does he want to see me? I touch my hair again and regret it. Feels like straw and the color…the color was once one of my favorite things about myself, but now the red is hidden underneath layers of mud. Looks like dirt. There's dirt all over my hands. No wonder he didn't want…

"Echo. Talkin' to ya."

"What?" I swallow when I catch his expression. His head is tilted to the side and his right hand is absently touching the X scarred into his skin. I can see it clearly now in the light of the fire. It refracts light, catching and bending it. "I was just…"

"Would give my left nut to know what you're thinkin' right now. Got this crazy fuckin' look on your face. Like you don't even mind sittin' with me."

I don't know what to say to that. I swallow audibly and am embarrassed by the sound all over again. "Do you *mind* sitting with me?" I squeak.

His hand tightens around the deer leg he's holding and all at once, he starts to move. He makes it halfway to his knees, his eyes glazed and unfocused, his chest making this terrible, hypnotic rumbling sound before he jerks, rubs his hand down his face roughly and plops back onto his ass.

"Fuck. Change the subject, Echo." He tosses the bone into the fire and doesn't look at me again. He flexes his hands and takes a few deep breaths, doing that counting thing again. "Don't buy your theory about the bodies, but I can't come up with one better. Also, don't think whatever gang was here coulda been taken out by Trash City, even with their guns. This was twelve…" He inhales deeply. "…fourteen Alphas, ten male, four female. No kids, no Omegas, no weaknesses with 'em. They'da been able to take Trash City, guns or not."

My lips purse. "Weaknesses? Are you saying that *I'm* the reason you couldn't take Trash City before?"

"Nah, but you were part of it."

"I'm not a weakness." I wrinkle my nose.

He smiles at me and it's a condescending, impish thing. "Baby, you've got no fuckin' clue. Now, go to sleep before I do real bad things to you."

"But you…"

"Sleep, Echo."

I open my mouth to ask what kinds of bad things he means until I realize that that sounds every bit like an invitation and I don't want a repeat of last night. I don't. Really. I clamp my mouth shut and start to slide under the blanket.

I watch him start to lie down, too, but he doesn't even bother with the blanket pile he's sitting on and simply stretches out by the fire. He props one arm under his head and crosses his feet at the ankles.

I hate him I hate him I hate him.

But I'm also confused. I feel like a weepy teenager. Maybe he put something in the tea. Yeah, that must be it, because all I really want to do right now is offer him to come sleep in the dry sleeping bag with me and envelop me in his heat. Maybe, it's because of the sex. Maybe, it's because until last night, I'd only done it with one other Beta guy before and it had been so quick it hardly counts. Adam would probably be horrified if he knew.

Alphas, from what I've heard, have sex for sport starting at ten. But for Betas, no one wants to get attached to someone who might get taken to a City one day… We don't start — *they* don't start — having sex 'til they're older and are sure they won't ascend.

"Omega, sleep," he orders and I wonder how he knows I'm awake when his eyes are still closed.

Embarrassed, I wipe my hand off on my pants and lie down on my side only to wince when my injured arm gets in the way of my getting comfortable. I try a few positions before the Berserker's voice cuts across the quietly crackling fire. "How's your arm?"

I sit up and wiggle the fingers of my left hand. They're swollen to shit and hurting. "Fine."

"Fuck." He rolls onto his side and comes around the fire to kneel beside me. He eyeballs my fingers and curses a second time. "Get undressed. Need to redress your wounds."

"I'm fi…"

"Can smell the fever startin' to set, Echo. Let you get away from this earlier today, but I'm not fuckin' around. Need you to take off your clothes. Don't make me order you."

My lips tighten together and anger reminds me who he is and what I am and how this shitty *thing* works between us. Wordlessly, I start to strip. While I do, he rifles through one of the packs I put together until he finds a pot. He fills it with water from the Alphas' forgotten jugs and sets it over the fire. When the water's boiling and I'm down to a tee shirt, he stirs leaves and bark into it.

He also feeds what looks like roots and bark into the fire directly, burning them just enough that he can catch the ashes in a small tin. He adds a little water to the ash, stirring until it's thick. When he returns to me, his gaze is focused on my wounds as he applies his poultice to the stitches slithering across the top of my forearm and over my shoulder, where Lou and Angel had to open me up and add plates.

I'm swollen bad and the pain isn't great. Everything is all purple and blue and yellow and bruised and I get the sense that it isn't healing properly.

"Fever, huh?" I say.

He just grunts. His face is grim determination as he wraps strips of a kinda clean shredded tee shirt around my arm, securing it tight. His fingertips and the strange electricity they send rumbling through me are the only things that help distract me from the agony of it. Occasionally, he curses under his breath.

"You ever been hurt this bad before in Paradise Hole?"

I shake my head.

His jaw clenches harder. A vein pops across the center of his forehead. "Lie back. Need to keep your arm elevated." He props my pack under my arm and presses his fingertips to my chest until I'm lying prone. Then he wraps my top half with the sleeping bag before unzipping the bottom half and fanning it open.

"Gotta get to work on the stitching here. Won't take too long." Cool air rushes against my bare legs, but heat lines the insides of my knees — his own knees make that heat as he kneels between my spread legs.

I close my eyes, hatred a distant memory as I think suddenly and ravenously of other things. "Echo…" His voice is deep and magnetic. "Can't have you goin' into heat now. Don't need you triggerin' my rut."

Just the words have my thighs quivering and I whimper wildly when his fingertips touch my left knee. "Echo…"

"You…" My voice is super loud and wobbly and embarrassing. I lift my injured arm to cover my face with it, but he reaches across my body and presses it gently back down, which only succeeds in bringing him closer. My head is *fucked.* When I inhale the scent of blood and his skin, I damn near moan.

"Omega, *still.*"

"It's not my fault," I say and I'm nearly teary again as I say it. It's so humiliating. "Being an Omega sucks."

He chuckles and the sound doesn't help. My skin sizzles. His hand slides behind my neck and lifts. I blink my eyes open to the sight of him way, way too close to me, pressing a metal cup to my lips and whisper, "I can do it myself. I can do all of this myself."

"Sure you can. Drink."

I drink. After the cup is empty, he goes back to my legs and I lie down and stare up at the bright patch of stars peeking through the muted grey clouds looming high overhead. I almost never see stars. There are nine of them visible in the smallest sliver between the clouds. I count them again and again in the hopes of distracting myself. But it doesn't matter. Because a question's already entered my mind and the words are on the tip of my tongue. They launch themselves out into the open, firing with no safety to stop them.

"Were *you* ever hurt this bad in Paradise Hole?"

His hands on my thighs stop in dangerous places, just inches below my core, which is covered by a swatch of sleeping bag and nothing else. These Alphaholes didn't leave behind any panties in my size, apparently, and my Trash City panties are so dirty they've nearly disintegrated.

"I was, but not in Paradise Hole. Pain started when they got me to Dark City."

"Why?"

"They wanted to know where my sister was. Wouldn't tell 'em."

He doesn't say more and I can tell by the bunching of the muscles in his back and neck that he doesn't like talking about this. A small bulb flickers in the long, dark chasm of my chest.

I slam my hand on the light switch, turning it off, but that bulb flickers regardless.

"She was an Omega?" I repeat, needing to hear the confirmation again.

He nods.

The bulb glows brighter. My hand slams harder. My heart squeezes. "What happened to her?"

He doesn't answer me for a long time. A *long* time. Instead he rips up more tee shirt and wraps it around my thigh — too tight at first, but he gets the pressure just right the second time. I move my hurt arm again — now that it's no longer bound to my chest, I can't seem to stop myself from doing it — and again, he catches it and presses it back into the pack.

Because of that, he's leaning over me, our faces only a couple feet apart when he says, "The Fates got 'er."

"No." I jerk, trying to sit up, and whimper at the pain it causes me.

He rolls his eyes and mutters, "M'I gonna have to sit here all night to make sure you don't move this shit?"

I don't answer right away. His face is too close. I can smell his scent and the hints of blood beneath it. "You could just order me."

"Only wanna order you when you need peaches. Don't wanna have to for this. Don't push me to it."

Peaches. He rolls the word on his tongue, making him sound like he's trying to fuck me with his tongue. "Then maybe you should stay."

"That an invitation?" His smirk doesn't return, like I thought it might.

My throat closes. No, it would be good if my throat would close, but it does not. Instead, I wheeze out a sad, pitiful, "N-no?"

His eyes flash and I jerk, moving my injured arm *again* and earning myself a growl. "What did I say, Omega?"

I recognize that the right half of his body is clothed and the wrong half of mine is clothed when he slides under the blanket beside me. Or maybe it just seems wrong because they're not both the same half. I replay the feel of his bare chest pressed against my bare chest along with everything else that happened last night in the dark when I was totally out of it, but not so out of it that the memory won't be branded into my skull forever.

"You shouldn't…" I jerk.

"You want me to get up?"

"I don't, um…you…I don't like you."

"Noted."

"So don't um…"

He dives down towards me and I squeak as his lips find my ear and he inhales directly into it, scattering my thoughts like he's blowing tumbleweeds across the vacuum of my brain. "You want me to fuck you and I'm not gonna do it, Omega, so shut that shit down. Don't move again. Just leave your arm elevated on the bags and go to sleep."

He lies down next to me and it takes about five seconds for me to realize that the pressure of his body against my body is going to make me explode. Grasping for anything, I shout, "The Fates?"

"The Fates." Shoulder pressed against mine, I glance at him from the corner of my eye and see him staring up at the sky blankly. The stars are now absent. I wonder what he sees. What her face looks like in his mind's eye.

"How old was she when she ascended?"

"Ascended early. Too early. She was seven. I was ten. I hadn't ascended yet. When they kicked her out of Bog City, I went, too."

Seven. No. *No no no no no.*

"Holy shit."

If I'd been seven when I ascended, I'm not sure what would have happened to me. I'd have died right away, either claimed by a bastard Alpha then — *at seven* — and used however he saw fit, or thrown into Paradise Hole to be torn apart by scavengers, gangs, or even animals. And that's only *if* the cold and the hunger and the thirst didn't kill me first.

"How long did you make it…in Paradise Hole, I mean?"

"Seven days." He laughs bitterly and thrusts a hand angrily back through his hair. "Not nearly as long as you."

"I'm four times older than you were."

"I shoulda protected her better."

I balk and start to rise up onto my good elbow. "You were *ten* and a Beta."

"Stay down. It doesn't matter. Shouda done better. Shoulda done better for you, too."

My jaw works, opening and shutting. The stupid light in my chest flickers more rapidly now, the bulb gaining in brightness.

"On your back, Omega, don't make me tell you again."

"You were tortured by Alphas trying to find out where she was hiding?"

"Echo, on your back. Not gonna tell you again. And yes. Was small. They didn't think I'd ascend to an Alpha, let alone a Berserker. They had no idea what I'd do to them when I did."

"What did you do to them?"

"Same thing I did to the other Alphas who were gunnin' for you. And Echo, *now*." He reaches across my body, rumbling as he does and, even though I quickly hasten onto my back, it's too late. His chest is pressed up against me and it feels like he's trying to use his whole self to blanket my body. He reaches across me and repositions my arm on top of the bag. With him on my right side lining my back and the fire on my left, I'm practically sweating in this cold night.

"Are you…" My throat feels unnaturally dry. "Are you gonna stay here all night?"

"I was invited, remember? Besides, you lost your sleepin' alone privileges. We'll see if you earn 'em back by tomorrow." It's a joke, I can tell by the intonation of his pitch, but for once, he doesn't smile. His eyes are still distant.

My Omega's desire to comfort her Berserker wins out. I tilt my face away from him, in defiance of that instinct, but I still whisper, "You never know. Maybe the Fates spared her."

"Don't," he exhales against my cheek. "Don't. You know as well as I do, that's not how things work in Mirage City."

I do know. I do… Because everyone knows that the Berserker who has control over the Fates that live in Mirage City is the most monstrous of them.

The Fates are Omegas with extraordinary gifts. No one knows exactly what they can do, or where the limits of their powers end, but what is known is that the Berserker who runs

Mirage City has figured out how to enslave the Fates to Mirage City forever, and I do mean forever. Because the other thing the Fates figured out how to do is defy death.

Their immortality is gained by consuming the souls, powers, and life forces of unclaimed Omegas — Omegas that their Berserker hunts down so he can live forever alongside them. So far, the Mirage City Berserker and his Fates have lived three hundred years. And if he's the one who discovered Adam's sister and took her, there's not a doubt in my mind that she was killed by his Fates immediately.

"Did you ever…"

"Did I ever go to Mirage City to find out? Course I did. Was the first thing I did after I took the Dark City throne and killed the Berserker sittin' on it, the one who tortured me in his search for an Omega. He never did get one…

"Mirage City Berserker refused to see me, but I saw the Fates. All four a' those smug fuckers told me the same thing — that they killed every Omega brought to them and they didn't even remember her. They didn't remember killing the most important person to me. I…"

He chokes, struggling, and my heart squeezes. I hear a small strange rattling and, for a moment, I wonder if this is a new sound all his own until I realize that he's not the one making it. *I am.* It's like…I'm trying to purr like he does. Is that…is that even possible?

He releases a breath and I don't miss the way his hold tightens around me. He nuzzles the side of my neck and I'm grateful he doesn't comment on the strange sound emanating from my chest. The only thing worse than the fact that I'm making it at all is that it's so pathetic.

"I'da struck them down there — or died tryin' — if they hadn't…" He breathes hot air against my skin and I dig my heels into the ground and fight to ignore the pressure and softness and heat of his lips against the curve of my shoulder.

"What?"

"Nothin'." He kisses my stitches very lightly before pulling back. "Go to sleep, Echo."

He gets quiet, but he isn't sleeping and I'm definitely not sleeping. I can't stop thinking about what they might have told him to stop him from trying to murder them all — attacking a Fate is effectively a death sentence. Though maybe, if they were there alone, unprotected without their Berserker to order them…

"Was it a prophecy?" I've heard stories about the prophecies the Fates give. They can't see all of the future, but they see enough of it. As kids, the Betas would tell me stories about the Fates, and November would always correct them. *They aren't all-knowing*, she'd say, but with how much they do know, I've never really understood the difference.

"Sleep."

"Scouts from Grasslands said there were five."

"What?"

"Five Fates. You said there were four."

"Scouts're wrong. Everyone knows there are four Fates. Saw 'em myself. Stared each of 'em in the eye. Made each of 'em tell me that they killed my sister. And I saw that none of 'em were lyin'."

"You can see lies?"

"Can smell 'em."

"No, you can't."

"Then how'd I know you knew already that there were trolls under that bridge?"

I frown. "Why did you walk directly into the trap then?"

"Thought I could negotiate, like with Trash City. Didn't expect the Alphas, or the darts."

"What did you trade Trash City?"

He huffs in my ear and the sound is one of pleasure, even if it's slightly strained. He whispers, "Who knew my Omega'd be such a fuckin' chatterbox. Go to bed, Echo."

His Omega. *His*. I hate how much I like the sound of that. I've never been claimed by anyone. I wonder…I had to have had a family, once. Did they claim me at some point? Did they even try? Or did they toss me into the Grasslands orphanage the first chance they got? I guess it doesn't matter. This is where I ended up. In a sleeping bag with a Berserker in Paradise Hole. Just my luck.

Adam sinks down beside me, the tension flowing from his heavy bones. The space blanket crinkles beneath him with each breath he takes. I can feel each one on my shoulder. He's rumbling a little, loud enough to drown out the sound of my own strange purr, and my eyes are closed but I'm nowhere near asleep. My fingers — my good fingers and my bad ones — have minds of their own. While my bad hand fights to stay rooted to the pack in an elevated position, the fingers of my right hand are wandering.

I hope he's asleep and that he doesn't notice, but I also hope he's awake and responds. Because I'm terrible. Because I'm horny as fuck. Because I never felt as good as I felt last night and I want more and I want him to want more, too, even if we hate each other. You can fuck and hate each other, can't you?

Lying on my back while he's on his side facing me, I stroke the back of my knuckles across his abdomen. Like it's an accident. I brush the button of his pants, wishing that there was some world in which it would be sane for me to free it. But I'll never have that kind of power over him. He doesn't want me. He wants only my gifts. And he's the Berserker. It's up to him. Everything is. He's already said no to me once tonight.

I pull my hand away from the dangerous button on the front of his pants, but he catches my wrist. I freeze and tip my head to the right. His eyes are closed, but his nostrils are flared and he's breathing harder than he was when we had the brilliant idea to share one sleeping bag.

He doesn't move forward or retreat, but remains perfectly still.

Goosebumps break out over my body and, in a voice that's soft and wobbly and sounds like it belongs to a weepy teenager and not to the Omega who survived six weeks on her own in Paradise Hole, I whisper, "Adam?" My voice breaks and so does he.

The rumbling in his chest vibrates against my outer arm. He grabs my right hand — that treacherous hand — and pushes it away from his belly onto mine where he traps it beneath his heavy palm. I clench, suck in a breath, and then suck in another. He starts to move our intertwined hands down, down, hitting my pubic hair and continuing. My eyelids are already fluttering, my heels digging into the ground. I whisper his name repeatedly.

He says nothing but his firm touch keeps my shaky fingers still as we near my clit and softly brush over my too soft skin. I start to arch, but his other hand sweeps under my hair and applies deadly pressure to the back of my neck. "Still. No bruises." He kisses my temple so, so gently.

I nod and squeeze my eyelids together as I try to obey his commands. It's difficult. My legs strain the edges of the sleeping bag, wanting but unable to spread further apart, while his fingers shove between my legs, guiding my own fingertips into my body. He inserts two, and just into my entrance, before the tips of his fingers join mine in my own heat.

"Warm," he rumbles against my jaw. He nips at my skin with his teeth, but doesn't break it.

I turn my face towards his and search for lips, but slam my teeth into his bearded jaw instead. He redirects me with his hand on my neck, tilting me up and slightly more to the right so he can deepen the penetration of his tongue. I open for him, wanting him in, wanting it with a hunger I've never felt in all my life.

"Warm," he says roughly, breaking the kiss only long enough to say it before searing his lips over mine once more.

His fingers are pushing in and out of me, deeper and deeper, holding mine inside, forcing my own hand to move with him. The angle is wrong though, and I won't come like this. I feel it ebbing, the shore is too far.

"Adam," I grunt.

His rumbling intensifies and I drown in it. He wrenches away from my mouth and lifts up the blanket. "Fuck you, Echo. Stay still for me and I'll give you what you need."

He's on top of me a second later, his hand working the button I had earlier tried to free. His head drops forward and he kisses me again, mouth on mine, heat blistering. He rakes his teeth across my cheek, devouring the space behind my ear.

At the same time, he slides a hand underneath my ass and pops my hip up at the exact angle his cock will need to find my G spot. And suddenly it's *there*. Right there. There's almost no space at all for his knees between my legs. We're all smashed in the sleeping bag together. I'm surprised it doesn't rip.

"Echo," he breathes and his cock presses against my swollen, sensitive heat.

"Adam…"

He meets my gaze and it frightens me, the connection between us. He opens his mouth, like he'll say something profound, but he chokes instead and pushes inside, filling me with a dizzying pressure my whole soul is starting to recognize. *And lust for.* I want this. I want this even though I hate him and I'm pretty sure he hates me.

But you don't have to like someone to do this. Right? Unsure about so very many things, I'm slow to respond when his mouth comes for mine again. I let him pull kisses out of me. I'm not really…doing anything. Just letting him make me feel good, and I feel a little bad. I don't know what to do with my hands, really — well, my hand. The other one he's holding down against the pack, straying only occasionally to massage my tits through my shirt. I don't have a bra — not an Alpha gang necessity, apparently — and I know he can feel how hard my nipples are.

His cock makes slippery, sloppy sounds as it pushes in and out of me in sweeping, gliding strokes. Its fullness creates a pressure I can't escape and I moan on every thrust and gasp on each retreat. He doesn't move in the figure-eight motion, which I miss, but in thrusts and circles. He knows to keep our pelvises close, though, because the pressure on my clit…the pressure on my clit is *insane*.

I lift my head as much as I can and bite his shoulder. He hisses and shoves me back down. I lift up again and sweep the flat of my tongue over the place I bit, licking deer blood off of his skin in the process.

I tilt my face back and his pupils get big, real scary big, and I suddenly feel an urgency in my chest that I can't beat back.

"Don't fuckin' do it, Omega. Do not go into heat." He starts to pull his cock out of me, the pressure of his thick shaft straining the lining of my core.

"Don't," I plead.

"Omega, you're disobeying me. Don't wanna deal with an Omega in heat out here in Paradise Hole." *Deal* with me. For some reason, the stilted way he's speaking strikes me as distant and cold.

Why is he like this? Why does he give me what I want without taking anything for himself? He isn't…isn't letting himself go. He doesn't want me. But why? Am I really so terrible or is it something else? What if there is some*one* else? What if he's…oh my god, what if he's *with* someone? What if he's in love with another woman? Maybe *that's* why he offered to put me up in private accommodations and leave me alone when we get back to Dark City. Oh my god. Oh my god…

He's married.

I freeze and close my eyes and try to pull myself away from this catastrophe, but my pussy doesn't care if he's married to someone else or not. It chooses this moment to squeeze. "I'm almost...Adam, please...I'm coming...I need..."

He thrusts inside of me and brings one hand between us to circle my clit. He rubs too hard with his rough fingertips, hard enough to send pain shooting through my hips, but apparently I like Pain just as much as she likes me because I break apart anyway and go flying into outer space.

I want to kiss him, but remember that he's got a wife and I'm just the pathetic piece of shit who's been coming on to him even though he's given me no encouragement. *Just orgasms. Pity orgasms.* Like a *favor*. It makes this *favor* he's doing for me even more embarrassing.

His lips are perfectly soft against my cheek when he gives me an open-mouth kiss. His tongue and teeth pull and push their way down my jaw to my mutilated neck, which he kisses with pure tenderness.

I rattle and shiver, leg muscles spasming, lower back burning, heels digging into the slippery sleeping bag, stretching it to the point of its maximum resistance. I'm panting as my conscious mind reenters my body and the Alpha pulls his erection out of my heat. I groan as the fullness is taken away from me. I want the knot, but I don't get that either.

He rolls onto his back and rubs his face roughly and I close my eyes and wish I were dead. "I'm sorry," I choke.

"Should be. Not the time or place for this shit. Wrap it up and get your instincts under control. You're better than this, Omega." My chin wobbles. "You go into heat out here and I can't stop myself from goin' into rut, I could really hurt you. More than I have already. You're not healin' right. Need to get you to the fuckin' doc and figure out why my venom isn't…" He grits his teeth — I can hear them grind together — before exhaling in small breaths. He's counting again. "Four…" he says out loud. I guess that's as far as he makes it.

He rolls onto his side, facing away from me and I stare up at the stars, wounded and confused. I don't know *how* to get my Omega instincts under control. I thought *he* had to control them. I didn't even think it was up to me.

"You cryin'?" he barks.

"No."

"Omega…"

"I don't like being called that."

"Think I like bein' called Berserker?"

My chin wobbles harder. I am so embarrassed. I've never been so embarrassed and my head is starting to pound. "We're never doing that again. I shouldn't have asked you in the first place."

"Jesus fuckin' Christ." He slips out from under the sleeping bag, landing lithely on his feet, and starts to walk away from me. He rubs his hair in mechanical gestures as he stomps off, only to storm back again just as quickly. He points a finger at me angrily. "Try to run, I'll hunt you down and punish you and I swear to god, Omega, you won't like how."

"You…you're a…jerk!"

"That's all you got?"

"Fuck you! When the trolls dump your body in an unmarked grave, you won't find me crying over it!"

His jaw stays clenched, but a muscle ticks in his cheek. He reaches down and grabs his crotch. "Fuck." He turns away from me and shakes his head again. "Better," he grunts. It's the last thing he says before the shadows get too thick for the firelight to touch him.

Staring for a moment longer at the darkness he vanished into, I shake my head and try to break out of my post-orgasm trance. I also use the opportunity to try to pull my legs together. The feel of their wobbly and wet insides does something to me and makes my stomach cramp. I want to be fucked again, longer and more thoroughly. I want him to come deep inside my body, knot me, take me… *Fuck!*

I start to roll onto my side until I remember that my left arm is supposed to stay elevated — for the swelling, according to him. Him. Adam. What a dumb name.

No, it isn't. The name is *nice*.

"I wonder if his stupid wife likes it." I mutter nonsense to myself and turn my head away from the fire. The sound of his stomping footsteps fades and I'm so upset about what just went down that I actually drift off into an angry dream state. I jolt awake, confused, because there's no light at all. And the heat of the fire and from his body is gone. I'm cold.

I shiver and when I open my eyes, I see a fox with its head lowered, staring at me from no more than three feet away. The strangest thing about it, I think to myself as it scampers off, is that it's the color of snow falling from the black sky. I've never seen an all-white fox before. Maybe, Adam is right. Maybe, I really do have a fever.

ADAM
PARADISE HOLE

WE MOVE THROUGH THE WOODS AT A PACE I SET. IT'S hard for her, but she doesn't complain and she doesn't fall back. I'm worried. The scent of fever on her skin got worse overnight. Came back after the fire was out to find her passed out like a damn brick. Not even lying down next to her on top of the sleeping bag was enough to wake her. I'd have thought it peaceful, had the sight of her arm not scared the piss outta me. *She's running out of time. I did this to her.*

"Did you see the fox last night? It was white." Her voice startles me and I glance over my shoulder to see her face lookin' at me without a worry in the world and I know that she's only got no worries because her eyes are kinda glazed and her stare's a little dazed and her typically brown skin is now paler than a damn ghost's.

I did see the white fox, I saw three of 'em and I thought it was strange, but I hadn't done anything about it or thought to mention it out loud. I glance at her over my shoulder and watch her push her way through some thorny brambles. She's gettin' all tangled in a way that's dumb for a woman who can literally manipulate the earth.

I turn around, stomp toward her and rip them out by the root. "Saw it. Let's move. Only a day away from a shower." And medical care. "Maybe less." Maybe more, if she gets worse.

"Dry sheets, too?" She smiles like she's on fuckin' drugs and it freaks the fuck outta me. She's lookin' at me like I'm a friend and it alarms me far more than the scent of fever on her skin.

"Course." I pull out another thorny bush, but she lifts her hand.

"Leave it," she says.

"Why?"

She shrugs and stares at the thing, the leaves glossy and dark, each as small as the claws on my pinky fingers. She drags her hand over them and is looking up at me, so she doesn't see it — the way they bloom so suddenly. Yellow flowers blossom amid the thorns. I damn near fall into rut right then but, like last night, I force myself to stay strong and fucking' brace through it.

That peach tree isn't so far away. But to get there, she's got to fuckin' *live.*

"Echo," I grunt, needin' her to stop. My voice is too loud — I fuckin' hear it — and she jumps, staggers, and falls into me. I catch her by the back of the neck, bracing one hand against her stomach. I inhale deeply. She smells good under all that filth, yeah, but she also smells like she's enterin' delirium and she sure as fuck's talkin' like she is. Not used to hearin' her talk like this. So freely. Like I'm somebody she actually wants to talk to.

Can't mean nothin' good.

"Echo, you needa ride me again."

She makes a sharp squeaking sound that I don't understand until the blush rises in her cheeks, stainin' the space underneath so many damn freckles. How'd she get so many? I'm startin' to like the look of 'em. Wanna count 'em. Wanna lick 'em.

"Fuck. Not like that." I shake my head to avoid grinnin' at her. Ain't the time for that. She's hurt and slow and we're so fuckin' close to Dark City I can breathe in the power that fills the air. Where my Berserker beast is home, even if all that power makes me feel unsettled. "Get on my back and strap in. Gonna carry you in my beast form the rest of the way."

"I can walk," she pouts.

"Can't."

"I'm walking right now, Adam." Adam. Fuck. I didn't do anything to deserve hearin' my name in her voice now. I open my mouth to answer her, but she speaks first. "Adam. If you added an M to the front then it would be a palindrome. You know, spelled forward and backwards the same."

The fuck is she talking about? Ramblin' the way she is almost makes me feel cheated out of hearing my name, knowing she didn't mean anything by it. Sorta wish she had, though. "Echo, you're sick. Need to carry you."

"I don't want to ride you. I mean — on your back." She resists, trying to pull her arms away, but I drag her against me carefully and this time, I can't help but chuckle at her rising heat.

"Gonna ride me any way I want you to, but I promise you, Echo, it's gonna feel good."

Her breath against my chin tastes sweet when it tickles my mouth. I lean in closer, likin' the smell of her lips, rememberin' what they taste like. Girl's clumsy, clearly inexperienced, and if that doesn't just please the shit outta me, bein' the one to teach her how to kiss. Fuck if I don't want more of it. Disorientation grips me fast and hard and disappears just as quick. Suddenly feel like a different Alpha than the Berserker I was when I first saw her in the woods, lookin' down at a very different Omega. It's the fever, at least that's what I tell myself, the glaze to her eyes givin' her that hint of vulnerability that makes my Berserker instincts kick.

"Promise, baby," I whisper, leaning in close so that the back of my neck starts to pinch with how low I'm tiltin' it, but she's a nasty fucker and won't cross the little bit of space I left between us.

I can feel her leanin' in, though, that subtle pressure in the balls of her feet. She wants to. But then she has to go and stab me in the fuckin' throat with her words, which nearly decapitate me clean. "Do you talk like that to your wife?"

What the… I belt out a laugh so loud it hurts my sides. My head tosses back. I ruffle her hair and, probably a little harder than I should, scoop her legs and crush her against my chest. Jealousy. It's a raw fuckin' emotion and it makes my stiff cock ache hearin' it from her now.

"Yeah, that's how I talk to my wife," I tell her, just to fuck with 'er. What she doesn't seem to realize is that the only wife I'll ever have is the Omega in my arms. And fuck yeah, this is how I'll talk to her now and forever.

Wearin' boots a size too small, my feet plod through twigs that snap and leaves that crunch. Everythin' here is kinda dry, which is a welcome relief compared to the swamps behind us remindin' me way, way too much a Bog City. *Adam.* I jerk to a stop.

"You say somethin'?" I ask, knowin' she didn't. The Fates' warning whispers in my ears and, distracted, I look over my shoulder. Nobody there though. Start to walk faster.

Meanwhile, Echo murmurs, "Adam…Madam…My friend Hannah was the first person to tell me about palindromes." Forgot about wives and jealousy, she's back to ramblin'.

"That so?"

"Yeah. I always wanted a palindrome name. I thought about telling people my name was Aurora, and if you took out the U it would be Arora, and that's a palindrome. I mean, back when I could still change it. Did they do that in your compound? Give every Beta a name on the Greek Alphabet? Most people changed theirs in Grasslands."

"You lived in Grasslands?"

"And Prayersville."

"Fuck." Both Beta compounds are among the best a Beta could get, but neither is good enough for a Beta who'd become an Omega who'd become mine. "Don't like that."

My grip tenses around her, but she doesn't seem to mind. Makes me fuckin' nervous. Her grip is lax around my neck and she's busy starin' up at the trees instead of at my face, even though I'm close enough to kiss 'er. Though I know that's not her fear. I'm also close enough to bite 'er.

"Grasslands was when I was little, I...I don't really remember it, but November took me to Prayersville when I was thirteen. I lived there ever since."

"Crossed Paradise Hole when you were thirteen?" The thought fuckin' floors me.

"You crossed Paradise Hole when you were six." She shrugs. "And no. I didn't. Ruby City Berserker picked out a bunch of Grasslands orphans he wanted. They were taking us back to Ruby City on their ships when a group of Betas intercepted them."

I snarl. "Gonna kill that fucker." I refuse to imagine what the Berserker of Ruby City had in store for her.

"You can't. He died when the current Berserker took his place."

"That's right," I say, registerin' her truth.

"Her name's N'Dogo. You should know that. She's famous. One of the only female Berserkers." Suddenly Echo giggles and the sound is so unexpected it makes me flinch. "Don't tell me I know more about the Berserkers of Gatamora than you." Her eyes meet mine and she's smiling slightly in a way that's upsetting.

"You dyin'?" I ask instead of answering her.

She laughs again. Fuck.

I start to slow down. "Need to put you on my back, Echo. Gotta run. You're not gonna make it."

"Echo. Such a dumb name." I set her down on her feet and she wavers wildly, reaching for a pack on her back that isn't there. I'm wearing both of 'em. She complained at first until I gave her back her dagger, but she didn't stand her ground long enough for me not to be worried.

"What do you think about Aneena?"

"Echo's better."

But she's not listenin'. Instead, her gaze gets even more distant and her lips murmur a word that makes time come to a complete standstill. "Or Noon. Pretty, no? And it's a palindrome."

"You fuckin' kidding me?" That knife she used to slit my throat with her jealousy? She retracts it and guts me in two quick moves. "The fuck did you say?" I step away from 'er and she wobbles, reachin' for me, but I don't let her get close.

"What?" She blinks her glossy eyes up at me and I fuckin' wanna gouge 'em out.

"What in the fuck did you just say to me, Omega?"

"I…" She looks around, scratches her head. "I just…he says…the man in the cave…" She makes a face and shakes her head and tries to focus on my gaze, but can't seem to find it. Like she's talkin' to someone else. "He said Noon. Noon… pretty. It's a palindrome, too."

"Fuck you." My hands form fists and I look around, takin' another step back, glancing around wildly. I don't smell foreign scents, but this Omega's got gifts — maybe more power than she lets on, maybe this novice Omega act is just that — a fuckin' act. Maybe she's cloakin' more power, more gifts, a partner, another Alpha, *one she actually wants to be with…*

"You got a partner out here with you? Somebody you're workin' for? That whole shit back at Trash City an act? You belong to them? That why you know so much about their guns? Why you got so many theories? You even from Prayersville or Grasslands? Or are you Merlin's fuckin' puppet?"

"What…I don't…I'm confused…"

"Don't fuckin' play me, Omega!"

Her eyes squeeze together and her shoulders tense by her ears. She shakes her head, lookin' like she's tryin' to reorient herself and when she stumbles, I catch her even though I wanna rip her head off at the neck.

I squeeze her shoulders in my hands and watch as she blinks up at me, tears clearin' from her eyes as she battles back her pain and her delirium. I glance at the arm in question, hatin' it and hatin' her. Hating the fuckin' Trash City scum that shot 'her. Hatin' the words comin' out of her mouth that have no provenance I can make sense of. *Can't be an accident.* Can't be a fuckin' coincidence that she's here, talkin' shit about palindromes without knowin' that Noon was my sister.

She looks at me for a long time, her face sunken in a way it's usually not. I look over her freckled cheeks, wondering how there could be so many freckles on a single face, wondering how her lips could be so full and fucking kissable. She bats her eyelashes. They're a darker red than her hair and glossy with unspent tears, with death creepin' nearer and nearer.

She's a fuckin' spy, traitor, here to kill me. Somethin'. I can't let this vulnerability get to me any more than it already has.

"What?" She blinks again and again and her hands reach for me, but I don't let 'er touch my chest, my heart. That's what she's reachin' for, to gouge it out with her nails. The fuckin' witch. "I…" She swallows and glances around, managing to look lost in a way that makes my stomach muscles squeeze together and my stupid heart kick.

"How the fuck do you know my sister's name?"

Her pupils contract, becoming impossibly small in the forest brown of her irises. Her brown skin turns white in the cheeks, making her eyes look like she's been socked good a couple times. Would likely be one of the lesser injuries she's gotten out here. *Pull her close.* No. I've survived hell. I'm not gonna let this little fuckin' Omega be the death of me. *I refuse to allow the Fates to be right a second time.*

She looks between my eyes, but I don't move. I'm not givin' her an out from this.

"Noon? Your sister's called Noon?"

"Omega!" I roar and my attempt at calm is shattered. I lash out and grab her by the throat. I hold her tight, watch her struggle. "Tell me who you're workin' for and I promise, it won't hurt."

"Hurt…the cave…what?" She squeezes her eyes together, shakes her head and grabs onto my wrists. She's fightin' because she's too stupid to ever let go. *Too fuckin' brave. Too fuckin' righteous.* If she's been playin' me this whole time, I don't know what I'm gonna do about it. She's gonna turn my whole world upside down and I might not survive it.

My instincts are all I got. They're all that's kept me alive. That and my resilience to pain, my size and my brutality. And my want. I've wanted her so fuckin' bad since the Fates first told me about the red-haired witch I'd give my life for. But I'm not givin' it if she's gonna take it from me like this. Like a fuckin' coward.

"You a coward?"

Her eyes clear in a sudden burst of lucidity and she karate chops her arm down against my wrist, not hard enough to dislodge my hold, but hard enough for her other arm to rebel against the bindings holding it to her chest and make me worry.

"Don't move your fuckin'…"

"I'm not a coward! You're a coward. You're a big, ugly, stupid coward. I don't know your sister. I don't know you. I don't know the man in the c… I…" She rears back like I slapped her and looks over her shoulder so quickly, it's like she was called. "Do you hear…"

"Echo, I'm not fuckin' dealin' with this shit." I exhale in a rush and rub my hand down my face. "Need a fuckin' minute." I turn away from her and start to crunch my way through the forest. I need to breathe — and not air stained with her scent, either. I need real fuckin' oxygen. None of that dripping cunt-scented crap that makes me wanna do real bad shit to her and even worse shit for her.

"You know I'm…I'm not going to be here when you get back," she shouts after me.

I throw my head back and cackle. "Run and it'll hurt worse than the first time I caught you."

Don't turn around, don't turn around, don't turn around.

"I…I only have one other arm and one other leg for you to rip off. You can…have them," she slurs. "I'm gonna die in Paradise Hole and it'll be thanks to you."

I turn around and advance on her, moving until her nose is pressed up against my chest and I'm practically shoutin' down at the top of her rat's nest. Sure there's shit livin' in her hair by now. "Not gonna die here, Echo, but you will in a

Dark City cell if you don't give me what I need. How'd you think a' that name? Not a common one. I wanna know. Don't fuckin' test me. I've got ways to get the truth outta ya."

"Yeah, like ordering me around like a *coward?*"

"Nah. Don't need to be a Berserker to bring you to heel. Already own you."

"You don't own…"

I grab the front of her sweatshirt with one hand and shove my other down the front of her pants. I push through her thick nest of curls, find her lips, as soft as two petals, and shove two fingers into her tight cunt.

She makes a choking sound in the back of her throat and grabs my wrist. She pushes me away, but when I curl my fingers and gently, so fuckin' gently, pulse them inside of her, she shakes violently and curls in on herself, collapsing against my chest.

"Could drive you into heat with my fingers alone and still stay standing on the other side of it. Could drive you into heat and leave you hurtin'. Could do it over and over."

"Stop…" she chokes. "Stop it."

I start to pull my hand back but she squeezes my arm. "Just a little higher," she whines in a voice so high-pitched only my Berserker and the dogs can hear it. "Don't…"

"Gonna purr for me, Omega?" I whisper against her ear.

She tilts her head back, face shining up at me, eyes blurry and rimmed in red. Fuck. Smell of her fever hits me like a smack in the face. I rip my fingers from where they wanna be and suck 'em clean. *Filthy*. Delicious.

Her pupils expand and contract like a telescope. Heat blooms under her ashen cheeks and I can't fuckin' think. It's a lie, what I told her. If she goes into heat, I might not be strong enough to stop my rut. Need distance from her now. Can torture her later.

"Just — " I exhale in a rush and swipe my hand down my face, inhalin' the rich scent of her cunt as I do it, then push my wet fingers back through my hair. Don't make it far though. My hair's in tangles around my shoulders, a fuckin' mop. My beard's even worse. "Wait here. I need a minute," I repeat.

I let her go and stomp away from her through the forest. I walk and I walk until I can no longer hear her breathing. 'Til I can't hear anything but the sound of the wind movin' through leaves, the gentle hum of machines workin' in the distance. We're so fuckin' close. I can suffer not knowin' who or what she really is until we get to Dark City. *Who she is? I know who she is. Pssh. She's Echo. She's not spyin' for shit. She's alone. Like me.*

And I punished her for it.

I exhale shakily and rub my chest, trailing the rough pads of my fingers over the soft silk of my largest scar. I close my eyes, picture the slim, pale face of a little girl who's even younger than I am, but who looks like our mother. Evelyn. Noon. Both dead. Both Omegas. Omegas aren't meant to survive this world alone. What am I doin'? The control Echo's got over her gifts is shaky at best. She's sick. She's confused. *She's workin' for them*. Nah. She's lonely.

And I left her alone for what? For *shit*.

"Fuck." I turn around and lurch back in the direction I came, trees starin' down at me like they know what I've done and disapprove.

"A…Adam?" A whispered word has me hustlin' faster. Sounds further away than she should be.

"You runnin', Omega?" I shout.

I make it back to the copse where we separated and see her kneelin' a little ways off, through the trees, in a patch of light that could only generously be called sunlight. The trees are thinner around her and I can see her lookin' away from me, off into the distance. There's somethin' strange about her expression, though…

Her face is suspended in disbelief, her mouth wide open, her eyes huge. She's watchin' somethin'. Somethin' I can't see until I clear the next cluster of thick tree trunks…and my Berserker form pulls forward the moment I see what she does.

He rips out of my skin, shredding the pack on my back, exploding out of all of my badly stitched clothes at the same time that Echo's shaky voice screams, "Adam!" And at the same time that an Alpha dives through the air, hands extended to claws and mouth open, fangs he *shouldn't* have reaching towards her. *Those are Berserker claws…Berserker fangs… and they're gunning for my girl.*

I release a feral roar and kick my back legs harder into the soil, springing up and colliding with the Alpha's chest so fuckin' close to Echo, I can feel the breeze her body creates as she lurches back in terror, makin' a fuckin' fool a' me. *She's no spy. She's* mine. *Two halves of a lonely whole.*

I take the Alpha to the ground and land in the dominant position. I don't hesitate, but slash my claws over his chest once, twice, and on the third stroke, I aim for his throat and relieve him of it. His skin tears easy — too fuckin' easy.

I look down at the mess of bone and flesh in my hands unable to understand what's so *wrong* here. I don't have time to analyze it when Echo screams again. I turn my back on the corpse and move into position in front of her only to find — Jesus Christ — thirty Alphas have formed a loose ring around us. Formin' a solid line between the trees, they have us boxed in.

The fur on my back lifts and a low growl slips from between my teeth. My claws clack against each other as I dig them into the soil and my thoughts fire, trying to piece together what it is that I'm seeing.

Echo, even feverish, is quicker'n I am, because it's her small, frightened voice that whispers, "Adam, I think they're…they're dead. The Alphas are all dead."

I glance down at the corpse I just dismembered and then at my own claws. *Blood? Where's the blood?* There isn't any. His bone and flesh had crunched so easily, like a sand castle disintigrating under a harsh sun, and inside had been nothing but brittle jaundiced bones and black flesh. But more importantly, there was no blood. But it isn't fuckin' possible. Echo can't be right. They're *moving*. How can they be dead…

"Adam, they're coming! Look out!"

The Alphas, finding their new target in *me*, charge forward as one. The first three I'm able to bat away easily, but the fourth and fifth and the sixth jump onto my back and stab and bite and claw with Berserker fangs and Berserker teeth. It doesn't make sense. They aren't Berserkers. They look like Alphas, larger than Betas, but they aren't beasts…

I slam into a tree and dislodge the three clinging to my fur. One of them gets up and, with sightless eyes, swivels towards me. His lips peel back from thick ivory fangs and he runs at me even though he's got a fat chance in hell a' winnin'. I'm a *Berserker*.

But...he might be dead.

I smash my fangs through his brittle, dry skin and the taste of it — oh fuck — the taste of it... Tastes like rot. My gaze sinks, changing from long range to near view, and I see maggots and flies festering beneath the torn ligaments as I kick his body back and spit out his skull. His limbs, splayed on the ground like a broken swastika, still twitch.

I ignore the bile that burns the back of my throat and rip a chunk of flesh out of the incoming Alpha's shoulder. As he staggers back, I grab onto his arm and rip the entire thing free. The socket that's left behind is a mangled mesh of what looks like forest twigs and beef jerky, but the bastard just keeps comin'.

I cut through another half dozen when I feel myself first start to drag. I know I can't shout at Echo to tell her to run, either. We're near the Dark City Highway Lines, finally close enough that, if she could get there, she'd be spotted by my scouts, and if she gave them my orders, they'd protect her. But I can't risk morphin' outta my Berserker form to tell her shit. Not when all fuckin' eighteen of 'em are surroundin' me now and I'm the only fuckin' thing between them and Echo.

Claws score my back. Fangs sink into my thigh. Venom — *fucking venom* — spreads through me and I roar as the first bolt of delirium reaches my brain, turning my sight hazy.

The Alpha at my leg suddenly slinks away and I spare the only second I got to look over my shoulder. He's pinned to the ground by vines, but gettin' through 'em doesn't take much.

Behind me, backed against three trees that don't got enough branches to climb — even if she had strength for that — Echo's on her knees, tryna fight. Sight of it breaks my fuckin' heart and makes me goddamn wild.

I turn and catch an Alpha by the jaw as it races towards me, fangs dripping with a venom that's black when it should be silver — and shouldn't even *be* at all. My paw is skewered by one of his fangs, but I ignore the pain of it as I wrench down and left and tear his jaw clean off. I rip free his longest tooth, toss the bones aside, reach through the gaping mess of his open mouth and impale his skull with it.

Eyes — murky yellow eyes — remain open wide as the body keels to the side, the dead thing finally still.

I keep fightin', tearin' my way through the wreckage. I manage to kill another four dead things, but I'm…I'm slowin' down. Whatever was in that fuckin' venom was lethal and they're closin' in on me, backin' me nearer and nearer to Echo, who's gruntin' and gaspin' with the effort it takes her to call forward her gifts, but they're not enough against these creatures. I'm not enough. *Unworthy.* Failure.

No. No, it can't fuckin' be. The Fates promised me, I'd give my life for hers, but if I die here and now there's not a chance she'll survive this.

I'm too busy gettin' chewed alive to notice the ground rumblin' at first. Got my fist shoved deep inside an Alpha's stomach, his bones shootin' up towards me like dry-ass confetti, when a growl distracts me and I look up and finally see 'em.

The bears.

I roar, but the sound just blends into the symphony of fifty fuckin' bears stormin' through the forest, headed straight towards us.

ECHO
LOST

CAUGHT BETWEEN A NIGHTMARE AND A DREAM, I WATCH as humungous bears pound towards us down the low ridge. They're white. Pure white, the color of freshly fallen snow. They're unafraid of the undead Alphas, unafraid of my Berserker, and they don't stop. Three of the remaining dead things turn to face off with them and release these horrible shrieks that don't sound like anything I've ever heard before. The bears roar out a response and attack and the result is wonderful and wretched.

I'd call it a bloodbath if there were any blood other than Adam's — and he. is. bleeding. He's bleeding so much. But some of what's dripping out of the wounds on his back is *black*, almost like the Alphas — the dead things — have their own form of undead venom, too.

Meanwhile, no matter how he tears at them, the dead things don't bleed at all and even the ones he dismembers somehow find their way to their feet and come forward again...and again and again. My eyes feel hotter than my skull, which feels too tight. My skin feels like it's roasting away from the frame beneath it and my injured arm is throbbing with a pulse that doesn't match the wild ricochet of heartbeats dancing up my arms.

Pain stands at a distance, no longer of use to me, while Fear sits up close, her long, cold fingers wrapped around my neck. It's the closest she's ever been, and it makes no sense. "I'm sorry, Adam," I say as he limps to meet his next opponent, tackling two Alphas to the ground as they lunge for me. He's protecting me and it's killing him. No one's ever protected me before and I hate the sight of it. Why doesn't he give up? "You're gonna die…don't die for me."

I reach my hand forward, but the vines that shoot out of the ground are difficult to manipulate and don't come to me like they should — like they did when Adam ordered them into existence. My head isn't clear, isn't calm, I can't concentrate. I need an order from him, but he's in no state to give it.

And then the bears are on us. I scream, prepared to be ripped apart by their jaws and their claws, but the bears go only for the Alphas. The bears claw the Alphas to shreds, but a few bears are bitten and with each bite of a dead Alpha's fangs, the bears fall right away. But they don't bleed, either.

They just…vanish.

And when they vanish, six more bears take the place of the fallen. They come in waves that overwhelm and subsume. Two bears and six Alphas roll into me and Adam roars, moving to intercept them, but one of the Alphas I thought he killed is rolling back onto its feet — its one remaining foot — and sinking its claws — from its one remaining hand — into

Adam's neck. He roars in pain and drops down onto his belly no more than six paces in front of me. The Alpha sinks its fangs into his shoulder, black venom exploding everywhere, and Adam howls.

I scream and reach for him, lunging up onto my feet, but the sight of a white fox distracts me. I glance right and no — it isn't a fox, it's a woman. She's pale as a sheet from her skin to her hair to her bright eyes, the color of cool water. She's crouched on the ground, her hair in ratty tangles around her arms, falling all the way to the ground. Her eyes are pinned to me.

For no reason I can think of, I shout, "Help him, please." Why this Fata Morgana should choose to help a half-dead Berserker and a more than half-dead Omega, I have no idea.

She jerks her head. *No.* Adam roars again.

"Please!"

She stiffens and narrows her gaze and looks at me like she despises me. "Move," she hisses.

A sensation like wet concrete shifts in my body. I shake my head and rise up onto my knees. A vision comes to me and I'm in a cave. I can see the man who lives there — I can see his mouth, it's moving. *Freya.*

"Freya!" I scream. "He's mine!"

The white-haired woman who looks every bit nymph — or forest witch — rises up onto her feet, looking terrifying, looking enraged. "I summon you, Omega!" Her voice comes out as a whisper on the wind, her accent confusing and silted, almost like these are the first words she's ever spoken.

Her hand reaches towards me and the concrete feeling in my chest liquifies to mercury, heating my bones, poisoning every bit of me. "Bring the dead ones down!" She disappears and a bear stands where she did a moment earlier and lunges to meet the dead Alphas charging for it. The Alphas take it down.

I choke on the scream that tears out of me as the last eight Alphas — one missing an arm, another, half the skin on its right side so it's just bones wrapped in white and pink strips of meat — turn to face me. They take slow steps forward and I know I'm dead and —

You're not alone.

The thought penetrates my stomach and Fear frowns down at me, shaking her head. She tries to reach for me again, but I lift up my hand and there's a dagger in it. *One he gave me.* I point it at the Alpha coming towards me — three bears close in on him from the back, so I point it at the next undead.

The air seems to slow, time hiccupping for just a single, tremulous moment. And then it happens. Vines wrap themselves around my arms, around my whole body, and they're controlling me as much as I control them as I plunge to the ground, blade-first. I stab it into the soft, yielding soil.

The Alphas hesitate, like they're waiting for something to happen as they watch me with their milky blue eyes. But Adam and I are still losing. The bears are still disappearing. Adam is still pinned to the ground. *He can't die, not for me. I won't survive it.*

Something like that will tear down all of my conceptions about him and Alphas and Berserkers and what it means to be an Omega. And then what will be left? Pain? Fear? Maybe, not even them. Maybe, all that will be left is a void that's begun to fill with things like compassion. Things like *tenderness.*

The vines wrapped around my arms hug me close, but they don't pull, they don't pinch. They seem to fit around my body like sleeves would if I ever had clothes that fit. And as I stare at the back of my hand, I start to notice something strange.

New vines grow, these soft and green. They twirl around the brown rope vines that snap and bend, and on all of them appear little flowers. *Flowers.* I've never seen a flower before this.

The ground in front of my blade splits open with no prelude or hesitation. It just opens like a huge mouth that gobbles up bears and Alphas and dirt and trees and everything else as it widens, splitting all the way up to the ridge in the distance. The Alpha who'd been in front of me tries to sink his claws into the ground and claw his way back up, but Adam gives him a kick in the face that sends him flying down, down, down…

Adam.

"Adam!"

Adam's clawing away from the huge split in the earth, flinging the Alphas off his back as he moves towards me, clawing and fighting his way over the rumbling dirt. His brown and honey fur is matted and streaked with black, inky venom and dark red-brown blood. I can smell it and it reeks of bloodlust and metal as he comes to cover my vine-entrapped form, his beastly body smothering mine while the whole world in front of us swallows up everything — all the undead Alphas and their dead bodies, and all the bears, except for one.

I blink and the bear vanishes, becoming a woman once more. She watches me from the edge of the trees where the split doesn't reach her. I can hear clawing and inhuman shrieking coming from below, muted as the sounds are absorbed by the soil. I can hear them coming closer though, and I meet the witch's gaze, only I know she isn't a witch as her ice-blue eyes look me over. *She's an Omega.*

I inhale deeply as Adam's huge, furry limbs fold around me. I exhale, relieved to just be wrapped up in them. Even if we both die like this, and it's likely we will. My fever is setting in, but I keep staring at the Omega that was once a bear, and the longer I stare at her, the easier it feels to breathe through the agony streaking across my chest.

"Move," dark lips whisper. The cave is clammy and cold.

Omega.

"Omega."

Omega.

I press my palm against the soil. The flowers growing across the back of my hand are already dead. The ground shivers as the dirt moves, sealing up the great scar in the soil until it never was. Until the only evidence that something happened here is fresh, overturned soil speckled with bright green vines that weave in and out of it like stitches. I know all about stitches.

The Omega tips her head down at me and disappears on my next blink. Time passes. Feels like a lot of it. Adam is still in his Berserker form. His breathing is shallow.

I open my eyes and jerk. The Omega is kneeling on the ground directly in front of me. She looks at the knife hilt reaching out of the ground like a tombstone with no epitaph. Short of her, no one will know what happened here. Adam and I are going to die. Not alone though, as we've both always been our entire lives. For the first time, we'll be together. *We have each other.*

"You saw…him, too," she whispers, "the man…in the cave."

I nod. "Freya."

"Echo." She licks her lips. They bloom pink for a moment before returning to a paler shade. And still, they're the only bits of color on her. She does look like a witch. Like the witch of the woods. Maybe she's the one the other Alphas at the troll bridge were looking for. "We…must find the…others."

"Others?"

"The Fallen Omegas. We cannot defeat them if we are just two."

I sigh, confused and very sure that this must be a dream. Or the afterlife. Because she's speaking in riddles, but in a pleasant way that makes me feel so much less alone. Even less alone than I do in Adam's beastly grasp. "Defeat who?"

"The dead army."

"We just did."

"No." She shakes her head and then her head snaps forward and I hallucinate that she's a fox, but nope…she's back. "You need to see. Go to Mirage…City and then…come find me in the cave." Her stilted speech gains in volume the longer she continues talking. It still takes me too long to piece her words together, but that's not her fault. That's mine. I'm fading. *Dying, probably. Maybe even for good, this time.* "I will meet you there…when you are healed. Come alone. Don't bring your…Berserker. You must kill him."

"No."

She snaps at me with fanged teeth and I wince, but when she rears back her teeth are square and normal. I must really be losing it. "You should have killed…him now. Take him into the earth…with the others."

"He's mine," I say, forcing my eyes open a little further. I meet her gaze and see her snarling at me, her lips pulled back, her fingers bent at unnatural angles. She wears claws on her fingertips. She looks like a wolf, or just half. "I decide if and when to kill him."

"Decide soon."

And then she sprints off into the murky, grey daylight most definitely wearing the skin of a snow-white fox, the crafty little witch that she is.

Meanwhile, Adam isn't moving and I'm not sure if I can move. But I don't sleep. I fight. I keep fighting until the daylight begins to dim around us. I keep fighting, but the fight is only mental. I can't move. My limbs are all weighted and his warmth is intoxicating, dragging me down and making me feel all kinds of cozy. *I guess it's not a bad idea to just die here.*

It wouldn't be, if it weren't for the sounds…no, not sounds. *Voices.*

I whimper and Adam's arms tighten around me, surprising me. He hasn't shifted out of his Berserker yet and part of me thought that the forest witch was stating redundancies because Adam was already dead, but turns out he's fighting from his immobile state just as hard as I am. *We're not so different.*

"Berserker Dragnovic!" Smashing feet on the forest floor approach.

I whimper again, but Adam releases a roar — a pained roar that makes my chest burn and my muscles contract. Hearing him suffer makes me want to fight harder, but he holds me down.

"Dragnovic!"

"Berserker!"

A family of deer scampers across the clearing in front of me, moving so silently and swiftly I jolt. Blinking, I almost miss them. But how could I? They're all *white*. Never seen a white deer before.

A beat passes, then the stomping gets louder. More of a crashing, really. And then faces. *Alpha* faces. I shiver and recoil into the heat of Adam's body. He starts to move — tries, but fails. He releases a pained sound again and the faces turn towards us. Six of them, and these are very much *alive*. Welcome to my nightmare.

My eyes close and I try to bury myself deeper into his bloody, furry body. I'm terrified, but Fear isn't responding in the way she's supposed to. She's still frowning at me from the trees I didn't topple.

"Jesus fuck!" one of the Alphas — a younger-looking guy with dark brown skin and lean muscles stacked on top of an obscenely tall frame — shouts. "Dragnovic!" He starts running first and the two Alpha females in the group move in line behind him, their hands on their weapons.

"Form a perimeter!" the blonde Alpha female with the heavy braid shouts.

"We need a stretcher. Fuck…" The only man who doesn't obey the blonde is a redhead with pale, clear skin. Instead of running to form a perimeter, he drops to his knees in front of us and covers his nose with his hand. "Fuck! Alphas, mask up. He found his Omega and her scent is strong, even beneath the blood."

He pulls a red bandana out of the back pocket of his black jeans and ties it around his narrow nose and wide mouth before reaching forward to touch me. His hands come near me, but Adam's massive paw closes around his wrist.

"Fuck! Berserker, you're alive. Can you change back to your Alpha form? I won't be able to work on you like this and we sure as shit can't carry your ass."

"I think if he could do that, he'd have done it by now," I hear myself croak.

The sound of my voice comes as a surprise to all of us. The redhead curses again. "Fuck. Omega, how did this happen?"

"Dead army."

"What?"

"That doesn't matter," the blonde says as she approaches, a piece of torn fabric wrapped around the bottom half of her face. She's got blood on her arms, scratches, too. It makes me wonder what kind of trouble they encountered in Paradise Hole trying to get to their Berserker. That they tried at all surprises me. I'd have thought that a pack of Alphas would be too eager to fill the vacuum.

"What can we do in lieu of a stretcher? Sierra, you got that axe? Good. Start taking down trees — any that are left…"

"Whiskey, Sierra — hold up. I don't think you need to do that," the young Alpha says. He bends down and picks up a vine — vines woven together to form a hammock large enough to fit a Berserker beast.

And me, too, if there's space. *And I did that.*

"Where'd that come from, Vi?" The woman called Whiskey says. They all look around, the ones I can see, but I don't bother to offer an explanation. "Fuck it. Who cares. Let's go."

Do I want to go? My heart starts to pound. No, I don't want to go. But I definitely don't want to stay.

"You think the Omega did that? Looks too perfect for it to be made by nature," Vi says.

"Musta," Whiskey answers.

It's weird hearing them all talk in that strange Dark City accent. All except the dark-haired woman — Sierra — who speaks like she's from one of the southern cities, Shadowlands or Gold City, maybe, but not so far south as Hjiel.

"Adam," I croak in a terrified whisper.

He moves, shifting, becoming even bigger. The Alphas complain about it, bickering among each other in a way I've never heard before, except for once…back at Grasslands, way, way back. One of my earliest memories. I met siblings. True siblings. They bickered like this. I left for Prayersville shortly after meeting them. I wonder what happened to them.

Despite their bickering, the Alphas still load him onto the vine stretcher I created in my subconscious and they load me up with him because he doesn't let me go. He doesn't let anyone touch me. He just clutches me to his chest like a kid holding a teddy and that's alright with me. Fear follows as they carry us through the woods, but only at a distance.

ECHO
DARK CITY HIGHWAY LINE

ADRENALINE AND MY HEART SLAMMING AGAINST MY ribcage keep me awake even though I can tell by Adam's heavy breathing that he passed out a long time ago. The moment they got him — us — onto the stretcher. *He trusts them*. The thought freaks me out. And that terror doesn't go away as we make it out of the forest and to a place I've never been before — that I'd never have dared go out here in Paradise Hole. *Dark City Highway Line.*

Scavengers only travel by Highway Lines to die. That's where Alphas roam.

On the Highway Line leading to Dark City, Whiskey pulls a huge brick of a radio out of the thin survival sling she wears over one shoulder. Surprising me, she's able to get a connection. That doesn't happen often in Paradise Hole. I've only ever seen Trash City use walkies, and they're only short-range. But she must connect to somebody, because after about an hour of jogging down the road — and yes, I mean jogging while holding up a Berserker in his beast form and a malnourished Omega — a caravan of vehicles cruises up to us.

Alphas carrying guns swarm out of the trucks and immediately set up a perimeter, as if awaiting an ambush at any second while the redhead who Whiskey calls Peate makes everyone put on masks. He talks about separating Adam and I into two different cars but I start to cry the moment he suggests it and the sound must wake a sleeping Adam, who roars out a battle cry that's so terrifying it makes me pee a little bit.

Peate is a sneaky bastard, though, because he pulls a needle out of his back pocket and plugs the pointy end into Adam in a dozen places. Then he and some of the Alphas who've joined us move Adam into another car. For me, I just get the one shot, but it's enough for my muscles to turn to soup and my body to fill with the most wonderful euphoria.

It doesn't knock me out though, at least not right away. I'm wide awake in the back of an SUV barreling down the Dark City Highway Line when I glance up through the tinted window and see Dark City's massive stainless steel wall, pocked and scarred and burned in places from rebellions long past. And then the gates embossed with a massive name, DRAGNOVIC, swing open wide enough to devour before swinging shut, caging me in.

I force my eyelids to stay open and see everything. The city doesn't start for a while, and that surprises me. There are houses out here, stores, low buildings that look like they're saloons from another era. We pass through suburbs, too. Industrial areas that have actual industry, and then industrial areas that have been converted into more restaurants and stores and living spaces. There are people in them. Buildings, grocery stores, pharmacies, even a school. I don't see very many kids on the playground right now, but there are some. They're laughing, playing, like they have no idea what goes on outside of these walls.

I'm crying again and I don't know why. Peate, kneeling on the floor of the backseat beside me, continues cutting me out of my clothes. He's been cussing like hell and trying to do what he can to doctor me with the supplies he has on hand, but when he notices my tears, he asks me if I want more drugs and I shake my head, then, at the sight of the first skyscraper, nod.

I'm so overwhelmed.

I've never seen anything like this before. It's insane. It's huge. Beta compounds are nothing like this. Paradise Hole is nothing at all. We drive until the main part of Dark City — the downtown — passes and suburbs pick up again. We drive up to a gate and then through it, down a driveway that lasts miles and up to a house… I don't see much of it. Everything's getting dark.

"What did you do?" I croak.

"Just a mild sedative."

"I changed my mind."

"Too late for that." His eyes flash to me. They're light brown, maybe hazel. He's a pretty man. Too pretty. He doesn't have any scars. Not like Adam and me. "Besides, you need to sleep."

"Where's Adam?"

"The Berserker needs to heal."

"I don't want to be alone."

"You're not alone," he lies to me. He gives me an awkward pat on the shoulder, a piss poor excuse for comfort. I cringe away from it and he chuffs, "Promise you, we won't hurt you, Omega. You're our Berserker's Omega..."

"You're gonna use me. He's gonna let you as soon as he wakes up."

Peate chuckles low and gravelly. "He's been waitin' for you his whole life and talkin' about you ever since we got the report that an Omega with red hair had been spotted in Paradise Hole. Poor bastard was shittin' himself with nerves, tryin' to guess what you'd be like, the shit he'd buy for you to make you comfortable here. Doubt he'd let anybody use you for anythin' other than worshippin' — though y'all were gone a long time. You do somethin' to piss him off?"

Only a hundred things. "He's gonna put me in the dungeon." I start to get all weepy because, well, I guess that's just the kinda week I'm having. *Weeks*. Ten of them — or has it been twelve by now? It feels like I've known Adam for a lifetime.

"Doubt it."

"I knew his sister's name. The man in the cave told me..."

"Jesus Christ. Gonna up the sedative."

"Just give me my knife."

"Your knife?"

"He gave me a knife. It's mine. I want it."

"Sorry, kiddo, we searched the grounds, but we didn't find any knife."

I sniffle and blubber some other things and Peate looks down at me with his warm brown, maybe hazel eyes and nods politely at everything I say while readying the needle.

The back doors to the SUV open and Sierra's face appears alongside Vi's and a plethora of black-masked Alphas whose names I don't know.

"Peate. Dragnovic's wounds." She shakes her head. "You need to see this."

Dragnovic. That's his last name. I knew that already, but I never called him by it. What if he dies before I ever get to call him by that dumb last name? What if I die? What if he dies and leaves me here all alone?

Peate starts to climb out of the back of the van while Alphas I don't know start to move in, crowding me. Fear claps her hands in the front seat, drawing my attention to the sight of her face flashing in the rearview mirror.

I close my eyes and fight against the delirium that grabs me and pulls me under, like the earth pulled those zombie Alphas under earlier. What were they? *Dragnovic.* What happened to him? *Adam.* Is he okay? Am I? *When did Peate stab me with that needle?* Will either of us be? I ask Peate and Sierra all these questions, but no one can hear me because I'm no longer awake.

ADAM

DRAGNOVIC MANOR
DARK CITY HIGHLANDS
DARK CITY
FINALLY.

"WARD! I'M GONNA RIP YOUR ARMS OFF. COME HERE." I jerk against the chains wrapped around my arms from wrist to fuckin' shoulder, locks the size of bricks holdin' 'em together and anchoring me to the edges of the damn bed.

Peate's walkin' fast as he reenters the room with more med tape. He's holdin' it high above his head, shakin' it like he's comin' to the damn rescue when all I want are *fewer* adhesives holdin' me back.

"Ward!" I roar at the female scientist in charge a' this damn operation. The only Beta in charge a' anything in my city, right now Penelope Ward's about three moves away from becomin' past tense.

"You'd have chained you down, too, if you'd been the one tryna operate," Ward huffs, layin' down another thick sheet a' gauze over my right ribs and gesturin' at Peate to apply the tape.

Peate is out of breath as he rushes to obey her. "You were movin' all around, callin' out for her, even in your sleep..."

"Look like I give a fuck about the goddamn wounds, Peate? Ward!" I pull against my bindings. The metal and plastic bedframe's only got a few more moments of life left in it. "Ward, you unlock these chains or I'm tearin' this bed apart!" I can feel her in my lungs — the only her in the goddamn world — weighin' 'em down, weighin' *me* down, poisonin' the air and seepin' into my blood. *She's hurtin'. Need to get to her fuckin' now.*

The golden beads in Ward's hair clatter softly against one another like chimes as she shakes her head. "Dragnovic, she's fine. I don't know how many times I have to say it, she's with Loveless and Rogers and she's safe. Her injuries are being treated and she's going to make a full recovery. Her fever broke last night…"

"Then why the fuck is she scared?"

"How would you…" Ward's eyes get huge. She blinks. "How do you know?"

I pull up in one swift movement and the rails of the hospital bed tear off like the bandages being placed over my wounds with such care. I surge off of the mattress and my left knee buckles the moment my feet hit the floor. I lock it, straighten, grunt, breathe enough to calm my spinning thoughts, then I move forward and I don't stop, not even as IV needles tear free of my arms and doctors shout at me, tellin' me shit I really don't care about.

"Your blood," Peate shouts as if I'm not aware a' the fact that I'm leaking. I feel it. Blood spatter drips onto the marble floor and it's the wrong color. It's blacker than it should be.

Ward's shoutin' at me about stayin' still, processin' shit, testing — that she needs me in her lab to do all a' that — but I don't give a fuck. I know where I need to be.

I throw open the double doors, heavy wood swingin' wildly at my back as I stagger out of the white sterile lab-converted-into-a-hospital-room into the black oak hall. Peate, the fuck, is followin' me. Doesn't seem to know when to stop because I'm about to kick in his fuckin' teeth.

"You're still bleeding, Dragnovic! The wounds aren't healing like they're supposed to. Ward's been running tests but she can't figure out how to get the poison outta your blood..."

"Not poison. Venom," I mutter, rounding the next corner and swiping my palm over the vein scanner. The unassuming wooden doors that no one would know are armored and armed swing open in front of me, but I don't make it ten feet into my open living room, draped in dark carpets and heavy oak furniture, before I sense it — a sharp and crushing emptiness. *Any room I enter feels emptier without her in it.*

I swing my gaze around, still not believin' it. "She isn't fuckin' here. Why isn't she in my house? Where is she?"

"Venom? The fuck are you talkin' about, Dragnovic?"

I spin to face him and latch onto his neck, squeezing hard enough for my claws to bite into his skin. Dark red blood wells beneath my claws, the *right* color, a reminder of Echo and what we went through together. I lift until his feet nearly clear the floor while pain ripples through my core. The whole thing probably hurts me more than it hurts him.

"Where is my Omega?" I throw him and he canters back into the wall, knocking over a painting of my Berserker beast and sending it to the floor. Rage is a painful thing to hold onto when it's coupled with fear and desperation. And it's worse when those sensations don't belong to me alone because for the first time since I bit her against her will, I can actually *feel* the bond echoing between us. Like a current, like a poison, like a drug, it spirals through my skin and clouds my thoughts with magical things. *With flowers.* With the acrid scent of her filth and the unbearably sweet scent of her cunt.

"Jesus, Dragnovic… I mean, Berserker. Dragnovic, I just…" His his cheeks turn ruddy. His hand massages his throat and he swallows hard as he blinks down at the blood staining his fingertips. "Yeah. Shit. Sorry. We didn't bring her to your private flat, we put her in the main house. She was talkin' some shit about you hating her and wanting her in the dungeons. We didn't know what to think, so we figured it was a better spot to put her, for now…"

I growl, frustrated with him and even more frustrated with her. I leave him there, return to the hall and race down to the far end where another oak doorway leads to a large winter porch. I nearly crash through the glass doors that lead to my private garden, though the name is…off. Garden? Pshh. It's just rocks. Rocks and a few tall trees with black trunks and grey leaves. What's Echo gonna think when she sees it? She, who can make gardens grow from the center of her palm?

It's a winding path down to the garden house from the main house. The main house, Dragnovic Manor, is the first house anyone sees when they approach the property and is where I meet with my sheriffs and the other useless Alpha fucks who work for me. The garden house is where Betas who work for me conduct their business. That's where they put my

Omega. Not in my bed, but out here with the help. Like that's what she is to me. A tool. Not my queen.

I enter through the kitchen, startlin' the cooks. Pans fall. Glasses break. Betas workin' there shout apologies after me, but I don't care about the shit they're cookin' when I've caught another far, far more tempting scent.

The smell a' earth and so many flowers. Nectar and sap, honey and syrup. I throw open the doors to the third-floor guest bedroom and see Echo against the far wall, fightin' in a large king sized bed where she's been restrained to the wrought iron headboard. My own restraints clatter behind me like the metal sleeves of a wizard's cloak. When I see her face, I go fuckin' insane at the sight of her terror.

And twice as mad at the sight of her seein' me and exhalin' in relief.

"Adam, please..." She yanks up on her good wrist and I can see she's rubbed it raw from pullin' and the fucker, Loveless, didn't bother to untie her.

My claws slash through the bindings as I haul my ass up onto her bed, the metal rail a' my hospital bed draggin' across her lap. I shove it off her and brace one arm on either side of her body. She's wearin' nothin' but a paper-thin hospital gown, same as me, and I'm shocked by how fuckin' frail she looks in it.

"Jesus, Omega, you always this fuckin' pale?"

"You're the pale one," she says, but her teeth are chatterin'. It's cool in here, but not cold. I edge closer, hoverin' over her, not missin' the way she shrinks beneath my shadow. I damn near howl in triumph when she balls her hand into a fist and touches it to the center of my chest. She paws at me tentatively, like she's tryna pull me even closer than that.

The fuck did they do to her?

"Echo, you..."

"Shh." She lifts a finger to her lips and scoots even closer to me. Against the blood red silk sheets, the dirt smudges on her face stand out in relief. She's fuckin' filthy.

"Need to get you cleaned up, baby." I lift a hand and tuck a strand — nah, a clump — of hair behind her ear. She doesn't seem to notice, her gaze shiftin' around to the edges of the room and the med staff movin' around in it.

"Shh! They can hear us."

"Who? My crew? Just tryna heal ya, Echo."

Her brows furrow. "They chained me up. Just like Trash City."

"Not like Trash City, I promise. These are my guys..."

"And gals," Loveless shouts from the edge of the room. I ignore her with a growl — a warning to stay the fuck out of what's between me and my Omega.

"But they...they separated us." She bites her lips between her teeth and tips her forehead down. If I thought she had somethin' livin' in her hair before, I'm sure of it now and I grunt — anger is the only thing keepin' me from laughin'. "I told them not to, but they did it anyway. I didn't know where they were taking you and I..." She sniffles, then she clears her throat loudly to try to compensate for the fact she's clearly about to cry. Fuck. Fuck this. Fuck everyone.

"Omega, don't you fuckin' dare."

Her eyes flare with challenge before dropping to my chest and filling with water all over again. "But you're hurt, too.

You got bit and you're not…not healing…and I didn't know where you were going. If you'd be alright…"

"Echo, don't start pretendin' you care if I'm hurt. Pretend any better and I might start fuckin' believin' you, and you don't want that."

But she isn't listening. She shakes her head and rubs her eyes. "It's not right."

"Omega, I'm fine."

"I can't…can't sleep."

"Haven't slept?" Rage spikes again, threatening to peak. My hand in her hair curls around the back of her head. I clutch her to me and shout over my shoulder. "Everyone, get the fuck out!"

Ward stands in the doorway next to Loveless, both women lookin' seven shades a' concerned. "Dragnovic. We need to keep testing…"

"Ward!" My voice changes and twists, softened by the way Echo shakes in my arms, by her gentle concern, by the tears on her face. Her vulnerability splits me open. I'm nothin' but sand swept away by the wind. "Loveless, wait. Can I move 'er?"

"Let me just check her…"

"Need to move her. Not keepin' her here."

Loveless sighs and pushes her glasses up onto the top of her head so that they get tangled in her thick, dark curls. "Look, I can remove the IV line. Just make sure she gets these morphine tablets every six hours and these antibiotic tablets every twelve."

Carefully, making no sudden movements, she approaches the bed and unties the ropes from around Echo's wrists and unlocks the cuffs from around mine. As she works, Echo cringes away from her and hides her face in the center of my chest. I hold her close, terrified of and loving her closeness. With my Omega and I both now free from the prisons of our beds, Loveless shoves three pill bottles into my hand.

She complains about me tearin' my stitching as I snatch the pills from her and scoop Echo up off of the sheets. "Don't care about stitching," I tell her. Right now, I got my Omega in my arms and she's holdin' onto me as tight as her shaky arms can, which scares the shit outta me since she's claimed to hate me more than a couple hundred times so far.

I just want her safe, alone, close, with me.

Down the stairs, I exit into the gardens and take a deep breath — that cuts short when I hear Loveless chasin' after me. "Dragnovic! Just…Berserker, wait!"

I gotta loyal core staff. They know they can talk back to me, talk shit, cuss and call me by my last name. They also know I'm only *slightly* less likely to ignore them and do whatever the fuck I want when compared to anybody else in my city. That's why they know to call me Berserker when they absolutely *need* my attention.

I pause, even though it hurts. Echo inhales sharply like she's been hit. Her toes curl and she cringes away from Loveless, like the tiny Alpha with very light brown skin stained by a sun we don't see when we live in the dark might hurt her. I feel like I'm standin' beneath that sun now and my skin flushes with heat that surprises me. My cock starts to stiffen in the most infuckinopportune goddamn moment… *Fuck.* I inhale a little deeper, wonderin'…

Echo mewls like she's in pain and I jerk up and try to hold her a little further away from me. "What the fuck?" I hiss.

Loveless manages to look a little sheepish. "I gave you antibiotics, morphine and heat suppressants. You're holding them now. Some of the Alphas who brought her in could scent it and started to get…well, let's just say there's a reason Vi, Barbero, and Peate are keeping themselves and the other Alphas out." Wanna break something. *Bones.*

"You mean to tell me you kept me sedated while my Omega went into heat?"

She takes a step back, her eyes widening. She lowers her gaze to the ground and starts to wobble. "Ward…we…your injuries…"

"Fuck my injuries. If other Alphas were sniffing after my Omega, it's my duty to challenge them for the right to her."

"But you'd…you'd have died. You weren't even conscious…"

"Then I would have died!" I roar. My hands tighten around Echo, but I stiffen, straighten, and try to relax my hold. My temples are pounding. I need rest. I need to calm the fuck down. But now that our bond is fucking…*there,* I can't breathe. I can't think. I'm excited, but more than that… I'm scared. "Tell them to meet me in Battleground in an hour, after I get my Omega settled."

"No." Echo's voice is hard — almost as hard as I remember it in Trash City. I look at her face, into her eyes, and read fear there that steels my resolve to murder somethin'. Until she grabs the tattered tips of my still matted beard and yanks on it. "You promised."

"Promised?"

She nods. "You wouldn't leave me. You said that. Don't you remember?" Tears again. Too many fuckin' tears. Each one is a chisel to the heart. Nah, fuck a chisel. A pickaxe.

She's talkin' about when I fucked her. The first time. She's never brought it up before, choosin' to forcibly forget. I know she didn't want to want it. That she's acknowledgin' it at all freaks the shit outta me. Makes me glad for the heat suppressants quite suddenly because if she went into heat now, there's no chance I wouldn't topple over into rut right after and, given the state a' my body and hers, it'd kill us both.

"Didn't forget, Omega."

Her eyebrows crinkle and she sniffles and I don't know if she's assured, but she nods anyway. "Then stay. Please?"

Fuckin' cut my legs off at the knees. "I'll stay." *For as long as you let me.*

I turn from Loveless and, as I walk, throw the bottle of heat suppressants towards the stream off to my left. It hits the bridge and shatters. "Don't need these anymore. She goes into heat, she's got her Berserker."

ECHO
DRAGNOVIC MANOR

THE BATH WATER IS SO HOT IT'S IMPOSSIBLE TO SHIVER, and I would be shivering if I could. Fear is standing in the corner, partially hidden by swirling mist. But she's still batting her eyelashes at me and waving with all of her claws. I'm so out of my element here. It makes me miss Paradise Hole.

Wait — is that coconut oil shampoo?

Alright. It makes me miss Paradise Hole a *little*. I reach for the bottle and flick the cap open with my thumb. Even though Adam let me take off the brace, I was given specific instruction not to use my injured arm — an instruction I immediately forgot. The swollen fingers of my left hand try to close around the shampoo bottle instinctively, but I hiss, fumble, drop it into the bath. It's an *enormous* bath, built for someone — several someones — much taller than me, so the water comes up to my chest. I lose the bottle immediately. I'm going to have to dive for it. I take a deep breath and start to sink.

"The fuck are you doing?"

The door slams shut and Adam wades towards me through the fog, looking like a spectre himself. An angry one. I glance in the corner for my BFF, but as soon as he appeared, she winked out of existence.

I exhale shakily and lift my injured arm. My jaw works. His eyes flash to my swollen fingers and his face crumples. A low growl rattles out of his chest, throaty and deep. It's not a purr. It's far from it and when I inhale, I smell pure *aggression.* How it's become so discernible to me in the span of a few days is confounding and annoying because it doesn't inspire fear. Oh no. My Omega instinct is pleased by his violence and I'm so, so grateful for the hot water surrounding me. Means I'm wet anyway. And he can't smell it. I hope he can't smell it.

"Talkin' to you, Omega." Omega. Oh no. Means I'm in trouble. I sink further into the water and he lunges toward the bathtub.

I squeak, but the attack doesn't land. Instead, I feel a brush of air as he rounds the enormous marble monstrosity he calls a tub and gently cradles my arm, two fingers pinching me around the swollen wrist, two fingers pinching my bicep. He lifts my arm out of the water and sets it on the once cool, now warm towels lining the broad marble side of the tub.

It leaves me in an awkward position and I feel more awkward when he abruptly shucks the pants off of his hips and plunges into the bathwater beside me, leaving just a few feet separating us. I look at him and he looks at me.

"You broken or somethin'? That morphine get to your head?"

He reaches across the space and tries to touch my forehead. I flinch away. He freezes and crumples his hand into a fist. "Echo, say somethin' or I'll order you to."

"I just..." And then it hits me — what's so *wrong* about him. And it hits me *hard.*

He's showered and shaved and washed his hair and combed it and he's...oh my seven saints...no. No no no no no. The Berserker — *Adam* — is absolutely gorgeous.

He's all tanned, scarred skin layered over the most arresting bone structure I've ever seen. High cheeks, hard jawline, straight nose, full freaking lips. His eyebrows twitch and so does the tip of his nose. He reaches for me again and this time, I'm too slow to avoid his touch. I'm not even sure I want to.

His blunt fingers are rough in texture, but gentle in pressure. My eyelids flutter. "Hey. You don't have claws."

"Don't."

I try to lift my injured arm and take his hand in my two, but he gently presses the injured one back to the towels, leaving me to try to contain his massive hand in my much smaller one. I look down at his palm draped over mine, fully obscuring it. His hands are cleaned, the nailbeds pristine. When did he have the time? His claws have been cut short.

"Why don't you have claws?"

"Cut 'em."

"Why?"

"Tired a' hurtin' you."

My chin starts to wobble. My pussy lips start to clench.

"Don't do it, Echo. Can't go into heat. Not yet. You need another suppressant?"

I nod vigorously.

He gets up, water sluicing off of his body and I try not to look. Fail. Try again. Fail again. His body is stunning. Six and a half feet — seven? — of pure, stitches-wrapped muscle. The black stitching looks gruesome and brutal and my chin starts wobbling again. My eyes get hot. He comes back a moment later and I get a second look at his wounds — not the newest ones, but the X across his heart — and the waterworks start up again.

"Fuck. Echo, please. You gotta stop with that shit. Makes me wanna…" His cheeks get red, but he doesn't finish. He hands me the pill and a huge glass of ice water.

My mouth is sticky with saliva as I choke the white pill down, humiliated and not for the first time. Of course I need the suppressants. I'm about to go into heat and he has a wife somewhere on the property.

"But you shouldn't want me."

He gives me an incredulous look.

I feel my face heat even more than the surrounding bathwater, which is nothing but pure divinity. "You can't smell it," I stutter.

His eyebrows pull together. They're the same blond-streaked brown as his hair. His beard is a shade darker. At least, it was. I miss it…but that doesn't stop me from wanting to scrape my dirty, broken nails over his clean-shaven cheek and jaw. Those angles… oh god. But I hate him. Except I don't. Not anymore. I don't know what I feel about him, but it's not hate. It's something more dangerous.

"Smell what, Omega?"

"You…" Sniffle. "You keep saying I shouldn't go into heat. But you can't smell it in the bath…"

His eyes widen and his nostrils flare. Immediately, he edges away from me. "Don't need to smell your pussy for you to send me into rut. Tears are just as bad. Fuck, maybe worse. Makes me wanna make you feel better in the only way my Berserker knows how. If you don't get your shit together, you're gonna send me into rut and there won't be any comin' back from it. For either of us." Because he has a wife, and that'll mess things up.

"What's rut?"

"Fuck." He rubs his hand down his face, water droplets clinging to the tips of his eyelashes. "You don't know enough. I can't explain it to you, either. Not without goin' into rut right here. Right now. I'll find someone to give you a crash course. Promise." Because he can't do it himself. Because he has a wife.

But…even if he does have a wife, I don't want anyone else.

"I want you to teach me." I don't want to talk to anyone else. I don't know when I stopped *not* wanting to talk to him, but I guess I'd rather it be him if I have to talk to anyone. "You don't have to have sex with me. I know you love your wife…"

"Omega, quiet. That's an order."

A chill floods my bones and I open my mouth but I find that I can't get any words out. My tears dry up, morphing quickly into anger. I shove a wave of water at him, which he snarls at. He surges towards me, then slams back into the wall of the tub. The marble is this gorgeous white and pink and brown swirling pattern, layered over the entire outside of the tub, floor and half the walls. I liked it before. I liked him before. Seconds before.

But this is a good reminder of why I'm an idiot and he's a bastard.

I look away from the sight of him with his eyes closed, chest heaving, hand rubbing roughly down his face. I snatch a fresh bottle of bodywash off of the edge of the bath and move over to the opposite edge, as far from him as I can get. I try to use my tongue to flick the cap open, but the taste of coconut bodywash isn't as good as it sounds and I gag.

The bottle is ripped out of my hand and I'm in motion, fighting even as I continue to choke on the taste. I'm easily overpowered. He grabs my good wrist, spins me around and plops me down onto his lap while he sits on the bathtub's inner bench. His cock is hard and huge against my back, which arches. I make a fluttery sound that I hate and I don't like at all how I feel strapped to his chest. It reminds me too much of the first time when he bit me.

He lowers his mouth to the curve of my neck and I whimper. Fear slips into the bathtub opposite me. She preens, satisfied, as she watches the two of us.

"Took the stitches out."

"Mmmm!" I grunt, wiggling my shoulders. He holds me tighter.

"Told you once I'd never bite you again. Not gonna repeat myself. Gonna have to trust me."

I shake my head.

He grabs my neck from the front and roughly exhales against the side of my face. His forehead tips to touch my temple. All of his muscles tense up, like he wants to squeeze the life out of me, or burst into tears, or both. And then he shoves me under the water.

I come up a second later, shocked, which makes me slow to process what he's doing now. He's dunking under the water with me and is setting the bodywash back on the side of the tub. In his hand, he's holding the shampoo instead and is he…is he washing my hair?

"Can talk, Echo," he says as the shampoo bottle farts somewhere above me. He thumps it down onto the edge of the bath before diving into the thicket that is my hair. All my red, frizzy strands are trying to loc themselves together. His blunt fingers massage my scalp in a way that sends feeling sizzling down my back, electricity shooting through my muscles, and fire through all of my thoughts.

"Ung," I grunt, making this and other stupid sounds.

He's shaking a little behind me, but I don't ask him if he's laughing. I don't have to. I can feel his breath on my cheek. Smells minty. I've had only a root to use as a toothbrush for weeks up until I got into the bath. A real one was the first thing I asked for. I'm shocked I've got teeth at all, let alone sort of straight, kind of white ones. Must be those good flossing techniques November instilled in me.

When he keeps shaking, I jam my elbow into his abdomen and try to pull my hair out of his hands, even though his touch feels heavenly. He jerks me back against him by the hair, sending pain shooting through my scalp, and he keeps me there. His chuckling stops. His minty breath mixes with mine. We're both breathing harder than we ought to be for two filthy people in a bath. Well, one filthy person.

"You can talk, Echo. Hope you never stop talkin' to me."

I slam my elbow back into him again and this time, he releases a light grunt. Pain steps through the doorway, only she isn't here for me this time. She's here for him. *You can't have him.* I close my eyes.

I'm breathing harder and I jolt when his lips brush the top of my cheek. "I'm sorry, Echo. Shuddna done that." He squeezes my hip, pulling me against his stiff cock in a way that makes my belly muscles contract. He's hard for me…but he doesn't want to be. "Forgive me?"

I shake my head vigorously, splashing hot water over him. He might have had a chance at forgiveness in the small window of time between depositing me in the tub and responding to the earlier knock on the door — the pounding — but I was too freaked out sitting by myself, wondering if he'd come back, to process whether or not I'd forgiven him for Paradise Hole and the shit that went down there.

But now that we're no longer in Paradise Hole, I don't like the imbalance between us. And for him to shove it in my face like that? It makes my tears dry up and my jaw clench. I don't like his orders. I don't like that he has…people here, a wife, allies — *friends* — and I don't. I don't like that he's clean now and I'm not. Makes me feel…less. Even less than I know I am already. *I'm just an Omega.*

"Alright, Echo. Gonna make me work for it." He starts washing my hair again, fingers firm and careful and dangerously addictive as they press into my scalp and tug carefully at the biggest knots. "I can work for it."

He holds the front of my neck, under my chin and jaw, while he works his fingers through my hair with his other hand. He massages my scalp for a while. A long while. A silent while. But it's…not unpleasant. Fear starts to fade, resurfacing only when he gets out of the bath, drains it and then leaves while it refills. Fear taunts me while I shiver waiting for him to come back.

"Comb," he says as he shuts the bathroom door quietly. He holds up a flat, wide-toothed torture device in front of me, even though I didn't ask.

Moving back into position behind me, he starts to try to pull it through my hair from root to tip, the fucking psychopath. I elbow him hard enough for him to yelp. It makes him sound like a little kid and a burst of laughter shoots out of me — a sound I've heard only once before, when I saw him in those awful stolen pants out in Paradise Hole.

I cover my mouth with my bad hand, but he pushes it aside, back to the edge of the tub. I'm deeply embarrassed by my laugh — both that I let it out, and by the sound itself. It's so ugly. Out of use, out of practice. I swallow it down, but Adam spares me by chuckling himself instead of laying into me about it.

He takes the wide-toothed bone comb to my hair again in the same bad way he tried before and I scowl. "It's tip to root!" I turn and try to take it from him, but he's smiling and my insides turn to rubber. It's not fair. It's really not fair. I miss his beard. Underneath it, I could pretend he really was a hideous monster.

"Tip to root? What, too much of a pussy to handle root to tip?" His voice twists salaciously and I scowl again.

"You're gonna rip all my hair out." I reach for the comb, but it brings my chest closer to his…close enough for my nipples to brush his sternum.

He doesn't react except for a slight tensing of his jaw. His smile stays intact. He looks so…different. "Lemme do this for you."

"Why?"

"Been such a good Omega. Wanna take care a' you." He separates my hair into sections, four big clumps. And then he sets to work. "My job." Little by little, he works the wide teeth of the comb through the matts that make up my red curls. At the same time, he works his calm through my anger, gently teasing it out, too. "A job I been suckin' at."

"Wh…what?"

His hand stills on the back of my neck where he'd been kneading it firmly, gently, coaxing me into leaning my weight against his hand, letting him hold me. "I don't wanna fall into rut because I haven't won the right to breed you. Did, but then I lost it. Twice. First time, when I couldn't bond you. Second, when I couldn't protect you from other Alphas…"

"The dead ones?"

"Dead or alive, I still woulda lost you to them if you hadn't…"

"No. No." I shake my head fiercely and close my eyes, hating what he's saying and hating that I can't just…*agree* with him.

"Echo…"

"No, it was *my* fault."

"*Echo*." He spins me on his lap so that I'm facing to the side, my hip pressed to his cock. The comb is somewhere stuck in my hair, so he has both hands free. One gently cradles my injured arm while the other one tips my chin up, forcing me to look at him. "Listen to me. None of that shit was your fault."

I touch his chest, place my wounded hand over the scar on his heart, focusing on it so that I don't have to meet his eyes. "I couldn't use my Omega instinct…"

"'Cuz I hurt you. And you did save me."

"I wanted to…but the other Omega. She saved us."

His brow crinkles. He pulls me closer, and even though his dick is hard, sex and instincts and what we want from each other, the only thing we want from each other — *at least, the only thing I want from him* — are pushed aside for the moment. "How?"

"You didn't…you didn't hear her?" I flick my gaze up to his. He looks murderous.

"Nuh."

"Oh."

"What she do, Echo?"

"She summoned me."

His front teeth slam together. His fangs elongate. I tense, panicked, and try to jerk away but he holds me still. "Not possible."

I nod. "She did. She told me to bury them in the earth and I did."

"Fuck me."

"She told me to bury you, too."

"Fuck her."

I sniffle. "But I didn't." I called him *mine*. I claimed this Berserker in front of another Omega, binding him to me in a way that *matters. Maybe, that was it. The moment that changed everything…* And yet, that claiming is the only significant bond between us because I'll never be his wife. He already has one of those. Where is she?

"Why?" He looks so concerned, I want to smooth the wrinkles out of his forehead with my tongue — my hand, just my broken fucking fingers. But I don't. I might have bound him to me, but he can't even do the same. He has a wife. Besides, he's a Berserker. I don't even want him to. Yeah…the taste in my mouth isn't jealousy. It's just toothpaste.

Right.

I try to pull my hand away from his chest, but he holds it there and inhales so deep, I rise on his chest. "Why, Echo?"

Frowning and suddenly angry, I snap, "Are you going to force me to tell you again?"

"No. But I wanna know."

"Maybe because I figured at least one person in this gross city wouldn't want to see you dead."

"That person you?"

"*No.*" I clear my throat and ignore the butterflies in my stomach. No. I dive in there with them and rip off all their wings. "Your wife might, though."

"My wife." He smiles again, slowly this time and it's a haughty, cocky thing.

"Did you forget about your wife?"

"Course not. Couldn't forget about her if I tried to cut her outta my thoughts with a knife." His gaze is moving over my face lovingly, longingly, a tangible caress. It's like he's never seen anything more beautiful than me and I know that's wrong. It's wronger than wrong because we're talking about his wife. Or are we? I…I don't understand.

I blanche, flush, get hot and clammy all at once. And the way he's smiling at me…I hate it. Makes me want to cry. Makes me want to jam my thumbs into his eye sockets. "She wouldn't have liked seeing you get eaten."

His face does something horrible then. Tragic. Wretched. Even my good friend Fear stands up from the tub and runs out of the door, naked and screaming. His expression gets all *mushy*. His eyes soften and light up, they even *crinkle* at the corners. It's awful. His smile gentles and he loses all of his cocky demeanor until he's just…an attractive stranger covered in stitching and scars. A stranger who used to be a Beta, too. Once. *Only, he isn't really a stranger anymore.*

"Guess not," he exhales *dreamily*.

"What's that supposed to mean?" He reaches for my hair again instead of answering and I block his touch. "She wouldn't like you combing my hair, either."

"Why not?"

"Because!" Because it's too intimate. "Because if you were my husband, I wouldn't want you touching another woman. An Omega, especially." My thoughts flash to the Omega in the woods and I lose control of my tongue. "Like the one in the woods. She was more powerful than me."

The expression on his face flickers. "She was. Her manipulation of the animals was…impressive."

I burn with embarrassment. *Meet me and the man in the cave.* My thoughts flash to a place that's cold and damp but strangely beautiful. I've been there before many times, but only in my dreams. "She was stronger than me."

He nods. "Stronger scent than yours, too."

I slap him. It comes out of nowhere. I hit him in the jaw-neck, like that's normal.

He looks at me, shocked, and then he laughs so hard it scares me.

"You…your wife wouldn't like you sniffing after another Omega, either! I mean, any Omega," I shout, as if that's a reasonable kind of explanation. Meanwhile, my cheeks flare in a blush I can feel all the way down to my toes.

"Nah," he says, wiping his eyes with the back of his wet hand. "Guess not."

He repositions me on his lap, lifting my right leg and spreading it around his hips so that I'm straddling him. His cock swipes across my opening and tantalizes my clit, but he doesn't…come in. *Because he has a wife*. But he still holds me in a way he shouldn't, kneading my bunched lower back muscles, abusing his power, or maybe just…using it.

I don't imagine his Alpha or Beta wife or whatever she is has much say over where he sticks his cock. He's a Berserker. One of the world's only Berserkers. She probably expects it, or doesn't care. I shouldn't either. I shouldn't…but the thought that his wife is another Omega makes me want to tear his heart out of his chest, shove it down her throat and strangle her with it.

"You shouldn't…"

"That Omega in the woods doesn't hold a candle to…my wife." He grins, then tucks a lock of hair behind my ear. He rubs his thumb over my bottom lip and bites his own. I wonder if he realizes he's even doing it. It makes it hard to concentrate on anything but not falling into heat. Like Heat is a thing standing outside the door, banging both fists on it, demanding entry. All I can do is hope that the cross beam holds.

"My wife is strong. The strongest woman I know. Her scent is thick enough to swim in. She's more beautiful than the goddamn sun. She's smart and brave and a fuckin' ass hole in the best possible way. The Omega in the woods is a fuckin' shadow compared to her because my wife…my wife is fuckin' *everything* to me." He starts to pull me in close, but I shove myself back, holding him to arm's length.

"That's…that's why I shouldn't be sittin' — I mean, *sitting* — here. Like this. Your wife…she's…" My voice is choppy. I'm scared. There's something about his words, the way he's looking at me, talking to me, even about his wife, that makes me think…no… I search helplessly for Fear in the corners of the room, but she's not there. I don't understand this or him or anything.

"Gonna deserve you, Omega," he sighs, like he can't feel my aggression and jealousy and rage at all. Or like he doesn't care. I bet that's it. He's probably used to ignoring his wife's, too. Yeah, that's it. He's talking about her like he loves her. So…so why is he saying this shit to me?

"Wh-what?"

"I'm *going* to deserve you." He punctuates each word, enunciating carefully, before he shocks the hell out of me, leans in and presses a kiss to the tip of my nose. "One day, gonna deserve you. But for today, gonna start with this."

He pulls the comb out of a matted chunk of my hair and I yelp. He grins and I glare between his stupid face and the stupid comb, fighting back a tenuous lip twitch of my own.

He smirks and pushes me back around so that we're back to front again and, as he starts in on my hair, sending pain shooting through my scalp, I shake off thoughts of his wife, for now, and offer him something unexpected.

"I didn't expect you to defend me against the dead Alphas," I whisper.

"Don't say that shit to me. You think I can't?"

"I…" I flounder, confused. I'd meant the words as a kindness. "They were monsters — *zombies*. They smelled dead. You…you killed them and kept killing them and they kept coming back. You killed each of them a hundred times…"

"Think I can't protect you because a' these?" He jerks on my chin and leans back so that I can see his largest set of stitches. The wound starts just below the X over his heart before circling down over his abdomen in four short, but deep wounds that are all gruesomely stitched up. *Bite marks. These are bite marks.*

"No. I said, they weren't…"

"Doesn't matter what they were or weren't. Alphas form packs to share one Omega between them. I'm a Berserker, not a fuckin' Alpha, and I don't share. If I lost you to a damn zombie horde, or another fuckin' Omega or a pack a' trolls or Alphas or whatever the fuck, I…" He chokes. Shakes his head roughly, the tips of his hair darkened from the water, dark brown and wet and sticking to his skin. He releases my wrist and grabs the back of my neck and crushes his mouth to mine.

His lips are bruising. It doesn't feel good. I don't care at all. My body responds in kind. I roll my stomach and I lean into him, but he holds me back with his other hand between my upper ribs. I gasp when he breaks contact. "Have to kill me first and make sure I stay dead, because if those fuckin' zombies taught me anything, it's possible to come back. And *you* are the first one I'd come for. The only one."

He's breathing hard. I'm breathing hard. Our breath is minty as it mingles and my shampoo smells like a beach paradise. It drips down my forehead, but he rubs it away before it gets into my eyes. I think of his wife. I think how she means *everything* to him and I recoil from the idea that maybe he doesn't…actually…have a wi…

"What were they?" I whisper.

"Don't know. Sent my Six back for the bodies."

"Your Six?"

"Six Alphas loyal to me. Ones who really run the place."

"Like your pack?"

"Don't fuckin' say the word, Omega." Omega again.

He kisses me deeply one more time, but this time, I'm the one to break it. I don't like being his Omega. I…want to be more than that. *I want to be more than that to* him, *too.*

"We need to find out what they are and where they came from."

His eyes sparkle. I wonder why. I wonder if it's because I said that horrible, ill-fated word that I know he likes. "*We* do."

"And Trash City."

"That, too."

"And the Omega in the woods. I think she's the witch Gang Mountain is looking for."

He rumbles deeply. "Yes, Echo. But not tonight. We're busy tonight." Just when I think he's going to say something salacious, he whips the comb out of nowhere. "Gotta take care a' my Omega."

"You don't..." I start, but he doesn't let me finish before he whacks me on the top of the head with the hard piece of bone. I scratch his neck in retaliation and he laughs. I laugh too, and for the first time in months, Pain and Fear remain utterly silent all night long.

ADAM
DRAGNOVIC MANOR

"YOU KNOW THAT'S NOT RIGHT. THAT'S NOT THE WAY it's supposed to work. It's like *you* didn't bond *her*. *She* bonded *you*."

I'm gonna kill 'er. "Didn't ask your fuckin' opinion, Alpha," I shout at Whiskey while she and Sierra lean against the library wall, amused gazes flicking between me, behind Ward's desk, and Ward, who sits where any other patient would ordinarily be seated.

Peate's present, too. So are Balcazar, Barbero and Vi. The whole damn Six even though this is — was *supposed to be* — a private fuckin' meeting between me and Ward. Wouldn't have let the other fuckers in to overhear me discussin' all the ways I'm broken and inadequate were they anybody else, but somehow, along the way, these Six I came to trust.

Most of 'em I met as Betas. Back when I was in the dungeons bein' tortured as a kid, Balcazar was brought in and tortured in the cell next to me. Whiskey was already shoved into the cell across from us. Some fuckin' idiot claimin' himself a prophet thought she and Balcazar would ascend as Omegas and tried to put both of 'em through the barbaric Omega trainin' the previous Berserker had put in place — a practice meant to *ensure* that any Omegas would be the ultimate tools of submission. They rebelled and, when the first Alpha laid a hand on Whiskey, she killed him. She'd been thirteen.

We met Barbero not too long after. He was a Beta servant and would slip Balcazar and Whiskey extra food. Eventually, when he saw the state I was in, he did the same for me.

I ascended as Berserker three years later, before the other two females got their Alpha forms. I freed 'em. They've been in my debt ever since and, when Barbero ascended a few years later, he joined my Six, too.

Whiskey fell in love with Sierra back at an Alpha Ball, of all fuckin' places, and brought her in. Peate earned my trust over the course of two decades apprenticin' as healer to the triage doc, Blake. He retired and Peate took over as my main war doc, the only medic of my three lead docs — Ward, Loveless and Peate — who comes out with me into Paradise Hole. Paradise Hole's too dangerous a place for women and Betas and Ward and Loveless are both. Can't afford to lose 'em.

Vi was the last one to come on. Found him only six years ago tryna drag his ass out of Paradise Hole to our gates. He was young — only eleven — and because he was young, he'd been used bad by a rogue Alpha gang despite bein' an Alpha himself. I helped him heal and, a few years later, took him huntin'. We razed the gang from the earth together, just the two of us, and he's worshipped the ground I walk on ever since.

I trust these fuckers, which is why they're here. And it's because I respect all of 'em that I'm embarrassed as shit.

I slam my fist on the table, though there ain't a lotta meanin' behind it. "Omegas can't bond and I did everythin' I shoulda."

"You sunk your fangs into her neck without her consent and you think you did everything you should have?" Ward blinks and the beads on the ends of her braids rattle in a way that I hate. I wanna rip 'em all off.

Whiskey and Sierra got their heads together again, whisperin' and drivin' me up the damn walls. "You got somethin' to say, *ladies*?"

"We were just talking about getting out of here and doing a little biting of our own," Sierra teases.

I frown. She still speaks with a Golden City accent which drives me fuckin' nuts. "How long you been livin' here and still talkin' with that awful twang?"

Whiskey flutters her lips like a horse. "Don't bite my mate's head off just because you can't control yours. Heard you've been fightin' these past three days." It's been three days. And in the few hours she hasn't been sleepin', she's been askin' me questions I can't say yes to.

Because the psychopath wants to go back into Paradise Hole.

She's after some guy she saw in a dream who was in a cave. She's not goin' and she's definitely not goin' for a guy. If anything, I'll go, find her cave guy and bring him to her in pieces.

"Shut the fuck up. Ward, gimme somethin' I can work with."

She holds her tablet up to her face and I can see little numbers and notes in tables and spreadsheets reflected in miniature off of her dark eyes. "Well, I'm still trying to synthesize the unusual properties of the poison in your blood..."

"Venom."

"...so, at the current moment, I can't explain the *venom* of these alleged zombies who attacked you and your Omega..."

"Alleged?"

"...but I can tell you why biting her didn't bond her to you."

"Why?"

She balks, squawking like a damn chicken. "Is he serious?" She glances around. The only person present who isn't one of the Six. I'm not sure how much I trust her, but I trust her expertise on this.

She looks at me when no one answers. "Are *you* serious?" She makes a chuffing sound and twitches in her chair. The tablet in her hand tumbles onto the slate carpet and she makes no effort to reach for it. "I suppose you'd just stomp into an Omega's nest uninvited, too, then? You're a barbarian! Everyone knows that in order to successfully bond an Omega you have to be invited."

Her eyes bulge out of her head as her face flames with heat. Surprised it doesn't shoot out of her damn ears. Meanwhile, I'm sure my face is burning with equal embarrassment. "Fuck."

"Just ran up to her and bit 'er?" Vi's scowl hurts even more than Ward's outrage. In a grey thermal, his arms are crossed tight over his chest. His eyes blaze and guilt rams its way through me as I imagine the kinda shit he experienced when he was on the outside. Did Alphas bite him too, without his permission? Am I no better than the gang we razed to the ground?

I fumble, "She tried to kill herself. Stabbed herself in the thigh. I thought if I didn't use my venom, she'd die and I didn't want…" My voice breaks. I clench my teeth together and dig one of my shortened nails into the wood a' Ward's desk, gouging a chunk out of it that's much smaller now than it woulda been if I hadn't clipped my claws. "Didn't want that."

The room falls completely silent. It's silent for a while… until the footsteps. They come stompin' down the corridor and, judgin' by their gait, I know who it is already. For as determined as my Omega is, she's distracted easily by the things in these halls. Paintings, mostly. She doesn't know they're mine. I mean, that I painted 'em. I like hearin' her praise 'em too much to tell her the truth of it.

Step, step, step, pause. Five more quick steps. Another shuddering stop. Another step. Three more. And then, "Adam! Adam. Adam, I want to go to…Paradise Hole…" Her words lose steam when she bursts into the room and glances around at the Six Alphas occupying it, and one fierce Beta, too.

"Jesus, what are you wearin', Echo?"

I rise to standing and glare down at my Omega, struttin' around my estate wearin' nothin' but a plush white blanket.

She hugs it against her chest with her one good arm. And Jesus, dressed just like that she's never looked more fuckin' beautiful.

Had I ever thought her anything else? I'm momentarily shook. Color has returned to her cheeks, which are flushed a more robust brown and glowin', makin' every one of those damn freckles stand out in relief.

Her hair is washed and actually forms curls now that she's run some conditioner through it. They drift halfway down her back in a massive waterfall that I get to comb out every time we shower. Even though the swellin' in her bad arm has gone down and the doc says it's okay to use it a little more, I don't tell *her* that. Whoever thought I'd like brushin' a chick's hair? Only she isn't a chick, is she? She's my wife. And she's an Omega nearin' heat standin' in a room with six Alphas I'd rather not have to disembowel.

"Christ. Everybody out!" I round the desk and approach Echo, but she backpedals until her body is wedged in the doorway, blockin' anybody from leavin' through it unless they touch her.

Even if they wanna take the piss all day with me, these Six know better than to breathe on my girl. This leaves 'em standin' there awkwardly in the middle of the study, books stacked sky high starin' down at 'em like they're curious what the fuck is gonna happen next. Vi, who's closest to the door, moves one inch forward and I snap my fangs at him.

He looks back at me and his skin is dark so I can't see the red in his face like I can in Echo's, but I can feel his heat. "Errr…"

"Back the fuck up," I bark at the same time Echo stammers and shakes her injured arm around at *my* Six, at *my* Beta healer, like they're hers. They are. She just doesn't know it yet. "You all owe me some answers."

"Owe you?" Whiskey stands up from where she'd been leanin'. She takes in a deep breath and a low growl picks up in my chest.

"Whiskey, you think 'cuz you gotta mate I won't tear your throat out?"

Sierra frowns at me. "Get a grip, Berserker. No one wants a piece of your Omega, even if she does smell so good."

I growl at the same time Whiskey does, roundin' on her woman. She plants both hands on the bookcase on either side of Sierra's head and drops her lips to the mouth of the slightly shorter female. "You're *my* woman. Don't go sniffin' out an Omega, if you know what's good for you."

"Tell me you don't smell her," Sierra says flatly.

Whiskey hesitates and that hesitation is enough to make me feral, even as she whispers, "I smell *you*."

The two women make out against the wall. My Omega is entirely unfazed by it and keeps her glare pinned to me. Her blush rolls up and then back down. "You promised me we'd look together." Her voice shakes. The scent of her heat — and her fear — rolls off of her and infects the room.

Makes me feel like shit and also like hurtin' somethin' for her.

"Echo." I move directly in front of her. Her scent. Fuck. Her scent…

I shake my head to clear it and take three steps back, balling my fists against my sides and then crossing them over my chest and shoving them under my armpits. I touch her and we're gonna rut right here and she hasn't invited me to bond her and, even if she had, she hasn't had time to nest yet.

"Been three days and you been sleepin' most of 'em. Ward's still tryna synthesize my blood and figure out what was in the dead Alphas' venom to make it so I couldn't heal. We're still waitin' for your heat. Your arm's still a fuckin' wreck..."

"I can use it more now," she says weakly, showing her arm to me as if that somehow erases the glaze that covered her eyes the moment I mentioned her heat.

I want to touch the blue brace that wraps up her wrist almost to the elbow, but the scars above it...they give me pause. The stitches were taken out of her shoulder and neck, but my gaze can't help but snag on the pink scars that disrupt her brown, freckled skin. *Fuckin' failure.* I don't deserve to breed her, even if it's just to service her in her heat. I take another step back and flex my hand, look away from her scars and her bandages.

"Know it. But you can't go back into Paradise Hole like this to look for some guy you met in a dream." Can't go period. But that doesn't need sayin'.

She frowns, blinks, then chews on the inside of her cheek. Her gaze flicks past me to Peate. "Did you find the bodies?"

"Barbero led the team."

We all turn to look at Barbero. He glares at Peate — he's a quiet one and tends to avoid the spotlight at all costs. Right now, can see a fierce heat flamin' his cheeks.

"Barbero," I grunt. "My Omega asked you a question — the *Dark City Omega* asked you a question."

He clicks his tongue against the backs of his teeth — tooth at the front is chipped and he rubs his tongue over it often, a nervous tick — and nods. "Found the bodies. Dug up two so far, but they're down there deep. The team's still lookin' for more, but it's slow goin' since it started rainin' out there yesterday."

Ward adds, "The two that were recovered were brought to my lab this morning. Loveless is still preparing the first for autopsy, but we did go ahead and remove the incisors from both corpses and started extracting venom for analysis."

"Incisors?" Sierra says. "Like…Berserker incisors? In Alpha bodies?"

"Precisely. And that isn't the only unusual thing about them. The *venom*, as Dragnovic called it, is *similar* to a Berserker's but…not entirely the same. It has fascinating properties. Much less viscous than that of a Berserker's, once it hits the bloodstream, it doesn't coagulate or even allow the existing blood to do so. The venom is poisonous, for certain, and over time would weaken its prey to the point that dehydration would kill it, if another predator didn't get to it first — think more like a black mamba bite to the foot, rather than to the face. That makes this…this *venom* less poisonous than a Berserker's — and be lucky for that. If it had been one of these…these…" Her hands flail wildly as her lips stutter and stumble over the word, refusing to say it, but left with no other choice. "…*undead* Berserkers who bit you, you'd be dead."

"So, you believe us now?"

"About what?"

"The zombie army."

"I..." Ward's expression shifts. She looks away from me quickly and tucks her hair behind her ears. "I most certainly don't believe in zombies, but until I can come up with a more scientifically accurate descriptor, undead will have to do."

I huff out a laugh, though the shit isn't funny. Especially not with Echo's eyes shimmerin' even glossier than they were. Her lower lip trembles.

"Don't," I bark louder than I needed to.

She flinches and looks at me and sniffles and says, "I'm not doing anything."

"Y'are."

She wipes her nose with her hand and her blanket wrap sinks. More of her chest becomes visible and I lurch forward, but she manages to grab it. I start to sweat. She's got freckles on her chest, too. I haven't had a chance to count 'em yet. Lick 'em. Taste 'em.

She says, "What about Trash City?"

"Truck's on its way now," I tell her.

"Shouldn't it be there by now?"

"Trouble on the road."

She shudders, her pupils contracting. She looks like she's gonna start shiverin' any second. "What kind of trouble?"

"Y'don't need to worry, Echo. Promise."

"More dead army?"

"No," I bellow, takin' a step toward her. I just can't help it. I reach out for her and put my hand on her shoulder, feelin' the small, rounded bone and squeezin' it. Fuck. Heat runs up my spine before racin' down again. My tee shirt feels too tight and my jeans, way too fuckin' tight. *Just let go of her.* I slide my palm up the smooth curve of her neck and wrap my hand around its delicate nape. Fuck.

"No dead army," I growl low. "Just gangs."

"*Just* gangs. Nothing *just* about gangs."

"Know it. That's why you're not goin' into Paradise Hole…"

"That's not fair. You can't keep me…" She gasps at the same time I grab her. She's let go of her blanket again and her tits come into full view — or woulda, had I not crushed her against me. Good place for her, because I'd have to gouge out the eyes of any of my Six who saw her chest bare except for *maybe* Barbero, who's the *only* Alpha in the room without an affinity for women. Maybe. Probably, though.

Biggest problem now is that with the way she's wedged against me, I can't see those magical tits, either. And she hasn't shut up. "I saw something important. I know it. I feel like something's coming. Something huge. And I know the man in the cave and the Omega in the woods can help. Please, Adam…" Fuck no. She can't do this. So fuckin' unfair.

I wrench her forward by the neck and bend down, bringing her forehead to meet mine. "Fuck you, Echo." I rub my cheek against hers and make her a horrible vow. "Take you to do whatever the fuck you want. Just gotta do one thing for me first, baby." She smells so good. Like a magical garden separated from me by only this one blanket, like a veil to the next world that I could so easily snatch away and cast aside.

Her eyelashes flutter. "What?" Her chin quivers. She's holdin' her breath.

Her want makes me ravenous. "Put on a damn shirt," I grumble, voice thicker than it ought to be.

"I don't have one. I-I still don't have any clothes that fit me."

I huff, like I didn't do that shit on purpose. Her words give me an idea and I peel away from her, yank my tee shirt off over my head and quickly whip it down over hers. I thread her arms through the sleeves and carefully bunch the blanket around her hips. Oh no. This look is even worse. My shirt gobbles her up, the light grey makin' her skin pop like she's standin' underneath a spotlight. And it's *mine* and so is she. I inhale fully, lungs a' burstin'…and I exhale just as deeply.

"Really?" She blinks brightly, eyes so fuckin' innocent it scares me. This can't be my Omega who stabbed herself in the thigh.

"Really what?"

"You'll take me back into Paradise Hole to find the man in the cave?"

"Maybe."

She pouts, mouth twisting to the side. "As soon as my arm is better."

"You tryna negotiate?"

She takes a step forward, the damn witch, and her hand — locked in the brace — reaches out and touches my chest. With the tips of her healing fingers, she traces the X the monsters of my youth carved over my heart. "No, I'm not. I'm not asking either. I'm going into Paradise Hole to find the man in the cave and I want you to come with me to investigate *together*, like we said we would." And then she looks at me — really looks at me — and even though she's blushin' hard, her words release like artillery and every bullet finds its mark. "You're *my* Berserker. It's your job."

"You manipulating me?" I snarl. Would be a problem if she thinks she can, because it's gonna work. It's workin' now.

"Maybe?"

Yeah, it's definitely workin'. I take a step forward and scoop her off her feet, wrapping one arm around her ass and carrying her high against me. She yelps, kicks her feet in the blanket like she's tryna dislodge me, but she's not tryin' so hard because she also laughs. Her laughter is awkward and loud and magnetic. We're back to bein' alright, it seems, and I love it. Fuck, I also love it when we fight.

I turn my back on the Alphas in the office, forgettin' them entirely until Whiskey calls out, "Dragnovic, are you forgetting the Ball?"

"Ball?" my Omega says.

"No."

"No, you haven't forgotten it, or no, you've forgotten it?" Whiskey asks.

Balcazar snorts, "Give the man a fuckin' minute. He hasn't even bred his Omega yet and she fuckin' reeks."

"Balcazar," I bark, both as a thanks and a reprimand.

I start towards the door again, and Sierra shouts after me, "Invitations have already been sent. The Omega Ball's gonna happen whether you want it to or not."

"Ball?" Echo whispers again directly into my ear. A chill shudders through my bones as her breath brushes my earlobe and sweeps down my neck.

I let go of her with one arm and use my free hand to comb her curls behind one ear. I debate lyin' to her, then decide I never want to lie to her about anythin' ever again. "To announce my Omega. Ball's for you."

"But I don't want a Ball."

"You think I do?" I do. "Hundreds a' fuckin' people on my property. Wanderin' my ballroom, oglin' my girl?"

She fidgets in my grip, her toes wigglin' somewhere in the blankets, ticklin' my calves. "Your wife won't like that."

A bolt of laughter bursts out of me and I can't stop. Gets worse when, from the room behind me, Barbero of all people whispers to Vi, "Did she just say his wife?"

"Think so…" Vi answers.

"No, get the sense my wife won't — doesn't like Balls," I tell her, shakin' my head.

"Then wouldn't it be respectful…to her not to have it?" Her fingers are interlaced in the tips of my hair, gently pullin'. Oh yeah. She's a master manipulator and I hope to god she knows it, because if this isn't an act and it's just *her,* then I'm more doomed than I ever thought possible. The little Omega's got me turned to putty and wrapped around her fingers, like a kid makin' traps with string too complicated to untangle because they all lead back to my heart.

"Yeah, probably. But can't do nothin' about it. Invites were sent the moment we set foot in Dark City. Every Berserker's gotta announce his…"

"Or her!" Whiskey shouts down the hall.

"…Omega. It's tradition. A stupid one, but even if I did kill the Berserker who sat in my seat before me, I wasn't strong enough to tear the entire system down. So if I gotta go to this damn Ball, then you can be damn sure my Omega's gotta come, too."

"And your wife?"

I grunt, well aware that, by now, Echo's gotta know that the jig is up. She knows that my only wife is the woman in my arms. But whatever. She wants to keep playin'? I'll play. "Yeah, she's gotta come too. Team player, and all."

"She sounds…generous."

"Wouldn't go that far. Now come on, takin' you to bed."

"But Adam," she whines, pullin' herself closer to me usin' my neck. I squeeze the back a' hers and try not to breathe. She's too near to heat.

"Echo, not another word." Over my shoulder, I shout to the Six. "Proceed with preparations. My Omega and I will be ready for the Ball. Anything urgent you need either of us to attend to between now and then, kill it."

Grumbling and laughter from my Six is what I leave behind when I carry my Omega outta the hall.

"Where are we going?" Echo says as I round the next curve and carry her through a servant's passage that's never used, rather than through the main hall, where my staff roam freely.

Lowerin' her in my arms enough to be able to whisper into her hair, I say, "You stopped takin' the suppressants. You're nearin' heat."

I climb a flight of stairs down and then another, then push through the door that leads me out of the manor and onto the enclosed winter porch, then finally out into the garden. Echo's been spendin' time in the garden house, even though it's Beta quarters — *servants'* quarters.

I haven't asked her why she's comin' out here and I don't mind. The manor feels like it's still got stains of the Berserker before on it, and I don't like the idea of those stains rubbin' off on her. Also don't like her near so many Alphas, comin' and goin'. And I *hope* she's been comin' out here to nest… though, knowin' my Omega, that might be too much to hope for.

"About the Ball. I just…I'm not ready to be out with a bunch of Alphas. I don't want that."

"Gonna be with you the entire time." My fuckin' house shoe sinks into mud. Goddammit. I glance around the misty world wrapped around us, wishin' it were possible to shield my Omega from it. I never took care about my garden before and I had to pluck the flower Omega from the Omega garden. Fuck.

"What is it?"

"Nothin'."

"You're thinkin' something." She taps my temple with one short nail. "Thinking," she corrects, but I heard it and grin.

"Don't tell me your Berserker's rubbin' off on you, Echo." I laugh as I lower my gaze to the retina scan, then shove the front door to my garden house open. I step into the quiet and lock the door behind me.

"My Berserker isn't…but maybe Adam is…"

A needle of need cracks through my armor and pierces me with the pointy end. I bleed, but that's fine, she could bleed me dry if she wanted.

Wait. Wait, she's injured. Wait, I'm *injured.*

"Am I rubbing off on you at all?" She asks, and the tentative vulnerability in her tone is too much to take.

Fuck waiting.

I move forward roughly, slamming her into the wall, though I've still got presence a' mind enough to cradle the back of her head. My mouth charges towards hers and I bite her lip, not hard enough to draw blood, but I want to. God, I want to.

I rear back and force her chin up, then kiss my way down her chest. I'm panting against her collarbone, feelin' her body shiver in my grip. She's needy, my little Omega, and and even though her lips are slack with surprise, her hands are pullin' harder and harder on my hair. She's tryna move me back up her body, but I can't have it.

She moans, "Adam." Alright, maybe, I can.

I taste her lips, pluckin' at 'em more gently this time around. Trying desperately to be gentle…or somethin'. "Tell me if I'm hurtin' you, baby. Please."

"Oh god, Adam. I need…need…"

"Take me to your nest." Fuck. That's not what I meant to say. I wanted her to invite me herself.

"I…what?"

"Your nest. Know you're buildin' it here." When she doesn't say anything, I take the reins of control in a death grip and pull the fuck back. "Fuck." I come up gasping for air and her body drops down the wall. She clings to my shoulders with both hands, but I gently remove her bandaged arm.

"No, Adam. Please. I want…don't be an asshole."

"You don't want me in your nest, that's fine, I know I don't deserve it. I know I might not ever, but I thought…for the first time…you might want to do it where you feel safest and most comfortable. If that's not what you want, I won't ask to see your nest again." I rub my hand up and down my face, struggling to meet her gaze and the look of horror in her eyes and the blush staining every inch of her cheeks.

"You want me to send Ward up here? There's more heat suppressants if you need 'em."

"No!" She grabs my arm the minute I so much as flinch like I'll turn towards the door. Her eyes are still huge and I can hear her heartbeat through her chest like she's havin' a damn panic attack. "I told you already I don't like the heat suppressants. I want…I want…" She gulps in air like she's fuckin' drownin'.

"Want what?"

"You know."

I frown. "What is it?"

And then the damn woman runs off.

And the fool that I am, I chase her.

"Omega?"

"Don't call me that."

"Echo."

"No. Omega."

"What?"

"That's the problem, don't you see? With the Ball, with everything. I don't know how to be that…that thing. I know Paradise Hole. I could be the dirty, filthy Omega in the forest because that was me. I can't…can't belong to a Berserker because I don't know how to do the…the things! I can't even control my powers. *You* control them."

"Omega," I say a little louder. Been repeatin' it the whole time she's talkin' and now I realize where she's led me — to the guest bedroom. At the sight of the nondescript wooden door, my restraint meets its short end, like a truck smashin' directly into the side of a cliff.

I can't bear it another fuckin' second. My fingers stab back into my hair again and again. The distance between us ends tonight. I'm not goin' another moment without her body welded to mine. All the time. Short of Ward stitchin' the two of us together, I want her as close to me as fuckin' possible. Forever.

Forever?

Yeah. Forever.

"The fuck you talkin' about? You're learnin' and so far, you've saved our lives multiple times. Doin' fuckin' great, baby." Better than great. She's been exquisite. I'm the failure. *Unworthy, unworthy, unworthy.*

She stands in front of me looking at me like I've grown ten heads and all of 'em have fangs drippin' in black venom. And she keeps standin' there starin' at me until even I start to get fuckin' uncomfortable. I rub the back of my neck and try to ignore the heat crawlin' up it.

"Echo, you don't gotta do nothin' you don't wanna do. You're home now."

Her eyes get even bigger and when I drop my head and stare into them, I see that her pupils are almost fully blown and have taken almost all of the warm mahogany with them.

"Echo. For everythin' that happened in Paradise Hole, I am sorry." I glance at her neck, and then lower at her thigh, which is only partially covered by my tee shirt. The blankets she abandoned somewhere on the stairs and ain't no fuckin' way I'm gonna go back for 'em. "Everythin' but findin' you and draggin' you outta there. That I'd do again a thousand times."

"You almost died. I heard what Ward said. If it had taken any longer for your Six to find us, you probably would have…"

"A thousand times," I repeat with a slow nod. "A thousand times." I drag my finger over her jawline, flicking her chin gently.

She bites her lower lip and backs away from me until she hits her bedroom door. "Just…wait here. Don't move. Please. Okay?"

I nod and cross my arms over my bare chest. Her gaze drops down to it, moving over my pecs and then my abs, and I can't help but tighten them. Her gaze drops lower still and my hard-on dares to hope. But then she disappears behind her bedroom door, wedging herself into an opening so narrow, it's impossible for me to see any of the room behind her. I hear shufflin' though.

"The fuck is she doin'?"

She's in there for so long, I run through a laundry list of possibilities, have time to whittle it down to three, then scratch 'em and start over.

"Adam?" she calls through the door, from a distance.

"Here."

"You…you can come in now."

I don't hesitate.

I push open the door and close it quietly behind me. Her room's big. Not as big as mine, which has large French windows that lead onto an arched veranda overlookin' the garden. The walls in here are a soft jade and the floor's cream-colored carpet. The bed sits on the right wall occupyin' a ton a' space with its four posters, but right now it's been stripped. All the sheets are missin' and behind it, the armoire doors are thrown open. All the shelves are bare, every blanket and pillow that once occupied it now piled in the center of the carpeted floor.

She's taken all the pillows and formed a circle with 'em that she's covered in the blankets. There're textures of all kinds in a chaos of colors and she kneels in the middle of it wearin' just my tee shirt. Her palms rest on top of her knees and her face is tilted up at me and, with glossy eyes and red, puffy lips, she says, "I don't know what I'm doing…I made a nest. It's so dumb. Do you like it?"

I should have known it was a nest — her nest — the moment I looked at it. I should have…but I didn't. The nests I've seen before have been…different. At Omega Balls, usually, the Omega being introduced will create a prop nest of towering and magnificent proportions. I've seen nests made entirely of tufts of down, knotted together thousands of times over to create beautiful, intricate mosaics and patterns. I've seen hand-stitched silk laid to cover entire rooms. Furs from animals whose species no longer exist. Melting candles formed to stand twice as tall as I am carved with symbols representative of the Omega's gifts that the nest belongs to.

The last Omega Ball I attended was in Gold City — that one where Whiskey found, seduced and fucked Sierra. There, the Omega had created a nest of furs which she surrounded by glass she'd created herself, with her own powers. Pillars and chandeliers that took single droplets of light and broke them into infinite shards of infinite colors.

The Omega daughter of the Glass Flats Berserker invited us to a demonstration of her gifts unlike any I've ever seen.

She created a waterfall inside the opulant Glass Flats castle, the nest built of driftwood and silk floating in the pool the waterfall created. I've seen Omegas build nests worthy of gods and all of their children.

What Echo's built here? It's a mess. And her presentation? In just my tee shirt, with a bandage on her arm, lookin' up at me with tears in her eyes and hope in her bated breath? A disaster.

I slip off my shoes and step forward until the tips of my toes press against her nest's outer edge. Then I lean forward, over the barrier made of pillows, crouch down and cup her cheek. "It's the most beautiful nest I've ever seen."

Her lips twitch and when she blinks, a tear springs free of her left eye. With my thumb, I capture it and spread the glitter it creates over the rest of her high cheek, counting freckles as I go. One, two, ten, fifty…

"You gonna invite me in?" I keep my voice easy, casual. Don't want her to know I'm about to shit myself with anticipation of her answer. Because the way she's lookin' at me? She might just say yes. Can't believe it's been a month since I met her. Since I took one look at her and she tried to kill herself. Since Trash City. Since we camped together for days on end, scavenged lost shit, ate dried meat over pitiful flames. Since she pulled me outta that river and gave me a piece of herself — her acknowledgement. And I gave her a piece of myself — my adoration.

"Yes," she whispers.

"Yes what?" My hands drop to my belt and I unfasten it with a snap. Her gaze drops to it, distracted, and I arch over her again and slide a finger under her chin, tilting it up. "Yes, *Adam*," I command.

She inhales, her little fists balling in her lap. "Yes, Adam."

"You invitin' me into your nest?"

"Yes, Adam."

"Wanna hear you say it. Wanna hear the words. Wanna hear you beg."

I'd worry about scarin' her off if my cock weren't ragin' in my pants and I could think straight. She's just as likely to fight me as she is to fuck me, but this time, I get lucky. At my words, her thighs squeeze together and she licks her lips. "Come into my nest, Adam. I'm inviting you. Please, come in."

Her voice breaks and she blushes and she's never looked so fuckin' gorgeous. I rip my belt off and step one foot beyond the ring of pillows into her nest, and then the other. Then I take my belt and lower it, slide the open loop around her neck…

Her eyes bulge in panic when I pull it taut and she reaches up toward my hand, like she's gonna stop me. I hold her gaze as I do it, and no, I don't stop. Never knew I was into this kinda shit, but lookin' at her, I realize I need somethin' more from her than her acknowledgement.

Need her trust.

Even if it's just a piece of it. A moment.

A deep growl starts up in my chest, but I will it softer until it comes out as a rumbling purr. I soothe my Omega. And then I offer her a wounded truth.

"I purred myself to sleep when they kept me in the cells," I say out loud, though I don't mean to. She blinks and her lips part. "I could purr, even as a Beta. Shouldn'ta been able to, but I could. Never done it for anyone else but you."

She stares up at me, the black band of my belt wrapped around her slender throat. Her chin that was wobblin' a second ago firms up and her jawline hardens. She drops her hands back to her knees.

I rip my button free and undo the zipper with my free hand. I pull my cock out and jerk my chin toward it. "Love this nest, Omega. Love seein' you in it. Love seein' you in it in our house."

"Our house?"

"Yeah, baby."

She starts to shake her head and rage makes my purr trip back into a growl for a second before I catch it. Acknowledgement and trust don't yield acceptance and commitment. But I'll get there. I'll get *her* there. Just need a minute. Just need to rut.

"Gonna show you how much I love seein' you here on your knees. But first, need somethin' from you."

"What?" She chews on her lips and I grin, fuckin' wild with anticipation and hunger and heat, and my purrin' gets louder. I can scent her arousal strongly. *Flowers. Fuckin' flowers.* "Nah, baby. That was good, but want more. Open your mouth for me, Echo. Gonna take my cock."

"And your cum?"

Fuck. The word…hearin' her say it. I fist my erection and tighten my hand at its base. Might blow a load all over her face… Yeah, wanna blow a load all over her face. Not yet, though. First load is goin' straight down my Omega's throat. Haven't come in her yet, and I'm dyin'.

"Keep your hands on your knees and you'll get my cum. Now open."

She opens her mouth and stares hungrily at my flushed cock. Careful with the belt in my hand, I give my Omega what she wants.

She lifts up onto her knees, still keepin' her hands on her thighs, like I asked. Feedin' my cock into my Omega's mouth one inch at a time until she chokes on it, it takes all the willpower I got to stay standin'. Her mouth is wet and hot and her tongue strokes me from base to tip. I moan and tilt my head back, then shiver. No. Gotta watch. Can't miss a second a' this.

I growl, looking down to see her looking up at me. Fuck. She holds my gaze as her head bobs up and down my length, as if seeking my approval. "Harder."

She sucks harder, her mouth clamping down on my length until there's no air left in her cheeks. Nothin' but sloppy, wet heat. "Fuck you, Echo." I throw my head back and roar as I slide back, my free hand comin' around to cup the back of her head — as if the fuckin' belt wasn't enough.

I gently pump in and out of her mouth, the feel of her lips heavenly. She scrapes my cock with her teeth and I tighten the belt as punishment. She looks up at me mischievously and I grunt out a laugh. Seems the filthy little Omega likes this.

"You're tryna trip me into rut, aren't you, Omega?" Because it's clear she's fallin' fast and hard into her heat. Her pupils are blown and her head is bobbing up and down vigorously on my dick. She can only take half my length and her fingers are twitchin' and jerkin' on her thighs, lifting up every few thrusts, like she keeps forgettin' the orders I gave.

Requests, not commands. Because she can move them if she wants.

Careful. Need to be more careful with her.

But not today. Not right now.

With one fist in her hair and the other on the belt, there's nowhere for her to go. She's at my complete and total mercy. "Gonna come, Omega. You gonna take it?" She nods and sucks harder, her cheeks suctioning.

I growl, "You want it? Lift the tee shirt. Spread your legs. Let me see that sweet Omega cunt."

She obeys instantly, moaning as she separates her knees and givin' me a view I'll never forget.

"Fuck, Echo. You're hurtin'."

No way she isn't. With wetness like that, coverin' her from bush to rosebud, she's gotta be. Her curls are soaked and I can't fuckin' wait to bury my face in 'em and clean her up completely. Fuck. I hold for a moment, tryna get my shit together and stop the rut from takin' me. I feel it come in a surge and separate it from the urge to come, makin' it possible for me to do the latter without the former.

Cum shoots out of me down her throat, my balls fuckin' expanding and throbbing. My lower back aches and my thighs go ramrod straight. I can't move. All I can do is fuckin' pray I don't trip into rut, try to focus on a point in the distance that helps me pull some of my awareness away from the pleasure I'm receivin' from her.

It's working.

It's barely working.

I relax the belt around her neck, but pull harder on her hair, forcin' her throat to work around the throbbing head of my dick. It's clear she's never done this before and that pleases the shit out of me because I'm absolutely certain that if she had experience with this, I'd have to hunt down every man she ever serviced and collect their skins for her nest.

"That's it, baby. Choke it down. Swallow…swallow again…" I grind out. "Again." My growl softens into a purr as I stare down at her and watch her body buck as she struggles to take everything I've been savin' up for her these torturously long days. "Look at me." She's got tears rimming her eyes when she obeys. "That's a good Omega. You please your Berserker so fuckin' much."

She whimpers slightly and, when I pull my erection out of her mouth, she glances at it desperately and tries to chase it. I pull harder on the belt until she looks up at me, red in the face, before freeing it. Damn, it's hard to move. She's lookin' up at me with stars in her eyes like I've given her a damn gift, and maybe I have because I realize in this moment I'd give her my life. The Fates were right. Paradise Hole is where I needed to go to find my wife.

But remember what else they said? Paradise Hole is where I'll die for her, too.

"What?" She says when I don't speak for a long, long moment. Thinkin' about the Fates has got me weak in the knees. *They're wrong.* They're never wrong. *This time, they'll have to be. Because I'm not givin' her up. Not for death or for anything.*

"Wife," I purr.

Her eyes bulge, color flushes her cheeks, and she gasps, "Adam!" She yelps in a panic, hands flying to her crotch as her whole body bowls over.

"*Wife,* turn around. On hands and knees, present for me."

She does what I command even though it clearly pains her and it pains me to watch her suffer. I don't stop her, though. *This* is the moment I did not know every year, every torture, every lonely fuckin' moment, I'd been workin' towards. This is it. My prize. My penance. The treasure in my arms. Not an Omega, but Echo. Not any Omega, but this one.

I drop to my knees behind her and rip her tee shirt up the back. She jerks against the movement, but I grab her hips to hold her in place. I position my cock at her entrance and look at the bulging, veiny shaft against her pussy, so swollen and wet. "Wife," I groan and then I slam forward into her, offering her no quarter. Our hips come together and my cock bathes in her center. "Holy fuckin' cities."

"Adam," she mewls, her hips writhing as she tries to find her own pleasure.

But I need a fuckin' minute.

Sweat breaks out over my forehead and my hands are shakin' on her skin. I hope she can't feel it. Wanna be strong for her. I flex and clench them.

"Adam…" My Omega's in pain. And I'm her Berserker. I need to move. Need to please her. It's my job. What I was built for.

I rumble deep in my throat, the sound comin' out strong and clear. I start to move in and out of her, slowly at first, but rapidly picking up speed. Hazy light, colors and sensations dull my thoughts for minutes…dozens of them at a time. *No, no. Don't fall into rut.* I wake to the realization that I'm fuckin' her hard — harder than I should be — but like the good Omega she is, she braces her forearms on the floor and takes it. *Fuck. What about her injured arm?*

I wrench out of her body on a moan, which she shares, and flip her onto her back. She blinks up at me, no irises to be seen. Her pupils have exploded. My name is on her lips. Over and over, she says it. Like a plea. One I plan to answer.

Wrenching her knees up to her chest, I lower myself down and dive into her center, face first. The taste of her is fuckin' exquisite and I fight my rut like it's the most powerful enemy I've ever faced because it is. Zombie Alphas be damned. I bury my chin in her cunt and devour her clit. I eat her from asshole to pussy lips, nipping and tasting my way down her thighs until her whole body shakes apart and she screams my name to the skies. And then I do it all over again.

After I wring a third orgasm from her, and then a fourth that she valiantly fights against, I press gentle kisses to the scars dotting her leg — all five. The knife and all my fangs. I batter my Berserker's beast back when he wants to rise and bite and bond, because she hasn't asked me for it. Until she does.

"Bond me, Berserker."

"No, wife."

I prowl back up her body and reenter her body. I slam between her thighs and let her savage me. She bites and claws and throws her head back. I let her take whatever pieces out of me she wishes. I let her pupils blow and her breaths grow short. I let my purr rattle out of me deep and slow. I push into her and out of her and keep my wits about me, a little. I don't let myself fall fully into rut. I can't break her. I refuse.

"Bond me, Adam."

I waver, glance at her neck, see the scars. I squeeze my eyes shut and lower my body to hers completely, breathe in the scent of her hair, and then I explode. I come into her deeply and her thighs quiver around mine as I grind my hips against her clit and force another orgasm from her body. It's mine. She's mine. All of it. My nest. My Omega. *Mine.*

Fuck. Rut's coming on faster. I fight. I fight… *I'm losing… not for the first time…*

I grab her tit in my hand and flick her nipple with my thumb while my reality spirals and fractures. I taste the sky. I taste infinite gardens. "Gonna fill you with my knot, Omega. Don't move away from me. Don't wanna hurt you," I grunt as the pressure — oh fuck, the *pressure* — surges around the base of my shaft, inflating it 'til it'd look like I've got two sets a' testicles, one right at the bottom a' my dick that's now knotted up deep inside her.

Her face twists. I see it in a haze. Her hand flies out and hits the nest above her head and what I see…is strange. *Were the sheets always green and purple?* I remember whites and reds but I don't remember greens and purples. I shake my head, wonderin' if I'm fallin' into rut or madness.

I hug her shoulders tight and squeeze her underneath me as my seed explodes into her body and my knot holds us together so I can come…and come…and come…

And she comes spontaneously. "Adam!" She yelps in a panic and grabs my hair so hard it hurts.

I grin as pain lances through me, but I'm grateful for it. Helps alleviate the pressure in my groin. Knottin' an Omega is said to feel good and it does, but it feels so good it hurts. Comin' and comin' and comin' like it's never-ending. I'm afraid it won't end, but more afraid that it will.

Slowly, her whimpers bring me back. She moans in my arms, half asleep already as the first wave of her heat fades, givin' us a reprieve. Who knows how long it'll last. Hopin' for at least twenty minutes. Enough time for my knot to deflate. And then another ten minutes would be solid. Enough time for me to get her some water and somethin' to eat. Need to feed my Omega.

The need comes on so strong, I'm up on wobbly legs the moment my knot releases enough for me to be able to pull out of her completely. We both cry out like lonely children the moment we're parted. So hard to leave her. So fuckin' hard. I stumble into the middle of the room, disoriented. Where's the door? No light. Whatever.

I'm gone and back in minutes. The house is empty, as I made sure it was, givin' orders for Alphas to make space for the Betas to do their work in the manor from now on. I ransack the kitchen, confused as shit as to where shit is as I've never been in here before, but as I grab some necessary supplies I can feel that there's somethin' wrong.

I hurry back to her with a plate and pitcher in my hand, open and close the door, but somethin's off. I look at her form on the floor and my chest seizes. Darkness has fallen and I can't see anythin' except the chaos of pillows that are spread all across the floor, her nest ruined in the frenzy.

I can only remember bits and pieces in clarity — sensations more than anything else. I thought I was careful, but maybe I hurt her. If I did, don't know what that'd do to me. "Omega, did I hurt you? What the fuck is all this?" I set the tray and pitcher down on the sideboard, but there's *stuff* all over it — shit that wasn't there minutes ago when I was just here. "Omega," I bark, voice stern and much louder.

I'm feelin' clearheaded now, stronger and more capable of thinkin' rationally. My erection is back to only bein' half hard and fading rapidly. I'm ready to whisk her to Ward. "Omega!"

"Mmm shut up, Adam. I'm sleeping," she groans.

Wild with relief at the sound of her voice, I lift my hand to the lamp on the sideboard, needin' to see with my eyes to confirm her diagnosis. Need to see she's alright. I flick on the lamp and my gut hollows, my head hollows, my cock stiffens to a fuckin' tire iron and I inhale the scent, identifyin' it. *Flowers.*

The whole room is covered in flowers.

"Omega. Run!" I roar and she jerks up and meets my gaze in the same moment that I fall to my knees.

She must read the urgency in my tone because she staggers to her feet and runs to the door, covered in delicate green vines and flowers in every shade under the sun. She pulls her way through them and I hold myself back, physically grabbing onto the vines winding across the walls for as long as it takes her to clear the threshold.

Then I come undone.

I enter rut.

And I give chase.

ECHO
DRAGNOVIC GARDENS

"OMEGA, ARE YOU ALRIGHT? TALK TO ME, PLEASE."

"Shh Adam. I'm sleeping." I feel like we've had this conversation before. Many times.

"Echo, you need to wake up right now."

"No."

"I bit you…" He chokes. "I fuckin' bit you."

"Bonded me. Yes, you did." I nuzzle further into the softness beneath me. It's chilly out here. Out here? Yes, we're outside. Not without shelter though, no. The shelter I provided. I will always provide. "I asked you to."

"Fuck that. Echo, need you here with me, baby." His voice is hoarse, ragged from the rattling and the roaring he did all day and night. He fucked me sideways and I'm ready to sleep for the next seven nights — days, too. He was ruthless and relentless. Never seen him look like that before, with such mania in his eyes, such desperation. *But there was devotion there, too.*

He kept talking about the flowers. And every time he whispered the word, I felt more and more flowers bloom around us, not surrounding us like the cocoon, but attempting to blot out the sky. It became my job — my whole job — to ruin the world with petals, like the rubble of the Hanging Gardens of Babylon. I didn't call on any powers, I didn't summon any gifts. I just…breathed. Adored and let myself be adored. Adorned and let myself be adorned. I forgot about hate. No, I didn't forget it. I left it outside the gates.

I breathe and I hear the sounds of life flowering around me. My Berserker's voice hitches, like it's done already so many times. I hear him sniffle and grin, but I'm still unwilling to open my eyes, even to see my big bad Berserker in tears. "Are you crying?"

"Berserkers don't cry. Now get up, Echo. Not gonna ask again."

"You gonna order me?" I wait. A lot hangs on this moment.

But he doesn't miss a beat and says, "Nah. Gonna tickle you." His fingers dig into my sides and I yelp at the unexpected sensation.

I scream bloody murder and bat at his hands.

"Jesus Christ."

I open my eyes and my Berserker lies flat on his back, his arms out to either side, strapped to the ground at the wrist by heavy black vines. They're as thick as snakes and frightening. I start away from them and Adam's eyes crinkle. He laughs. "Can't be scared a' shit you fuckin' created." He lifts up using his stomach muscles alone and all the vines, even as big as they are, snap. He reaches for my face and cups my cheek, tilting my head to the side so he can see my neck. "You… y'aren't bleeding."

His thick eyebrows come together and the concerned expression makes my lust flare. I shove on his shoulders with both hands until he lies flat in the bright green grasses. They're high. Overgrown. Lush and unlike anything I've ever seen before. Grass like this doesn't grow in the bogs of Paradise Hole. His eyes explode with starlight as I lithely swing one leg over his hips and then reach between my thighs for his length. It's hard. It's always hard.

"Mine," I whisper.

He starts to lean up, but a vine snaps out of the ground and latches around his throat, dragging him back. I think of the belt he placed around my neck, the thrill of it, and meet his gaze in challenge. He swallows and bares his front teeth at me — not teeth, fangs. They're all glistening with silver venom that drips back into his mouth and I'm not afraid of it. The rational part of my brain thinks I should be, but I'm not.

I reach into his mouth and he jerks his head back — tries — but there's nowhere for him to go, not without toppling me and breaking the vine and taking away my control. I pull my silver-coated finger back and suck on it hard. Adam grabs my hips and his fingers dig into the flesh of my ass, but he doesn't push or pull as I lift myself up, position his veiny red erection at the dripping entrance of my brown lower lips, and sink onto him as much as I can.

I take him all into me, remembering the Beta I fucked in Prayersville and immediately forgetting him. *What was his name again?* Adam. *What did his face look like?* Strong and tan, with hard cheekbones and tangled brown hair thick enough for my fingers to get lost in. *What did he smell like?* Like ancient Berserker warlords on the hunt, ready to steal, pillage and destroy.

The fingers of my once broken hand slip past his lips and smear the venom across his front teeth. His fangs elongate, four of them looking like the fangs of a massive, mythical snake. I press my thumb to the sharpened tip, feel his resistance, but I push past it. I break my skin and red blood releases into his mouth while silver venom slips into my bloodstream.

"Oh fuck, that feels good." I throw my head back, grab his hand on my hip and shove it against my clit. With one featherlight touch, I come instantly.

I shiver out an orgasm while this beautiful raging fullness fills and fuels me. I open my eyes and I see yellow, which doesn't make sense to me at first. There is no sunshine here.

"Flowers," I whisper, sounding like Adam, just as reverent.

The sky is full of flowers. Whatever happened last night to the ground surrounding us has spread its arms up to create a dome that hangs high over our heads. Flowers cling to vines and drip towards us. White petals fall from the vines and drift in the lazy breeze that permeates the patchy parts of my creation, but that's okay, because more flowers just come to take their place.

I'm so warm. Beneath me, Adam's chest is heaving. "Can't leave me like this, wife."

I blink down at him and see that his pupils are blown again. I struggle to keep myself upright and nod, arm shaking against his chest where it's planted over his heart. The vine releases his neck without me having to do anything more than *want* it. Adam doesn't have to command me at all.

He moves the instant the order's been given, circling one arm around my shoulders and cupping the back of my head while his other hand pushes us up off the ground, revolving us until he's on top of me.

"Careful with your arm, wife," he says, calling me that word again in a way that's purely deferential and without mocking.

It makes my eyes glaze, being claimed like that. It makes my pulse hammer knowing that he's been claiming me in this way for some time. It makes my cheeks burn to know that he was teasing me all along — that there never was anybody else. It makes my lungs sear remembering the things he said about me. My heart hurts, it's so full.

"Sure it isn't hurt?"

He tries to gently place it to the side, but I shake my head and make quick work of the straps. I shuck them off and toss them to the grasses.

"What are you doin'?"

"It doesn't hurt anymore."

"Doesn't fuckin' matter. Keep the bandage on."

"You didn't bite me, Adam. You *bonded* me. I asked you to." I blink, eyes surprisingly dry. Seems like a moment this new weepy Echo would cry, but instead, I don't feel defeat or fear. All I feel is excitement.

"You asked me to?"

I nod. "Begged you to."

"Fuck. Wish I could remember it." He slides into me deeply, stretching my sloppy pussy even wider. It's already gaping for him, ready to accommodate him twice over with how he worked me all through the night.

"Do it again, Adam."

"Nah."

"Please, Adam."

"No, wife."

I hitch, shocked by his use of the word in a way I imagine I will be every time. The moment passes and I comb his hair behind his ears with both of my hands, admiring the way my left arm moves, despite the scars that decorate it. "Berserker, please bond your Omega. I'm begging."

His fangs jut out of his mouth like he's lost control over them and he lunges for my neck. He bites down hard, mouth fully covering the place that he bit me that very first night, back when I was a scavenger and a stranger and he was nobody but an enemy to me.

I scream in rapture, in absolute delight. He roars and curses and sniffles because my Berserker is a cupcake. A murderous cupcake. And that fills me with violent satisfaction that carries me all through the day and into the night.

The entire time, flowers fall around us.

ADAM
DRAGNOVIC GARDENS

"WOW, HE EMERGES FROM THE DEAD."

"Just in time, too…"

"Do you know how much work it is to plan a fuckin' Omega Ball? We've been receiving delegates in Dark City for the past three days and you've been totally MIA."

"We put them up in Dark Tower — that's where we moved the venue. Figured you're not in a state to host."

"Not to mention, we got so many fuckin' RSVPs…"

My Six are all talkin' at fuckin' once and givin' me a fuckin' headache. Not lookin' at me either, which drives me nuts, but starin' at their computer screens like somethin' in there could ever be more important than what's goin' on in the real world. Here. With their Omega.

"Move the venue back here. Get it ready."

"What!" Four of the Six scream at once. Two are missin'. They all swivel their chairs around and silence reigns for a full sixty seconds.

Slowly, Vi stands up from the desk he's got positioned in front of the bay window. Our home office looks so damn stereotypical. Dark oak flooring. Soft, comfortable leather couches. Ergonomic chairs, stools, keyboards, desks, everything. My people are nerds. But they're alright.

"You…*okay*, Berserker?" Vi says, sounding strained.

Yeah, they're alright.

I nod absently, know I need to get some food. Already fed my Omega, though, and put her back to bed in her nest, and that's what counts. Need to feed me now, though. My body's hurtin'. Never felt like this. Never knew a body could feel like this. Like I been totally wrung dry yet could respond to my Omega's call for anythin' in a second.

"Jesus," Sierra stands and glances to Balcazar, who's got nothin' to say apparently.

It's Whiskey who I can count on to voice the group's collective thoughts. "How much…" She swallows, her face gettin' red before turning white as a sheet. "Did you fuck so hard you lost thirty pounds?"

I glance down and fuck, she might be right. I look thinner than I remember feelin'. Then again, was there a time before bondin' my Omega? Not sure, but if there was, it don't fuckin' exist to me.

I stomp through the door on the right into the mini-kitchen and throw open the fridge. I grab a hunk of meat, don't know what kind — a leg a' lamb, maybe? — and start gnawin' on it as I reenter the office.

Gesturin' with the bone, I say, "Follow me."

They glance between each other, but Sierra shakes her head. "Should I cancel the venue? They're gonna be pissed."

"Don't cancel the venue," Whiskey barks at the same time I say, "Cancel the fuckin' venue. We're doin' it here."

She throws her arms out to the side and huffs, exasperated, "We don't have anywhere here to do it. Dragnovic Manor is packed since you moved all the Betas in here, the northeast side is under construction, the garden house is out of the question after you and your Omega ruined it and…"

"Come."

I take another chunk of meat off the bone, chew, swallow. Bite, chew, swallow. I drop the clean bone off on the carpet as I make my way down the hall. A Dark City bureaucrat squeaks as he nearly trips over it. "Brute," the Alpha mutters under his breath. I don't turn and I don't apologize and I don't skin him for the insult.

I can hear my Six shufflin' after me, speaking in hushed tones under their breath as we go down, down through the regular hallways to the large double doors that lead out onto the winter porch that spills out into the garden.

I shove on the doors. Nothing happens.

"You barricaded the doors shut. Nobody's been able to access the back wings of the compound for five days. Or willing to risk it. Hell, we didn't even know if y'all were alive."

Five days. It's been five days. She has a six-day heat. I grin, fuckin' exhilarated at the thought that my Omega's got a six-day heat and I'm the lucky fuck that gets to service her for the rest of our lives — at least, for as long as her heats last and then some.

"He's scaring me," Sierra whispers to Whiskey and I realize I'm standing still, staring off into the distance wearin' a huge fuckin' grin. And nothing else.

I shake my head and flowers fall at my feet. They're pink. Bright pink.

"You bleedin', Dragnovic?" Balcazar points at the ground where the flowers lie against the dark grey carpet. She doesn't understand.

"You have to see it," I grumble before leanin' my shoulder into the door and pushin' as hard as I can.

The double doors strain and, when they part an inch, I can see a few skinny trees have been uprooted and laid across them. Hm. Guess I really didn't wanna be interrupted. I reach through the door and kick the trees over. The door gives a little more. There are vines crisscrossin' over the entry, too, and I draw my Berserker form forward and protract fresh claws long enough to be able to slash through 'em. The door gives a little more, but I'm also not feelin' my best fuckin' self.

"Little help here," I grunt over my shoulder.

The others step in line beside me and with one coordinated shove, we crack the doors wide open and spill out onto the stone porch. The whole thing's been overrun. The porch is no more. Now there's just green grass and wildflowers growin' as far as the eye can see. The canopy stretches from the top of the house out…out all the way to fresh trees in the distance blocking the garden house from view. The dome she created towers above our heads and vines drip down towards us bearin' flowers. So many fuckin' colors. Orange and blue, purple and yellow, pink and red, white and multicolored, too.

"Oh my god," Sierra whispers. She's got her hands clapped over her mouth, starin' around at everything.

At the edges of the dome, thick vines spiral up, braided together, as thick as tree trunks. They support the frame of this magnificent space that's the size of a football field twice over.

I watch my Six move out into the beautiful carnage. In patches, the grass comes up to their shins; in others, it's flat and I can hear the sounds a' their sneakers and boots crinklin' over vines and flowers. Must be millions of them. Billions.

Barbero hasn't moved away from the door and when I look back at him, he looks fuckin' terrified. He looks like he's about to bawl like a baby.

I jerk my chin out towards the others in the field, toward Vi who's crouched down to inspect a small thicket of rosebushes that are growin' in no particular order, without reason. There is no reason for this. There is no reason for her power to be so limitless. It scares me a little bit. *Scares me that someone else might covet it.*

"How..." Whiskey's blabberin' to my right, her hands planted on her hips, her gaze goin' everywhere and nowhere at the same time. "Did she...I've never seen an Omega with gifts like this."

Sierra adds, "Most work small-scale — remember Gold City's Omega? She could bend glass, but rumor has it only one piece at a time. Apparently the decorative nest they had on view took months for her to create."

"And the Town of Teeth Omega...she could only move objects a few feet," Barbero says, taking a few terrified steps forward. He flinches every time a vine beneath his feet crunches or breaks. "Dragnovic." He looks at me, his face gettin' kinda pale. "This is huge. She's got Fate-level gifts."

"Know it."

A suspended silence brings chills with it that make me clench my teeth. Fear. This is what fear feels like.

"Alright," Sierra snaps, movin' us away from more dangerous topics. "It's settled. We'll cancel Dark Tower. Get the event team out here to scope this place. Will the...uh... foliage die in the next three days?"

I grin. "Not if I keep fuckin' her in it."

Sierra laughs. Barbero chokes.

Vi looks up from where he's still kneelin'. Face scrunched, eyes glowin', he says, "Don't wanna share this with the others. She's our Omega."

I feel heat brush my chest, right over my heart, and I grab at it. I'm deeply touched. "Nobody's seen flowers before, except maybe in Mirage City." Where the Berserker who controls the Fates can tap into powers as far-reaching as they are unknown.

"Can't keep 'em locked away."

My Six are all starin' at me with small smiles on their faces. Vi still looks like he's about to cry and Sierra looks like she's up to somethin'. "What?" I bark.

"Can I plan the wedding? Please, please, please!"

I laugh. "Not gettin' married. Woman can't stand me unless we're fucking."

"Have you tried bein' nicer?" Whiskey says, unhelpfully.

"I bonded 'er."

"You did?" Three of 'em — except Vi — say simultaneously.

"Did."

"And did it…"

"Healed 'er. Her bones mended themselves, the tissue and fat that was drained out of her leg filled itself. Only things it didn't heal were her scars." And I hate every one. Tried askin' her if she wanted Ward to take a look at 'em, but she wouldn't have it. Said she liked 'em. Said she made it look more like — I choke up at the damn thought — she said it made it look more like we belonged together.

My wife is a goddamn romantic.

Even if she's a scavenger, a survivalist, a goddamn bitch who lets me get shot by trolls, and is just as likely to stab me in my sleep as she is to kiss all my scars and kiss away all my fears, so sweet and tender.

"What did it feel like, bondin' an Omega?" Vi whispers.

I don't answer right away. My face gets hot, though. *Like drinking nirvana. Like finding an elixir to defy death. Like everything I ever was exists now outside of my body. Exposing and frightening. Empowering and enlightening. Like swallowing the sun.*

I grunt, "Can we just get a fuckin' move on with this goddamn Ball? Don't want a big thing. Just want people to come, eat, drink, and leave. Don't want anybody lingerin'. Now where's the rest of you? Where's Peate and Balcazar?"

"Peate's with Ward, still in the lab, and I sent Balcazar back to Paradise Hole," Barbero says, swiping a hand back through his messy curls. His eyes shift over my body, lingering on my hair. I can feel I got leaves and twigs and flowers stuck all in it, but I don't move to free 'em. I like 'em. "They found somethin' odd about the bodies."

"What isn't odd about 'em?"

"More odd."

My head cocks to the side, hatin' that I'm bein' distracted…but still curious. "What?"

He looks uncomfortable, somethin' he rarely ever looks. "Two a' the bodies. Well, they got…they got Dark City markers."

"What?"

"One of 'em had a brand. A Dark City brand. We traced it back to one of the founding Dark City houses and when we brought in Ellery — " Ellery bein' the matriarch of one of the oldest families livin' in Dark City. A loyal supporter, and since I took over she and her family have always been good to me. That's why killin' their oldest son in Paradise Hole had been hard. "She identified the body as Benjamin's."

"That's not possible."

"What isn't?"

"It isn't Benjamin. She got it wrong."

Sierra pipes up, removin' her hand from a huge yellow blossom hangin' low. "There's no mistake. She was sure."

"I saw Benjamin alive in Paradise Hole four…five weeks ago."

"You what?" Whiskey's eyes bulge.

I nod and glance in the direction of my house, where my heart lies. "He was after Echo. I killed him."

The Six exchange a look. We all share in it. We all arrive at the same conclusion. "Then that confirms it," Vi says, voice as soft as ever. He stands up from the roses, crosses his arms over his chest and manages to look deeply perturbed. "Somebody's out there reanimatin' Alpha corpses."

"That isn't possible," Barbero rebuts, but even he doesn't sound sure.

"Ellery was sure?" I say.

Whiskey whispers, "Swore it on her life. We were there."

"Then the Omega was right." Sierra whistles. "It's a dead Alpha army."

"She was right about more than that." They open their mouths to start arguin' but I cut in. "She suspected Trash City of supplyin' the bodies. They had guns. They took the bodies of the Alphas I killed and killed the rest I didn't."

"Who are they sellin' them to? Who's doin' the reanimatin'?" Vi says.

"Don't know who's doin' the reanimatin' or how, but there's only a few powerful enough for it."

"You don't think it was an Omega…" Sierra says, then registers the look on my face and drops her arms. "You think it was a Fate."

I turn away from them and start stompin' towards my own private residences, where my heart sits. Over my shoulder, I say, "Keep plannin' the Ball. Just make sure Mirage City Berserker gets a special invitation."

ADAM
DOWNTOWN DARK CITY

ECHO LOOKS SO FUCKIN' CUTE — CUTE — AS SHE stares out of the dark tinted window at the city, her face all pressed up against the glass. She keeps foggin' it, then wipin' away the fog with the flat of her fist rather than just pulling back a few inches. I don't suggest she does, though, because every time it makes me laugh.

"That's Dark Tower, where we were gonna hold the Ball before you turned our place into a fuckin' palace."

"I did not. I just grew some flowers," she says absently before saying more loudly, "What's Dark Tower for?"

I shrug. "Mostly business shit. Lots of offices in there. We hold conferences there sometimes, galas, balls, host delegations from other cities."

"Are Betas allowed to go?"

I clench my teeth, heat traveling through my abdomen. I shift my weight between my hips and my ass squeaks against the seat. I'm embarrassed. "No. Betas aren't allowed in Dark Tower."

She pauses for a moment. "What about Omegas?"

"You are the Dark City Omega," I say, punctuating each word with menace. "Can do whatever the fuck you want, Echo. Go wherever the fuck you wanna go." Just not into Paradise Hole.

As if she's thinkin' the same thing, she shoots me a withering look over her shoulder. It's fleeting though, because then we take a turn and pass an open-air market. "What's this?"

"Farmer's market."

"Farmers. There aren't any farmers in Dark City."

"No, but we get a lotta traders in from Shadowlands and Glass Flats. Sell their crazy artisan, hand-crafted shit here at Greenie's Square at insane fuckin' markups, but it doesn't seem to matter. People like the shit."

"Hm."

The fact that Echo doesn't have anythin' snarky to say for once catches me off guard. "What?"

"Nothing."

"Don't nothin' me, Omega. What're you thinkin'?"

"Nothing."

"Jesus Christ. Echo," I say scoldingly.

She huffs, "Can't I keep anything to myself anymore? You're so fuckin' — fucking — nosy."

My lips twitch at her pronunciation. Yeah, my little Prayersville Omega has some Dark City down in there deep. Wants to come out and I'm not about to punish her for it. She's so fuckin' cute. "I know you, Echo. Know when you're sad at me, mad at me, and right now, you're a little bit a' both. What'd I do?"

"It's nothing you did. It just reminds me of the markets in Prayersville. Except there, we barely had stuff to barter. Here, there's like…dresses and fancy-looking stuff…*soap*, for fuck's sake. I just…" She shakes her head and sinks back slightly in her seat. "Betas don't get fancy soap. Betas get to trade their only pair of shoes in exchange for shelter for just one night."

Knowin' she's speaking from experience pisses me the fuck off. Makes me want to go back to Trash City and skin Merlin alive. But…is it really Merlin's fault? No, it's not.

"You wanted to live good as a Beta, you always coulda gone for Shadowlands." There, the ruling Berserkers have always kept to the old ways, letting Betas keep their children and work alongside Alphas.

She balks, "You mean make it through Paradise Hole?"

I don't answer.

"Were you not there with me trying to cross a tenth of the distance I'd have needed to cross to get to the ports?"

Still don't answer. Her glare cuts.

"And even if I did make it to the ocean, I'd have to cross it somehow. You know the coastal cities don't let Betas ride boats. Not for free. And it's a fare that no amount of rabbit pelts coulda bought me. I'd have had to pay a fee on my back. Maybe. Or work in the…"

"Shut the fuck up, Echo." The thought of her on her back, her legs spread for some horny fuckin' sailor… Jesus Christ.

"And you know that Ruby City pirates catch ninety-nine out of a hundred unmarked boats that try to pass between the northern and southern island. Even after all that, I'd just be back where I started."

She lapses into silence and I glance down and see the back of my hand is covered in fur and swallow my next growl, trying to curb the urge to kill something for her. To do something for her. But what?

Maybe, nothin' my Berserker's beast can do, though… Maybe, it's somethin' she needs from me as the ruling Alpha that I am. The thought sits and lingers in the silence that exists between us. Not an unpleasant silence and I like that about my wife — she can challenge me all she wants and bring out all kinds of unearthly thoughts and feelings in me, but I don't get the sense she hates me for my failings.

"It doesn't matter, anyway."

"What doesn't?"

"Even if I made it to Shadowlands, it wouldn't matter. Everybody knows Betas do fine there, but women don't."

"Women…" I know what she's talkin' about and wish I could contradict it. Stereotype is that the Berserkers of the southern island are still quite patriarchal. Women can exist as Betas or Alphas just fine and get any role they want…so long as it's not in a position of authority. "At least they can keep their kids."

"I guess." She shrugs.

"What? You don't want kids?"

She tenses visibly and hugs her sweater tighter around her shoulders. It's black, like the leggings she's got on and the tight tank top that clings to her curves and looks like it'd be so fuckin' easy to rip off.

Got a clothing delivery this morning she seems happy with, but I'd love to send 'er out shopping and see what she came back with. Sure she'd surprise me if she had a credit card and free reign. Hell, if I sent her off alone, she'd probably come back with no clothes at all and somethin' else weird instead. She doesn't care about this shit. She hasn't had a chance to. Same with kids.

"Are we here?" She clicks her tongue against the backs of her teeth and reaches for the door handle.

"Locked. Keep it locked," I call up to Sierra, who volunteered to drive us for the day.

From the front seat, Sierra chuffs, "Are you kidding? Why do you think I'm here? I've got to report all this to the boss."

I chuckle and watch Echo's face turn even pinker. Her freckles look like they're darkening along her cheeks. Her shoulders curl inward. My bark turns into a full laugh, "Shut the fuck up, Sierra. Ignore her, baby."

"Baby?" Echo scratches the seat between us. I reach over and take her hand.

"Yeah, baby. You want one?"

She rubs the space between her eyebrows with her free hand, unable to stop fidgeting. "I don't know. I…never thought about it. Do…" She swallows. "Do you?"

"Only if my wife decides she wants one. Eventually. Maybe, she and I can talk about it again when we don't have a horde of zombies on our heels."

She laughs at that and pulls her hand out of mine. She reaches for the doorhandle again and rolls her eyes, tension sloughing off of her at talk of the undead caused by talk of creating life. "Sounds good, *baby*. Can we get this over with?"

I look up and see the row of fancy-ass boutiques in front of us and nod, but my mind and heart have both stalled over what she called me. I clear my throat and have to force the words out, "Uh, yeah. Gotta get outfitted for this shit."

"Oh golly gee, I can't wait." Her voice drips with sarcasm like venom that makes me choke.

"Sierra, the door. Echo, get the fuck out."

"Aww, aren't you two cute?" Sierra says as I slam the door behind me and usher Echo out of the car, across the sidewalk and to the glass door of the luxury storefront, out of the path of prying eyes. Dunno why, but I'm feeling sensitive about her bein' out in my city. Not just because I don't like Alphas sniffin' after my Echo, but because I worry she won't like it and I want her to like it. Want her to be prouda this place. Her new home. Prouda me.

She digs her heels into the sidewalk and physically reaches out to try to block her way forward on the glass doorway as she looks left and right. "Do we have to do the dress thing? Just pick something out, I don't care."

"You actin' like you're late to somethin'."

The wind ruffles her hair. Her curls. They don't look quite silken yet. Needa cut. But they look a helluva lot better than they did when they were tangled with twigs and leaves and mud out in Paradise Hole. Paradise Hole. What fucker named it that?

I comb my fingers through the softer curls that frame her face. She jerks away from me before looking up and meeting my gaze. "What are you doing?"

I smirk, "Touchin' what's mine."

Her skin glows just a little brighter when I say that. She shuffles between her feet, looking uncomfortable, before cocking her chin down the sidewalk. "I want to explore. I've never seen a city before."

Hm. "Hm." Don't know what to do. Don't wanna deny her, but I don't feel like sharing her, either. "Dress first, then we'll grab a coffee."

"Grab a coffee?" she says, turning to face me. Her face is a picture of incredulity and laughter. Still, she acquiesces and lets me push her backwards through the automatic door. "*Grab a coffee?* Did you really just say that?"

The air conditioning washes over me, blasting my hair around my face. I tuck it back behind my ear and Echo surprises me by reaching forward with both hands and untucking it. "The fuck are you doin'?"

"Touching what's mine, Berserker."

"Cheeky fucker. And yeah, what? You don't like coffee?"

"Grab a coffee." She turns from me and scoffs. "Sounds almost as ridiculous as this place looks." She wanders to a rack of dresses and pulls out one covered in black sequins. "This is the stupidest thing I've ever seen. It must weigh like thirty pounds. How are you supposed to run for your life in this?"

"Don't think you are."

A throat clears to the left. "I can confirm that." The sound of clicking confuses me at first. It's been a long time since I've heard the sound of heels against marble. This whole place is fancy as shit and Echo looks so outta place beneath the lights, amidst the velvet settees and the racks of glittery dresses and silky suits. Gilded mirrors reflect Echo's annoyed expression back to me a thousand times over, and also paint a vision of a well-dressed woman approaching with her hand outstretched.

"My name's Pri. I'm the designer." Her black hair is thick, silky and long. She wears a sleeveless tunic in white that contrasts against her darker brown skin. "Nice to meet you. Welcome, welcome. I take it by the look on your face, you aren't into dress-up. I can get you outfitted quickly if you come with me."

Echo follows the woman after a beat, almost surprising me with how quickly she acquiesces. And the fact that she doesn't look back at me at all. I miss her when she's out of sight, taken away from me into a dressing room. Don't fuckin' like it. Don't fuckin' like it at all.

I take a step to follow her when a soft voice says, "Berserker Dragnovic. If you could follow me." A younger Alpha who looks an awful lot like Pri stands before me in a suit tailored to the nines, reminding me of why I'm here. "We have your suit prepared. We just need to finalize your measurements."

"Let's get to it, then."

True to his word, the kid — actually, a man with a young-lookin' face — gets me in and out in less than half an hour. By the time I'm finished changin' into and then out of my suit, Echo's ready, as well. "Where's the dress?" I say as she bolts to the front door.

"Uhh…"

"We'll deliver it to Dragnovic Manor along with your suit," Pri calls, practically running to catch up to Echo.

"I don't get to see it?" I wanted to see it. "Can't picture you in a dress."

Echo blushes hard. Fuck, I love how she blushes. Her skin is such a soft brown and the pink that illuminates it is so fuckin' cute. Makes her look so healthy, too. Makes me feel safe…like we're out of Paradise Hole and we're never goin' back.

Because we're never goin' back. *You lied to her.*

"It's nice. Pri did a…uhh…good job. It's fine. I mean, it's good. I like it. You'll like it. Can we just go?"

I feel a corner of my mouth cock and I run my fingers back through my hair. Hardly feels like my own, it's been so many weeks that my hair was just as fuckin' tangled as Echo's was out in the mud and the bleak dark. Uncertainty shimmers through me. *She's not gonna like it when I tell her I'm not goin' with her out there at all because she's not goin', either.* I wonder if maybe, things have changed since I bonded her. Maybe, she doesn't want to go anymore… Yeah. Right. Because that sounds like the stubborn Omega I'm bound to and determined to one day marry.

"Yeah, we can go. Ready to grab that coffee?"

"In Prayersville, you get coffee from the cantina. Tastes like piss. I only drank it once. Are you telling me that you go proactively to a place to get coffee? It's like a thing people do in the city?"

I laugh and gesture her down the street and we make our way down the sidewalk. As we walk, I keep my hand on her lower back, wanting to tuck her against me completely and struggling to fight the urge.

The sky's grey — typical — but it doesn't feel as dark as it usually does. Maybe, it's her hair, red as fire, glittering against the black backdrop of her coat. Maybe, it's the pink still dusting the tops of her cheeks and the tip of her nose. Maybe, it's… "What are you staring at, weirdo?"

"My wife."

She just shines brighter. I pull her into me, switching sides with her and placing her closer to the buildings. "What are you doing?"

"Makin' sure if somebody crazy swerves off the road, I get hit first."

She snorts, "You wouldn't get hit. You're a Berserker. You could stop any car."

"And I'd have to. Not gonna see you get hurt again. Ever." Gonna keep you out of Paradise Hole, to start.

She elbows me in the side. "Stop it."

"Stop what?"

"Trying to make me like you."

My turn to snort, now. "Don't have to try, Echo. You already do." I pull her to the left and underneath the awning of the coffee shop. It spreads across the sidewalk, a deep burgundy, beneath which round tables and plastic wicker chairs stand mostly full of happy customers. We enter through the front door just as an Alpha couple walks out. They've got a small Beta child between them. Their own. Something about that fact doesn't sit right with me, but I can't pinpoint it, least of all when Echo comes to a complete stop and distracts me.

"What?"

"Those are all different kinds of coffee?" She points up at the old-school blackboard hung above modern bronze machines and appliances. Calligraphy scrawled in chalk marks dozens of different types of coffee and flavor combinations.

I smile as I push her up to the front counter, not missing the stares and whispers at all, but happy she's distracted enough she doesn't seem to notice them. "Oh! Berserker Dragnovic. Hello. Welcome. Is this…this is…is this the… your…" The barista swallows so hard she starts to choke. Though there are six other baristas behind the bar counter, none of them come to her rescue, so Echo and I wait until she's downed half a glass of water and can speak clearly enough to be understood.

"I'm so sorry…"

"Not necessary. I'll take one of everything for your Dark City Omega."

Echo's laughter clacks through the greyness of the day, slaughtering it mercilessly in ways I never managed to as a Beta or an Alpha or a Berserker, no matter how I willed it.

Drunk on coffee a half hour later, she stumbles out onto the sidewalk and runs straight into a passing Alpha. He's on the phone and quick to utter an apology, without giving her a second glance or recognizing me beside her. She apologizes back just as dismissively before turning to me.

"That's so stupid. A whole shop just for that stuff? And it was full! And what is pumpkin spice? Pumpkins don't taste anything like that."

"You've never had a pumpkin," I mutter, following her wherever she wants to go.

She opens her mouth, ever quick with a retort, then punches me playfully in the arm. *Playfully*. Fuckin' hell. I'm done for. "You neither." She sticks her tongue out at me and I nod in agreement.

"True. But that's how I know it might taste just like that pumpkin spice shit."

"I'd bet my bottom dollar it doesn't."

I swoop in on her, wrap my arm around her back because *fuck it,* I've kept my hands off of her for too long. I sink my fingers into her ass cheek and haul her up against my body, pulling her high enough I could steal a taste of her mouth, but I don't. Because it's a taste I want her to give me.

"I'd bet on that," I whisper.

Her pupils dilate. Her scent blooms around me. "I… thought my heat was over." Her wrists fall lazily onto my shoulders and I rub the bridge of my nose across her jawline.

"It is. What you're feeling now isn't your Omega, Echo."

"What do you mean?" she says, completely breathless.

"It's just you."

She gasps, grabs hold of either side of my face, looks at my lips and licks her own and leans in…and then she jerks back. Eyes glued to somethin' happenin' over my shoulder, she wriggles until I'm forced to release her from my grip. I don't see what's claimed her attention until she starts towards it — the Alphas standing on the corner up ahead, a Beta man and a Beta boy on the ground beneath and between them.

The Beta boy is in the street and an oncoming car has to swerve to avoid him. The father is reaching for the boy, shouting, but the Alpha closest to him places a leather-soled shoe on his shoulder and gives him a kick, forcing him back, away from the child he'd been trying to protect.

Several triggers fire in my chest, reminding me why I don't come out into the city. I've been out here. I've also seen worse. Reminds me of when I was a Beta boy but, in this moment, it makes me think of the conversation Echo and I just had about kids. What if that were me? Tryna protect my own kid? Not even sure the two males are related but the thought still claws its way into my skull and grabs ahold, and I find my feet moving faster down the sidewalk.

"Echo," I call, panic firing as I realize that my Omega had the same idea at the exact same time I did. And she's moving faster. "Echo!"

But Echo's already at the corner, her arm outstretched. The Alphas turn to face her and I feel my Berserker rearing, ready to enter beast mode and obliterate them if they touch one strand of hair on her head, but Echo's far more than two steps ahead. Her fingers curl and the sidewalk *crumbles.* Thorns branch out between cracks in the concrete and even Echo is forced to a stop when they unfurl in long brown and black vines and fully encircle the Alphas, creating what look like bird cages around them. Big, beautiful, and terrifying.

My heart thumps and the taste of chicory and fear floods my mouth. *This is my Omega and she's a breathtaking and savage thing.* I come to a stop at her side and see her covering her mouth with her hand. Her eyes are enormous, pupils tiny in the midst of so much brown. So much warmth. So much violence.

I take her hand by the wrist while the captive Alphas scream and gently lower her hand back to her side. "Berserker Dragnovic! Berserker Dragnovic! Help us! That female…the Omega…control her!" Ignoring the Alphas in a way I *never* would have before, I lace my fingers through Echo's and approach the Betas on the ground.

The Beta boy kneels next to his father now, just outside of the ring of broken concrete. I stretch my hand down to help him up, but he flinches, holds his hands over his head, and cowers from me.

Shame.

I've felt it before, before Echo. I know I have…but I can't ever remember feelin' it the way I've felt it since Echo came into my life. Bitin' her against her will, hurtin' her…yeah, those were lows. But this? And knowin' she's seein' this? The hole I dug myself has dug itself deeper. And worse, I'm frozen on the spot, not sure how to proceed. Don't wanna touch the boy if he's 'fraid a me. Don't wanna leave my hand suspended in the air like a fuckin' dick.

And then Echo moves. She edges her body half in front of mine and pushes my wrist down, just like I did to hers earlier. She slides her fingers along the boy's arm and I notice that his clothes are a little dirty, his sweatshirt not as clean as it should be. Shame. It hurts my chest, like a bruised heart beating.

"You're okay. It's okay. They're not gonna hurt you," Echo whispers.

The boy opens his eyes and Echo helps him stand. I reach for the man and he hesitates before touching me. Everything hinges on him touching me. He looks up into my eyes, his blue eyes small and hesitant. But…he's still brave enough to try — or maybe, he just senses my desperation. I want him to prove this to me, to Echo, to himself. I want my wife to like me.

He looks to Echo, and then his gaze drops to where my hand is still laced with Echo's, before he takes mine. *Relief.*

"What happened here?" I can feel his bones through his thin skin as I haul him up onto his feet.

"The boy…he's my protégé. We're working for the paper. We do the deliveries." It's only when he gestures to the courier bags on the ground and the newspaper spilling out of them that I register what he means. "The Alpha lords…" Alpha lords. Do they really deserve such a title? "They accused the boy of being my son…said I needed to report him to our…to the Dark City Berserker. I…refused…I mean, he isn't my son…"

The man is lying. I can tell. I can tell that Echo can tell because her hand squeezes mine as if pleading with me and I fuckin' hate it. I ignore Echo for now, though I want to take her over my knee, but I know that's not gonna convince her of who I am and what she means to me as much as what I do next right now, right here.

I step forward and take the man's shoulder in my hand. His blue eyes fall to the ground between us and he starts to shake just a little bit before I say, "You and your son don't need to register yourselves and you don't need to put up with this harassment. I'll help you gather your things and then my driver will take you anywhere you need to go."

I call Sierra and she pulls up to the curb while the Alphas go quiet in their cages — quiet, yet I can feel their rage. It's a rage my Berserker longs to explore…to match. That they *dare* in the presence of my Omega is…well, I'd love nothing more than to set them free and let my *true* form take over.

I block Echo from helping gather the newspapers up and do it for her. I hand the heavy bag to the boy and whatever cash is in my pocket to the man. At least a few hundred dollars. "For your family. And there's my number in there, too. Any Alpha asks you to register yourself again, I want you to call me directly. I'm changing things. Betas don't need to give up their kids anymore." I'd decided this earlier, but hadn't decided to announce it so publicly until then. Didn't wanna piss off the Alphas, my Six counciled…

My Berserker's beast has got other fuckin' plans.

In front of me, the Beta's jaw drops, revealing a mouth full of crooked teeth. "Are you…when…when did this happen?"

"Now. 'Cuz of you. 'Cuz of her." I raise my voice, pitching it loud enough that the Alphas trapped in their cages — and the gathering crowd — can hear me. "Betas are no longer second-class — I'm gonna make changes. Until then, I catch wind of any Alpha causin' trouble for Betas, they'll have to answer to her."

"Who…who is she?" an Alpha female asks. It's the same one who was walkin' out of the coffee shop earlier with her Beta kid. She's got a hopeful look on her face, too and it makes me realize that I didn't need to be so chicken shit. I didn't need to wait for Echo to challenge me to make this change. Some Alphas will be pissed…but others, some that give birth to Betas, at least, will support me. They want more for their kids, too. If it were me and Echo's kid, I know I would.

I nudge Echo forward, slightly in front of me so that she's surrounded by an arc of Alphas, me at her back, the Beta males behind me. Traffic in the streets has stalled. The world feels utterly still as she swallows *audibly* then says, "I'm the Dark City Omega."

As talk on the sidewalk explodes and Alphas fight each other to introduce themselves to the Dark City Omega, Sierra drives the Beta males home — or wherever the fuck — leaving me to fight off the throngs and Echo and I to grab a cab. It's dangerous, and I ordinarily would have waited for Sierra to come back, but after hearin' her openly acknowledge her position beside me, I fuckin' can't. And not just because of the Beta kid holdin' his momma's hand, starin' up at my Omega with fuckin' awe and adoration.

It's 'cuz I'm in awe of her, too.

We don't make it through the front door of the garden house before I shred her fuckin' annoyin'-ass tank top off her body. Echo shocks the shit out of me by pouncin' on me right back. She throws herself at me and I catch her against the stairs. She kisses me hard, pullin' on my hair, trying to pull me into her body. She's kissin' me somethin' fierce, so fuckin' desperate it scares me.

"Wh…what you thinkin', Echo?" I say, breaking away from the seductive taste of her mouth long enough to ask.

It's dark on the staircase. None of the lights are on. Her tank is torn down the front already, revealing her black bra. I yank it down until her tits spill out the top. They're begging to be suckled, my eyes trying to look everywhere at once. But then she sniffs and my heart stutters.

"Talk to me, baby."

"Stop it," she whispers, her breath mingling with mine as she rakes both of her hands back through my hair, holding it out of my eyes.

I freeze. "Don't need to fuck you if you're not feelin' up for it."

"Not that, you big idiot."

I bark out a dry laugh, "Then what?"

"You…what you did for those guys. What you said…"

"I meant it." I swallow hard, pull one of her hands away from my face and pin it above her head. I lean in and kiss the center of her forehead. "Spent so long tryna fight for power and then spent the rest of the time livin' in fear of somebody takin' it that I never thought once about what to *do* with it.

"But you're right. I can do better than fuckin' Shadowlands. *We* can do better. What the fuck's the point of ruinin' the lives of Betas? Why the fuck should they live like they're less than? Why the fuck did we? If we hadn't — if we'd had good Beta parents in nice Beta communities — I'd probably be a lot smarter and you'd probably be a lot nicer than we turned out to be."

Echo doesn't laugh like I thought she might. Instead, she rebels against my grip, grabs the side of my face and wrenches me into a kiss. She bites both my lips, wraps her legs around my hips, pulls me in close…

And then she pushes me away, just a little, just enough to brush the most breathtakingly tender kiss between my eyebrows. She kisses me again right there, in the same place, and then harder. Her lips brand me. They're so hot and I can feel that heat travel all the way through my body down to my toes. It sears through me. It sears me. It brands me and binds me and I know that everything Ward and Loveless said was right, is true…

I didn't fuckin' bond this woman.

She stole my soul and bound it to her.

"Stop it," she whispers. "Just stop, Adam."

"What?"

"Stop trying to make me fall in love with you."

My heart hiccups in my throat and I rear up and back and meet her gaze and then explode. I just fuckin'…combust. Her clothes are gone and so are mine and I take her on every stair, every surface, everything, until I completely unravel. And it's got nothin' to do with her heat or my rut and everythin' to do with her thorn-covered vines and the cage they've built around my heart.

I fuck her somethin' fierce until flowers fall from the rafters of the garden house like rain that chases away all the ghosts.

I CLENCH MY TEETH TOGETHER SO HARD, I'M SURPRISED I don't break them. I'm pissed. I'm beyond pissed. I glare at Adam so hard I'm surprised he doesn't wither beneath my stare, and I hate that I'm a little impressed he doesn't. Vines rise from the floor of his room and latch onto his ankles.

He lets them and watches me dully as he says, "Omega, gotta wear it."

"What happened to changing outdated and fucked up traditions?"

"Doesn't happen overnight. Besides," he shrugs. "Kinda like this one."

"Fuck you. I don't have to wear it…"

"Wrong."

"…I don't have to go to your stupid party…"

"Your party…"

"I don't have to do anything." I coil the vines up his legs, shocked by how easily they come to me. Since caging those Alphas on the streets of Dark City, it's felt less like drawing water out of a deep, deep well and more like flexing my fingers. The vines come so easily to me now that it scares me sometimes. All the time. Every time.

What scares me more? When my vines come for Adam, they don't produce thorns…

"You're not a child. Don't make me punish you like one."

"What is that supposed to mean?"

He raises an eyebrow. "Bend you over my knee."

He drops his gaze to my hips and I burn all over. I open my mouth, seconds from dropping to my knees and begging him to order me to present for him, when the doors to the room burst open. "Don't you dare!"

Sierra throws herself between Adam and me with both arms spread to the sides, like a referee at a boxing match prepared to block us from going at one another. "Do you know how long it took Meredith to do her makeup? If you mess it up for the third time, she'll skin me and kill you both."

Adam grins and I hate the way it makes everything below my waist dissolve. I'm a puddle of melted knees, looking at him like this. I can't believe I confessed to falling…no…it was a moment of weakness, nothing more. Right now, I've got a clear head and I remember that the Berserker of Dark City is really just a dick with occasionally good intentions and a suit perfectly tailored to his trim hips and his broad shoulders.

Way too perfectly tailored. I bite my bottom lip, hating Pri in this moment.

He clears his throat and my gaze pulls back up to his face. His beard's grown back in and that's not helping, either. I told him never to cut it and he's a man who understands direction. It's an unruly mess, almost as bad as his hair, and the contrast looks absolutely deadly against that suit, which is all crisp lines in overlapping shades of grey.

The dress Pri fitted me for arrived earlier and a woman called Meredith helped me with my hair and makeup, but she had a bit of a rough go of it. The first time Adam came into my room and saw me in a tight black dress with spaghetti straps and a slit all the way up to the hip, he advanced on me wordlessly, grabbed the dress by either side of the slit and tore it all the way up the side. Then he bent me over the vanity.

Pri, being the clever woman she is, sent me three backup dresses. The second dress didn't survive Adam's lust either, so we're on the third now — a maroon number that weirdly doesn't clash with my red hair and that has long sleeves. I hope, for my own sake, that we don't have to go to dress four because it's dark green velvet and makes me feel like Garden Girl, much less like the Omega of Dark City.

I'm the Omega of Dark City.

I swallow hard, fists balling and clenching as Adam's glare fixes itself to my dress's deep V. "Sierra, you're going to move out from between me and my Omega. My Berserker doesn't like that shit."

Sierra curses, but backs up to the door. "Just…stay calm, Berserker."

"The fuck am I supposed to do that when my Omega's bein' a naughty fuckin' girl?"

I feel heat flood my face and take a half step back that pulls Adam a full foot forward and makes Sierra curse again. "Dragnovic…" she hisses in warning.

I'm getting hotter and hotter and push my hair back over my shoulder and fan my neck. My hair…it's actually been *styled* for the first time in my life. It's been coiffed into curls that fall all the way down my back. Half of it is up in braids and twists that look kinda pretty, keeping it off of my face.

I can't really wear makeup with all my freckles…at least, that's what Adam said. He took one look at me with makeup on and I thought he was gonna kill Meredith. Then after he fucked me the first time, he told Meredith to wipe off the shit. She reapplied lipstick, blush and some smoky eye makeup that makes my eyes itch. I haven't worn makeup before in my life. Have never worn a dress, either. Not sure I like it, but I do like the way Adam looks at me when I'm wearing it.

"Everybody out," Adam orders.

"No way in hell," Whiskey says, making me jolt. She appears like a spectre in the doorway behind Sierra. "You two need adult supervision."

Adam glares at Whiskey, but she doesn't back down. She stands at the door, keeping it propped open with one foot, and adjusts the lapel of her suit jacket since she refused to wear a dress. Calling it a suit is even a bit of a stretch. In all black with a leather sling crisscrossing her chest underneath her jacket, she looks ready for combat.

Finally, he sighs and removes his suit jacket. He tosses it to her and unbuttons his cuffs, then begins methodically rolling up his right sleeve. Oh. My. God. Why is this so attractive? I've seen his forearms before, but watching the starched white material move slowly up, up, up over his tanned, scarred skin, watching the muscles ripple beneath it, standing taut, and then relaxing…oh my…

I glance at the vanity behind me, looking for a weapon. I grab the mirror and hold it out in front of me like a sword. Adam smirks, "I look like Medusa?"

"What?"

"Not gonna use a mirror to turn me into stone."

"I still don't get the reference."

His eyes glitter with something a little different…a little more like sadness. He swallows. "You be good and I'll give you storytime before bed tonight."

I just firm my grip around the mirror's handle when he lifts two fingers and gestures at me to come. His fingers move in this quick motion that reminds me way too much of the way it feels when he uses those fingers inside me.

"Stop it," I hiss.

He actually gets a surprised look on his face, maybe at the volume of my tone or the accusation. "What am I doin', wife?"

Wife. There it is again. And once again, I ignore it. "You know what you're doing?" I say, voice pitched as a question. "You're trying to distract me and it won't work. I'm not doing it. I'm not wearing a fucking collar!"

I point my weapon at the thing on the sideboard. Glistening black platinum, it shimmers menacingly. Adam takes it in his hand and lifts the chain it's attached to. "Every Omega has to wear one."

"Decided by who? You stupid Berserker Alpha bastards! You said you're changing things, so change them, because I'm not doing it!"

"Look at it like a piece of jewelry," Sierra offers.

"You wear it then!"

Sierra frowns and a blush rises in her cheeks. "You know what? On second thought, we'll be waiting right outside." She backs out of the room, pushing Whiskey along with her, and closes the door with a quiet click. I don't dare watch her go, too focused on Adam and worrying about a potential ambush if I let down my guard.

His smile has slipped into a frown but his focus is unflinching and I'm worried — real worried — that I'm not going to make it out of this with my pride intact.

He opens his mouth, but I gasp, "Don't make me, Berserker. Please. Don't do that."

He grunts and there's anger in his tone, but I don't get the sense that it's directed at me. "You think I wanna have you chained to my wrist all night?"

"Yes."

"Damn right. Want you chained to me so that way I can watch every single fucker who's gonna look at you too long so I can remember whose convoy I need to ambush on their way back to wherever they came from. You're mine to protect and mine to serve. I'm your Berserker..."

"Then why do *I* have to wear the collar?"

Adam exhales through his nostrils. They flare and his jaw sets. He takes another step towards me and I lunge to meet him and whack him on the outside of the wrist with the mirror's edge. "Jesus, woman. Look, I'll make a deal with you."

"I don't wanna deal."

"You will when you hear the terms."

I wait.

Adam grits his teeth and I know what he's going to say before he does. "You wear the collar just for tonight and I'll take you to find the witch in the woods."

"The Omega?"

He nods jerkily and I can tell it takes his whole damn being to give me this thing that I've asked for.

"You already promised me that."

"We'll leave day after tomorrow."

I freeze. Yeah, he's made general statements, but anytime I've brought it up, he's brushed me off, saying that we need to wait for my arm to heal and then after it healed, for Ward to finish her analysis of the venom and then after she finished her analysis, for the Ball…there's always something. He's never laid down a date before.

I replay his words, wondering where the trap is. Finding it, I narrow my glare and firm my grip on the mirror. "*And* we'll find the man in the cave." He came to me again last night and he sounded so sad. So desperate. In pain.

"No."

I frown.

He frowns.

We frown at each other.

I glance at the stupid bangle dangling off of his fingertip and frown even harder. "If I wear that thing, you *have* to take me to Paradise Hole *until* we find Freya." And once we're there, I'll convince him to take me farther.

"The Omega?" I nod. He also frowns harder. "How d'you know her name?"

"I told you. The man in the cave. He has more to tell us, too. More about Trash City and the Fates and the Alpha zombies."

"Reanimated corpses. That's what Ward's callin' 'em, anyway," he grumbles.

"Zombies." I insist.

"Don't matter. Not gonna see him. You got this one shot to go see your Omega, too. After that, window's closed."

I glance at the stupid collar, knowing that he means it. He'll do anything I want when he's fuckin' my brains out, but even at the height of his rut, on this, he won't budge. He does not want to go back into Paradise Hole. Neither do I. But the dream keeps coming, harder, stronger. Since my heat ended, I haven't slept through one single night.

"Fine," I growl.

Adam blinks, looking surprised before determination takes over. He crosses the room, gaze traveling up and down my body as he stalks towards me. "You look pretty," he says, like petty words will distract me from wanting to carve his heart out of his scarred chest.

"Fuck you, Alpha."

"Berserker."

"You're being an Alphahole right now, so I'll call you Alpha."

His low laughter rumbles in my ear as he circles behind me and gently lifts my hair off of my neck. "Call me Alpha again and you'll pay for it."

"I'm already paying for it."

"Nah. Tradin' for it. But call me Alpha again and I won't just collar you, I'll walk you into the damn Ball in front of all those people crawlin' on your hands and knees, like my pet."

I shiver, an unexpected surge of wetness slipping down my leg. I can feel Adam's chest brush my back. He stiffens behind me. "Fuck you, Omega."

Yes, is all I can think, though I whisper, "Don't."

The latch on the collar clicks into place and I swallow as the smooth platinum settles around my throat, fitting far, far too well. "You're mine to do what I like with, this night and every other. Don't forget it."

He arches over me and plants a kiss beside my ear, his lips warm, leaving behind soft dew. He bites my ear just enough to break the skin, just a little bit, but it's enough for the venom from his fang to sink into my blood and poison me with a desire difficult to fight through.

"Is this how you talk to your wife?" I beg, trying to distance myself from the situation.

And then I hear his slight intake of breath seconds before the burnished platinum cuff clinks into place around his wrist. A delicate platinum chain connects us.

"This is exactly how I talk to my wife." His warm breath brushes the top of my head, through all my many red curls, and then his voice cracks when he whispers, "When will you call me husband?"

I close my eyes, trying to block out the pressure in my chest. I feel grief…a grief that might be his or mine or shared between us…just a little bit. Like a whisper through one of those old tin can telephones we made when we were Beta kids living in the Grasslands. They were the only toys we had. The memory hurts because it fills me with both happiness and sadness in equal measure. Or maybe, neither. Maybe, just… *longing*.

I turn in his grasp and step out of it, the chain stringing itself taut between us. I step back as far as the chain will allow. "When we're equal."

He winces and looks down, a look of consternation furrowing his brows. He opens his mouth to speak, but doesn't. There's nothing to say. I know that. *He* didn't write history and make things for Omegas this way. Why then am I still so disappointed?

"Can we go now?" I say and I reach between us for the chain and give it a good yank.

Adam's gaze shutters and his lips tense. He nods down at me once and then leads me to the party.

Torture. It's pure torture. "Yes, a pleasure to see you, too, N'dogo." Ruby City Berserker is here with her Omega. A male, one of the few. She fought hard to claim him and shows him off whenever she gets the chance. I don't suppose my Omega likes seein' him in the um…attire she's selected for him, but whatever makes them happy is their own business.

"He's wearing a dog costume," my Omega says the minute we're excused.

"Was." I nod, answering in the affirmative.

"And he looked like he liked it. He was panting and woofing."

"Like a dog."

"Yes. But wasn't he hot? It was entirely made out of plastic. Could he even breathe?"

"*That's* your problem with it?"

She nods. I look over her shoulder and down into her eyes. She tilts her face up to me, so open, so damn wild. So fuckin' beautiful. "Whatever gets them off in the bedroom ain't a problema mine." My lips twitch and I can't help but chuckle. Try to rein it in, though, as I scan the crowd of assholes assembled, lookin' for the ones I invited. Technically, I invited everyone. But I'm lookin' for the ones I shoulda killed a long time ago.

"What's wrong?" she whispers, pivoting her body towards mine.

"Nothin'."

Her wide, inviting gaze turns to a glare. "I know something's wrong. You're practically strangling me."

She rolls her shoulders back and I drop my hand from where I'd had it positioned around her neck. Holdin' her just above the collar makes me feel less like I'm leadin' her around like a pet — less like a piece of shit. *Unworthy*.

"Sorry. I'm sorry," I repeat, clearin' my throat and strugglin' to meet her gaze. *When we're equal…* I fought so hard for my seat, I…wasn't expectin' to have to share it. But I need to make space. I need to learn. I need…her. Just her. And I want her to look at me like I'm *somebody*. "Nothin's wrong. Just gotta take a piss."

"I'm not following you into the bathroom."

"Think a Berserker holds his own dick when he takes a piss? Nah. That's what Omegas with soft hands are for," I try teasing, try to move us back onto safer ground.

She smirks, taking the bait, "Good luck with that. You've seen my hands before." She lifts her palms and waggles her fingers at me, showing off her calluses with pride. I think she might be the only woman in here without their nails painted, or their hair dyed. Still managed to put a little bit a' makeup on 'er though. Not that she needs it. She looks good all the damn time.

I take her left palm in mine and rub my thumb across its battle-hardened center. "You think I meant you? Nah, baby. Why d'you think I invited so many Omegas here?" I chuckle, continuing to tease, knowin' my Omega doesn't like that she feels jealous of me, and knowin' I like it far, far too much and I'm…feelin' wounded. I'm a selfish fuck to do this to her just so I can feel the reassurance of the fire that sparks in her eyes.

My cock stiffens in my suit pants as she turns to face me and I open my mouth to laugh it off, but she's quicker than me. She lunges, crossing the distance between us until her breasts are crushed against my chest. While I flounder, she reaches between our bodies and grabs my erection through my pants so hard I go numb below the waist. I grab her wrist with my free hand, but she just squeezes tighter.

"*Fuck*," I hiss, drawin' out the word. "Omega…"

Her gaze flashes. She bites her front teeth together and pulls her dark reddish brown eyebrows together over her speckled nose. So many damn freckles. Wanna draw star maps across all of 'em, creatin' constellations meant for me alone. "If you let another Omega touch you, I'll cut your balls off while you sleep." I feel them…the vines…liftin' up from the floor and glidin' over my shoes, comin' up the legs of my pants and wrappin' around my shins. Fuckin' savage, my Omega. I wonder if she even knows she's doin' it.

"And if an Omega touches you, I'll take her down." I shiver when the vines reach my knees and it takes all the willpower I got in me to keep standin' as I fall so fuckin' hard for her. "I'll tear her to pieces."

My voice is thick when I speak, but I force myself not to twitch, not to let her know that I'm a little freaked and creeped out by her — and aroused more than both. "Don't think her Alpha'll like that."

"I'll kill him, too."

I lean towards her, well aware we're bein' observed. Eyes follow my Echo wherever she goes. She's the star a' the night. Star a' this whole fuckin' galaxy. "Can't go around killin' Alphas in Dark City. 'Cause me a tonna paperwork seein' as you're the Dark City Omega n' all."

"Then treat me like it."

Oh? That a challenge? I grin and her brow flattens, her face transforming from rage to a skeptical concern.

"I…" she starts.

I grab her by the waist, shove the high slit of her dress aside, bypass the flimsy scrap of fabric that passes for her underwear and slip two fingers inside of her. "You mean like this?"

She squeals, grabs onto my upper arms and brings our bodies together, tryna hide herself from view. "We're in the middle of people!" she squeaks, voice hiccuping with restrained laughter as she forgets her vindictiveness and her hurt.

"Like this, Omega?" I whisper. I move my hand slowly, gliding in and out of her wet heat. She's so fuckin' wet for me already. I glance up and see eyes watchin' us from near and far. Catch Sierra's gaze. She's talkin' to a pack a' Alphas from Rookery and the Omega with her neck chained and her head bowed between them. Gettin' Echo into the damn collar was hard enough. Teachin' her that she's supposed to keep her gaze down in a sign a' submission the whole damn night woulda been impossible. I grin savagely at the Alpha pack, meetin' each of their eyes as I work my Omega into a fuckin' hurricane.

One hand possessively around the back of her neck, my lips pressed to the top of her head, I hold her firm while her left knee buckles slightly and she clings to me. "You're the only Omega for me, wife."

"Mhmmm," she moans.

"Shh. You make a sound, I stop and leave you like this."

"Fuck you, Alpha."

I release her immediately, slap her clit, pull my hand out from under her skirt and look away from Sierra cuttin' me with a glare and the pack Alphas gettin' all agitated. "Paradise Hole's good for breedin' murderous little Omegas, but not very obedient ones."

Echo's chest is heavin'. She pushes her mussed curls back over her shoulder, combing them behind her right ear. She shakes her head and I can see her dilated pupils strugglin' to focus on me. My cock is in full-fledged agony, but I draw up the techniques I learned as a Beta for dealin' with torture. I pull out a box, take off the lid, move my pain into it, seal it shut, walk it down a long stretch a' hallway, open a closet door, stick it on the top shelf, turn out the lights, and slam the door shut, leavin' my cock — my pain, my frustration, my agony — behind me.

I exhale through my nose, tryna keep up the appearance that I'm unaffected. She gets one whiff of vulnerability from me, my Paradise Hole Omega's goin' in for the kill. "You… you're…" She sniffles.

I lift my hand to my mouth and lick my fingers clean. Her pupils dilate further and the box I got locked up in my head? Yeah, that fucker pulses with its own heartbeat.

"Why do you like to provoke me like that? It…it isn't nice."

Fuck. She shakes her head, comin' down and tries to step away from me. The chain jangles between us and she glances at it and *fuck*. There it is. She breaks me just like that. She doesn't even have to try. I wrap her chain around my fist and reel her in until we're nose-to-nose. I slide my hand over her cheek, cupping the back of her neck.

I exhale in a jerky breath, "Because it's fuckin' funny, you thinkin' I could ever look at another Omega when I got you. You…" I lick my lips. The words comin' out of my mouth fuckin' hurt. "You gotta know how I feel about you."

"Jesus, Berserker," Balcazar says, tearin' me outta the moment with her hand on my shoulder. She gives me a yank and I woulda reprimanded her for it had her next words not frozen me in place. "Your Omega's scent is even gettin' to *me* and now might not be the best time for it. Guests of honor have arrived."

The ease in my bones turns to somethin' knotted and feral. Thoughts of my dick in my Omega's not-so-soft hand die instantly. "Thanks." I'm starin' down into my Omega's eyes and several different thoughts coalesce at the same time.

I invited the Fates.

With the Fates come the fuckin' Mirage City Berserker and he's known for wanting to collect the most powerful Omegas.

I have a powerful Omega.

And then one final thought: Am I a fuckin' idiot?

I glance over the hundreds of heads mingling in Echo's garden and see a light shining from the far end of the space. There is commotion there and I know that he has arrived. I don't have much time to get Echo out of here to safety while I confront Mirage City about the zombies his Fates created.

"Fuck." I shake my head, wantin' Echo outta here, but not wantin' her to know why. "You…you want me to finish what I've started, you go to the bathroom and make yourself come."

She just stares.

"Go, Omega."

She pouts and she looks so damn cute when her bottom lip juts out. "I…you…"

I swoop down and capture her earlobe between my teeth, then suck it into my mouth until I feel her body sway towards me. Happens right away. I bite down hard enough to break the skin, affectin' her with my venom while she distracts me with the taste of her blood. Dark and bitter with an aftertaste like caramel, it's sinful and… Focus. *Focus!*

"Go, baby."

"What are you hiding from me?"

"Nothin'." I step back and watch her shift uncomfortably, the color still high in her cheeks. She frowns at me, but I don't let her displeasure — or her arousal — distract me from keepin' her safe. I unclip her chain from the cuff at my wrist. Feels wrong doin' it in every possible way. I rub the metal around my wrist over and over and don't look at it as I say, "Balcazar, take her. Make sure nobody bothers her."

I hand Balcazar the chain and Echo looks at the Alpha woman with a blush in her cheeks. "You don't have to hold that..." she starts.

"I do. Any Omega with an open chain means her Alpha's declared her free for use by any a' the guests."

Echo's eyes bulge out of her head. She holds the backs of her arms and she glares up at me with accusation, with a disgust that reminds me of my promises to change all this shit. "I know," I hiss. "And I'll fix it." I'll fix all of it. The zombies. Maengor and his Fates. Trash City. The man in the goddamn cave. The witch a' the woods. I'll make it all better for my Omega.

"Don't box me out," she says. "You said we'd do stuff together."

I grimace and nod at her once. *I'm not.* It's on the tip of my tongue to tell her as much, but I don't want to lie to her. I promised myself I wouldn't. So I don't say anything at all. I cock my head towards the manor and give her my back. I stalk off, refusing to acknowledge the look a' hurt on her face. Hurt and disgust.

I rub my fingers over my scalp roughly, undoing all the good work the Beta female Meredith put into taming the mane of my hair. A Beta server walks by and I swivel, swiping a highball glass from the tray and draining it. Bitter and brutal, the alcohol carves a path down my throat that makes it easier for me to breathe. *Don't storm after her.* I can't storm after her. I don't have Maengor's head on a platter yet. All I've got are half-truths and empty promises. *Unworthy.*

"Berserker Dragnovic."

The glass in my hand cracks. I drop it and turn towards the dark, chilling voice calling out to me. But it's not the monster, I'm searching for. Instead, I see a face that's equally surprising. "Berserker Yaron."

His eyes, the color and intensity of a storm cloud, bore into me. I fight not to narrow my own gaze against the invasion, but he is a male who wears power like a cloak and, after the Mirage City Berserker, is the most powerful Berserker among us.

And he keeps no Omega.

He better not be sniffin' after mine. "You flatter me. It's a far journey from the south island to Dark City." My hackles rise, the urge to challenge strong. I settle, though, when his gaze remains firmly tacked to me.

"I need to speak with you." With no further prelude, he stalks past me to the edge of the garden, disappearing beneath the hanging branches that mark its circumference.

I take one last glance over my shoulder, searchin' for Echo in the crowd, but I don't find her. Frustrated and disappointed *in myself*, I turn and follow Berserker Yaron into the dark, his black cape rustlin' in a slight wind. The sound a' his cape slashes like a whip and is louder than his footsteps even though he's in boots — heavy shitkickers that clash violently with the fact that the rest of his attire is shot straight from the Dark Ages. He's in black riding pants and a black tunic that's unbuttoned to his pecs. He turns to face me when we're almost a quarter mile out onto my property, out from underneath my Omega's flower dome.

He walks until we're halfway across a bridge that overlooks the now black waters of a still creek. There is no moon overhead. I see him best through the eyes of my Berserker. I don't like how he watches me from beneath his prominent brow, the wells of his eyes deep. His hair is dark, streaked with grey at the temples, his clothes are dark, his beard is a shadow on the bottom half of his face and he's just taller than I am, leaner though. Wouldn't hesitate to kill him if it came to it, but somehow, standin' with him here on this small wooden bridge in a place I'd bring Echo and find it romantic, I don't think it'll come to that.

And then he says the last words I'd have thought to hear from him. Words that floor me. "What do you know of the dead Alpha army?"

ECHO
OMEGA BALL

THE GROTESQUERY THAT THESE ALPHAHOLES CALL A Ball is made more abhorrent by the fact that I. staged. the. venue. I'm so mad at Adam I could gouge his eyes out and I plan to try as soon as I get him alone tonight, away from all these people. Their eyes on me make me itch and I stay in the bathroom for as long as I can. Balcazar waits outside. And she keeps waiting.

She knocked once a few minutes ago, or maybe it was longer than that… How long was it?

I frown at the door in front of me and stand up from where I'm seated on the lid of the toilet. I go to the door and even though *I'm* the one in the bathroom pissed off and *she's* the one outside supposedly watching me, I'm still the one to knock on the back of the door and shout, "Balcazar, are you still there?"

No response. Not even a whisper.

"Balcazar?" What the fuck? "Are you alive?" I realize I need an audience for my tantrum, which isn't so much a tantrum really as it is a call for justice and humanity.

Though what is humanity in a world of Alphas? She'd probably punish me worse than Adam for the thought that Omegas and Betas should somehow enjoy equal rights. At least more rights than caged animals.

I'm not a fuckin' chump, despite how complacent these last weeks have made me outside of Paradise Hole. I know better than to believe Adam can change things for Betas and Omegas in Dark City, if he even plans to try…if he even wants to. It's still hard to reconcile this…disappointment with how I feel about him. I…like him. I like him more than I should. Even when he's a dick to me. Maybe, even more then. Because it's the same defense mechanism I have. I understand it and even find comfort in it.

But I don't like when he lies to me. There was some reason he sent me away with Balcazar. I want to know what it is. I should probably follow and confront him, instead of wallowing in here. But…

"Balcazar?"

When I still get no response, I turn away from the sleek modern bathroom that's all marble countertops and bronze fixtures and pop my head outside into the hallway. In this part of the castle, the hallways are all dark wallpaper embossed with designs I can't make out and black and white swirly marble flooring. It's fine, but what gets to me are the paintings. Some of them are landscapes — most are landscapes — but they're quite abstract, a little sad, and mostly filled with longing. Or maybe, that's just what I see when I stare at them for too long. Whatever the case, they all make me think of Adam.

I can hear the party still in full swing through the glass double doors hanging open to my left. The crazy garden that Adam insists I conjured up while fucking him stretches from the winter balcony out all the way to the garden house. The green dome glows, illuminated by the lights strung up beneath the canopy. The Beta orchestra is playing on the far side of the space while waiters weave in and out of the crowd carrying trays covered in opulence. There are hundreds of Alphas here, but I've only seen a few Omegas, identifiable by their collars, and so far all of them have been female except for the man in the dog costume, and not one of them has met my gaze.

"Balcazar?" Across this open space is another bathroom, but the door remains shut even as I will it open with my mind. Too bad my gifts don't extend to manifesting people in front of me because that would come in handy right about now.

I glance right, down the hall. It's dark because — of course — it has to be dark. Then I look left, towards the winter balcony and the brightly lit festivities beyond it. I chew on my bottom lip, weighing my options, knowing I'm going to need to make a calculated decision or hang out in the bathroom for the rest of the night.

Voices come from the dark end of the hall. I crane my neck towards them, hoping to hear familiar tones, but I can't make them out clearly. Spying the lightswitch hanging between two paintings on the shadowy edge of darkness, I make my choice, take a calculated risk, grab the end of my goddamn chain, ball it in my fist and scamper over to the switch.

I flip the switch up and down and nothing happens. Cursing to myself, I repeat the process a dozen times. "Balcazar?" No answer. The voices at the end of the hall have gone silent. "Fuck me."

I turn, prepared to run back into the bathroom and wait out the party there for all the craps I give, but I slam nose-first into a chest. A male chest. A *Berserker's* chest. And I know instinctively who it is.

I slap a hand over my mouth and step back, my once wounded arm gathering the chain to my chest. He grins and his eyes twinkle with a devilish gleam. "It is a pleasure to meet you. My Fates have told me such wonderful things."

I don't give a shit who this man thinks he is, or what he thinks my status is as an Omega. I'm from Paradise Hole and I won't be intimidated. "I know who you are and I will defend myself, Berserker."

"What makes you think I would come all this way to quarrel with a little Omega like you?" He laughs and takes another step forward and I notice that his voice is strange and melodic, belonging to someone much less gruff than he appears. "I come for bigger fish." He takes a step forward, but I hold my fucking ground, even as his scent fills my nose and confuses me. He smells like something rotten.

Like something dead.

I repress a violent shudder and firm my shoulders by my ears. "I may hate the bastard, but make no mistake in thinking I won't defend him, too. He's *my* Berserker to hate and neither of us will have anything to do with you." I step back. My chain rattles as I lift my hand and point my fist at his nose. "We don't concern ourselves with the *dead*. Only the living."

I lift a brow in challenge, but his expression is doing something…else, something that makes me wonder if he's listening to me at all. He'd been watching me with wide eyes and a soft, condescending smile, but as soon as my last word was uttered, that smile dipped.

His whole glowing aura slips, like a record skipping, or a slide on a petri dish shifting momentarily out of place before the magnifying glass refocuses. What is this disease I'm left looking at? Sallow, jaundiced skin barely clinging to its skeletal frame. Black and brown teeth rotten in their skull. Bone-thin, liver-spotted hands. Eyes…the eyes are still bright though.

The monster that is the feared Mirage City Berserker lunges abruptly towards me and I freeze, going cold to the bone as his hand returns to its previous form — glowing golden and perfect — and strokes just the outer edge of my arm so lightly I'm not even sure we're touching. I can feel only the raising of hairs on the back of my forearm.

I open my mouth to tell him he's not allowed to touch me and that I'll fight, but I find that I can't move at all. My tongue goes stiff in my mouth and acute terror and paralysis take over every inch of my body. I can't call for help. I can't draw on my gifts.

The Berserker's full, flushed lips twitch — I can feel the movement a breath away from my cheek. He leans in even closer and as he speaks directly into my ear, darkness begins to eat away at the edges of my vision. I feel myself plunged back into that icy river. I feel my skin scraped off of the bone by the Trash City docs. Every pain and every horror I've ever lived comes cascading back in bright, violent slashes. The attack is so violent, I know I won't survive it. I clutch at my throat. *Adam.* I want to call for him. Because in my final moments, Adam is the one I want most. The only one.

I'm falling and the Berserker before me is whispering in a voice that is not the one he used before, "You search for the man in the cave. Don't. Because if you find him, Adam will die. It's a trap."

And then I pass out.

ADAM
OMEGA BALL

"I'M HEARING REPORTS THAT MY OUTER VILLAGES ARE being attacked and that the bodies are being stolen for…nefarious purposes." His voice is flat. Skeptical. "I don't believe in these…purposes, but what I do know is that several Alphas within my territory have disappeared. I want to know why and who is taking them."

I meet his gaze in the dark. Look him over. Assess quickly. Decide that I don't trust him as far as I can throw him, which isn't very far considerin' he stacks up pretty decent against me, but I know he's not workin' with Mirage City on this. So I feed him a truth, just a partial truth, but enough to test the waters. "To make zombies."

He releases a gruff snort, nostrils flarin'. "Do you deign to mock me, young Alphalord?"

"No." And I know the last male Alpha who did had his cock sliced off and fed to the crows. The last female Alpha? Her tits. At least, that's how the stories go. The torture chamber beneath his castle is infamous. And antiquated.

Wouldn't want to fall into it for any reason. Here, in Dark City, our punishment mechanisms are far more modern and efficient.

"Then tell me what you know. Who is taking the Alpha bodies and for what purpose? Who is raiding my outer lands?"

I open my mouth, fully intendin' to tell him about Trash City and the Alphas that attacked Echo and I, Mirage City's likely involvement, the venom… But before I do, another question shines louder than the rest. "You're askin' me. Why?"

His stilted, ancient Shadowlands brogue clashes with the growl that rips out of his throat. "I heard another report, this one equally alarming. That only days ago *you* killed *Alphas* in Paradise Hole."

"So that's what the kids are callin' it these days…" I laugh darkly, richly, humorlessly, and rub my fingers through my beard. "I'd go ahead and call it unkilling, and before you ask me again, Berserker, I'm not mocking you. I'm going to tell you the truth of it, and you can choose whether or not to believe me."

And because I'm feelin' a little fucked that the Fates are here and that my Omega's pissed at me and that I've still got the taste of her cunt in the back of my throat and there's nowhere I'd rather be but between her legs and instead gotta waste my damn time figurin' out why Paradise Hole fucks are tryna kill Alphas, why Trash City's bein' supplied with guns and where the goddamn Fates and the Berserker of Mirage City fit into this convoluted fuckin' puzzle, I tell him.

I tell him everyfuckinthing.

When I finish, he doesn't move. Doesn't so much as flinch. He waits, as if expecting more — a joke, per chance? Me to tell him that I've just spent the past ten minutes lyin' to him? When I just stare back, he finally balks. "So, your current theory, young Berserker, is that the Mirage City Berserker is not only contracting villagers and peasants from my territories and vagrants from Paradise Hole to kill Alphas, but that he's then forcing the four Omegas in his territory known as the Fates to reanimate them?"

I nod.

The older Berserker hisses out of one corner of his mouth. He turns to face the stream winding beneath us and grips the rail of the bridge in both of his hands. He bears no scars. He grew up a very different Beta than I did. I try not to be resentful or cynical and remember that Shadowlands is a different territory than Dark City — than any other city on Gatamora — one in which Betas have more rights.

They can keep and raise their children, regardless of how they ascend, or don't. They can work any job they want. They can hold positions of power. They don't have to flee to compounds, or Paradise Hole… That's why, on the south island, there are no Beta compounds…

I think of Echo's words and frown. Why can't Dark City make itself a home to Betas as Shadowlands does? Why can't Dark City do better? Why can't I do better? He's not that much older than I am. But…he was raised to rule. He has all the experience. I don't know shit.

His cloak snaps in a non-existent wind. His hand flexes, Berserker claws momentarily flashing on his fingertips. "To what end?"

"Not sure yet."

"We should confront him." He reaches behind his back, beneath his cloak, and withdraws an axe the size of a fuckin' tire.

"Christ. You know there's no weapons allowed in my fuckin' Ball." My *Omega's* Ball. That's what I should have said. That I didn't irks me and I don't know why.

I shake off the discomfort and come around to the sight of his front teeth mashed together. His fangs peek out over the top of his bottom lip. They're longer than mine and I feel my hackles rise, my Berserker yearnin' to challenge the Berserker in its presence. It's not used to bein' made to feel inferior. I'm *not.* At least, that's what I tell myself.

I take a step forward and a surge of aggression rolls off of the male that makes venom flood my mouth — not the bondin' kind, the killin' kind, though they're one and the same. The muscles across my chest ripple and the buttons on my collared shirt strain. Three buttons down, the strings tryin' valiantly to keep my shirt together pop. I start to stretch. He lifts his axe.

"Do not test me, boy."

"Not the enemy, friend," I sneer, "but you're in my house. Put the weapon down."

I start to transition, but the bastard insults me by remainin' in his Alpha form. "I have no need of my fangs and claws to slaughter a baby Berserker and I have no desire to, either. But I will."

He opens his mouth and his wicked fangs flash. I open mine and issue a deadly rattle. And then just when things move from dangerous to deadly, a soft voice calls out, "The scent of an Alpha's aggression is a lovely thing, is it not, sisters?"

I turn and shiver back into my Alpha skin. My aggression doesn't abate at the sight of the female faces in front of me, but ratchets up to ten.

"The only thing better is a Berserker's." The second female that speaks devolves to giggles.

Berserker Yaron and I exchange a glance and, as if choreographed, we move at the same time to form a line at the base of the bridge, like we're about to go into battle. My mind skips. I feel a momentary spike of fog roll over me. This feels eerily like a premonition of somethin' to come… somethin' horrible.

"Omegas, what are you doing away from your Berserkers, uncollared and unchained?" Yaron's voice comes out deadly. He doesn't put his axe away.

I feel my claws stretch and bend, elongating with the desire to tear into the females coming towards me. Eerie and ethereal, they barely seem to touch the ground as they walk. "Fates," I hiss.

The Fate standing at the front of the group of four looks at me and offers me a small smile, behind which I can read nothing. She's known as Omora. "Berserker Dragnovic. Berserker Yaron."

She tips her head, her eyes unhurried as they look me over. Such an assessment would make my Omega rabid. The thought makes me smirk, until it occurs to me that Echo's been gone for some time. Where is she? I worry until I remember that I've got one of my most trusted Alphas with her.

"Fate," I say at the same time Yaron growls, "Omega."

Her gaze flits to him before returning to me. She has long, silver-white hair, streaked through with hard black, and these clashing colors present an unsettling contrast to the starch-white of her skin. Her eyebrows are just as white as her skin. Her irises are black.

Her Fated sisters look nothing like her, each distinct in their own way. The one to her left, Sy, has jet black hair, white skin and a hostile expression fixed to her obsidian glare. The one to her right, known as Odette, has dark brown hair that falls in braids to the tops of her breasts and medium brown skin.

And the last one…the one just behind the rest, who I know to be named Adoqhina, wears hair as red as Echo's with skin that's an eerily similar hue. She lacks Echo's freckles and has green eyes, but in so many other ways she reminds me of her. The look she gives me doesn't help. It's a scornful look that Echo's mastered and that gaze on me right now does nothing good to my bones. It makes me feel something treacherous — an unwillingness to kill her, because this Omega reminds me so much of my own.

"You two seem so tense." Odette wears a mischievous smirk that, by contrast, makes me want to cause her immeasurable pain. "Are you Berserkers afraid of the dark?" She flourishes her right hand and a sentient flame appears in the center of her palm. I tense.

"Is that a *threat*?" I hiss.

Yaron's voice chimes after mine, "Of course not, Berserker Dragnovic. If it were, it would be punishable by death."

He holds his axe to the side, but the Fate just cocks her head, the cocky little fucker that she is. "It's a fate far worse than death to kill an Omega, especially one that belongs to a Berserker of a different city."

"Especially when she's a Fate," Adoqhina continues, and the sound comes as a shock, a defibrillator straight to the chest. *She sounds like Echo, too*. My heart pounds and I start to sweat as the Fate who looks like Echo looks at me even as she speaks to everyone else. Her green gaze holds mine and she smiles, and I suddenly hallucinate holding her heart in my hands. I hallucinate Echo's death.

"Not when that Omega walks uncollared in a Ball. Dragnovic, have her arrested."

"I-I have questions, first." My lips come unstuck and my tongue, a thick block of wood in my mouth, manages to finally form words.

The Echo doppelgänger smiles at me in a way Echo never would. I force myself not to recoil. There's somethin' sticky and ugly in her expression whereas in Echo's, there's only truth — for better or for worse. *I treat her badly*. Fear grips my heart. Fear that I've done her too much wrong to ever repair in this lifetime, fear that she isn't standin' pressed against my back, her heart beatin' flush with mine, fear that she isn't close enough to protect, fear that something's just…fuckin' *wrong*.

"Of course, Dark City Berserker," Adoqhina says with a slight bow that feels mocking, rather than deferential. "We expected you would." She giggles — *giggles* — making her sound like Echo less and less.

Odette closes her palm and the light goes out, but only for a moment. She closes her palms, pressin' 'em flat together, and as she peels them apart fire crackles between her hands like the strings of a bow, suspended there by nothin'.

Distracted as I am by the magic in display in front of me, I don't react to defend myself when Omora steps forward, moving quickly and soundlessly, like a wraith. I sway. I wonder if Yaron feels it. The energy that pulses between them, through them — *out* of them — that affects everything it touches like sap, saccharine and seductive. It makes me want to close my eyes and lean in, give up and let them take me. *I wonder if this is what Noon once felt.*

Right before they killed her.

The once calm water in the river below sloshes and splashes, spray comin' up and over the railin' high enough to touch my cheeks. The world pulses around me once, twice, a third time. And then her voice *touches* me.

I can see Omora's lips movin', but her voice sounds in my mind a split second later. The delay is disorienting and destabilizing. I try to move away from it, but I can't lift my fuckin' shoes from the bridge, which feels like it's crumblin' beneath my feet, 'bout to send me into another river, only this time, Echo won't be there to keep me from drownin'.

"Omegas, whatever it is you believe yourselves capable of, stop this before I draw blood." I can hear Yaron beside me roarin', but his voice is dimmer than it should be and even though he's standin' right at my shoulder, it's like I'm seein' him through a filter. Purple and yellow spots slide lazily between us, makin' him look like he's ten thousand miles away.

"You cannot draw blood from us," Sy says so sibilantly, soundin' hardly more than a serpent herself.

Yaron raises his axe and it feels like I'm watchin' this shit happen in a dream inside a dream, everythin' caught in slow motion. He brings his blade toward Omora, who I didn't even realize is touchin' my arm, violatin' about a thousand rules atop the thousand rules she's already broken, but she doesn't flinch and his blade doesn't fall.

Instead, the axe is ripped from his grip by the lightest breeze. It thunks down onto the bridge beside him like the discarded toy of a child.

A boom that isn't a sound but a feeling fills the air and I close my eyes and I'm lost in a forest of Echo's lovely red hair.

"You will succeed in finding the army you hunt for," comes Omora's frightening whisper, *"but in your success, you will also find failure. You will fail her. We have seen it in the dreams of an Omega who came to us. Your life stolen at the hands of those you seek, your Omega gutted beside you.*

"The undead army will not be stopped by one Berserker or two or ten. And you will die trying. But if you hand her over now, we can save her. We won't kill her as we did the others. We have need of her. She can help us. Her gifts are strong — the strongest we've felt in decades, perhaps centuries. We will make her a Fate, teach her to control her greatness, teach her to wield it, teach her the art of immortality. We have spoken already with Berserker Maengor. He wants her for his harem. He wants her for a Fate."

Her grip on my arm tightens and my blood runs backwards through my veins, chilling me to the bone, unwindin' time until sunsets rise before me and sunrises set. My nostrils flare and I feel breath come hot out of my mouth, panicked, insecure, *weak*. I feel the muddy swamp risin' around my boots. Hear myself shoutin, *"Noon!"* See her shoutin' back at me, *"Adam."*

Noon uses a name only used by one other person on this planet. And now, here in the present, the Fates want me to give her up.

"Let us give her life and power and glory that you cannot. With you, she will only ever be a liability, crippled by your fears of inadequacy, your many weaknesses… But she dreams greater dreams. We do not need to see inside her mind to know this. Neither do you — she has told you, hasn't she? She wants to go back to Paradise Hole. She wants to run and be free. She who controls the earth cannot be bound by man or beast. Let us take her and protect her. Let us shape her into the Fated Omega that, with you, she will never be."

"No," I say, though the voice isn't mine — or it's mine, but from when I was a Beta, when I was a boy.

I shiver and recoil, frightened in a way I haven't experienced since before I learned to control my pain and my fear and my response to torture. But I wasn't trained for this. This is a torture not of the body, but of the soul.

Of the heart.

A soft sigh. The air around me ripples. *"Then she will fall at your side, her blood on your hands. We have seen it, Berserker, and we will not be able to stop it."*

"Berserker Dragnovic." A booming voice pulls me from the delusion.

I blink and the world refocuses. The Fates are nowhere near me, not even Omora, who stands over fifteen feet away. I jerk, blink, glance around and find that Berserker Yaron isn't at my side, axe fallen. He's behind me, axe still raised. The bunching of his eyebrows is the only indication at all that he's aware that anything is amiss.

"What..." he starts to say, meeting my gaze, but my attention is pulled forward by the sound of crunching vines and flowers.

"Dragnovic," the intruder says again and my entire body immolates as I register Berserker Maengor standin' on the flower-studded grass just before the bridge, his Four Fuckin' Fates on his left. In his right hand, he carries a chain, and at the end of that chain stands my Omega. I can't breathe. He smiles at me and in his smile I know that Omoro may be a fuckin' ass hole, but she's not a liar.

Echo's gonna die in Paradise Hole fallen beside me gutted if I don't do somethin'.

I gotta defy fate.

And Echo's not gonna fuckin' like how I do it.

ADAM

DRAGNOVIC MANOR

"I'M NOT GOING TO APOLOGIZE! I DIDN'T DO ANYTHING wrong. And what you did to Balcazar is fucked up! She didn't do anything wrong, either!" Echo writhes in my grip, thrashing back and forth, trying to claw and tear at me with her blunt nails, but she doesn't call on her gifts now and I don't know why. *Or maybe, I do know. Maybe, it's because she trusts* —

No. It doesn't matter. The only thing that matters is her safety.

My heart pounds out of time with the pulse throbbing across my forehead. I see red. All I see is red.

After tearin' the party apart and tearin' Echo's garden down, I beat the living shit out of Balcazar who I found passed out in the hallway where she shoulda been watchin' my fuckin' wife, then I beat the shit out of the rest of the Six who tried to stop me. Now the wreckage is outside and I'm haulin' Echo's insubordinate ass inside the garden house, up the fuckin' stairs, into her bedroom — *our bedroom* — where she shoulda been this whole fuckin' time, and then I throw her onto the bed.

"If you think for even one second I'm going to present for you, you're fucking crazy!" She shrieks, her red curls, fallen from their silken perch are now a tornado around her face. She throws an accusing finger up at me. It's unpainted. Why the fuck does it turn me on so much that her goddamn fingernails are unpainted?

"What are you doing, Adam?" she shouts, kickin' out with her legs, backin' up until she slams her head on the headboard. I reach past her, grab the wrought iron bedframe and rip a post free. To cage her complaints, I straddle her thighs, loop the loose end a' her chain through the iron post, bend the iron in my hand into a loop around another post in the headboard, usin' it to lock her in place. Now she'll never be able to get away.

There.

Done.

What I shoulda done when I brought her back to Dark City in the first place.

"What did you… Adam." Her eyes bug outta her fuckin' skull, which is small and shapely and far too fuckin' breakable. I slam a pillow behind her head and shove her onto her back, then I climb off a' her and rub my face roughly. I glance at the window. There's moonlight tonight, slippin' in through a break in the perpetual cloud cover. I hate it. Why tonight? We never see the sky here and the break in the clouds now makes everythin' that shoulda been romantic look suddenly sinister.

"Adam, look at me."

I head to the door, strides purposeful and determined. Get there and look back at her with a feelin' that's as unwanted as it is unexpected. Hatred. Hate her for doin' this to me. For makin' me weak. For bringin' me right back to that moment that I failed Noon when Maengor's fuckin' Alphas took her away from me.

"Her name was Noon," I say, though I don't know why. I look at her and watch her brows furrow and flatten, watch her rage spike and die. "My sister's name was Noon and that fucker…he had a squadron of Alphas come and take her away. Didn't want me around as a liability, so he gave me to Dark City, while he gave her to his Fates like a fuckin' steak dinner to a hungry fuckin' hound. They tore her apart."

"Adam…"

"Don't know how, don't wanna know how, but I'm not fuckin' givin' you to them. They say I'm gonna die for you and that might be fuckin' true — do it for you easy — but you're not gonna die, too."

"Adam!"

"Nah." Her panic gouges at my insides. I close my eyes, take a breath, then open 'em again and tell it to her straight. "I'm gonna go out and find the fucker and his Fates and do what I shoulda done a long time ago."

"Adam, please!"

"Gonna kill 'em."

"It's supposed to be both of us. You promised we'd investigate the dead army together."

"I'll be back in a few days. Maybe a week or two. Ward is gonna watch you 'til I'm back and, if I don't come back, gonna give her orders to have you taken back to Trash City and give that fucker Merlin whatever she needs to take care a' you."

"Adam!" She kicks her feet, bangs her fists on the bed beside her. She tries to sit up, jerkin' hard on the collar around her neck — a collar I promised her wasn't meant to cage her. Maybe, it's what I promised myself. *I lied and I'm fuckin' fine with it.*

I refuse to cower from the hurt in her gaze, but meet her stare straight on. Her brown eyes glitter light and bright and bore holes through my skull, but that don't matter. I'm a Berserker and she's mine and this is my right. *This is what she expected of a Berserker. This is what she feared. This is why she tried to kill herself rather than come with me.*

"You won't…*hurt* yourself when I'm gone." My voice trembles. Did she hear it? Hope not.

"You…" Her breathin' steadies and her voice hitches on the word in a way that makes me hesitate, wait, wonderin' what's comin'…fearin' it, too. "Adam, you are the worst thing that's ever happened to me. I hope you fucking die in Paradise Hole."

She called me Adam. Not Berserker. Adam.

I snarl, rage makin' my legs stiff and my venom drip more viscous down my throat. I can feel with acute clarity every place my scars shift against the fabric of my shirt and in each wound is a message in a bottle. They're all the same. They all read: Failure.

"Not gonna let anybody hurt you, Echo. You're my wife, my heart, the most important thing to me. Whatever I need to do to ensure your safety, I'm gonna do it. Even if it means I gotta lie, break promises and chain you to my bed. Not gonna be forever. Just until they're dead. Maengor and all his Fates and his army of the dead."

She settles back against the pillows, her left arm held upright where she grips the chain, revealin' a scar that cuts from the back of her hand down to her elbow. *I did that.* She inhales deeply and exhales audibly through her nose. Her nostrils flare, freckles dancin' across 'em. Wanna kiss her so fuckin' bad right now. Wanna pull her close. Want our bodies together one last time. Why the fuck does it feel like a last time?

I take a step forward.

"I will *never* be your wife." She looks at me with such revulsion, a stare I didn't even win from her the very first time she saw me and she tried to kill me by bringin' a tree down on my head — ten trees. Then, she looked at me like I coulda been any Alpha she hated. Now, she looks at me like I'm *Adam*, who betrayed her.

I feel like arguin', rippin' her to shreds, but I don't. Moonlight streamin' in through the window glints off the collar around her neck.

My stomach hollows, heart droppin' through the hole it leaves behind and into my ass. Feel like takin' a shit. Feel like killin' Fates. Feel like apologizin' to my Omega. I'll do all three, but I'll start with the Fates first.

"Gonna be back to fix this," I tell her, takin' a step backwards through the door, but as I close it to the sight of her stare, I know there's no comin' back from this.

The Fates were right. I lost my Omega.

The Fates were wrong. Didn't have to die to do it.

I lost 'er all by my fuckin' self.

ECHO
DRAGNOVIC MANOR

THREE DAYS GO BY. THREE DAYS GO BY AND I'M STUCK to the bed. I can't get off of it. I can't get out of it. I'm chained to the whims and will of a Berserker, left behind to be used and abused by him under the pretense of protection.

Three days of plotting and unsuccessful attempts at escape.

Three days of hate.

I hate him. I hate him with everything I've got. I *hate* him. I hate him even more knowing that I was so close to giving him a real shot — giving us a real shot. And I hate me for the things I said to him when we were in the back of that car, those lifetimes ago when he stood up for Betas and spoke down to Alphas and promised them things would change — promised me he'd change things because of me. That he'd do anything for me that would take him any amount of will or effort, any sacrifice to his pride, any risk. He's such a fucking…

No. Calling him an asshole doesn't cut it. He's Adam and I hate him with every piece of my broken heart.

I think about what'll happen when he comes back, replay it in my mind over and over. Think about the things I'll say to him, what I'll do when he finally lets me up off of the bed and gives me new clothes. I think about the promise I made him — no, the vow, the threat.

I *will* get out of here if it's the last thing I do. He'll have to build a dungeon like the one I've heard about in Shadowlands and chain me up to keep me from leaving Dark City because I'm not staying here with the lying Berserker snake, in his bed, in this house he calls *mine*, pretending to be a wife that I'm not and never will be because Adam is gone. He got bit by zombie Berserkers in Paradise Hole. He died along with them.

What happened in the thing that wasn't a nest but just a pile of rags on the floor doesn't mean anything. What happened in the car, out in Dark City at the coffee shop, doesn't matter either. What happened outside in the puddle he calls a garden matters even less.

My nipples stiffen as my body remembers the feeling of his. It all comes back to me in a blur, but now those memories don't feel like they did. They feel like scars that cut deeper than the ones he marked me with that very first night.

I shake my head, sitting up and pulling the blankets with me. It's cold and the breeze filtering in through the window the Beta servant cracked is icy. Underneath the blankets, I'm naked. No one gave me anything to wear after I kicked off my dress considering that, after Balcazar's beat down, no one's been willing to go against a single edict of the Dark City

Berserker. So far, the only explicit instructions he's given are to feed me and give me stuff to drink. I have to use a bucket for a bathroom that a Beta servant, standing in the corner, takes away from me after I've finished. It's humiliating.

Tears spring to my eyes and I think about trying to hurt myself. I glance at the lamp on the bedside table. It's porcelain. I could probably break it or the bulb and try to gouge my wrists open, but even that rebellion doesn't fill me with satisfaction. I don't want to die. I have a greater purpose. I can feel it in my bones. I have to get to the man in the cave. I need to find the other Omega. If I run into Trash City and get a chance to break Merlin's meaty neck, I'll take it, too. But more than anything, I want to know more about the dead army that the Dark City Berserker said we'd investigate together.

I don't often get the feeling that I matter, but I feel it now. That, somewhere in this convoluted puzzle, I fit.

I thought, for a second, I might fit with Adam too, and that I might matter to the Berserker of Dark City, just a little bit.

Fool.

The wind whispers through the window and I ignore it, but as time flutters past and the wind picks up, the darkness outside calls my attention. Carefully peering through the cracks in the fluttering white drapes, I can't see much. Just a grey skyline beneath which my shattered garden glimmers. Flowers still cover the space. Betas have been scavenging them like crazy. They won't live long though, I don't think. The flowers I conjured up to cover my own room when the Berserker and I fucked have all died since.

The wind picks up and I twist towards the window fully. There's a weird sound…I can't quite interpret it. I sit very still, trying to decide what it is, so I'm caught totally off guard when a swarm of bats explodes through the crack in my window, and flies straight over my head. There must be a dozen of them or more, and they're all *white.* Shocked as I am, a delayed scream rips out of me that's cut abruptly short.

The bats redirect to swarm my face. I reach for the lamp and grab it around its thick stem. I lift it up, fully intent on using it to defend myself with, but before I can bring it down, fingers circle my wrist, halting my progress, while another hand covers the bottom half of my face, muffling the word I shout next, *"Fruh…"*

I blink. It's Freya.

She sits so close to me she's practically on my lap, her nose damn near touching mine. She's as naked as I am and even though I'm made very uncomfortable by our closeness and our nakedness and the fact that she was bats a second ago, she doesn't seem to mind.

"This is where you have been?" she says, disdain on her tongue. "Acting as the…house pet of a Berserker?" Her voice is stilted, speech slightly odd, just as I remember it.

Her ice eyes flicker between mine like windshield wipers, swish, swish, swish. Maybe it's just the beating of my blood through my veins, moving triple time. What's more than triple time? A thousand times too fast for the pitiful body that contains it. And then her words hit me and I rip my head away from her hands and give her shoulders a shove. I don't push her hard, but she still flies back on the bed, like a sheet in the wind.

I glance over her. Her breasts and ass are small, her hips are wide, but she's covered in lean, sinewy muscle like she was once a swimmer. Maybe, she was. Or maybe, she's just a fish. She's been a fox and a bear and bats, so why not a dolphin? Though I've never made it to the ocean, I'd love to see one someday when I'm free of this place and *him* and the insidious thoughts I have of him when rare sleep comes for me. Dreams of forgiveness, of returning to the garden where we once lived…

I shake out of it and jangle my chain, sitting up a little straighter. "You fucker. I'm tied up, or are you blind as a bat?" Pun's very much intended, but she doesn't laugh at my joke.

She glances at my neck when I gesture to the collar and then at the headboard behind me. "You are…" She hesitates, like she's searching for words, and her hesitation lasts so long, it makes me wonder if it's not that she speaks with an accent…maybe she just doesn't have a good vocabulary in any language. "You are *weak*. You could have freed yourself… from this…any of the times."

"How? This is steel!" I shout before I remember that there are Betas lurking in the hallway outside, specifically planted there to monitor me. I drop my voice to a hiss. "I don't think *flowers* can break that."

Her hand comes out of nowhere and strikes me upside the face. She hits me! The bitch hits me! "You…you!" I can't even come up with an insult. Doesn't matter. She doesn't give me time to, anyway.

Instead, she's back up on me, nearly nestled on my lap again. No sense of personal space. "You are not…Fallen," she whispers, grabbing the sides of my face and squeezing until my lips pucker. "The man in the cave…sent me for you…but he must be wrong. You are not one of the Fallen. You are not one of us." She moves with the breeze and returns to the window in elegant, graceful strides that make no noise on the carpet. Not even a whisper.

My heart starts to pound and I feel a budding headache. I can't watch her leave. Because she's going to take something very important with her when she does and I might not recover from the loss of it.

"Wait!" I whisper-shout.

She doesn't stop, but touches the window frame and opens it wider. Her hand…her hand looks like it's disappearing into the wind…or growing wings. If she turns into a bat again, she'll be gone forever.

Desperate to keep her here, I blurt out the words that come to me without thinking. "I ascended three months ago. I don't know what I'm doing. If you tell me I can get myself out of this, then I believe you, Freya. I trust you. You're the only one I trust here. The Berserker, he…he lied to me. I trusted him when I shouldn't have. I should have believed you and killed him when I had the chance."

Her fingers smooth over the wooden frame of the window, tracing its square edge. She's deciding. Everything hangs on the now.

Tears grip my eyes, but she won't respond well to that. I don't know her at all except that she hates Berserkers and weakness, so I suck it down and infuse my voice with strength. "Freya, please."

"I see the…cloth you tried to use to free yourself. You are still thinking like a Beta, not an Omega…but a Beta cannot kill the undead. An Alpha cannot, either. Only…Omegas…" She gestures absently at the pieces of torn blanket I used to try to break the iron posts of his bed.

Bashfully, I confess, "I heard somewhere if you pee on silk, it becomes strong enough to bend steel…" My words sound about as lousy a theory as it turned out to be. Instead of busting out of here, all I got were pee-covered sheets.

"Why did you not use your instinct?" She looks at me over her shoulder, still touching the window frame. Still poised to leave.

"It's not strong…"

"You have control over earth, yes?"

"I can…"

"Yes or no?"

I swallow. Well, when she puts it like that… "I guess…"

"Yes or no."

"Yes." My voice comes out in a breath.

"And control over water, yes or no?"

I remember the river, pulling our bodies from the water and how little control I felt until I was summoned. The Berserker told me to bring the water, so I brought the water. It had been easy, but only under his command. "Yes."

She turns in a flourish, grabs the pitcher of water left for me on the bedside table and dumps it over the chain. Then she tosses the glass onto the floor where it lands with a heavy thunk, but doesn't shatter. She doesn't look back at it. She doesn't care. She stands over me like an archangel, an underworld demoness, her body covered in shadow while the window behind her creates a halo of her silhouette.

She grabs the chain at my neck and pulls it out from behind me. Taut, I stare at the droplets clinging to it. "Freeze the chain."

"What?"

"Freeze the water, freeze the chain." Her eyes narrow when I don't react except to stare at her like she's crazy. "That was a summoning, Omega."

I suck in a breath and, staring into her eyes, am lost to the disorienting sensations swirling through me. She is not my Berserker but, when she orders me, I feel that compulsion deep in my stomach, that urge, that essence, that force, that pull. Like a good Omega, I obey.

I inhale and glance at the chain when she drops it with a hiss. Cold radiates from the metal as the water crystalizes and I shiver as a chill shoots up to touch my collar and I shiver again as ice comes to cover the headboard and then the bed, and then the sheets around me. I clutch the blankets to my chest as memories of a lifetime of being cold creep in.

Fear and Pain slink out of the shadows, resuming their rightful places at my left and right hand. They're crowding me now and I feel my throat hitch, nerves getting the best of me. I've been without them for so long, it's both a hatred and a longing for them that keeps me from reacting right away when Freya takes the now frozen chain and yanks.

It shatters instantaneously. "You are not…a coward. Why do you…act like one?"

"I'm afraid of Paradise Hole," I confess timidly. Her genuine confusion only makes the pain in my chest worse.

"Why? You and I…we are Omegas of Mother Earth. In Paradise Hole…we are her favored children. We are home."

She starts to pull away, but I lift a hand, the one covered in scars. She sees them and looks at them as if she's never known injury before. Glancing over her quickly, I spy dirt dotting her lanky limbs, but no cuts or bruises.

"I can't protect myself."

"Then what are these gifts?"

"You've seen me. I can't control my gifts. I need a Berserker — or you — to summon them."

Freya's glare is hard, her expression is hard. Fear and Pain take one shared look at her and step back. They are useless in her presence. She will not befriend them with the ease I have. She sweeps her long, elegant fingers around the curve of my face without touching my skin, though I can *feel* a wonderful energy, soothing and warm, caress me like the aftershocks of an earthquake a second after her hand passes over the affected areas.

Then she grips my chin between her thumb and pointer finger, pressing it firmly. "You say you cannot control your gifts…but have you tried? Or do you give your power away to the breeder who cages you because it is easy?"

My mouth hangs open. Drool might be dripping out of the corner of my mouth for all I know, but I can't seem to care as this Omega takes an ice pick to my skull and pries it open. Thoughts escape like loose butterflies. I struggle to catch them. "But…but Omegas submit, Betas serve, Alphas rule and Berserkers own…that's the way…"

"That is *their* way. It is not mine. It does not have to be yours. The Omegas of this world do not have the power of the Fates…or their doppelgängers. That you…give yours away to a breeder is a waste," she sneers. "The man in the cave says you are one of us. I do not believe him, but if he believes you are Fallen…you might be. Your gifts are strong, in any case." She gestures absently to the window with her free hand, and I still see the image of her fingers painted across the air long after they fall.

She tapes my skull back together after shoving new information inside of it. It's bursting. My world unravels, but I manage to hang on to one word, only one, that feels the most important. "What is *Fallen*?"

"Not what, who."

"Who then are the Fallen?"

She drops her fist from my chin and extends it down, fingers slightly parted. It takes me a moment to realize she's offering me her hand. "Come. I will show you."

I stare at her palm and not a second goes by before I take it and stand. She grabs the front of the collar on my neck and pulls, and the brittle metal breaks, little pieces sprinkling my toes like glitter. I step over them, leaving them behind, along with the one little broken shard that I would have called a heart if I had one. But I don't. Adam made sure of it.

ADAM
HIGH PLAINS

"SEEM MORE AT HOME IN PARADISE HOLE THAN I thought you would," I tell Yaron. He isn't much for conversation, but the thought's been eatin' at me the better part of the past three days. Three miserable fuckin' days.

Three days without... No. Got nothin' to do with it.

Bastard refused to ride anything but his damn horse — a decision I came to understand after the first day when my bike crossed the first trap. It survived — all my bikes are built rugged — but four a' my Alphas' didn't. Slowed us down, huntin' the scavengers who set the trap and cuttin' their tongues out as punishment — a punishment Yaron approved of — but on day two we got stopped completely. The rain did us in.

Felt less like a dick, seein' as Yaron's horses couldn't make it through, either. Now we sit under a tent that he helped me and my Alphas build. Surprised me, too, seein' him do hard labor. Wonderin' if the idea I've got a' the bastard isn't entirely fabricated.

He continues cutting the apple in his hand apart with his black dagger. I watch him work, my left heel tapping out a beat on the tarp below. The stool under my ass feels wobbly and uncertain. Maybe it's just the air. Too thick. Maybe it's just my skin. Too thin. Everything fuckin' hurts.

I wonder what she's… No. No.

"I don't know why that would surprise you. I maintain the old traditions. My city has no walls. That is why it is not called Shadow City, but Shadowlands. Lands where Beta and Alpha villages remain intact and where, upon occasion, the problems of the north island and Paradise Hole bleed, crossing the sea to do so."

He takes another bite of his apple, chews, swallows. He glances down at my leg and I force myself to stop fuckin' tappin' it like a little boy tryna hold in a piss. He glances up into my gaze, his slate eyes a rich combination of evil and apathy.

"You, on the other hand, who was once a Beta boy living in the slums of Bog City, seem less at home in Paradise Hole than I would have expected." His gaze drops again to my leg. "Or perhaps there is another reason for your…hmm…" He pauses, his voice already movin' too slow…like this whole damn operation's movin' too goddamn slow.

I jerk up outta my seat. *If Echo tries to jerk up outta her seat, the collar could cut into her flesh.* The thought hits and scrambles the words I'd been poised to say next. I pull my satellite phone outta the inner pocket of my waterproof bomber jacket. Lined in fleece, it's warm. *Is Echo warm? All she's got to wear is that dress.*

I punch the call button and it goes straight through to my estate. "Berserker Dragnovic," Ward says. Strange, hearin' her voice on the line. Right now she's the highest rankin' person still in the City. And she's a Beta.

"Ward, how's she doin'?"

"Katrina just checked in on her. She's fine. I checked her vitals yesterday. All are within the normal range."

I scratch my jaw. Growin' out my beard 'cause that's how she likes it. *But will she still?* She's gonna have to. I'll make her. Gonna make it all right. Gonna take her back to that car where she said she was fallin'. Gonna make her fall. Crash. Burn. Just like I have. Gonna make her forgive me. Gonna...

"Wanna talk to 'er."

"You asked yesterday and she said no. Do you really want to debase yourself by asking a second day in a row and getting the same answer?"

Yaron snorts. Clear the fucker can hear everythin' on the call. I try to stay still, but I end up pacing even though, in this tent built for a dozen Omegas or six Betas or four Alphas or two Berserkers comfortably, there's nowhere for me to go.

"Yes."

She mutters so low I can't catch it over the sound of the rain poundin' down on the roof a' the lined canvas tent.

"Ward," I growl.

"I'm going, I'm going. I just think you'd benefit from giving her space. You did chain her to your bed and she didn't seem to appreciate your efforts to keep her safe." Sarcasm coats her tongue like a thick paste.

"Watch your mouth," I snarl.

Ward huffs, though I can hear that she's movin'. That's good at least.

I'm chewin' on my bottom lip again. Just about chewed the damn thing raw already. After the first time she rejected my call. *I'd rather bite off my own tongue and swallow it than talk to that Alphahole.* That's what I heard through the phone when I called yesterday. And instead of takin' a fuckin' breath, I'd shouted back, tellin' her that that could be arranged. Fuck me.

I rub my face roughly. It's just a fight, though. We fight all the time. When I'm back with her, I'll fix it. I'll fuck it outta her. I won't chain her up again. *That's what I told her the last time.*

"Do you hear that, Berserker?" Yaron's entire body is tense, alert.

He rises before giving me a chance to unchain my thoughts from the Omega I chained to my bed and walks to the tent's slitted opening. He rips back one edge of the canvas and stares out at the bleak, sodden world and the tents studding it. I move to stand next to him and, with a great show of force, pull my attention away from the crackly sound of Ward walking.

I stare at the greyscape that is Paradise Hole's high plains. We're headed in the direction of the Grasslands Beta compound now, one of the places where Echo grew up. Part of me wants to go there and raze it to the ground for their mistreatment of her, but I'm not so sure I'm in a position to do that.

"They are over the next rise," Yaron says at the same time that the phone in my hand makes a crackling sound, like bubble wrap exploding.

"Ward… Fuck!"

Yaron surges forward, moving out into the rain, water sluicing off of the pelt he wears fastened around his shoulders.

"Dragnovic…hear…can…it's…"

"Ward?"

"Dragnovic, my god…" The line cuts.

Fuck.

There's shouting coming from around the edge of the next tent where Yaron disappeared. I hesitate to follow him immediately, choosing that moment instead to glare at the plastic brick in my hand. My claws surge at the sight of it as I fight not to smash it into a million fuckin' pieces. Can't hear Ward. Ward's gone. And on *this* shitty end of the line, the shouting's getting louder…louder…louder…*Bang!*

Gunfire.

"Fuck! Six, to me!" I shout and I hear the sound of boots squishin' over the waterlogged ground. It's rainin' way too much for the plains, this far east a' Dark City. *Somethin's off.*

Maybe everythin'.

And still, this is where Echo wanted to be. Right here beside me, gunfire screamin' through the watery world. But I remember what happened last time. Last time, she got fuckin' shot. It's better she stays where I put her. Yeah…

Better for me.

Because when that bullet ripped through her shoulder, she didn't make a sound. She took it all like a fuckin' warrior, a savage that I shackled, a beast without a Berserker's build but no less deadly. And it hits me then, just like a bullet…

Echo says I draw her gifts out of her…but she draws my strength out of me, too. I may be unworthy when I'm alone, but how can I be when we're together? Because she may be made of many unsettlin' and sinister things, but there ain't a doubt in my mind that all of 'em have worth. And if I make her stronger, maybe I got worth by proxy. When I chained her, did I cut the legs out from under us both? I shrug outta my jacket, lettin' it hit the muddy ground, frustrated and pissed off and unsure as I move out to meet my Six as we all converge with Yaron and his people.

"Beasts, hold! Scavengers, hold your fire!" Yaron shouts, Stallin' my Berserker's beast from takin' over.

The tents fall away as I rush around 'em and I see Yaron standin' at the base of a low hill, his cloak snappin' in a wind that's characteristic a' these parts even if the rain isn't. Alphas and Betas wearing crimson approach him from the back on all sides, made up of his elite team — like my Six, only they call themselves Crimson Riders — me and my Six and another fifty Alphas from Dark City. Together, we're seventy-eight total and even though Yaron only thought to bring eighteen of his Riders to stand against the dead army — bastard still only half believes it exists — we more than outnumber the scavengers makin' their way down the hill towards us.

"Why'd you stop?" I growl as I step up to Yaron's right and watch the scavengers climb slowly down the hill, weighed down by the weapons strapped across their chests, the many layers they're wearin', and the rain soakin' 'em through.

"The flag." He juts his chin towards the flag carried by the scavenger in the front. It's white.

Well, it was once white. Now, it's closer to black, but the message still stands. In observing the flag and the one who carries it, I narrow my eyes. "Unfuckinbelievable."

Yaron shouts as I storm forward, "You know these Betas?"

"*Betas* is a generous fuckin' term," I snark under my breath before shoutin', "You've got some fuckin' balls on you, Merlin, I'll give you that much! But I'm gonna tear 'em fuckin' off, disembowel you and take your eyes back for my Omega."

I stomp through the muddy terrain, rain slickin' my hair against the sides a' my face, slidin' underneath the collar a' my tee shirt and soakin' me through to the bone. Don't give a shit about that, though. I'm about to tear through my clothes. My Berserker is fuckin' agitated at the sight a' her. *Maybe, if I tear Merlin inside out and offer Echo the corpse, she'll forgive…*

"I've got a flag," Merlin blurts, finally lookin' up from the careful way she'd been walkin' down the hillside. She waves her sopping flag pitifully and tries to rub the hair out of her eyes, but the ragged blonde strands remain stubbornly plastered to the outside of her obnoxious fuckin' goggles.

"That rag ain't about to save you…"

"Hey!" She flips open the flap of her coat and levels the barrel of the automatic weapon in her hands at my chest. A machine gun. It's an even nicer model than the last one she had.

"You dare point a weapon at a Berserker!" Yaron's voice hits me like a wall and both Merlin and I stagger. I glare at him over

my shoulder as he whips open his own cloak and reaches for the axe strapped to his back.

"Wait! I have information you want." Merlin's finger on the trigger looks happy, but she stays her hand. That alone I find troubling. She isn't the kinda woman to wait. She's more of a shoot first, kill the bastard, sell 'em to the Mirage City Berserker so his Fates can reanimate 'em, then ask questions later kinda gal.

Yaron doesn't know her. He doesn't notice, but I stand back watching, concerned by a sensation that there's something absolutely not right about this. Those lingering questions are what keep me from actin' on every impulse I have to kill the blonde trigger-happy fucker.

Yaron glares between Merlin and me — between her gun and me. The water in his hair drags black tendrils down the sides of his face and forehead like spilled ink. "Trash City carries weapons." I don't answer and he hisses under his breath. Sounds more like a prayer than a curse. "Jesús!"

A tall Beta male with black hair trots up to us. "Berserker." He bows to Yaron, then to me, and, to Merlin, shows a mouthful of sharpened teeth.

"Ride to Ruby City. Return with the rest of the war contingent we left stationed there."

Unlike my Six, he doesn't talk back. He nods sharply, red cloak flapping in the wind, and says, "The entire contingent? You don't want anyone left behind to guard the ships?"

He seems to consider, then says, "Ruby City are our allies, but they are known to ally themselves to Mirage City as well. Bring me a hundred more Crimson Riders. Leave a sparse few behind to defend the ships and send the rest to return to the south island. Keep an eye on the ports and set the villages on high alert. Betas capable of fighting should arm themselves and prepare to defend their lands in the absence of my full war party. It seems that our *ally* Dragnovic was telling the truth."

"You doubted me?" I ask as Jesús disappears in a breeze.

"I did. Scavengers with automatic weapons and Alphas back from the dead make for difficult digestion." His slippery gaze slides to Merlin, who shifts the barrel of her gun to him. He snarls, "But if you did not exaggerate about this, then perhaps you did not exaggerate the rest."

I grunt, "Don't flatter me now."

"I didn't."

"Hector, relieve the scavengers of their guns."

Hector, an Alpha about Echo's height with thin legs and arms, struts forward, approaching Merlin first. When she gives her gun up, my suspicion inflates like a balloon prepared to burst. "The fuck are you doin', Merlin? How'd you find us?"

"Are you kidding?" She spits as she watches Hector and two other Alphas remove guns from the other dozen scavengers at her back. "You thought we wouldn't know about two Berserkers joining forces and roaming across Paradise Hole?"

"That don't answer the fuckin' question."

"Grasslands compound told us. They've got scouts all over the area," she says with a shrug.

Wrong. Wrong. Wrong. "We would have seen them."

"No, you wouldn't. We Betas have been livin' in y'all's shadows for a long time. We know how to avoid the sun." She looks Yaron over in a way that seems threatenin' and I know he feels it too when aggression and a growl roll off of him in response. Merlin's lips flutter and she lifts both hands palm up by her face as if she's only just remembered who the fuck she's speakin' to. "Look, I didn't come here to get robbed. I came here to do you a favor."

"Ha!" I laugh, loudly and theatrically. "You shittin' me right now?"

Can't see her eyes clearly underneath the foggy goggles, but her lips form a thin white line. I'm still searchin' for signs a' deceit as she says, "It's not a favor for you. It's for Echo. She's in trouble."

Rage pummels through every inch a' me. I open my mouth and my jaw distends, the bones rearranging themselves. My hand follows my jaw's lead and starts to grow fur, becoming more beast than man. Merlin swallows hard, drawing my attention to her throat. I snatch it and lift until her feet hover off of the ground, kickin' uselessly, and her face turns beet red.

I hiss, "She's at home in bed where she needs to be. If you think for a second that I believe anythin' comin' outta your lyin' mouth, you're a fuckin' fool."

One of the Trash City fucks who hasn't had his weapons confiscated yet comes at me with the barrel of his gun lifted. I lunge out and grab it, rip it out of his hand and toss Merlin to the ground. She's coughin' and chokin' but still aware enough to know what's comin' next.

"No! Don't!" In the exact same spot she shot Echo, I fire. Her scream rips through the day and brings the night. Seems darker when I next blink and I recognize that I've shrunk back down into my Alpha skin, leavin' my Berserker behind. Rain slaps at my cheeks. The world feels unsteady beneath my feet.

"You believe these scavengers a liability?" Yaron asks, voice flat but not bored.

"Thousand percent. And this fucker right here can't be trusted for shit."

Merlin writhes on the ground, the scavengers behind her lookin' less worried than they should. I recognize a couple of 'em and, when I look up and make eyes with the doc, I snarl. The coward that he is, he ducks behind the taller woman standin' to his left.

"We should kill all of 'em."

"Then you'll never get to her in time," Merlin pants. "Lou! Get your ass over here." The coward does as he's ordered and starts patchin' up her shoulder only this time he's usin' clean packets of gauze and sterile tools all marked with Dark City's logo — shit *I* fuckin' traded her.

"She's not lying, you know." I look left. Angel. The medic girl. I never got a good read on her… I still don't. "Echo was lied to. The witch in the woods is leading her to her death."

"Fuck you. The Dark City Omega is in her bed where she's supposed to be."

"We're just telling you what we know. What we heard, anyway." She shrugs, like she doesn't have a care under the goddamn sun. "The rest is up to you."

Yaron's boots crunch over the ground as he steps up behind me. "This one speaks with an honest timbre," he says, speaking so low only I can hear him. "If she is lying, she does not know it."

I'm troubled by the same thought. My chest is heavin', like my skin is stretched too thin across it. "Whiskey!" I roar, callin' for the rest of my Six along with 'er. Needin' 'em. I turn and see her already on the satellite phone a few paces away. Vi holds up both hands as if to ask for me to settle, maybe ask for more time. I can't figure out which and I can't manage either.

My heels are tappin' out a frantic beat in the mud and my heart. My heart…

Whiskey turns to me, eyes round in her face like the two oversized button eyes of a doll. They're chilling. "Ward… I got Ward on the line. She says Echo's gone."

My blood slows and I collapse into my open grave then let the dirt shower over me. I blink and realize my body hasn't moved — just my spirit. Yaron at my side asks the question I don't want him to. *Failure.* "Why would an Omega traverse Paradise Hole without a guard?" *Unworthy.*

"She's lookin' for somebody," I whisper.

"Beta family?"

"No. A man in a cave…"

"Did you say cave?" Merlin blurts, voice loud and oddly stilted.

I nod, the urge to run her through strong, though not as strong as the urge to tear out my own heart. Echo is too far away from me.

"Then we know where she's gonna be. If she meant a cave, and not just some hole in the dirt — a proper cave — then there's only one outside of the southern cave systems near Ruby City. Only one over by Trash City." She speaks between labored breaths, her gaze hot on mine and filled with anger that contradicts every helpful thing she's sayin' as Lou finishes stitchin' her whole. The blood on her shoulder is incriminatin' and so is the violence in her eyes. She's lyin'. Know she is. Maybe not about what she's sayin' but about somethin'.

But I don't have any other leads.

I narrow my gaze and approach her, and the Beta insults me by not backin' down. She holds my eyeline until I grab her by the neck, bruises already formin' where I grabbed her moments ago. "You hurt her in any way, or take any part in whatever the man in the cave is plannin' — or the witch — I will take you back to Dark City, hold you in a cell, take you apart piece by piece and leave you to choose between starvation and eating your own flesh."

Her eyes flash with heat and her hands twitch. Her lips pull into her mouth and she finally looks away. There's fear there. Lies. Deception. Hate. I don't know what piece Merlin's got on the board, but I don't want her to fuckin' play. She cheats.

"You want to reroute and go for your Omega," Yaron says.

"Yes."

Yaron waits a long beat. His voice is even when he speaks and his words surprise me. "It would be best not to separate our forces as my reinforcements have not yet arrived. We will join you in this but only with the guarantee that, immediately afterward, we approach Berserker Maengor..."

"Mallory, Karamoko — take a group a' seven to follow us on foot. Bring Trash City with you. Don't let this one outta your sight." I grab Merlin by the back a' her neck and toss her toward the two Alpha males I've instructed to stay behind. "The rest a' you, pack up your shit. Fuck the rain. We ride now."

THE FORESTS OF PARADISE HOLE LOOK EXACTLY AS I remember them but, traveling with Freya, are entirely changed. We don't speak much — try, *at all* — so I'm left to watch her and the things she does. Such incredible things.

We move slowly because every few miles she calls out and animals come to us — all kinds of animals, big and small. They bring her their young, their old, their sick. The sick she…she…

A wolf limps up to her. The first one I saw terrified me. Now, after two days, I'm used to it in a way that makes me feel like I've been doing this my whole life. She steps past the wolf pack that accompanies it — her, the wolf is a *her* — and Freya bends one knee.

She sinks down in front of the creature, slides her hand over her flank, reaching her back leg. The wolf howls and, when Freya's finished petting her and murmuring softly into her ear, the wolf bows her head to Freya and leaps away utterly uninjured, unscathed, unafraid.

The wolf Alphas show her their bellies. The bears that come trotting up to her greet her like friends. Small rabbits cocoon her body when she sleeps so she never goes cold. And even if they weren't there, it wouldn't matter. She can transform into any creature she wants, whenever she wants. Her gifts aren't an extension of her body, like mine are. She *is* her gifts, they are her, and there is no separation between them. She doesn't have to reach or call for them. They just are. They're beautiful as she is beautiful. I've never seen anything more beautiful in my entire life.

Freya approaches a tree and bends down. At its base, a baby bird lies featherless and screaming. It must have fallen from its nest and appears to be in pain. I look up and see that the nest is now empty, its family gone. Freya lifts the tiny creature and covers it with both palms and I get closer, peering over her shoulder to watch her work. She whispers under her breath. The air, which I imagined would rile up in the presence of this magic, is still. Humid, flat.

And then Freya digs a small hole in the dirt at the base of the tree and tucks the small bird inside. It isn't screaming anymore. It's lifeless.

She starts to cover it with dirt and I panic, reach out, grab her shoulder. She hits my arm, knocking me away, and glares at me somethin' fierce. I try to keep the tears out of my tone, but it doesn't work. I'm watching the bird, willing it awake. "Why'd you do that? Why didn't you bring it back like you did the wolf?"

Freya's eyebrows soften over her face. She returns her attention to the bird and covers it with care. With love. "Most believe that there is…just a thin line between life…and death.

This isn't true...between life and death, there is a vast divide...an ocean. If a life is close to the shore, I will save it. If it is too far from the shore, I help ease its transition..."

"But you could," I stammer, mesmerized. Horrified. I crouch in the dirt, the wetness of the soil soaking my pants through at the knees. It rained so hard the past few days. "You could bring them back, if you wanted."

"I do not want."

"But you could. You could save it."

She spins and is suddenly in my face, her nose a hair's breadth from mine. "It is not saving it...it is...ruining it. Too far out to shore, you come back...but not healed. A ghost. Tortured. I have *tried*. I have seen..." Her voice cuts. I feel my heartbeat race in my chest. My hands form fists against the earth and a shiver racks my frame. "Whichever of the Fates...reanimates the Alphas has the same powers I have. The only thing that separates us...is this *want*. I do not want to see the living suffer. This is why I heal. I do not want to see the dead suffer, either. This is why I give them peace."

She pulls back and mutters more to herself that I can't make out. It doesn't sound human though. More like the soft whistles songbirds make. Maybe it is. Maybe she's still speaking to the bird in whatever language they share.

I stare down at the newly turned soil long after she pulls her pale hands away from its darkness, turning over her words, turning back time. I think of Adam and the hate that fuels me and wonder, against the chaos of life and the beauty of death and the ocean between them, if hate has any place in this tenuous ecosystem. *No. I don't think it does. But then, does love?*

"Come." Freya turns back to face me and the light above her is brighter than I've ever seen it. I can almost see sky. Not quite, but nearly.

I shake my head. She frowns, but before she can speak, I say, "Want is not what separates you."

"What?" Her pale, almost invisible eyebrows furrow together over her sharp nose. Her pale pink lips purse.

"You said want is what separates you from the other Omega, the one who brings back the corpses. But you're wrong. It isn't want. It's…" I choke, struggling to form words that feel so suddenly damning.

Her expression twists even more. "What?"

"It's love."

She stares at me but I can't read her at all. She stares for a long while though. And then all she says is, "Come."

I trudge after her, exhausted, beat. I didn't bring nearly enough supplies for this, grabbing only clothes enough for three days and no food at all. Freya knows where water sources are, but the one time I even hinted at hunting an animal in the forest, she screeched at me like some kind of crow-meets-howler-monkey, the sound so loud I thought I'd burst an eardrum, and it was enough for me to know better than to ever bring it up again. So, I don't. Instead, I forage with her for nuts and berries and I eat them all happily even though I'd kill for a steak.

Not gonna mention steak to Freya if I want to live long enough to find the man in the cave. Not gonna complain about the stitch in my side, the way my feet are killing me or how much I miss sleeping in a bed, either. It was only a few days, but it's incredible how fast I got used to city living. I'll forget though. Or at least, unlearn it. Just like I'll unlearn all the rest. Even if hate and love play no part in our story — in *my* story — I know already that a life of captivity would make me little better than one of the undead. So yes, I'll unlearn Adam, too. *Adam who?* There is no Adam. There's only the Berserker of Dark City and he has no Omega.

"We're here." Freya's voice comes as a surprise and I move faster, climbing the small incline, which isn't so much steep as it is treacherous. My boots sink into the mud up to the ankles. The chill has already seeped in through the leather to dampen my socks and claim my toes. Still, they're a helluva lot better than rabbit skins, though.

Reaching the top of the muddy knoll, I grip the straps of my backpack and step in line beside her. I track her hand with my gaze and shake my head. "This isn't right," I say. "There shouldn't be a cave here."

She ignores me and marches forward into the clearing where there's just a massive hole leading into the ground. "Come."

"Freya, I'm serious. I've been all over this part of Paradise Hole. I've been *here*. The only caves are in the south. There are a few caves in Gang Mountain and up north on the way to the Glass Flats. This isn't supposed to be here and I don't want to go in. It doesn't feel right."

"The man in the cave won't speak to me without you," she hisses, her feet black up to the shins from the mud. The tips of her hair are black, too, as black as coal. Fitting, since her eyes are diamonds, clear as ice and cutting. "And I need to know why..." She shakes her head and starts again, this time even more severely. "There should not be another Omega with my gifts. I need to know how to stop her."

"But this…"

"She…*unalives* the creatures of Paradise Hole." Her severity does nothing against the grief that rolls through me as it finally clicks. *Those creatures are her family. Her friends.* Not ever having had either of those two things, I don't really understand, but I don't need to understand to know Fear. To know Pain. I feel hers acutely and it hurts me, because she feels Pain and Fear on behalf of someone else. I've never felt that, so focused on looking out only for myself. *That's not true. I've felt it before. I felt it for Adam.*

"Fuck." I rub my face roughly and take a step down the muddy incline towards the hole. There are rocks here out in the open, forming the mouth of the cave. It doesn't make sense. I point.

"There *aren't* rocks here," I say in contradiction of what's directly in front of me. "This is a forested area away from Gang Mountain. There shouldn't be rock formations."

She grabs my extended arm by the wrist and shoves my hand down. "I have been inside. It is safe. The man in the cave is a…friend. He waits for us, but he does not…doesn't have much time."

"What does that mean?"

"He is far from the shore." She pauses, as if lost in thought. Then she shakes her head and moves further down the incline. "Come."

I approach the open hole that looks like the actual entrance to Hell, wondering how much I trust Freya. I decide that I do. Sort of.

A little.

I trusted Adam too, though, and look what happened.

I stare between Freya and the hole, worried and wondering if, after Adam, my instincts aren't a little frayed…is this a trap? Just like Adam and all the things he promised?

"Why do you wait?" she says to me from the shadows as she climbs nimbly over the rocks down into the below. The way she moves confuses the crap out of me until I notice that the bottom half of her legs resemble that of a goat's. She has *hooves*. The woman has hooves. How can you *not* trust a woman with hoof feet? Huh? *Huhhh?*

"Fuck me," I say with a half laugh. "If I die, I die…"

"You are not going…to die," Freya says, responding to a whisper not at all meant for her, but for me and my sanity, which has evidently gone bye bye.

I move forward awkwardly, slipping over mud-covered boulders until I'm able to see a scattering of twigs and vines and rocks leading down into Hell like an earthen staircase. It makes the rocks easier to navigate as I follow Freya, who skips on her goat legs from boulder to boulder while I make my way down, down, down in between them.

The rocks get bigger and eventually the ground rises up above my head. I stare back over my shoulder at the entrance to the cave. I haven't gone far, but the opening manages to look very small from here.

The quality of the air doesn't help. It's thick and misty and warmed by the earth surrounding it. When I round the next set of rocks, I see why. There's a lake down here.

The cave is wide and the lake spreads to reach nearly all of its curved edges. A narrow path rings the lake, wrapping around the inside of the cave wall. Freya follows it right, without hesitation, as if she's done so many times before. I follow her around the rocky ledge away from the light, towards the dark.

There aren't any other entrances into or out of this place that I can see and the primary light source is the hole in the ground that's far behind me now. The light passes through the mist, turning the world white and then dark and then… the palest yellow. And it has nothing to do with the light from Paradise Hole. This light comes from the glow.

An ethereal, yellow warmth emanates from behind a stone. I round it and find a man leaning against a large boulder stroking a floating orb. He holds the ball of light lovingly in his lap, its murky exterior emitting fog and light. It's strange, not just in its strangeness, but because it casts no shadows. He keeps it close and smiles as we arrive.

"Ah. The Fallen Earth Omega. We meet at last. Freya has told me quite a bit about you." He smiles wide enough to show all of his white teeth and looks directly at me. I'm simultaneously soothed and petrified.

As far from the entrance of the cave as we could be, we stand on a wide, flat stone ledge. It's much wider than it appeared from the other side of the lake. A small camp has been set up here and the man holding the orb sits at its center. It looks like a camp that's only meant to last a few days, though I know that can't be. He must have been here for weeks. And he's… Wait. I…

My gaze, which was trapped by his for these past moments, tears free and hovers over the place where his legs should be. I don't understand it, at first, and then my mind catches up to me. They're *missing*. His pants deflate high around his thighs. I don't see any blood anywhere. Maybe he was born this way. Maybe the army of the dead got to him. Should I ask him? No. That's rude. Or maybe, it's more rude to pretend I'm not thinking about it…

"I wasn't born this way."

I jump and glance at the water where Fear completes a lovely, lazy backstroke.

"And no, I cannot read your thoughts. I can read your future and I saw that you were going to ask me about my legs. The answer is that the Fates took them."

I have so many questions. I open my mouth to ask the first, but I don't get it out. Instead, he replies, "For the blood, of course." He gestures to the mats laid out on either side of the now dead fire. It looks long dead. Days dead, if not weeks. "You have many questions and I will attempt to answer them all. But first, have a seat."

Numbly, I sit across the empty firepit from Freya who looks with frustration between me and the man lying back on a blanket-covered stone. "You said bring her and you will…you would tell me of the Beast Fate. I do not want to hear the rest of the story."

Can she feel it too? The walls watching us?

I glance around the edges of the cave.

"We have some time," the man says, his voice a calm, gentle lull, much like the waves lapping in the lake. I glance across it, searching for the exit, but the mist is so thick I cannot see the far shore.

I jerk as an invisible pull draws my attention up to his eyes like a hook to the chest. It pains me, though his eyes are brown and kind enough to soften the sting of it. His skin is tan. I don't know how young he is. Or how old. He looks like…like a kid, with skinny arms and soft lips. But his hair is matted, brown streaked through with grey, and his skin is wrinkled and bruised all over.

Freya tsks. "We don't. The animals are restless. There is something coming. Something big. I need to know how to defeat the Beast Fate. If I can defeat her, I can stop the dead army…"

"No, Freya, you cannot. We've been through this before." He speaks to her like he might a child.

Freya's lips open. Her fist clenches on her bare thigh. She's still not dressed. Over the last two days I got used to it, but seeing her now next to this man who's fully clothed, I'm reminded. His clothes are deep red and look like they were, at one time, expensive. They're tattered now, covered in dirt and other dark things and, in places, shredded.

"Who turns them does not matter…I can still destroy the Fates. Not just my own."

"Not alone." He coughs into his hand, his lids batting slowly, making them look heavy, making his every movement seem pained. "Never alone."

I'm so confused, I don't understand the conversation being had. A whimper escapes my throat when I mean to voice a demand. "What's…what's going on?"

The man raises a hand and Freya settles, even though her own fists remain clenched and her eyes continue to blaze. "There is a war brewing. Mirage City is coming for the world and is using a dead army to do it."

"He wants to take over the world?"

"He..." The man smiles. "Yes, *he* wants to take over the world." He chuckles to himself until a look of pain crosses his face. He places the orb of light on the ground at his right hip, but keeps one hand resting on it.

"What can he possibly hope to accomplish? Claim new territories? He already has the largest city, outside of Shadowlands." Then again, wanting more land has never stopped an Alpha male before. "Besides, the cities are well established. They won't be easily taken."

"No, not easily, but they *can* be taken by force."

Freya cuts in, her expression sharp as she flits her gaze to me dismissively. "The more Alphas fall, the stronger the dead Alpha army becomes. Eventually, there will only be undead. Undead and us. The survivors...no, the Omegas will be killed for the Fates...the Betas who survive will serve Mirage City. Alphas who survive will be enslaved...as they should be."

The man nods, but his gaze never leaves mine. "Yes, as they should be. Don't you agree, Fallen Earth Omega?"

I frown at the moniker and at his words. "No one should be enslaved. Not Fates. Not Alphas. Not even Berserkers."

And then a shiver of a thought enters my mind and it's terrifying because I know one thing with absolute certainty — this thought doesn't belong to me. Sibilantly, it says, *"Yes."*

"Alphas have no purpose," Freya spits, like she didn't hear it, too. "Berserkers aren't worth their skins."

I shake my head, trying to snap out of it.. "I, um..." Fail. Total fail.

"Alphas...Alphas are the scourge of Gatamora. Breeding is all that they're..."

"Enough." I round on her. "Alphas can hurt and destroy and hate, but they can also be hurt and be destroyed and be hated. They can also *love* and be loved. All Alphas were Betas once." My voice cracks and I struggle to meet Freya's gaze with the hate — or something — I feel towards Adam still weighing on me so heavily. I swallow hard. "They may not be birds, but they can still be loved."

Freya hisses and speaks to me, but all I can hear is *his* voice in my head, echoing there like a summoning. *"I was right to wait for you."*

"Alright, Freya. Calm. I will tell her about the Fates and the Fallen and then I will tell you all that I know about the Beast Omega," he says aloud.

Freya settles, though her nails are now digging into her legs just above the kneecap. She looks like she's a second away from pouncing on me, and I have one hundred percent confidence that she'd be able to kill me in one of her animal forms with a swipe of her hand. *No.* A small doubt pierces my line of thinking. No. I don't lie down. Not for Berserkers or for Alphas and not for Omegas.

I am not owned because I am my own.

I stare Freya down, even as I speak to the man. "The Fates are the ones responsible for making the Berserker's dead army."

"You are mostly correct." *"The Fates are responsible for* resurrecting *the dead army."* "The first of the Fated Omegas was discovered by the Mirage City Berserker three hundred years ago. That is as long as they have been in his service. Together, they are the Fated Omegas of Fire, of the Mind, of Beasts…" He tips his head towards Freya and then towards me. "...And of the Earth." He rests his gaze on me and it is filled with an implication I don't like. *"And there is one other of which they do not speak. The Omega of Death."*

I wince at the conflicting and overlapping words, without understanding what he means — spoken or unspoken — and why I've been brought here to hear this. "What does this have to do with me? I...I'm not a Fate."

"No," Freya sneers, sounding exasperated. "You are like me — a counter to the Fates — at least he thinks you are. I think he is mistaken."

The man smiles kindly and rolls his head as he looks between us. His breathing is shallow. The light in his hand flickers. "The Fates are powerful Omegas that get stronger with every additional Omega life they drain. But what only a privileged few know is that the Fates have another reason for collecting newly ascended Omegas and tearing them away from their families...ripping their bodies from their souls..." His voice doesn't echo in the cave. Why doesn't his voice echo? Mine does. Freya's does.

Fear swims closer to shore and flashes her fangs.

"They search for their doppelgängers, their counters as Freya says. The Omegas whose powers match their own... They've been searching for centuries. They've eradicated dozens of their own doppelgängers — Omegas that they've termed the *Fallen*. It's rather poetic, don't you think? Speaks to their hubris." He laughs and it's a dark laugh, a sickly one. A little deranged.

"They believe themselves *fated* to save the Omega race. Because the Fallen can rise to match them in strength, they represent a threat and must be eliminated." The light below his hand flickers again and, as he speaks, his voice comes out more labored.

Quietly, gently, I say, "Is that what happened to you?"

Silence falls between us. It's pronounced and so oversaturated with sadness, the air can take no more. "No. I am not one of the Fallen. I am just an Omega who was ripped from my Beta family by Mirage City Alphas after I ascended and was brought to the Fates for their use. I was not strong enough to fight them. No single Omega is. And I have only the gift of sight." *"That is what I told the Fates. They do not know that I possess this ability. Say nothing of it. I only have moments left to live. I've been saving all of my strength for this. For you."* "They took my legs for the blood. With it, they can prolong their own lives by stealing my life force." *"The blood also binds us. They can hear everything you say and see everything you do. They have stolen my eyes and now, see through them."*

"Who?" I shout, startled. I look over my shoulder. Nobody there but Fear. And she's close. Close enough to touch. Must mean Pain's nearby, too.

"Do not respond out loud. Just listen." "The Fates, of course. They want to rewrite the world and bend it to their will."

"You keep saying the Fates," I say, voice shaking. "But what about the Mirage City Berserker? He controls them and he wouldn't want to get rid of Alphas. Unless he wants to take all of Gatamora for himself…"

The man just smiles. "Yes, of course. I misspoke." *"There is no Mirage City Berserker."* He groans in pain, his chest heaving. The light flickers wildly and I jerk back and suddenly I'm not in the cave anymore. I'm back in the garden, back in Dark City, back at Dragnovic Manor attending my own stupid

Omega Ball moments before the world went to shit. I'm standing on high ground looking down at a bridge and my Berserker standing on it next to the Shadowlands Berserker. All Four Fates walk towards him past me, ignoring my presence.

And then I blink and I'm no longer on the hill, I'm down on the bridge and the Four Fates and the Berserkers are gone, no longer walking towards me, but the man from the cave is there. The Omega Ball behind him is entirely empty beneath my brightly lit flowery dome.

"Earth Omega, I am sorry to have to meet you here, but we are being watched," he says. His voice echoes here, where it shouldn't, even though back in the cave it does not.

"Where…where are we?"

"We are in the past. At the moment the Fates tempted your Berserker to betray you and succeeded."

"Betray me?" I feel slow. Confused… And then I hear a slight tinkling sound and look down to see the loose end of a chain that Adam told me he'd never make me wear again, and then locked me into. My stomach sours and becomes weighted.

"How did they sway him?" I ask.

"They gave him visions of the future…" He runs his hand back over his hair, which is silky smooth and full. His dark brown or maybe black locks cascade to his shoulders, which are full and cloaked in regal reds and blues. He inhales and then releases the breath in a gale, unburdened by it. Unburdened by something. "False visions, to be sure, but even false prophecies hold power."

His gaze flicks to mine and in this light, I can see that his eyes aren't brown at all but the brightest green, brighter than emeralds. "The Fated Omegas do not have the gift of sight, so they steal mine. That is why I am still alive. But not for much longer. They discovered my lies in a previous prophecy I told and cast me out. My final submission to them is calling for you through your dreams, luring you into this trap here in this cave."

A dagger of ice pierces my heart even though I know it shouldn't. Some part of me had known that this was a trap already. "To kill me?"

"Yes."

I take a step back.

He matches my retreat with a step of his own and his feet move in perfect sync with mine, as if he'd known I'd move before I did. "I'm not the one they sent to kill you. By setting the trap, my part has been played." He takes another step. A wandering flower crunches under his velvet shoe. He looks down at it and says, "This garden that you created is lovely, by the way."

"What are we doing here then? Stalling? Waiting for my executioner to arrive?"

"No. What the Fates don't know is that this trap isn't only for you." His green eyes flash with fire and wickedness. He grips the railing of the bridge in one hand, brown fingers appearing alien and gaunt, shadows stretching over us. The lights of my Omega Ball go out. "This is my last act of resistance.

I had a vision once at the very beginning, right when I ascended, right when the Fates first got to me. I saw their rise to power. I saw the fall of the Berserkers, the fall of the Alphas. I saw the grey, diseased wasteland of Paradise Hole spread and watched cities grow smaller and smaller. I saw Beta children culled from their families in even greater numbers as the Fated became obsessive and desperate in their search for the Fallen. I saw Alphas kept in chains and used for breeding or killed in genocidal numbers. I saw Omegas with wild powers come and go, killed by the Fates to create powers even more colossal and violent and monstrous.

"I saw a rule unending, one where the Fallen had no chance because they could never overcome Fates who draw on centuries-old powers harvested from dead Omegas. I saw the end of civilization and an unending madness.

"And I saw you. Your Berserker fell at your side, dying to protect you. You died at his side, regardless. I did not see Freya in this vision. She abandoned you and you died alone, hand reaching for your Adam, but unable to touch him. This is what the Fates told your Berserker on this night." He gestures around at the world with one hand and the shadows his body creates flicker wildly in the dark. I'm frightened, but Fear doesn't make an appearance. She must be even more frightened of *him.*

"He is a weak male and he believed them. He did not know it, but by believing the Fates and the prophecy they foretold, he took the first step towards realizing it. He locked you in chains." The chain at my neck tightens. "He abused your love."

"I don't love…"

"Love. Yes, he abused it. Your trust, too. But do not despair," he whispers and his voice fades in and out. The dreamworld flickers — I'm back in the cave — and then it holds and the garden around me solidifies and firms. I'm back on the bridge, only this time, the cool metal in my hand changes. When I look down, I see that I'm holding a bundle of brightly colored peonies and the collar around my neck is a chain of small yellow sunflowers, their faces tilted up as if I am the light.

"I saw something else, too," the man says with a smile, this one saccharine. "I had another vision. A world where Omegas and Berserkers ruled side by side. A world where Paradise Hole was restored, brought back to the oasis it once was. Covered in gardens just as magnificent as this that you have created here, because you created all of them.

"Yes," he says in response to my expression.

I'm shaking my head. "It can't happen. I'm not that strong."

"I'm not here to tell you what you are, only what I saw… I saw Beta families reunited with their children. I saw flowers, *unending fields of flowers*, grow." More flowers sprout from the bouquet in my hand, and then come to cover the rest of me, little green vines wrapping around my body and crawling over the bridge and then out over everything. I look up and, for a flickering moment, there is a strong burst of sunlight, then it's gone.

His face remains tilted towards the light that vanished, or never was. "I saw fires hold strong in the Rookery's coldest winters. I felt sunshine as truly as you feel your Berserker's touch and I know that you are the key to attaining it."

"How?" Does he hear how my voice trembles? No? What about my heart?

His eyes open and he looks directly into my soul. "You already know."

I take another step and the world around us flickers again. "You're crazy. I'm not strong enough to kill a Fate. They have unlimited powers..."

"False. They have, at their core, the same gifts as the Fallen — dominion over earth and water, fire and air, mind and spirit, animal and human, life and death. Together, each of the Fallen can defeat the Fate whose powers they share."

I'm still backpedaling, shaking my head. "But the Fates have the gifts of generations of Omegas. Gifts like yours. Like this. This is *incredible*. I can't fight this — I can barely control my own gifts."

He doesn't chase me this time. He only narrows his gaze and drops his proffered hand back to his stomach, which he holds. "They have what they've stolen, yes, but you also have something else. Something that they don't. Something that was freely given, that can never die, that is immortal."

Tears again. Those damn tears. I shake my head but I can't break the line of his gaze no matter how hard I try. My shoulders curl inwards and when I look down, I see that the flower bouquet in my hand has begun to wilt. Dead petals fall at my feet. I clench my teeth and press my wrist over my heart.

"I *can't...*"

"You can. Only you can steer *your* fates back onto the right path."

"I can't kill a Fated Omega and I *can't* forgive him. You can't ask that of me. *He broke my heart.*"

The world shudders and shakes. He looks up at the sky and suddenly a stone falls from it, smashing through the bridge between us. "I am not asking anything of you, sweet Echo, I am merely telling you what I saw."

Another stone falls and as it splashes into the river below, I'm wrenched from the dream and back into a reality where Freya's already standing and shouting. I don't know how long she's been shouting. "What happened? Where did you go? Why did your eyes cloud? Why did you not speak? What is this? What's happening?"

I can feel the ground beneath me, cold and hard. I can feel my heart pounding, cold and hard. I can feel something in my hand — it's a cold and hard metal chain — only when I look down, it isn't. It's long green stems and wilting flowers in a thousand different shades. *I brought the flowers with me.*

The man meets my gaze one last time before his eyes squeeze shut in pain. "You must take the path that Adam couldn't. Only by taking that first step can you save Adam, save Gatamora and replenish Paradise Hole."

His back arches, but he fights brilliantly against whatever binds him. He grabs onto the orb, digging his fingers into its shell. "Freya, you must not forsake the other Fallen. Find the other two. Only together can you survive the Fates."

"I do not need help!" Freya roars.

"Then you truly will be the Fallen…" His head shakes violently, like he's having a seizure. When he finally settles, I scream. He's…he's *dead.* He's a husk of a human with black holes where eyes should be, shriveled, dessicated skin and a lipless mouth baring bright white teeth.

The light in his lap flares violently and the man — the corpse — screams. Pain is here, but she's here for him, standing over him, her hands wrapped around him, squeezing. I lunge forward while Freya staggers back, holding her arm up to the light to fend it off.

"Freya, we have to help him!"

"You can't," the man wheezes. "They're here." The light under his fist is pulsing and, when I look into it, I can see colors moving…shapes…*faces watching me.* I gasp and lurch back, and Freya's arm wrenching me forward is the only thing that keeps the next rock that falls from cracking open my skull. *"Run."*

He seizes again. Tears well in my eyes. He grabs at his wrist with one skeletal hand and, with what looks like every ounce of strength he has, he yanks his hand off of the orb. He collapses and the sound of his body hitting the stones below is both wet and brittle and makes my stomach lurch. A gust of wind rolls off of the light source and, on its wings, carries the screams of a woman *or four.* The smell comes next and I actually do retch. I drop my hands onto my knees and open my mouth and purge a mouthful of berries and bile.

I blink away the dust that clouds my eyes and when I look up, all I can see in the sudden darkness is a lump where the man once sat. "Is…is he dead?" I gag.

Freya hisses, sounding every bit a snake. When I look up at her I can see that her nose is pointed and, in the muted light, her skin glistens like scales. "Yes. He's…not been near the shore for some time." She shudders — *shudders* — as her gaze assesses the pile where his body once was. "He was badly tortured." Another stone drops into the center of the lake, causing a splash that makes me jump. "The Fates need to be stopped." *And I'm the key to how.*

I close my eyes, hands still braced on my knees, and shake my head. "What was his name?" I whisper.

"What?"

"His name. What was it?"

"I don't know." She looks at me incredulously, as if that question is utterly absurd.

Rage claws at the backs of my eyes and I growl, forcing myself up to my feet. "He risked so much for this. For us. It doesn't make me a monster to want to call him something."

"He risked much for nothing. He died and said nothing of what he promised."

I unfurl to my full height as needles shoot my spine through with awareness. "He spoke to me in my mind…" *He said to run.* "We need to get out of here now. The Fates set a trap for us."

"What?" she shouts, voice echoing. Rocks plunk down from the roof of the cave and land in explosions or splashes. I look towards the entrance, wanting to get to it something fierce. "Why would he speak to you? You're *weak.* You are nothing compared to your Fated counterpart. I am strong — much stronger than mine. I can actually kill the Beast Fate and stop the horrible way she's ruining my forest!"

"I…" I ignore the bit about her calling me weak. I can't refute it. After having seen her these past days, I know what a powerful Omega — a Fate, or a Fallen — can be capable of. I'm nothing like that…*but I have something else*. "We have to go."

"No. I want to know what else he told you."

"It doesn't matter." *Because I can't…I can't forgive Adam. Just like I can't kill a Fate. Just like Freya can't form alliances with weak Omegas like me.* "We're doomed."

"We are…" she starts to yell, then abruptly stops. Her face angles towards the exit and her eyes change shape no less than a dozen times. Suddenly, her mouth opens and she releases a loud bird-like shriek. She vanishes in a flurry of feathers and, when I hear the beating of wings a moment later, I know that she's left me.

Sparing one last glance at the pile where the man once lived and died and idled somewhere in between, I offer him a world of gratitude, then start after her. My legs burn with the effort of trying to find my way up and down and around the edge of the cave in the dark. I know my shins are going to be bruised to shit when all this is through but, as I near the entrance of the cave and start to discern the heavy sounds of bodies moving up above, I begin to suspect that bruises will be the least of my worries.

I'm surprised to find Freya waiting for me at the mouth of the cave in her human form, perched atop a boulder my shoulder height. "It is a trap."

"I know. But it was worth it."

She glares down at me, her body twisted into a position I know I'd never be able to get into or out of. "We are surrounded."

"Who did they send to kill us?"

"Mirage City Berserker sent dead Alphas to kill us."

I shake my head. "There is no Mirage City Berserker," I repeat, though I have no idea what the man meant. I met Berserker Maengor myself and yet…I believe him.

"What did he tell you?"

"That we need to work together."

She waits, then spits, "There is more. I want to know."

"I'll tell you if you help me kill them."

She scoffs loudly. "Is this blackmail?"

I shrug.

She scoffs again. "I will kill dead Alphas because I enjoy to kill dead Alphas. You, I will protect for your answers. Your Berserker I will kill if I get the chance."

My heart lurches. My pulse picks up. "My Berserker?"

"He is here. I can scent him on the wind."

My heart. Oh my heart… "He's probably here to punish me," I whisper. "Don't kill him, though. He's mine."

Freya snorts, seemingly satisfied with that answer. I know she interpreted it to mean that his life is mine, that I plan to kill him, but I'm not sure that's what I meant… She jumps off of the boulder and lands lithely on her feet. "Come, Fallen Omega of the Earth, let us kill the dead."

We emerge onto the rocky clearing just as the cave begins to collapse behind us in earnest. We stand together in a depression. Our enemies have the highground advantage. I take them in, strangely unafraid. The pinching of nerves at the base of my spine, the pounding of my pulse, the perspiration on the back of my neck — that's all for Adam. Freya's right. I can smell his Berserker beast on the wings of the wind even stronger than the scent of corpses.

Dead Alphas surround us, their sightless eyes cloudy but not blind. They stare straight at us, unmoving except for the slightest shuffling of their feet as they step shoulder to shoulder, knocking clumsily into trees in order to get into position. One, two, ten, thirty, fifty, a hundred, *hundreds. There are hundreds of them.*

But my gaze stops on Freya, white hair whipping across her face as she stares the dead Alphas down. I think about the man, turning over every word he said, what he asked of me and of her, of us.

If Freya can work together with me, I wonder if I can also follow the man's advice and turn away from hate. I inhale and as I scent Adam's Berserker form on the breeze, I take the next fork in the road I'd been wandering and choose a different path.

I lift the ragged bouquet of flowers in my hand and sweep them around at the dead Alpha army like a sword. My mettle settles. I exhale, "Well, come on then."

ADAM

FUCKIN' PARADISE HOLE

MY CHEST IS HEAVIN'. WOUND IN MY SIDE IS MOSTLY healed and the stitches that hadn't already dissolved were ripped out. "The bites," Yaron heaves, shiftin' slowly outta his dark grey Berserker form until the only grey patches on him are those at his temples.

He kneels naked a dozen feet away from me, separated from me by a deep fissure in the ground my Omega created, a scar on this already scarred earth. And now, a grave. Bodies of at least three dead Alphas lie buried there. Pieces of at least six other dead Alphas lie discarded around Yaron's bare feet.

I nod. "They bite you with their freak Berserker fangs, you don't heal."

I was more careful not to get bit this time. Yaron wasn't so lucky. His right arm is mangled beyond recognition and his lead medic, a Beta called Okayo, is workin' on mendin' it, his dark hands movin' rapidly over Yaron's bloodied flesh.

"Have you need of medical attention?" He doesn't let his pain show in his voice and my respect for him swells like the waves of dead Alphas that have been charging us and charging us and charging… Until we permanently killed all of the undead.

Yeah, I've got need of medical fuckin' attention, I think with a snort. Fought a zombie army and lived to speak of it. Can hardly put any weight on my left leg after two undead Alphas fell on top a' me tryna avoid the tree that came down on top of them, but I ain't worried about my injuries now. Ain't worried about anything, except the one thing.

"How many they send after us?" I say, chest heaving.

"Two hundred, perhaps. Perhaps fewer than that." He grunts as Okayo fits what looks like a metal torture device around his arm. He flinches, but otherwise doesn't react as he looks up at me and says, "Though they did not appear to be after all of us."

"They were after the Omegas."

"No. They appeared to be after *you* and, to a lesser extent, me. Did you not see the Omegas? They were avoided — I'd dare say *spared* — and were left open to attack the undead often and without retaliation. It was…unusual."

I turn slowly and stagger up to my feet. I survey the battlefield, tracking the carnage to a stony outcrop where I ordered all my Alphas to concentrate their efforts — where I ordered them to surround Echo. He's right. My Alphas had no problem gettin' to her, but I couldn't. The undead were after me makin' it impossible for me to pass.

But as I fought my way to her it felt…it felt like the earth was spinnin' around me most. *Was she worried?* Nah. She was probably tryna end me. Maybe, she just doesn't have the skills to satisfy her bloodlust. Guess I'll have to ask her myself. I leave Yaron behind and trudge forward across the graveyard.

The battle was just as brutal as the last and I know that we wouldn't have survived without Yaron's reinforcements. They showed up halfway through the melee and changed the tide, made it possible for us to overwhelm the undead that just wouldn't fuckin' die. Dark City alone wouldn't have been able to hold them at bay, even with our Omega fightin' on our side.

The witch a' the woods put up a good show, her pack of white bears thirty strong and regeneratin' constantly — five bears formin' for each bear that got taken down. When they died, they died in a pile of feathers. *Feathers*. Was fuckin' beautiful.

White feathers dancin' through the air. Green vines dancin' over the earth.

Moss formed over the rocks and flowers formed over the forest floor, trampled just as quickly, but again and again, they bloomed. As the earth tossed and pitched and dead Alphas were swallowed up — a couple live ones, too — and trees fell and water fell like needles from the sky, tearin' through my skin like sandpaper, I could feel *her*. She was everywhere. And I felt made stronger by her, too.

I killed at least thirty dead Alpha fucks all on my own. Took down more 'n Yaron did. He catches up to me and comments on it. "Your fighting was…impressive." He seems loath to admit it.

His gaze dances across the disrupted soil, past the living tryna separate the dead Alphas from the undead, though when I manage to get my wits about me, I'll tell 'em it doesn't matter. All the bodies gotta burn.

"Yours, too."

"Perhaps, but I am the more experienced Berserker. Your display was unexpected."

"Why? Shouldn't be."

"What does that mean?"

"I wasn't fightin' to live. Was fightin' for her." I meet his gaze bluntly and speak just as bluntly. "Besides, I got practice. Fought these fucks before."

He makes a disgusted sound — at which part of what I said, I'm not sure — but I ignore him and keep trudgin' past the bodies, towards a sunken place filled with stones. My Omega kneels in a muddy patch amidst the rubble ringed by a mountain of corpses. Whiskey's pushin' 'em aside already, orderin' Sierra and Balcazar around like she was born to do it. All of 'em are wounded and limpin', black dead Alpha venom and their own red Alpha blood smeared across their faces like they're warriors during an ancient battle rite.

"How you holdin' up?" Whiskey asks me as I trudge towards her. She hands me a pair a' sweats covered in mud. I shove 'em on, stumblin' as I do, but manage to keep upright and walkin'.

"Fine. Numbers?" I say, gaze fixed on that swatch of red hair, shinin' bright. My heart beats hard and proud at the sight of her lookin' up at Barbero and Peate. They're talkin' about somethin'. I wanna hear what she has to say.

"Not sure yet. Looks like we lost about half the original eighty we started with. The reinforcements Shadowlands sent fared better. Looks like they only lost a third, maybe less.

Hard to tell." She kicks an undead arm, one that's been dismembered from the rest a' the body because the only way to kill 'em is to tear 'em apart. "Echo's right. They really are zombies."

Sixty lives lost by Whiskey's estimate. Leaves our numbers at about a hundred combined with Shadowlands' forces, if she's right. That ain't enough to take on the Mirage City Berserker and his Four Fates. Four Fates against two Omegas…not enough to take 'em down, but workin' together, we might be able to get close enough to their Berserker to vanquish him. After that, the Fates are sure to turn to our side. Surely…right?

"Call Karamoko and get his status. We need the extra seven soldiers guardin' Trash City to help us here."

"I tried calling, but I didn't get through."

"Call him again."

"What should I tell him to do with Trash City once I get ahold a' him?"

"Kill 'em."

I march forward into the clearing where Peate and Barbero stare down at Echo and the witch, concern etched into their expressions. The witch is kneeling on the rocks, her body blocking my view a' Echo. She looks over her shoulder at me as I approach and her eyes flash into something more feline — no, serpentine. I don't hesitate, but push forward, even though there's an energy rollin' off a' her that makes my skin crawl.

"Echo," I say, voice scratched, and it has nothin' to do with my injuries at all. I'm *nervous.*

"She is unwell," the witch snaps.

"Back up, witch."

"I don't answer to breeders. Not like your Omega...who gives her power away. Stretched herself too far...too thin...all to defend a breeder like you. She should have killed you like she said she would." The insult slashes, but not as hard as the implication behind her words. Echo mighta wanted me dead at some point...but not anymore. Not if she was lookin' out for me. "She is weak because of *you.*"

"Weak? She hurt?" My heart. Jesus fuck, my heart... I surge forward, but the witch rises up to block my way. "Back the fuck up!" My voice is a roar that echoes. Somewhere in the distance birds crow. A flock takes flight into the daylight, blotting out the sky.

"I don't take orders from breeders. I will stay — she has answers I want — but she needs rest. Her powers drained her...took more than she had to give...for *you.*" The witch steps back and my heart takes a runnin' jump and dives straight outta my chest as Echo comes into view. She's got red blood on her hands and smeared across her ashen face. Her eyes are closed and she's got one hand pressed against her left temple.

"Echo!" I surge forward and the world vanishes as I drop to my knees beside her. I slide a hand beneath her hair and cup the back a' her neck. I grab her waist and then lift her gently and lower her onto the ground on her back. "Peate, what's wrong with her?" I shout.

"Couldn't see a wound...and the witch wouldn't let me near her to do a deeper..."

"Okayo! Need a medic!"

"I'm a medic," Peate rumbles. "And I'm telling you..."

But I'm not listenin'. "Echo...where you hurt, baby?" My hands canvass her body underneath her jacket. It's one a' mine. In any other circumstance, the sighta her in it woulda made me half wild. Right now, all I can see is the blood leakin' outta her nose and her eyes blinkin' triple time. "Echo..."

Echo blinks her eyes open, but doesn't seem to see me. Freaks the shit outta me. "Baby, you hurt? Where?"

"She is *weak*," the witch snaps over my shoulder.

Gettin' on my fuckin' nerves. "You're still here?"

She manages to look pissed at my words and hisses a response I really don't need. All I need right now is my fuckin' wife in my arms and a medic at my side. "I want to know what the man in the cave said to her. Why he even spoke to her...he could have told me, but he chose to tell *her* even though I am strong and she is weak."

"She isn't fuckin' weak," I shout back, lettin' myself get riled. "She's a goddamn fortress and if I hear you say it again, I'll rip the legs off your fox and beat you to death with 'em."

"She is weak!" the witch shrieks, her face transforming as she yells, becoming half-animal and fully monstrous. She shrinks back down to size and throws her finger accusatorially at Echo. "The Omega in the cave said so himself. He said she has no chance to defeat the Earth Fate by herself! I can defeat mine! Why didn't he tell me?" She thrusts forward and my Berserker comes out to play.

I'm all fangs as I roar back at the witch, talkin' down to my Omega this way. "I don't give a fuck if you're an Omega, a Fate, a fuckin' angel — you take one more step towards my wife and I will crush every bone in your body... You!" I point angrily at Okayo, who appears in the valley between the bodies at Whiskey's side. She's holding off what looks like the entire rest of both Yaron's and my armies as they attempt to peer in at the spectacle taking place here on the stones. "Get your ass over here."

Okayo smiles timidly at Whiskey, who responds with a sarcastic-ass thumbs up and a big-ass grin. His smile falls and he shuffles forward more meekly than Ward ever would.

I hold the witch's eyeline for another moment. It's a strange sensation. I've never met the gaze of an Omega for more than a split second before — every Omega I've ever met has been meek, cowed, collared and owned. But in the span of four months, I've met two who look at me like they'd like to gut me.

And…just maybe have the gifts to do it.

Then again…I look down at Echo…she doesn't need any damn gifts to gut me. She wants my heart? I'll cut it outta my own chest and hand it over. All she's gotta do is ask.

"Echo?"

She blinks up at me and frowns. "I saved you," she whispers.

"What's wrong with her?"

Okayo pulls his stethoscope away from her chest and his flashlight outta her eyes. He shakes his head. "Her pupils are responsive, her pulse is steady but weak. She doesn't appear to have had a stroke or an aneurysm, not a heart attack either. I think she's…"

"She's drained. You don't need an Alpha breeder to tell you that," the witch hisses.

Her arms are crossed over her chest and Okayo's gaze drops to them — no, past them, to her breasts which she covers. "I…I wasn't staring, it's just…I'm a Beta."

She hisses, fangs jutting out of her mouth, and leaps at him.

He releases a strangled cry, throws up both hands like he's unsure whether to catch her or fight her off, but before her weight can land, she transforms into a flock of small white butterflies. They scatter past us, silk wings brushing my cheeks. I cover Echo's body with mine, wanting no part of her to come into contact with any part of the witch.

The butterflies flap closer and closer together, spiraling like a reverse tornado into the sky until they meld into one single white owl who finds its perch on top of the pile of dead and undead bodies. She stays there and I decide I hate this witch and I'm fuckin' pissed at Echo for goin' into Paradise Hole with her.

From the moment Ward confirmed that she was gone, I deluded myself into thinkin' that this witch would have Echo's back, but it's clear she's about as reliable as Trash City and just as homicidal. Maybe worse. She hates me and all Alphas and there's some part of her that hates Echo for any ounce of empathy she's ever shown one of us. And this man in the cave? Whoever he is, I'm gonna skin him for callin' Echo weak, for gettin' into her head, for puttin' her in this position in the first place.

"I forgive you," Echo whispers, lips lookin' dry, voice crackin'.

I know I misunderstood her, know I did…and yet… "You…you forgive me?" Hope. It oozes outta me like pus from a goddamn wound.

She nods.

I stroke my hands back through her hair. Cradle the back a' her head. Lean down and brush my lips over hers…she doesn't kiss me back and rips her head to the side. "I forgive you. The man in the cave said I had to. But I don't love you and I can't trust you, not ever. Not again…"

My hope that had been soarin'…shatters against the pavement.

I wanna rip into her, cuss and curse at her. I open my mouth…but lookin' down at her lookin' up at me, I just can't. Not when her eyes are brown and perfect. Not when her eyelashes are a darker red than her hair is. Not when both are a darker red than the blood smeared around her nose, mouth and across her right cheek. Beneath it, it looks like she's lost freckles since I last saw her, like stars fallin' outta the sky. Wonder if I could track them to find the path she took out here in the rocks. Five days. Five fuckin' days she's been in Paradise Hole without me and she's okay. She may be guardin' her heart from me, but who gives a flyin' fuck about that right now? She's alive.

I'm so fuckin' grateful she's okay, I can't help but grin suddenly, madly, and I pretend I don't feel the water wellin' in the depths of my eyes.

Her eyes round, then narrow. I use the edge of my coat — the one she's wearin' — to dab at the blood under her nose. Just a nosebleed. Just a nosebleed… "Stop…" she starts.

I cut her off, takin' advantage of the fact her lips are parted. I kiss her deep and I can feel her inhale as her body starts respondin'…and then stops. A vine lashes outta the ground and wraps around my throat. It's a thicker vine than I've seen her wield before and it fills me with pride and devotion. I'm grinnin', the taste a' her blood on my tongue as I pull back. Her eyes are closed. I'm worried, but with my Berserker's ears, I can hear her heart beatin'. Soft, but consistent. She's just drained, whatever the fuck that means.

There's blood on her lower lip that I wipe off with my thumb.

Over my shoulder, I look at Peate and Okayo standin' together. "She really okay?"

Both medics nod and, fuck, it's gonna have to be good enough for me. I nod, a shaky smile tuggin' my lips a little wider between my cheeks.

"Got orders?" Whiskey asks.

I nod a second time, then scoop Echo up off a' the ground. Even though it hurts like fuck to move, I cradle her to my chest and don't let her go, even as my legs threaten to give out. "Get a tent up. Get a cot up. We're parkin' here until the Dark City Omega's back on her feet."

"I'm not the Dark City Omega," Echo whispers, eyes closed, head tipped back. I'm about to contradict her until her lips move. "I'm the Fallen Omega of the Earth."

"What, baby?"

She doesn't get a chance to respond, though I'm not sure she would have. She looks already half-asleep.

"Remaining here isn't prudent. We're in Paradise Hole and the Mirage City Berserker awaits his reckoning." Yaron has approached. He's found riding pants, but no shirt, and is apparently helping the other Alphas go through the bodies, separating the dead and the undead from one another.

"Nah. He can wait. But we need to regroup. Need reinforcements. Need to get rid a' the bodies."

"We'll burn the zombies," Whiskey says.

"No. No." I clutch Echo tighter to me, her light breath fannin' my neck. "Burn all of 'em."

"Absolutely not. The bodies of my Alphas will be returned to Shadowlands where they will await proper burial."

"Mean no disrespect, but any Alpha body that isn't charred is a potential enemy. You've seen with your own eyes that the dead don't stay dead."

Yaron hesitates as he stares into my gaze. His teeth clench and the microscopic pulsing of a vein across his forehead becomes his only sign of rage. One of his Crimson Riders approaches — the one called Jesús — and tips his head to Yaron. "Lord, what would you command us to do?"

"Make records of their identifiable marks. Then burn them all."

ECHO
PARADISE HOLE

I'M WARM AND DRY AND I'M NOT ALONE. THERE ARE people here. People I know. I can't say that they care about me, but they're not here to hurt me and that's more than I've ever been able to say for the ones I encounter out in Paradise Hole. I think about alerting them to the fact that I'm awake and can hear them, but my body feels heavier than lead and my mind's foggy to boot, so I just lie there and listen to them argue, too curious to fall back asleep.

"They what?" Adam. His voice is closest.

A voice slightly further away and that sounds like Whiskey's answers, "Told you, Dragnovic. We tried all their phones. No answer. Vi's willin' to lead a small team back now to see what happened."

"No. Can't afford to lose any more bodies right now. Need all the Alphas here. After we confront Mirage City, we'll go back for the rest."

"Think somethin' bad happened?"

"Know somethin' bad happened. Trash City set us up."

"Our good friend Yaron is on the war path," Balcazar butts in. "He says after Mirage City, he's razin' Trash City to the ground."

"Tell him Dark City's happy to help. Shoulda killed Merlin when I had the shot. Instead, I traded four truckloads of shit to the bitch. Won't make the same mistake twice."

A corner of my mouth twitches. I don't know what happened, but from what I understand, Merlin did some shady stuff — some *more* shady stuff. She deserves to die but somehow I don't want to be the one to kill her. That said, if anybody else wants to — and I'm sure they do — I won't stand in their path. Hell, I'll hand them the gun. But…I won't pull the trigger. Someone with that much will to live — at any cost — may just come back and haunt me as a ghost.

Balcazar and Whiskey chuckle. It's Balcazar who says, "Any Betas killin' Alphas deserve whatever Yaron's got in store for 'em…"

"You don't think he'll take them to his dungeons, do you?" Barbero asks quietly.

"Goodness," Sierra hisses. "A frightening thought."

"Trash City does the world a service…killing Alphas. Where they fail is giving them up to the Fates to bring back," a voice snarls and it's so vicious it takes me a moment to understand who it is. *Freya. What's she still doing here?*

There's a commotion which cuts this thought short. Whiskey curses. Balcazar shouts, "What the fuck! Why the fuck do you have a naked witch in your tent?"

"Where did she come from?"

"You all should leave now that she's awake," she shouts back. "Leave me with the Omega. Breeders are not needed here."

"She's awake?" Adam asks, tone entirely changed.

His words are followed by silence that makes me uncomfortable. I know they're all looking at me without having to open my eyes and I'm not ready to be subject to their questions or their scrutiny. I'm not ready for *him.*

"She is awake, though she pretends not to be. Pretending won't save you, Fallen Omega. I need the answers I am owed."

I release a small "oomph," already exhausted, before I carefully peel my eyes open. Adam's the first thing I see. He's sitting on a short stump just a few feet away from whatever I'm lying on — a cot, I think, based on the way it squeaks when I move — staring at my face with an expression that's as bright as the world beneath this tent is dark. Full of hope. It breaks my heart.

I sniffle and look away from him quickly. I struggle to push myself up onto an elbow, my whole body protesting at the movement. "Ow," I whisper.

"Shit. You okay, baby? Peate, take a look at her. We thought you weren't bit. Okayo said you weren't bit. Yaron thought the zombie fucks were tryin' not to hurt you. Was he wrong? Were we? Talk to me. Please…"

I hold up my hand as Peate's presence rides up against my right side, crowding me. I shake my head. "I'm fine," I lie. And it might be the biggest lie I've ever told because I'm not alright. I'm shaky. My limbs are all sore. I feel like I just ran full out for hours. My joints are creaky. My lungs burn.

"You're not fuckin' fine. Peate…"

"Peate," I snap. "Don't. I just want space."

Slowly, I feel him pull away. As he does, I finally find a seat and rub my hand up and down my face. "Where…where are we?" It's dark in here, but there's big lanterns set up throwing orange and white light over everything, and in the corner, looking so ghostly she shines like a light herself, is Freya. And as Balcazar said, she is completely naked. Against a darkness that's nearly black except for the bright green lattice of vines stretching over it, she looks like a ghost.

"You made a tree." The voice is Freya's, but it's unimpressed. She crosses her arms over her chest and continues to glare at me.

"I made a…a tree?"

"Yes. A tree grew around you as you slept. I think…you made it to keep…out your Berserker and the Alphas he travels with. But he is a dumb brute and smashed it." She flicks her pointer finger to the right and, sure enough, there's a gaping opening that's jagged on all sides. It's hard to discern the edges precisely because of the vines and the flowers that drape across it — that, and the Alpha bodies blocking the doorway. Adam's Six, as loyal to him as ever. When he chained me up, I wonder if any one of them tried to stop him. Knowing that they didn't embarasses me.

"Balcazar," I say, surprised to see her among them. "You're alive."

"And kicking." She chuckles.

I frown. "I thought Adam — Berserker Dragnovic — beat the life out of you."

"Not quite, though he gave it his best effort."

"And I already apologized for that," Adam pipes up. "I meant it. I shouldn'a…shouldn'a used my fist. Shoulda said shit…"

"No need." Balcazar's curls ring her face. She has them pinned back with a headband. So much of her forehead on display, it makes the crude black stitches crawling over it stand out violently. "I fucked up. I let Maengor get close to you," she says to me, tipping her head forward in contrition. "I'm sorry."

"I'm sorry," Adam blurts. I think he's talking to Balcazar until I glance quickly over to see his gaze pinned to me. It's haunted and wounds me. "You gotta know how fuckin' sorry I am. For Balcazar, for invitin' Maengor, for hostin' the stupid fuckin' Omega Ball in the first place. For the way I run my City and the way Betas and Omegas get treated in it. For all the fucked up shit I did and said to you in Paradise Hole. For…for the chain. For breakin' that promise, I'm sorry, baby." He swallows hard. "I'm sorry, Echo."

My face burns like a torch and I feel hard, hating tears swim across the surface of my eyes, but they're not tears for Adam or for Freya or for Mirage City. They're my tears, my anger, my frustration. "I told you already, I forgive you." The man in the cave gave his life to tell me the things he did, including urging me to work together with the Berserker of Dark City. The least I can do is forgive him and extend that olive branch…

I just can't do more.

"You…do?" He sounds skeptical and I…I struggle to meet his gaze, choosing instead to focus on his hands. They're clasped between his knees. He's got his elbows braced on them and is leaning forward as far as his little stool will allow for. His heels tap out a beat on the dirt. It looks like he's just itching to come towards me, but doesn't. I'm grateful for that.

I nod and swing my legs over the edge of the cot, fighting off a small dizzy spell as I do. "Yeah. I want to work together to take down Mirage City and the undead, like we said we would."

"Can do that."

I don't believe him and my expression must say as much because he continues before I get the chance to respond.

"Not gonna keep you in the dark anymore. Not even gonna try. Saw how that strategy backfired the last time." He laughs a dry, humorless laugh and fidgets in his seat.

Slowly, and without acknowledging his promises, I say, "I want us to work with Freya. Freya, I want you to work with us."

Neither Adam nor Freya respond immediately. After a beat Adam starts but Freya cuts him off, "I will not work with your stupid savage…especially not after…his betrayal. He is not trustworthy."

"Fuck you," Adam hisses, a surge of aggression rolling off of him and crashing into me in a way I have to fight. *I may not want to, but my body remembers…*

I cough, working to clear my throat. "She's right. Not about the name calling but she doesn't trust you and I don't trust you, either."

Adam's eyebrows lift and I scoff at his disbelief. "I'd be the biggest idiot in Gatamora if I let you get close enough to me to put me in chains again. Though, thanks to Freya, I'm more confident now that any chains you did put me in, I'd be able to break."

"Echo, I fuckin'…" He surges up onto his feet and clenches his hands at his sides. "When all this shit with Maengor is over, I'm gonna prove it to you."

I don't know what *it* is, but I don't care. "It doesn't matter. When all this is done, I'll still go back to Dark City with you, if that's what you want."

"If that's what I want? The fuck are you…"

"I want to make sure that you keep your word on the changes you said you'd make for the Betas. I want to see it."

"Of course you're gonna fuckin' see it. You're the Dark City Omega…"

Our voices are getting louder and louder, overlapping and thickening. The others in the room with us have faded into the floral background, truly wallflowers now. It's just us.

I shout, "I can still be the Dark City Omega but I can't be *your* Omega." Aggression charges the air. "I'll live in the garden house. I'll be available for events. You can live in the manor with someone new. Another omega…"

"That's what you want?" Adam voice is unrecognizable. It matches the set of his shoulders, which are bare and flash wounds made by zombie Alphas proudly. But no wounds grab my attention like X carved over his heart.

I close my eyes for longer than a standard blink, open them and meet his gaze. His gaze, that piercing gold mirrored in a face just as lovely. Right now it's cold. Colder than cold. And holding his eyeline? Harder than hard. But I need him to know that I'm sure. "Yeah."

His rage pummels the air. In my peripheries, I can see the Alphas in the door stir, agitated. Barbero backs out of the tree towards Vi, pulling Balcazar with him. Whiskey and Sierra huddle close. Peate has moved back to join them. "You want to see me with another Omega?"

No. "I don't care. I just know that if you're seen with an Omega it won't be me. The man in the cave wants us to work together. All of us. To do that I need to forgive you so we can move on."

"Move on," he says flatly.

"Yeah, move on. I forgive you but I can't love you again. The trust between us is gone, broken, over. We're over, Adam. Hell, I'll even fuck you during my heats if you still want to, but I won't believe in you. I trust Freya more than I trust you. I trust *Merlin* more than you. Both want me dead, I'm pretty sure, but neither's lied to me yet." I snort and glance at Freya who doesn't bother to contradict me. Instead, I'm a little surprised to see that she's backed up to the edge of the tree, too. Her arms remain crossed over her chest and she watches Adam with a frown. It's as I follow her gaze back to him that my heart begins to pound.

It's the way he's watching me. His eyes are huge in his face, his lips are drawn tight across his face, his mouth hangs agape. He's looking at me like something about what I've said has shocked him to his forgotten Beta core. That's when I realize that the air in the room is still thick, but it's not thick with anger anymore.

It's thick with lust.

"Fuck. We gotta get outta here," Peate says, but Whiskey grabs Sierra by the arm and hauls her against her body.

"Are you kidding? We're not goin' anywhere…"

I feel my cheeks heat though I'm not quite sure why. Ignoring the stiffness of my muscles, I sit up straighter on the cot and squeeze my knees. "The Fates told you that you'd find your Omega in Paradise Hole. It didn't have to be me and it still doesn't. It could be another Omega — it could be Freya, even." I'd be ravenous with jealousy at the thought if it weren't for the fact that Adam doesn't seem to see her or anyone else in the room — the uhh…tree — at all. He doesn't even seem like he hears me.

"Adam, are you…"

He lunges at me, arriving at the edge of the cot and landing on his knees. My knees are pressed against his chest until he parts them, pushing forward, his heat crashing into me. He doesn't make a move to grab my hands, but grabs either side of my face and crushes his mouth to mine. His lips are fire and silk and so heartbreakingly familiar. I whimper as our torsos collide and my fingers fumble lamely, settling on his bloodied abdomen. I'm not used to being touched. Am I even doing this right? He groans and makes a choking sound in the back of his throat and a smile threatens the corners of my lips, but I fight it. *He isn't used to being touched, either.*

Adam jerks back abruptly, breaking the kiss before it's begun. "Fates told me I'd find my Omega in the woods. But I fell in love with *you*."

Still struck dumb, I don't answer, not that he gives me a chance to. He traps my face between his hands and brings our noses and foreheads to touch. "Know you don't believe me, but I'm gonna spend the rest a' my life provin' it. I'm a bastard, Echo, in more ways than one. In all the fuckin' ways, but I love you with every bit a' my black heart. That's how I know this shit between us ain't over." He's breathing hard with urgency that scares the living daylights out of me, but his voice is soft and gentle and so are his fingers stroking patterns lovingly down the sides of my face and across my cheeks as he whispers, "You said *again*."

"Wh…what?" I hiss, so confused by the direction this moment has taken and distracted by his touch. *I've missed this.*

"*Again.* You said you wouldn't love me again. That meant you loved me once and if a worthless fuck like me could make you fall in love with me once, then I know I can do it twice…"

"Adam," I yelp, my voice strangling. Tears needle the backs of my eyes and my back muscles bunch and heat and my heart thumps and my lungs turn to lead. I try to push away from him, but he doesn't allow my retreat. I sputter, "I didn't…" He kisses me. "I don't…" He kisses me and grabs me by the back of the head to hold us where we are.

"Shut the fuck up, Echo. You said it's over, so *again* is all I've got left." He grabs my wrists and gathers them to the center of his chest, pulling back enough for me to be able to see his face. It's a smart move in this battle, because everything is a battle between us. This right here is how he softens the battlefield, with his red cheeks and redder lips and his red eyes. It's the gloss sheening his eyes though that make me so afraid, my best friend Fear runs right out of the room along with the other Alphas and Freya.

We're alone. I wish we weren't alone…

My heart is pounding rapidly — too fast to match his languid movements. Slowly, slowly, he brings my hands up to his lips. He kisses my filthy fingertips. "Not gonna let you take it from me."

His gaze locks with mine. I don't know exactly what he means by that, all I know is that the tone he's using is one that I've never heard him use before and feels designed to make me cry. *Desperate. It's desperation.* Desperate like a wounded Beta boy calling for his murdered sister in the night.

I shake my head and tug at my hands, but he doesn't release them. Instead, he leans forward. His breath flutters against my earlobe. He kisses it. Then he kisses the side of my neck where I can still feel the lingering pain of the platinum digging into my skin, carving the trust I had for him out of my body, like sucking marrow out of the bone. And before that, the mark he left behind when an evil Berserker bit a runaway Omega he didn't know in the woods.

"Don't take it from me." He kisses the other side of my neck, coming as close to me as our positions allow, like he's trying to absorb me into his skin. "Please don't take it from me, Echo." His voice cracks.

"I hate you," I tell him, only because it's true. Every inch of me wants to say no — every inch, but the one inch more powerful than the rest. And its in that inch and in his touch that I come to understand a solitary truth. He doesn't manipulate my powers, he *provokes* them. Because he provokes *feeling* in me. So much feeling. Infinite feeling. Most of it terrible. But not that last inch. Because it's that inch that feels so wonderful its very existence is in defiance of nature itself.

He inhales deep and quick. "Hate me like an Omega hates a Berserker…or like a wife hates her husband?" He doesn't give up. Just like I don't give up.

"Adam…"

"You don't have to answer now, just tell me again."

My head tips forward and I press my eyes to his shoulder, hiding there in a darkness that smells like zombie blood and him. "I hate you, Adam."

"Good." A wet laugh chokes him and he releases my hands in favor of grabbing the outsides of my arms and squeezing them. "Hate me, Echo. Because I love the way you hate me. Just so long as you only. Hate. Me." He pounds the words out, touching my hair, my neck, my back, pulling my hips forward to meet the wall of his body. "You hate anybody else like you hate me, it'll…" He doesn't finish. He doesn't need to. He just grabs my right hand and lays it flat over the X carved into his heart.

I squeeze my eyes shut tight, fighting the tears that threaten to destabilize me. A second passes before I give in. To all of it.

I rip my hands free of his grip and palm the erection pressing at the cotton of his pants roughly. He growls and I lunge for his neck, biting down onto it hard. "Jesus, Echo. I don't know if I…" I yank on the elastic waistband of his sweats and fist his length. "Fuck it," he whispers.

He leans back and yanks up on my knees. Caught off guard by the motion, I fall back and open my eyes to the sight of him prowling over me. The cot squeaks under his weight as he moves over my body, gaze roaming everywhere and nowhere before settling on my pants. He rips a hole in the crotch and pulls his erection free. He strokes it maddeningly.

"Fuck. Where's your underwear?" he says.

"Where's yours?"

"Gonna fuck you now." He starts to roll forward, angling his cock toward my damp lips. I wait for the familiar feeling of his body crashing against mine like a wave, but he hesitates. "Can I?"

I hate that he asks and fist a chunk of his hair. I yank, trying to pull him down to me. "Fucking is all I want from you."

But the bastard just smiles. "Say it again."

"I hate you."

I moan and he growls as he fills me up to his knot. My arousal is almost painful at the thought of feeling it inflate inside me, claiming me wholly. I roll my hips and he digs his fingers into my waist too hard as he pounds me down onto his body too roughly.

I reach back and gouge my nails into his shoulder. I bite and moan and claw. He doesn't relinquish a lot here, and the movement is left up to him. He picks me up and pulls me down and even though we stare deep into each other's eyes as we fuck hard, the moment is suspended in time, hung low like the moon on a cold winter night, so close to the horizon.

Everything is quiet…everything except our breath, the leaves that crinkle as they come to life on the inside of the tree trunk, and our voices repeating a quiet mantra over and over.

"I hate you, Adam," I tell him.

And his response. *"Again."*

31 ADAM
GARDEN OF ECHO

I TOOK MY OMEGA FOR EVERYTHING SHE HAD AND IT wasn't enough, so I had her again up against the wall of this castle she built around us because I wanted to see the way her red hair and brown skin and freckled fuckin' face looked against a wall of flowers and vines.

Then I had her again in the dirt.

Lyin' on the cot, her body draped over mine like a blanket, I'm idlin' on the edges of sleep…I need to sleep…but I'm wide fuckin' awake when I feel her carefully tryna lift herself off a' me.

"Where the fuck you think you're goin'?" I wrap both arms around her shoulders and drag her into my chest. I kiss the top of her head.

She stutters, "I…need to find Freya."

"The middle a' the night?"

"It's important."

"Fuck." I release her and fumble around in the dark for my clothes. Don't find much. What little that there were are shredded. I pull 'em on anyway and, usin' my Berserker's eyes, I watch Echo do the same.

I snort, "Can't make clothes outta flowers, can ya?"

She gives me a wary look that makes me smile wider. *I'm gonna win her again, or I'm gonna fuckin' lose limb or life tryin'.*

She doesn't answer and I watch her struggle to pull her shirt on and then to determine which way are the front and back of her pants. "Here. Let me." I help her dress because there's somethin' horribly fuckin' sexy about maneuvering her legs into garments that makes me want to do it all the fuckin' time.

Maybe it's because the act of puttin' 'em on and watchin' her struggle to get her hands through the arm holes makes me want to shred the clothes in half and just have her freckled body naked and pressed against me for all time. "Still need to count," I whisper.

She jerks up. "What did you say about my cunt?"

I laugh a lungful a' laughter, bend down and kiss her mouth just because I can. "I love you."

Her lips twist. She doesn't say anything. Just stares at me with jaded yet dazzling eyes. She's tired. She needs rest. She hates me. It's the middle of the night. "You sure this can't wait?"

She shakes her head. "I owe Freya answers. It's why she helped me fight off those zombies at all. I'd be dead without her, a couple times now."

"You held your own."

"She killed twice as many of those creepy things as I did. More than you." I frown, not liking that I got bested by an

Omega. I like the reverence and respect in Echo's tone even less. I've never heard her use it before.

"This important shit you gotta tell 'er?" I'm grumblin' and she gives me a funny look. She opens her mouth, like she might ask me about it, but then takes her questions another way. She doesn't wanna get close, but that don't matter. Gonna tear down that fortress she built between us even if it means I gotta pull it apart brick by brick.

"Life and death," she says.

I nod, havin' suspected as much. "And it affects everybody?"

"Yeah."

"Then we wake everybody."

She pauses in the doorway of her hollowed out tree castle long enough to look at me and gawk. "Everybody? You mean the Six, right?"

"I mean the Six, the rest a' my Alphas and all Yaron's people. Alphas, Betas, your Omega — everybody." I step up next to her and look down at her face, her perfect face, illuminated by this thing Paradise Hole begs to call moonlight. "You think nobody's hearin' you, but that ain't true. I hear you. And you been talkin' a different tune ever since you saw the man in the cave." *That fucker.* "Been usin' the word *together* an awful lot. So, don't stop now. You got shit to say, say it to all of us."

Her jaw snaps shut and she gives me a funny look, wrinklin' her nose before combin' the thicket of her curls behind her ear. Her fingers get tangled. She gives up. "Should we wake everybody up?"

"Just not the dead."

Her stoicism cracks and a smile breaks out over her face. She snorts, tryna stifle it, but in the end just gives in. She exhales and stares out at the world rollin' out beyond this tree, this strange little sanctuary. "Fuck you, Berserker," she says, parodyin' my own words back to me.

I grin like a goddamn loon, wantin' nothin' more than to go to her and shower her with affection, but I hold my ground. For now. I point left with my chin. "Go wake our Six. I'll handle Yaron's crew."

She doesn't say more as she brushes past me without a backward glance and I smirk, chest feelin' tight though my lungs feel airy. I can breathe in her presence. Without her, I been drownin' for days. The breeze that filters in through so many trees even smells like her. Huh. Feels like there's more vegetation surrounding us than there was when the battle began. Shiftin' my beast's gaze out at the world, I see that I'm not mistaken. I grin. The outside is just as stunnin' as the inside. Covered in flowers. Paradise Hole covered in bright patches of green.

I find Yaron awake, sittin' in one of those patches. He watches me approach, clearly able to see me as well as I can see him. "Your Omega has exceptional gifts."

I preen at the compliment, though it bites in equal measure. "She does." But she's not mine. Not anymore. "Dark City Omega's got somethin' to say to us. Let's get a fire goin'. Make space for your people. You seen the witch?"

He lifts a finger and points up at the tallest boughs of a nearby tree. I shout up at the white owl perched among its sparse foliage. "Echo's ready to talk to you. Whatever the cave guy told her, she's gonna tell you and me and everybody else.

Meet there on high ground." I point and she takes off into the sky.

We get a space cleared out slightly east, where the ground rises higher and drier. Alphas and Betas work together to get a ring of logs from the fallen trees Echo tore down arranged into a circle, a fire flaming brightly at their center. I sit next to Echo. Whiskey sits on her other side. There's space enough in this inner circle for about forty Alphas and Betas to cram in together, all in various states of healing.

Some've got bandages wrapped around their heads and arms and legs and chests, some lookin' unscathed, but not many. Maybe two. When space along the logs fills up, those that aren't too injured, or aren't still dealin' with the bodies — i.e. anybody that can still fuckin' stand — crowd in behind us. *Survivin'* we might be one-twenty, but *standin'* we're only eighty and a few.

I can tell the attention makes Echo nervous and take her hand. She jerks, as if outta instinct, but I hold firm, not allowin' a retreat. Because there's nowhere she'd go that I wouldn't chase after her…but I'm done chasing.

I meet her wary gaze and lean in, brushin' my lips over her earlobe as I whisper, "I'm here no matter what." Louder, I cock my head to Barbero, standin' just behind Whiskey. "We got booze? Grab it. I've got a feelin' we're gonna need it. Organize anythin' you can find to eat, too."

He leaves and I nudge Echo in the side. "You cold?"

"No, no. I just want to make sure Freya is here."

"She's here." I point at the log two over. This log has only three occupants despite the fact that there's enough space enough for six — Yaron, an Alpha with a bandage over his right ear and the left side of his chest, and a white owl.

The owl coos and Echo seems to take that as a prompt to start speaking. She begins explaining a long story, one in which an Omega is trapped by the Fates in a cave and takes her into a dream and tells her that she, the witch of the woods, and other Omegas called *the Fallen* will be the ones to take on the Fates and bring down the dead army and that, in order to succeed, they'll need to work together and with the Berserkers and the Alphas of the cities.

When she finishes speaking, the circle is silent. Wariness streaks across my chest. They don't believe her. I don't *not* believe her, but I don't know who to trust.

Yaron is first to speak after Echo goes quiet. "The Omega in this cave who turned to ash — could he not have been an illusion created by the Fates? I have heard tales that they can manipulate thought."

"It's possible," Echo says, swallowing nervously. She's got a blanket spread across her lap but she still shivers. I pull her closer, tucking her under my arm. I feel her resist at first, and then her weight settle onto me more fully a few moments later.

"But you do not believe this to be the case?"

"No."

Yaron stares at her brutally for a few more seconds before his attention shifts to me. "An Omega is not a likely source of reliable information. Two Omegas, even less. We should ignore these edicts and proceed as planned. Berserker to Berserker, we must confront Maengor. Should his Omegas prove difficult, then your Omega and the witch can be deployed as part of a larger strategy working in coordination with our armies."

"We aren't tools to be deployed how you see fit, Berserker," Echo spits in a tone that borders on disrespect and makes me tense. Berserker Yaron is known for his antiquated ideas on heirarchy and respect, obedience and...torture. My hackles are up, prepared to defend against any retaliation. "This isn't another Alpha War or Berserker battle. This is a *reckoning* of Omegas. A reckoning for your hubris, for your treatment of Betas and Omegas throughout history. If the Fates weren't so determined to wipe out the world along with you, I'd be hard pressed to tell them they're wrong."

"Silence. You speak of the murder and reanimation of Alphas as if it's a game. There are newly ascended Alphas missing from Shadowlands — *children*." His voice carries conviction that Echo does not try to dispel.

I don't either. Instead, I clear my throat. "There's no disputing that killin' kids is wrong, but most of us Cities have been doin' it for a long time to Betas and Mirage City has been doin' it for even longer to Omegas. It's *Omegas* doin' the killin' of Omegas. They want everythin' and if it takes four Omegas — one to match each of the Fates — to take 'em down, then we can't keep Echo and Freya and the other two as knights on our chessboards. They're our queens. And if we're the kings it's our job to defend 'em."

I lean my elbows onto my knees, wonderin' if my analogy made any fuckin' sense at all as I never played a game a' chess in my life — prefer games where I get to hit stuff — and hopin' for all our sakes that even if I'm talkin' shit, the stink at least got through to him. Hard to tell though. His face doesn't change at all.

And then he says in a tone that borders on violence, "There is no universe in which I will allow an Omega command of *my* army, least of all a gaggle of Omegas, one of whom seems content to spend her days on four legs rather than two and another who wields flowers in place of a sword. *Flowers*, my dear pet," he says, addressin' Echo again, "will not frighten centuries old Fates and they will not kill Maengor."

"Yaron," I bark, "Take care in how you speak to the Dark City Omega." My Berserker is strainin', wantin' out, wantin' blood.

"Take care in how you speak to *me*, young Berserker, or it will not just be her tongue I tack to my dungeon walls."

"This is how we all die," Echo shouts, breathin' hard. "This right here. If we can't figure out a way to treat each other like equals, then Freya and I are going to be harvested for our blood and our gifts and the two of you are going to end up as breeders chained in the Fates' basement and that's only if you're not turned into zombies, first."

"Jesus, Echo. Ain't makin' this easy."

"I refuse to entertain any more of this." Yaron stands.

Echo stands.

"Fuck." I stand beside her.

"Fuck." Whiskey, Sierra, Vi, Balcazar, Peate, and Barbero stand with me. Several of Yaron's Crimson Riders rise with him.

I snarl. Aggression fills the space. Yaron's shoulders swell and his hand snaps back one edge of his cloak. He reaches for the axe on his back, a menacing blade that has absolutely no fuckin' purpose since his Berserker form is his best weapon. The bandages crisscrossing over his skin shine bright white in the light of the fire. Ribbons of flame reach for the heavens.

And then Echo puts an end to it all. She shouts across the divide separating us, "I believe the man in the cave. He knew that we'd been set up for a trap. He knew that he would die for what he knew, but he still fought to tell us. He fought *for us*. For all of us. And I'm standing here now telling you that I will fight for him and I will fight for you. I will fight for *all* of you." She angles her body to face me and takes my wrist in her rough palm. She gives it a squeeze and I feel the touch all over my body all at once. "I'll die for you, too. For any of you." She finishes by looking at Yaron. "I just won't *un*-die for you.

"Freya and I can't kill the Fates and the entire army by ourselves." Freya's owl coos, but Echo waves her off. "We can't and you know it, Freya. But maybe, just maybe, if we get the other Berserker armies together and try to find the other Omegas, we'll stand a chance against Mirage City. I know you don't believe me about Maengor not being…well, Maengor, but who cares. Our enemy hasn't changed and neither has our strategy. All of us. Together. As equals. As One." She exhales and when Yaron doesn't speak, she flicks her attention to his left. "Freya. Are you with me?"

The fire crackles. The owl hoots again. Its head spins all the way around its neck and as it settles, it unfurls, becoming human. Several in the circle who haven't seen her transform before hiss. It's a strange thing, seeing a human that has shifted into something that isn't a Berserker.

She approaches the fire naked and, standing before it, her skin is so white it seems to shine, pure luminescence. "With all Fallen Omegas gathered, we do not need the Alphas. They are *weak*, irrelevant in the war of the Omegas." The Alphas start to rile again — fuck, even I'm growlin' at her assessment — but she ignores them and stares only at Echo. "But without all Four Omegas, the dead army will…get in our way. We can use living Alphas to reduce their numbers."

"We *did* reduce their numbers. We obliterated them," an Alpha from the crowd shouts to a chorus of agreement.

Freya hisses. "You know nothing. The army of dead Alphas number in the thousands."

"How do you know this?" Yaron barks.

"I have seen it. I spy on their city. I have seen fields of dead Alphas penned and ready, waiting for their hunger to be sated."

"Impossible. Mirage City would have no way of containing them. Word would have spread and my scouts would have heard of this."

"Clearly not."

Lifting his upper lip to reveal elongated canines, Yaron looks her in the face, but I don't see any love lost between them. I wonder about him — the Berserker who will take no Omega — and I wonder about her — the Omega who will take no Berserker. Not a match. But why? Is there more that makes an Alpha-Omega pairing than just our instinct to breed?

I look at Whiskey and Sierra. Sierra has her hand on the small of Whiskey's back. They are two Alphas, yet there is more chemistry in that one shared touch than in all the looks passed between Freya and Yaron even though they're only wearing a cloak and a pair of half-shredded pants between them.

My chest expands and Echo looks up at me. I'm already staring at her with wide eyes, confused by a sudden sharp, stabbing realization.

I wanted her from the start. Only her. Bein' an Omega had fuck all to do with it. And she never had a shot at freedom, because I never had a shot...

I lean in and kiss her tenderly. She's unprepared for it, and slow to react before I pull away. "Believe you, Echo, and I'll back you to the end. I'll convince Yaron. You work on Freya." I kiss the tip of her nose before straightening up, feelin' a weight shed. I sling my arm over her shoulder and reel her into my chest, her reticence be damned.

"We saw what happened today. An army that matched our numbers almost one-to-one took out half of us and that was *with* two Omegas fightin' on our side and no Berserkers or Omegas fightin' on theirs. They might be mindless Alpha zombies, but they're fuckin' hellions on the battlefield. If there's even a chance that there's an army bigger n' the one we went up against today, then with our numbers, we can agree that we don't stand a shot.

"Two Omegas, two Berserkers, and a hundred-some-odd Alphas ain't enough. We need a minute to regroup, gather the other cities to our cause, like the Dark City Omega suggested, and together plan for a war the likes of which no city's seen.

We keep searchin' for Omegas in the meantime as part of this strategy.

"We give ourselves a set amount a' time — Berserker Yaron, you got better relationships with the other cities, so I leave it to you to decide how long," I tip my head towards him, granting him a concession that a Berserker's not likely to make *ever,* and it is the only one I'll ever make him. I don't do it for him though.

"Freya, you're welcome to stay in Dark City until the time comes to wage our war as a guest of the Dark City Omega, so long as she's okay with it and so long as you don't cause my people, Alphas included, any trouble."

Freya looks at me with her upper lip pulled back in a snarl that I don't know how to interpret. She doesn't speak.

"We will also need to obliterate Trash City," Yaron says. "They are working with Mirage City and it is possible that they have done something with Alphas in our war parties. Paradise Hole cannot align with Mirage City. Paradise Hole creatures number far too many. They could, with their numbers alone, overwhelm us."

"I agree. Happy to coordinate a sweep a' Paradise Hole."

He nods, twirls the grey hairs at his temple with one finger as he thinks. "Gang Mountain Alphas are said to possess a force, as well. It would be good to align them to our cause."

"Agreed. So that settles it. We'll follow Echo's plan, gather the Berserkers to our cause and search for the missing Fallen Omegas in the interim. You two okay to wait, regroup, and go after Mirage City together? A united force?"

Both Yaron and Freya look at me. Both Yaron and Freya look at Echo. An eternity passes. Yaron concedes before Freya does and, when they do, I can tell that the agreement that's been struck is shaky and likely to disintegrate by mornin'. Ain't nothin' I can do about it now though but hope.

After the group wraps up a few more discussions and eventually, disperses, I lead Echo back into her tree and watch her climb onto the springy, flower-covered cot and slide underneath a blanket, still fully clothed. I look down at her longingly, but back away instead towards the door.

"I'll let you sleep."

"The man in the cave told me that the Fates fed you a prophecy…that that prophecy is why you betrayed me. What was it?"

Surprise stalls me. I struggle to swallow past the lump in my throat. "Fates told me I was gonna end up dyin' for you… that I'd fail you, just like I failed Noon, and that you'd die right next to me. Said I'd never be good enough for you. That if I gave you up, you'd get to be powerful. That you'd be better off without me." My voice is tight? Can she hear the terror in my tone?

"You believed them?"

I choke. "Fuck me, right?"

She blinks, betrayin' nothin'. "Hm."

"Hm? That's all you got to say to me?"

Her cheek ticks, like she's gonna smile. We're talkin' about her death and she's got the fuckin' nerve… "That's one eventuality."

"What's that supposed to mean?"

"If we do like we've planned and stick together, fight together, we'll win. The Fates didn't see that outcome."

"But only if you forgive me, right?" I try to smile. It fuckin' hurts.

She tries to smile. It looks like it hurts. "I think I'm supposed to…" She stops, voice catching. "I think it's gonna take more than that." She bites the inside of her cheek. "I just can't. I'm sorry."

Fuck that. So long as I've got a heart, it's hers. So long as she's got a heart, it belongs to me. "Go to sleep." I turn from her and start out the tree, heading for my Six and where they're gathered, but I'm stopped short.

"Adam?" I turn and see her propped up on her elbows. "If you don't have anywhere to sleep, it's dry in here. If you don't mind sleeping on the ground."

This time, I don't grin even though I want to. I turn around and make my way back into her tree and as I pass over the threshold and watch her flick her gaze away from me, a deeper resolve floods my bones. I settle onto the ground just below her cot and just before sleep hits me, I voice that resolve out loud to the star my universe revolves around — an Omega I pulled out of a trash heap.

"I'm not goin' anywhere." And I'll put a damn chain around my neck and shackle myself to her wrist if I gotta make sure of it.

ECHO
GARDEN OF ECHO

I WAKE ON AN ORGASM. WET HEAT STROKES MY CLIT. Sometime in the night — or is this day? — my pants were dragged to the tops of my thighs and a hard body pinned my legs down. Fingers spread my labia while his tongue massages my clit and speares my center with wild wanton. There's a finger in my asshole and it's thick — maybe his thumb?

I don't manage to take a full deep breath before I'm shattering.

It happens in warp speed, too fast to catch. My chest is heaving and stars play out in front of my eyes as Adam — it could only be Adam — chuckles darkly and sucks my oversensitive clit into his mouth and rolls it between his lips.

"Ouh," I chirp, legs spasming, but I can't retract them because he has me caged in the only way I'm happy to be caged. "Too sensitive," I beg.

He prowls up my body, resting almost his full weight on me until I'm half suffocated. He doesn't care. He leans in and kisses me and I try to dodge it. "You smell awful," I say on a poorly restrained laugh that makes him grin rakishly.

"Smell like your filthy pussy," he growls, going for my lips anyway. I don't pull away. I could…but I don't.

Heat builds between us, his tongue stroking mine, forcing me to taste morning breath — his and mine — and unwashed pussy. "Nasty," I whisper as he breaks the kiss.

"Disgusting." He reaches his hand between us, slapping it possessively over my core. "And I'm still hungry. Unless…" He hesitates, giving me a goading, teasing look with one eyebrow cocked. "Unless, of course, you don't want it."

I shake my head rapidly, unable to think about anything but the fact that I want it.

"Of course. Cuz this is all you want from me, right?"

He slices his tongue up the center of my most sensitive place and I freeze, back arched, lips parted, eyes glued to his as my thoughts scramble and I try to make heads or tails of what he's said. *That's what I told him. That I'd take him only for the title and only for his body.* I cringe, not liking that I said that. He's not a whore and yet, without trust, what else is there besides this?

He snarls when I say nothing and kisses me hard on the lips, bruisingly, *longingly*. "Don't answer that." He kisses his way back down my body and brings me to orgasm once more. "Love kissin' you when you're sleepin'," he says against my inner thigh. "Love that surprised little look on your face when you wake up screamin'. Gonna fuck you awake next time." He prods my asshole with his middle finger and I tense up against the invasion.

I reach down and comb my fingers through his hair. *What am I doing?* "I'd like to try that."

"Know you would." He grunts as he pushes up into a seated position and swings his legs over the edge of the cot. "You hungry?"

"I…what?"

"You hungry?"

"I…" I sit up and reach for the erection tenting the front of his sweats. He laughs and takes my hand by the wrist. "Later." He winks and I ignore the disappointment that churns in my gut and makes my pussy clench around a dick that isn't there. "Meant for breakfast." He stands and adjusts himself, but it doesn't help his situation in the slightest. God, he's huge.

And he was mine, once.

All mine.

But then he had to fuck everything up.

"Don't like that look. What you thinkin' about?"

"Nothing."

He doesn't say anything and I brush my hand over the flowers that cover the outside of the blanket. I grew more last night. Maybe, because of the community I felt forming. The hope that it will last. *It will. It has to.*

"You're so fuckin' incredible," he says out of the blue. When I look up. I see he's looking at the blanket, too, staring at the flowers like they're precious gems.

I just grunt. "I'm not. Freya, she's incredible."

"She's a fuckin' asshole."

I laugh at that and sit up straighter, reaching for my threadbare clothes — what's left of them, at any rate. "Yeah, but one doesn't negate the other. She's a badass and she's really cool."

"Cool?" Adam balks, one leg shoved into his sweatpants, the other proud and thick and looking so very delicious. "*Cool?* You hit your head on one a' those rocks?"

I laugh again and shake my head, trying to stop the familiar banter I'm so used to with him. *We're not together.* "She is. She handles herself like a one woman army. She doesn't need saving."

"Psh — you don't need savin'."

"You saved me," I begrudgingly admit.

"You were holdin' your own."

"I needed help. I always need help." I shrug. "But I felt a little more in control with Freya's help. Maybe, just with her there. She carries Omega energy. I can feel it."

"Good."

"You carry energy, too," I admit.

Adam hesitates before answering and I don't want to look up and see his face, looking struck. Lookin' humbled. I shouldn't be talking like this. Leading him on. Giving him hope. I hate him. I hate his hope.

"But even with all the help in the world, I still don't know what I'm doing. I may have the gifts, but I'm not good at using them. I know what I want to do but I can't make it happen most of the time. It's either a landslide or an earthquake or nothing."

"You're an all or nothin' kinda warrior. It's one of the things I love most about you." He laughs when I look up at him and give him a stern look.

"Adam…" I start.

"Nah." He shakes his head, runs his fingers back through his hair, tugs on the tip of his short beard. "Don't fuckin' think of changin' anything about you. I love it all. The way you move. The way you hate. I love all of it. I love all of you."

They throw me, the words coming out of his mouth. Like love-caged violence. That's who he is. And I need to put an end to it before we both sink into the pit where violence and love are left to battle it out to the gruesome, gory death. Right now, I'm not sure which would win.

"Look. Adam, I…" But I make the mistake of being distracted by him looking for his tee shirt. He can't find it because he wasn't wearing one. Still, he's got something around his neck. "What are you wearing?"

"Pants."

I can see that. The erection tenting the front of them is unmistakable. "Not that. Around your neck."

He stands up and runs his finger over the thing. "You like it?" His grin is wild and impish and I'm afraid of it. I glance around for Fear, needing her now, but she still seems reluctant to make an appearance.

"Adam…" My voice fucking shakes. Why does it do that?

"I gotta show the world I belong to the Fallen Earth Omega, don't I? Couldn't think of a better way. Made it outta your vines. Impressed? They're hard as shit to work with. Either brittle or so damn delicate. Makes sense knowin' who made 'em, doesn't it?"

Stop it. That's what I would tell him if I had words, but I can't find my voice. He's robbed me of it with a thin little band made of green vines coiled around thicker brown ones. I shake my head. "No one should own anybody else."

"And if I wanna be?"

I shake my head. My heart weighs me down like a brick. *Stop it,* I say, but I realize only after a moment that I haven't said the words out loud. I've said them only to myself.

"Enough." He ruffles my hair and cocks his head toward the light sky shining in from outside. "Heard some commotion out there. Think they mighta found somethin' to eat. Maybe hunters brought back somethin' good."

"Hunters?" Confused and disoriented and on shaky legs, I follow Adam at a distance, worried to get too close.

"Yeah. That a problem."

"Might be. Last time I tried to hunt in front of Freya, she smacked the shit outta me."

"She *what?*" Adam rounds on me, but I step past him, giving him an overly wide berth as I make my way out of the tree. I open my mouth to call Freya's name — to stop her from killing anybody — but the moment my eyes take in the world around me, the words I'd been poised to speak fail me.

"Oh baby," Adam whispers beside me, rage leaking out of his touch and his tone.

I look up at him, hoping he'll confirm what I think I'm seeing, because it can't be. It just…can't. "Adam?" I say shakily, voice like my gaze, filling with tears.

"Baby…" He moves forward and, when I don't immediately follow, reaches back and grabs my hand. He tows me to the first tree. He reaches up and his fingers make the fruit between them look so tiny as he plucks it. He bites into it, demolishing half of the somewhat desiccated-looking thing in one mouthful. He chews, swallows, throws his head back and laughs.

"Echo…" He presses the fruit to my mouth and I bite, chew, swallow and smile. "You did it." He brushes his thumb beneath my left eye while his other hand brings the pit to his mouth. He licks it clean.

"I made a peach," I whisper incredulously.

"You still think you need my savin'?" While I blush, he shakes his head and balks, "Baby, you made a goddamn fruit forest."

He's not wrong. He turns and sweeps his hand out toward the green that spreads and spreads, blotting out my vision and making me think of the man in the cave. I turn his words over carefully. *I saw flowers growing in Paradise Hole.* And there are a lot more than flowers growing here.

Peach trees form a dense forest around the hollowed out tree trunk. Tall, dry grass laced with flower-bearing vines form the floor of this orchard. The trunks of the trees are green, the branches are green, the leaves are almost electric. And as for the dark grey trees of Paradise Hole? They still stand, wearing robes draped in flowers.

Long strands of moss hang from the tips of all their branches like the tinsel some northern families use for solstice decorations. Ropes of vines hang between them creating a canopy that's every color of the rainbow. You can barely see the sky above it.

"You gotta peach in your pocket or are you just happy to see us?" Whiskey and the rest of the Six approach from the left.

Yaron approaches from the right. "Your Beast Omega is gone."

"What?"

"Fuck. When did she leave?" Adam asks, pulling another peach from the tree. He hands it to me and I gorge myself on it. The flavor is sweet, unlike anything I've ever tasted, even though there isn't much of it. It's smaller than my fist and the dark orange skin is fuzzy and a little wrinkled even though the inside is dense and delicious.

He's watching me again. "What?" I whisper, aware that Yaron is talking even though I can't hear him.

"You got some…" Adam touches my chin, leans in, licks the peach juice dribbling from the corner of my mouth. "Here. Tastes so fuckin' good."

"I know," I say, jerking back from the intimacy of the moment. "I've never had anything like it."

"Wasn't talkin' about the peach."

Yaron clears his throat. "Is this fruit your attempt at a peach?"

I look up at the Berserker and his hot, austere aura and feel a little embarrassed as he reaches for a branch above his head and plucks a fruit from it. The branches rattle. Another peach on another branch falls. His red-cloaked friend or helper or worker or whatever catches it on its way down and throws the whole thing into his mouth. He chews, chews, spits out the core, chews and swallows.

"It's supposed to be," I answer.

"Peaches are plumper than this, rounder and much larger. This is the size of an apricot. The taste is also much too sweet."

I feel my face heat and I can scent Adam's aggression rising, making my thighs squeeze. "I've only seen one peach before and that's what it looked like. Sorry…" I want to drop to my knees and present, but fight it.

Adam's hand slips around the back of my neck and squeezes. "That's enough, Yaron." And then to me, "You apologize to no one. You are the Omega of Dark City." Then again to Yaron, "Freya left?"

"My patrol saw a pack of white wolves escape into Paradise Hole this morning. Based on rumors circulating throughout the camp, it was your Omega."

"She's not his Omega." Realizing what I just said and the hostility with which I spoke, I quickly try to correct it. "She'd be pissed if she heard you say as much."

Adam's hand on my neck has a full-out spasm. His chest rumbles with a deep purr. My legs squeeze tighter. He whispers, "Fuck."

"If you insist on plunging into rut and triggering my aggression, I will be forced to challenge you as a Berserker," Yaron threatens. "I neither covet your Omega, nor do we have time for this. We need to dispose of the bodies and there isn't wood enough to form a pyre from the fallen trees. My Alphas are hesitant to begin cutting fruit-bearing trees in Paradise Hole and I share their sentiment."

"We could…" Adam starts, but I step forward out of his grip, cheeks on fire.

"I can build it." All eyes fall to me. I shrug, feeling nervous, a little rebellious, a little powerful looking out at my garden now. "I can try."

Yaron, who seems to struggle to look at me — maybe, because I'm an Omega and he hates Omegas, or maybe, because it's Alpha protocol not to look at an Omega claimed by another Alpha — finally gives in to the compulsion. He frowns. "Hm. Proceed." He chomps into the peach.

Several hours later, we watch the bodies burn, standing upwind and far enough away from the fire to avoid the smell. It makes my eyes water when I know they should be watering for other reasons. I should feel sad, but all I really feel is strangely proud and deeply honored at the sacrifice they made to come for me and Freya and fight against the undead that defy everything we stand for. They think she's gone, but I know better. I can feel her presence somewhere nearby, lurking in the woods, watching, waiting.

The bodies burn all night and, when I go back to the place the pyre once was, I see a forest has grown. Elevated and wild, the vegetation boasts things I've only seen in my dreams. But I've seen all of them in my dreams.

Humungous green beans the size of an arm with beans that are pink like brains and taste like cornbread. Stalks of blossoming bamboo weighted with flowers that hold big red fruits the color of beating hearts. Apple trees — I know what apples are, that's the only fruit we got in Prayersville — and grape vines. Peach trees above all else.

We have enough to feast without hunting, though some Alphas still do. I'm not able to stop them and Freya doesn't show her face. Her presence doesn't fade either. Not sure what to make of it. I have only hope and a feeling to go by.

On the third day, something else delays our departure as well.

A group of scavengers arrives. They don't even seem nervous about the Alphas surrounding them. Instead, their eyes are orbs, bugging out of their heads, taking in Paradise Hole as I've reimagined it. By the Alphas' best estimates, my little garden stretches about a mile in every direction. And it's still growing.

Adam is close by — he's always close by either making plans or making innocuous conversation. He comes to stand beside me, getting up from the moss-covered log we've been seated on for the past hour just talking and together, we face the scavengers Balcazar and Vi lead to us. He angles his body slightly in front of mine in a way that hurts my heart. I wish he wouldn't. *I'm elated he does.*

"Err, what should we do with 'em, boss?" Vi says.

Adam strokes his beard but, before answering, looks at me. "Do you think they're the scavengers who shot me?"

"That was Trash City."

"No, the other ones."

"Those were trolls."

"What's the difference?"

"The bridges and the backpacks."

He barks out a laugh and I grin in response, unable to forget our shared adventure. Finally, Adam strokes his collar and says to Vi, "You're asking the wrong person. We aren't in Dark City. This is Echo's garden."

"Uh...Echo?" Balcazar jerks her thumb at the men. There are three of them, all Betas, of course. Their clothes are rags. They look malnourished. "Y'all need a place to stay? There's empty rooms in the Dark City castle. You're welcome there." Adam balks behind me and Vi chokes on his next breath.

That choking devolves into a coughing fit, even after Adam claps him brutally on the back. "Until then, you're free to eat anything you find here. It's all up for grabs."

The youngest man is the one to speak. The others just stare slack-jawed. "We…we don't want to move into a city. We like it out here. We just…" He sniffles and rubs his nose with his dirty sleeve. "We just left Trash City and are looking for shelter. It's been wet n' cold." He speaks with a slight Dark City accent, leading me to think he might have been a Beta there, once.

I wonder if Adam thinks the same thing I do, because I'm surprised by what he says next. "Why'd you leave Dark City?"

He doesn't answer, but slinks back behind the two men standing with him. The older one sets his pale hands on the younger man's shoulders. "Alphas took my other son after he ascended as an Alpha. Later, we found him, but the only role that would allow us to stay close was serving his estate. We chose to leave instead."

"You had the choice to stay close to him and you rejected it?" Adam's tone turns sour and I feel my heart pinch on his behalf. He'd have made a different choice if he'd had the option of staying close to his sister. I'm sure he'd have done whatever he had to. "Your pride tore your family apart."

The third of the scavengers stands the meekest and as he speaks, he stares at his feet. "Yes. Maybe. We just…we wanted more than our status."

"You're allowed to want more." I reach forward. I take his dirty hand in my dirty hands and squeeze until he meets my gaze. "Even if it doesn't exist, you're allowed to keep looking. I'm happy to help try to make a shelter for you three out here.

Just know that we won't be staying much longer and when we leave, it might be a dangerous place to stay. More scavengers might come. There could be gangs."

His blue eyes dim and his face falls. The three scavengers share a look, speaking a language all their own.

Adam clears his throat behind me. "If you'd like, I can arrange new roles for you. Something you might like… better," he says through gritted teeth, "but that allows you to remain close to your kin."

Silence. "What kind of roles?"

Adam makes a sound like a horse and when I turn to look at him, he's rubbing a hand over his face and through his hair until it sticks up in several directions. "I don't fuckin' know. What d'you wanna do?"

They're quiet. Meanwhile, I can't stop the smile from claiming my face. Judging by the shocked expressions on Balcazar and Vi's faces, it's clear I'm not the only one surprised by Berserker Dragnovic.

"Look. I don't know how they did it in the old days, but I know that it's possible. Berserker Yaron's Betas don't serve. They're more…integrated. Don't know how, but I'll find out. I promised the woman I love that I'd make changes. So, I'll make changes. Don't want you lookin' anymore. Want you in Dark City," he says to the man — to the three men — even while pink touches his cheeks and his words skewer me. Because I know they're meant for me.

"It's not safe out here. Don't want here to seem like the better option. And you don't like it after six months, I'll think a' somethin' else. Get you safe passage across the Sea of Zaoul so you can settle in Shadowlands. Or better yet, my

Omega'll build a garden outside a' Dark City that's under my protection. A safe space for Betas, just…don't stay here in Paradise Hole. Alright?" He's rubbing his face again and everyone's quiet.

"Damn, Dragnovic." Balcazar whistles.

"What d'you say?" He plants his hands on his hips and glares daggers at the three scavengers who are totally speechless.

"Is this…for real?" the younger one asks.

"It's not a fuckin' joke."

"That is…exceedingly generous. My sons and I would like the opportunity to prove ourselves beyond…" The older man gestures at the dark rags he and his sons are wearing. "This."

"Will. Promise." Adam nods jerkily. "I'll come talk to you in a minute. Until then, Vi, help 'em get set up. Get 'em new clothes, too."

"There aren't many spare sets to go around."

"Just take the spares packed for me."

In a cloud of shock, the Alphas and Betas meander off into the forest. I immediately start off to follow them, but Adam grabs me by the arm and jerks me to his body. He presses his lips to the center of my forehead. They're warm. "Can't fix the world, but can fix my city. Need your help to do it, though."

"I…I told you already, I'm happy to help."

"Means you can't leave. *Don't keep lookin'.*"

And then my treacherous, small voice breaks on a whisper, "Don't leave me behind."

"Won't. Swear it."

"You already swore it once."

"Fuck you, Omega." He grabs me by the neck and tips my head back with the easy pressure of his thumb.

I stare up into his eyes and am betrayed again by my own words. "Why…" I lick my lips.

"Why what?"

"Why have you stopped calling me *wife*?"

I expect him to laugh, to tease or to mock me, but he doesn't. Instead, his expression stays hard and mean. "I'm waitin'," he growls, fingers tightening around my neck.

"For what?"

"For you to call me husband." He releases me and crunches over the forest in his retreat. It's the first time he's ever been the one to put distance between us. He touches the collar at his neck and breathes in a lungful of air that causes his meaty, scarred chest to inflate. I want to present for him. *I miss him.*

"Dragnovic, Echo," Balcazar says, crashing back towards us through the trees. "Another group a' scavengers showed up."

"How many?" Adam says, all business, like I'm the only one struggling.

"Four this time."

"Make 'em the same offer I made the last three. Make any Betas that show up the same offer."

Balcazar shakes her head. "Will do, but thought you might wanna meet 'em."

"Why's that?"

"They're from Trash City."

ADAM
GARDEN OF ECHO

IT'S BEEN FIVE DAYS AND WE'RE STILL HERE SORTIN' through the chaos that is Echo's garden in Paradise Hole. Yaron's gettin' antsy. I'm gettin' antsy. Echo seems to be comin' into her own.

Turns out Trash City ambushed the group a' Dark City Alphas I ordered to stay behind to guard them. The Alphas left behind are dead now, or so the defecting scavengers suppose. They said they signed on to follow Merlin, not to kill Alphas, and managed to escape in the brief scuffle that ensued. Woulda found it fuckin' hilarious that Betas would come to Alphas for protection against another Beta if I hadn't fuckin' met her myself, and if I hadn't lost good Alphas in the process.

Yaron wanted 'em dead, but the information they had proved valuable — and relevant to Yaron. Looks like Merlin is gettin' fuckin' bold. She's expandin' her reach and, accordin' to the scavengers, she's got access to a boat. She's goin' after somethin' on the south island, makin' Yaron's people vulnerable.

"Shadowlands, the city with no walls." I shake my head. "That's why Alphas built walled cities ages ago, cocky bastard." The knowledge that Merlin may be up to somethin' in Shadowlands has derailed our plans. Now, as soon as we leave Echo's garden, he's goin' after 'em. Plans to burn Trash City to the ground and root out any scavengers left in his territory. And I ain't plannin' on stoppin' him.

I shake my dick and tuck it back in my pants, done pissin' off the edge of the garden because I refuse to piss in it, even if it means I gotta sprint a mile to get to its nearest edge.

Echo thinks I'm crazy but she doesn't know how crazy I am about her flowers. I dream in flowers. I only ever dream about one other thing… what it would feel like to hold her trust in my hands one more time, how terrifyin' it would feel knowin' I could lose it so easily…like I have. Like I did. Right now, I hold nothin'. It hurts like hell, but in another sense, it's a relief for a fuck up like me. Nothin's easier to hold onto.

And fuck — what the shit is she doin' out here? Thought I left her back with the scavengers and the Alphas tryna cook food outta one of the weirder vegetables Echo created. Called it a squash, 'cept its purple, grows underground and tastes like a potato. Oh yeah, it's also three fuckin' feet long.

"Echo, hey. Get your ass back here, before I tan it." Red hair gleams between the trees, movin' further outta the garden and further into Paradise Hole. My heart jackhammers. My palms start to sweat. She leavin' me? She said I'd never hold her trust again, or her heart, but she said she'd stay, if for nothin' else than to hold me to my word about the Betas livin' in Dark City and to solve the mystery of Mirage City and their dead Alphas…she…fuck…

Did she change her mind?

I go through everything I did in the past five days that coulda been mistaken by her for somethin' else. Did I fuck her too hard, too rough, too much, not enough? Did I push too hard? Should I have called her wife? I like to think she seemed saddened by the lack, but I want — *need* — her to accept the chain around my neck before I take that leap again. Want her to claim me but *fuck*, maybe she can't. Maybe, there is no redemption and quick fucks and restrained smiles are all I'll get from her for the rest of my lifetime. It's not about me, maybe that's what she needs. Fuck. Every insecurity I got is suddenly etched into the black, wet trees before me. All my confidence I left in the garden at my back.

My boots sink into the earth as I step out of Echo's garden. It gets muddier the further I move. Echo's in black pants and a black sweatshirt — just like she was when I left her. She's runnin'.

I pick up my pace. "Echo, you don't turn around now and get your ass back over here, you won't be able to sit for a fuckin' week…" I'm gainin' on her. "Echo…" The distance between us closin'. "Echo, please!" She leaps. I lunge. My hand clamps down on her arm and she spins down onto one knee.

She looks up at me and I rear back, arm dropping from her shoulder as if burned. She's hot to the touch. This ain't Echo. She wears her hair, but her face is all wrong. Her skin is three shades lighter. Her eyes are bright green. And worse than all these things, she doesn't have any freckles to torture me.

She has a hard gleam in her electric eyes, the color of Echo's leaves. My jaw works, my mind soft and buttery and still trapped in the delusion that Echo was out here leavin' me while my fists hang limp at my sides at the horror of havin' touched another Omega. "Fate…" I whisper. *Earth* Fate, my mind corrects. Echo's opposite, if what the fucker in the cave said is true, which it is, because Echo believes him and I believe in her.

I drop into the ground as the earth opens beneath me and swallows me up to the waist. I start to transform into my Berserker, but pain shatters my mind and I roar at the agony of it. My mind blanks. I see stars, galaxies, new lifetimes. I drift in and out on a scream and when I come to, I look up at the dead grey sky and find myself surrounded.

The Four Fates form a semi-circle around me. Berserker Maengor stands among them. He looks down at me with *nothing* in his gaze — a gaze which I struggle to hold. My own gaze genuflects as I try to push my hands into the ground and lift up, but vines — black vines, thicker than any Echo's ever produced — explode from the soil and slap over my shoulders, coil up my arms, latch onto my neck. Their oily surface is covered in thorns and I can feel my skin tearing beneath them. My venom works through my system, racing to heal me. I can feel it in the frantic tattoo of my heart.

I blink, see a white blur moving behind their legs, keeping low and moving fast. I blink and I see Echo's face behind closed eyelids. I open my eyes and see her hair on a face that has no freckles.

Pain pushes through me and I remember my training. I remember every moment of being tortured. The way they sliced and cut and chewed. "We told you you wouldn't survive this," Adoqhina says, droppin' to a crouch so we're at eye level, her voice a cruel imitation of the one that I want.

"Yeah? Somebody else told me different." I push the pain in my mind into its box and store it in the cabinet where it belongs. It pounds, wanting out, but I don't let it. I meet Maengor's lifeless gaze. "Your dead army is nothing against the united cities. Already, Dark City and Shadowlands fight together. And your Omegas?" I laugh hard and theatrically until my thoughts splinter. "They're nothin'…nothin' against…"

Sy, the Omega with the black hair, releases a horrible screech. Everything goes dark, but not before I hear the sound of roaring behind me.

I come to a moment later, or maybe an hour. The Fates are gathered around Maengor, whispering to him, touching him everywhere that they can like sycophants crowding their idol. His gaze looks more haunted, but the pain has receded for a time. I can feel my Berserker banging on my chest with fangs and claws, trying to get out. I try to transform into my beast's form but the vines are impossibly thick and heavy and the pain is still present, now a pounding ache that radiates up and down my spine. Feels like the heavy hand of a vengeful god has just snapped it. I can't feel *nothin'* below the soil.

Somewhere in the distance, I can hear a fight happening. Who versus who, though? I need to get up and get to Echo. I inhale deep and smell death on the breeze and I know that Maengor and his Fates brought with them more of that dead army, just provin' Freya right. But what are they doin' here? Tryna take my Omega from me while I lie here bein' tortured? For what?

I roar and my hands find claws and my legs begin to swell in the loose, wet soil. It's fuckin' impossible to get outta these vines and outta the dirt, like tryna claw my way outta wet cement, but I fight and don't stop fightin'.

"Move, Omega! Do it! Do it now before he escapes!" Sy's voice is a shriek that spears my brain.

"Sy, compel her," Omora hisses. "Adoqhina, Odette — do not let him escape!"

Adoqhina and Odette, the Omega with the long, thin braids, turn to me and more vines latch onto my skin, but these aren't as strong as the last. I break through them. Wind starts to pick up and a ring of fire blazes to life, surroundin' me, the Fates and Maengor even though it isn't possible because even though there is no wood, there is no kindling and the ground is wet the flames burn hot and their walls rise high, but not so high I can't see over them as a group appears — the last group I'd wanted to see here. My Six, Echo, and the woodland witch.

Echo sees me and meets my gaze. She murmurs something, but I can't read her lips over the chaos running through my veins. Freya transforms, becoming a pack of white bears that shake the earth when they start to charge towards the wall of flames.

A screech splits my remaining concentration and I black out again, comin' to just long enough to see Omora charging forward to meet the bears. The flames part before her, allowing her passage, and as she throws herself past them, she hits the ground on all fours and becomes a black tiger, two at first, then six,then ten. Two a' my Six engage the tigers while Barbero and Vi rush towards me.

The animals and the Alphas tear into each other and the fire starts to flicker and dwindle, its heat makin' me sweat. I claw and scrape at the ground, which is workin' to suck me down and under. It's getting wetter, harder for me to claw through, but slowly, I can feel somethin' start to form underneath my feet — earth or maybe rock, *pushing. Echo's tryna free me.* I bark out a deranged laugh. *That's my girl.*

"That's…my…*wife*," I mutter, the word leavin' my lips and filling me with power. I rip through a vine bindin' my left shoulder and stop it from latchin' onto my neck and breakin' Echo's chain — that, and suffocatin' me to death. A vine shoots over my head and I snatch it outta the air, because I know who it's goin' after.

"Don't fuckin' think on it," I growl.

Adoqhina meets my gaze from within the ring of flames and I can see fire reflected there, burnin' in the green and I hallucinate a vision of Echo's garden set ablaze. She opens her mouth and grunts as she throws her arms forward, vines sproutin' from the ground behind me and goin' for my Six.

The ground tosses once before settlin' on a tremor. Adoqhina grunts and looks over my shoulder at Echo. I'm almost fuckin' free and Echo's got her arm up. The vines stop — literally stop, hangin' suspended in midair — but after a few seconds of impossible tension, they push forward by an inch, and then another, movin' through the air like magnificent snakes covered in shards of black glass.

As the vines push forward, the fire starts cutting a violent path towards Echo. She grunts and lifts her hand. The mud beneath her starts to swell and lift, lappin' at the flames, but if I can see it, the Fates already know it — Echo can't stop the fire and the vines both.

A stream of bright red blood suddenly bursts from her left nostril and her whole body bucks like she's been hit in the back with an arrow. Her hands spasm. I roar out a word that reeks of desperation as the vine plunges towards her. The blur of a body — one a' my Six, Barbero, I think — throws himself in the vine's path. Bloody gashes appear in his side as he takes a hit. He collapses and my Berserker roars a response that's caught somewhere between grief, gratitude and rage.

I tear the last a' the vines holdin' me back free and surge towards Echo — fuck the fire — but the air is suddenly too thick to cut through. I glance over my shoulder and see Odette's got her hands up like she's the one controlling the air and the flames both…

And it pisses me the fuck off.

I redirect and start towards her, fully intendin' to end this shit.

My claws dig the ground deep and I wrench my way forward on all four paws, one painful step at a time. I get closer and closer and closer… I'm within six feet a' her now. Echo musta been wrong about the Berserker of Mirage City because Maengor, the coward, stands just behind Odette, usin' his Fates as a shield like the bastard that he is. He's just starin' at me while the wind whips so fast and so hard I slide to my knees. He's got Sy standin' right beside him speakin' directly into his ear, but I don't bother with them — yet.

Right now, I'm close enough to this Fire and Air Fate to fuckin' wreck her.

I lunge and sink my claws into Odette's stomach. Her eyes roll back. The wind stills. Blood drips down my arm and I feel around for an organ — a good solid one to rip out through her ribs. But just before I can, Omora screams, *"Noon, now!"*

My blood runs cold and in reverse, cities toppling, civilizations long deserted. I withdraw my hand as Maengor sucks in a breath and takes a step towards me. I meet his gaze over the head of the Omega standin' in front of me. Dyin' by my hand. Odette. She falls to the ground.

"Noon, kill him!" Adoqhina echoes, but all I can see are the brown eyes starin' outta a' skull they don't belong to. They're light brown, the left one streaked through with a downward slash a' green. My sister had those same eyes. Shoved into a man's head who's supposed to be immortal, I understand nothin'.

"Noon, it has to be you. You must do this. Kill him. Kill the Berserker!" Sy's voice is shrieking louder now, louder and louder it builds until it bursts.

Maengor closes the distance between us. He lifts his left hand and presses just the tip of his middle finger to the space between my eyes. Lightning cracks down the middle of my body and voices screaming are the last thing I hear before I die.

Sy. *"Noon, he wears your Fated sister's blood on his hands like a glove! He is a malevolent, evil thing! He is a Berserker!"*

And then Echo's tormented shriek, *"He was a Beta too, once."*

THE MIRAGE CITY BERSERKER TOUCHES ADAM AND AS I watch him fall, the soul leaves my body and cymbals clash so loudly, they shatter all of my bones. Pain and Fear emerge from the trees on wings made of warped metal, dripping in Adam's blood. They lunge towards me, but they pause in their tracks, dig their heels into the ground and scramble backwards, halted in their approach by something bigger than they are, more menacing, more destructive, more terrible and terrifying than either or both ever could be, or ever dream of…

Love.

It screams out of me on a word, "Freya!"

She's suddenly at my side, a woman and not a bear. She's got a series of three cuts scoring her chest and she bleeds from all of them. Her face is that of a wild thing. Her eyes are magnificent rings. "We should call for the assistance of the Alpha army your Berserker and his ally…"

"Give me your hand!"

She stutters, looking a little afraid for the first time since I've known her — this time, afraid of *me*. But she obeys my command. She slams her palm into mine and I feel the energy that courses through our bones come together in a mystical and magical combination that no science could ever hope to explain.

I feel the water in the ground. I feel the rain. I open my mouth on a silent scream and energy tunnels out of me and I know what to do next and how to channel it. I shove my free fist into the soil and with my thoughts alone, I pull. I stab down and energy strikes the place where Maengor once stood, knocking him and the dark-haired Omega back and sending Adam's body flying away from them, towards me. The ring of fire dies. Adam's body lands in the mud, motionless. My urge is to go to him, but Freya holds me back.

"She wears his dead skin as a coat." She shakes her head. Her eyes are huge. She tries to scramble back and pull me with her, but I am stone. I grab her wrist and don't let her go. "Not even I can do that. We should run, Echo," she says and it's the first time she's ever called me by my name.

"Never!" I screech and I yank her forward.

I see her cause for alarm as I kick and crawl over the mud, dragging her with me. The Fates have fallen back, but the Berserker still stands and the skin Maengor once wore is just as I glimpsed it in that fleeting moment in the hallway by the bathrooms, right before he touched me and my reality faded. It occurs to me just now that maybe, just maybe, he wasn't trying to warn me away from the cave to deceive me. Maybe, he was trying to warn me away from the cave because he foresaw *this. Adam's death.*

No. Adam lives. *He has to.*

The only dead one here is Maengor himself.

Berserker Maengor doesn't exist. The energy rolling off of the corpse flesh is all Omega and it's more powerful than me, more powerful than Freya, more powerful than all of us.

The skin the Omega wears sloughs off of one shoulder like an old leather sack, stretched and distorted, grey and yellow in all the places it isn't brown. His suit is just as ragged and disintegrates as it begins fluttering to the ground. Something is *moving* underneath the skin and when the other shoulder falls free, I see what Freya did a moment previous.

A *woman* slides one shoulder out of the skin suit and then the other. It pools around her waist and she blinks her eyes open and looks from Adam to me.

"Don't you dare hurt him, Noon. He's still your brother!" I roar.

She's got long, medium brown hair and skin lighter brown than mine, but darker than Adam's. She has the same proud chin Adam has, but otherwise, I can't see anything similar about them. She stares at me. I claw forward, so close to him, separated by half a dozen feet. She wears a black tank top and black leggings and lunges towards Adam, who lies equidistant between us.

"No!" A vine shoots up out of the ground and latches onto her wrist. She looks at me, stunned, but a moment later the vine explodes open, tearing itself to pieces.

"Noon, come on! We need your help with Odette," the Fate with the red hair like mine says. She's the one who manipulates the earth. She's my counterpart. And she's too strong for me. Tears well in my eyes. I reach Adam's body and drag myself across it. I cover him with my own self and lay my head on his chest and I look up at Noon from this position, Freya's wrist lost to my grip as she has sense enough to fight her way free and pull back.

The pale Fate with black streaks in her hair appears at Noon's shoulder. "You did excellently. Come. The Omegas aren't to be touched. We will convert them later once we rid the world of the Berserkers who confuse them and threaten to undo everything we've worked for. Come, Noon. *Come*… Noon!"

But Noon is coming towards me. She has her hands outstretched — both of them, one aiming for Adam, the other for me.

"He still loves you," I tell her.

She touches Adam a second time and when she touches my third eye, I'm already screaming.

Darkness.

35

ECHO

PARADISE HOLE

I WAKE TO THE SIGHT OF FREYA'S FACE. SHE'S GOT blood streaming from her nose down her chin. The blood on her chest hasn't clotted at all. The converging streams mix together between her breasts. She's panting hard.

I breathe.

Sitting up, the world spins around and around. I can feel mud under my ass and the wind on my cheeks. The world feels lifeless compared to how it felt before, in the midst of the battle when I'd been surrounded by so much Omega energy. I can see how easy it would be to get addicted to that kind of power. I can see why the Fates made the choices they did.

And I know in my heart of hearts, I'm going to kill all of them for it.

"Adam!"

Freya rocks back onto her heels and tilts her face up towards the sky. She shakes her head. "He is too far from the shore."

"He isn't." He *isn't*. I know he isn't. "She didn't kill him."

"She did. She tried to kill you both. I don't…I don't understand…She is not a Fate and yet…she is more powerful than any I have encountered." Her lower lip trembles. "Than *me*. She is not meant to be. There are not meant to be Five Fates. We cannot defeat Five with Four, not when Death is on their side…"

"He's her brother!"

I roll up onto my knees and even though I'm shaking like a hollowed out reed, I'm ready. I'm ready… Even if it kills me. He can't die now. Not now. Not yet. "Don't you see? The Mind Omega keeps her under her control. Sister or not, she is one of *them* now."

"No. I saw Noon in there, just like I saw her in there before. *She* tried to warn me about the trap at the cave — about what would happen to Adam. I know it. She broke free. Something triggered her. She's still in there beneath whatever compulsion they've got her under."

I can see Freya's thoughts ticking. I push closer to Adam then scramble so that I'm kneeling with my knees pressed up against him, on his other side. "He dies, we've lost. He's the key to bringing Noon to our side. We *need* him, Freya. This is what the man in the cave meant." It isn't. He meant more. Much more. He spoke of love. But to speak of love between Omega and Berserker will not sway Freya, now. I'll have to sway her with talk of war. "We need *him* to bring them down — to bring her down. We have to try together. There's life here." There has to be.

Freya nods only once and I slam my palm over hers the moment she touches his chest. I feel it — his life force, still in there. I can feel him fighting to cling to it. I can feel Freya's energy working through him, trying to find that life and resurrect it. I can feel Noon in there, too, and I can't decide if she only thought she killed him fully or, with her second touch, she also brought him back.

"Come on, you bastard. Come on," I whisper.

I keep my eyes closed and I remember flowers. I remember growing them. "They're all for you, don't you know? I don't even care about flowers, but I know you like them. I saw you getting all teary eyed the morning after we bonded." I sniffle and laugh. "You're just a big crying asshole."

I bend low and press my ear to his chest. I pray for a heartbeat I don't yet hear. I can feel the presence of Alphas coming near and wonder who of the Six it is, if they all survived their brush with the Fates. I pray that they did, but I'd still give all their lives for Adam's because that's how selfish love is.

"Fuck you, Berserker." I sniffle harder and press harder with my ear and push harder with Freya's hand. I can feel vines starting to form a lattice beneath us, creating a platform between us and the ground, and then grass pushes through all of it and then flowers form on top of that. "I made you peaches, Alphahole."

I sit up and look at Freya's face. Her eyes have rolled back and there's blood running down both her nostrils, just like it's running down mine. The Fates are stronger than we are, even united. But we have to keep trying.

I pour my power through Freya's hand and she opens her mouth. "Yes," she whispers, voice rich with ecstasy. "I can feel you…everywhere…like touching Mother Nature…herself."

I can feel my own limbs shaking, but I still release all the energy I have. I'll fight to the end. "Take it all."

"Ouhhh," she opens her mouth and light pours out of her lips. It's beautiful. It's terrifying.

I feel my own body start to crumble and arch over Adam until I'm prostrated over him, cheek to his chest, staring at his face, his mangy-ass beard and his beautiful pink lips. His eyelashes are long and dark brown and his hair is a tangled mess of brown and blond swirls, like a river, like a current, like vines creating a lattice over the earth.

"I love you," I whisper, pushing myself up only enough to be able to kiss him on the lips. His mouth is frightening in its unresponsiveness. He always responds to me. Always. Even before he knew my name. Tears wet my eyelashes but I refuse to let them fall. I am one knot of hope, of desperation. I can't break apart.

"Husband," I whisper. "If you wake up, I'll marry you. I'll marry you tomorrow, please, just wake up…"

I start to pull back, but a pressure latches around my head and holds me in place. His mouth moves against mine brutally, cuttingly, with every intent to devour. With his eyes still closed, he grins and in a gravelly voice that's rich with pain, he wheezes, "Told you…I'd get you…to call me husband…even if I had to die to do it."

I bark out a hysterical laugh, wild with mania, and bury my face in his neck for an hour. For a second. His collar scratches my cheek as I pull back. "I hate you so, so much." I pound on his chest with the flat of my fist and burst into tears. "And I love you. There was no again, because I never stopped. Will…" I sniffle hard, feeling entirely deranged, undone and put back together with all the same pieces forming entirely new shapes. "Will you marry me, husand?"

His eyes are wet and he's got tears streaking through the mud that covers his face. "Fuck, yes, wife."

36 ECHO
GARDEN OF ECHO

WE GET MARRIED IN PARADISE HOLE TWO DAYS LATER — when Adam can stand on his own and after Freya and I both recover. We get married right there in the orchard I created. Peach trees surround us. A few dozen attendees, valiant warriors fresh off the battlefield, all sit on stumps, bodies broken, looking like they'd rather be anywhere else.

Vi got speared with a vine thrown by the one called Adoqhina.

Sierra got badly burned up her right leg by the Fate called Odette.

Whiskey and Barbero both got badly scratched up by undead Alphas.

Balcazar's doing okay for someone who got chewed up by Omora's pack of tigers. Luckily they didn't carry the toxic venom so, unlike Whiskey and Barbero, she healed faster and fully.

Peate's arm was broken when he successfully protected a pack of Beta scavengers from more undead.

Freya can't shift and still gets bad headaches, which is the only reason she's here at all, otherwise, I'm sure she'd be far away, trying to track down the undead Alphas that scattered when the Fates fled. Her rage and determination to kill the Fates burns hotter than ever but her fear of Noon and Noon's power has helped convince her more than anything that she can't take them all on alone.

Adam's relief at knowing his sister is alive is only just stronger than his guilt. I don't blame him and I don't know how to help except to promise him that there's hope to free her and that I won't stop fighting until she is. *We* won't.

We don't know what she's been through all these years, or even where. We don't know how long Maengor had her, if he ever did. We don't know how long Maengor has been dead for, or how long Noon or another Omega's been wearing his skin. So many questions still unanswered, but we will answer them. We will go after her, kill the other Omegas and, despite Freya's insistence to the contrary, return the Omega with dominion over death to the land of the living.

The scent of burning bodies floats intermittently past. The sound of Yaron chopping dead bodies into itty bitty pieces also sounds in the distance. He didn't want to attend and that's fine. No one does but me and Adam, the Six and the scavengers that survived the battle. I'm proud of the Alphas who fought hard for them. I'm proud that they fought for themselves, too.

"Do you, Berserker Dragnovic — "

"It's Adam."

"Adam," a Beta scavenger repeats. He holds an open book in his hands, but it isn't a Bible. It's just a dogeared paperback that's so badly stained it's illegible. I'm just amazed he agreed to do this.

"Stop interrupting," I say with a smile. My belted, oversized white tee shirt is hardly white, but Adam still looks at me like he'd like nothing more than to rip it off. I wear a crown of flowers on my head. He wears one, too.

He bites his bottom lip and shakes his head, then looks back at the Beta. "Continue. *Faster.*" With death on the breeze and flowers under our feet, we hold hands and grin madly at one another.

"Oh, uhh… yeah, right. Berserker Adam, do you take Omega Echo for your lawfully wedded um…Omega?"

"Yes. Definitely, a thousand times over."

"Only a thousand?" I tease, one eyebrow lifted.

"A fuckton."

I laugh. Several others laugh in the crowd. Vi tries, but the hole in his left leg makes it hard. He wheezes. Actually, most people are caught somewhere between pained groans and laughter. Adam's barely standing.

I'm barely standing.

My stomach hurts. My head hurts. My arms and legs are shaking. Going up against the Omega whose powers matched my own — as well as all the rest — was agonizing. But I'd do it again. I *will* do it again.

"And Fallen Omega Echo, do you take Berserker Adam for your lawfully wedded husband, to have and to hold, to protect and to cherish…"

"To hate and to love?" Adam finishes for him.

I smile cautiously up at the Berserker I love most in this world, the one I'd fight for against Omegas and Alphas and gangs and trolls and legions of zombies and Fear and Pain. "I do. And I vow that I'll never hate anybody like I hate you."

He gulps and ducks his head to meet mine. He slips a single finger beneath my chin and tips my head back and up. "Not what I wanna hear, Omega."

I watch the hope and fear dance in his eyes while a mirrored hope and fear dance in my chest. No longer Fear, but fear. She is faceless in the presence of something greater than herself, greater than Pain, and more magnificent than love…no. Just as magnificent.

Courage.

I smile more fully while the breeze carries scents of death and peaches to my nose and I exhale. I exhale it all. All the pain and rage and fear and hate that I've held onto for so long. "It's time," I whisper. I reach up to the vines around his neck and, with my fingers alone, I break them. "I trust you, Adam." I let the collar of vines fall to the ground, lost. "Please don't break my heart."

Adam's expression changes so quickly, I don't manage to catch every nuance. Only the elation shines through, the laughter, the awe. He grabs me around the waist and slams his chest to mine in something too brutal to call a hug. He sways side to side and buries his face in my hair. Against my neck, against the scars that still linger there from the bite marks that brought us together, he says, "I will never try to possess you, 'cuz you are your own. I will never try to own you 'cuz you are free. When you brought me back to life I understood that better'n I ever have. I also learned that if you're willin' to fight death for me, I gotta be worthy a' somethin'. And if I'm worthy a' somethin', why can't it be you?" He kisses my neck tenderly and softens his touch in a way that brings tears to my eyes. "I love you, wife, and I vow to protect and cherish the trust you have in me."

I squeeze his neck hard. And then harder. "I love you, husband."

The Beta awkwardly clears his throat. "So, I guess, you may now kiss your…"

"Out! All of you out!" Adam roars at the impromptu officiant and the forty or so half-wounded attendees who came out to witness our weird, wounded love heal.

"All of you, get the fuck away from here unless you wanna watch a fuckin' show." Groans rise up as the crowd attempts to disperse, though they move so incredibly slowly. Far too slowly. I'm hurt, but not hurt enough to stop this. "Had a dream last night I fucked my wife under a peach tree."

"Aren't you a little too injured to be fucking your wife anywhere?" I laugh.

"Hurt, not dead. But if this kills me, so be it. Know a couple a' Omegas who can bring me back."

"Not funny," I deadpan.

"It's kinda funny…" He sweeps his hand through my hair and leans down, presses his lips tenderly to mine. "Don't worry. I'm not going anywhere you aren't." The taste of him runs through me like a current that I feel to the tips of my toes as he lowers me down to a bed of flowers, beneath which I can feel the tendrils of the earth moving, so connected to me now.

A shard of sunlight peeks in through the grey clouds over his shoulder and birds chirp from the tops of funeral pyres and peach trees as we come together, his lips worshipping my scars, my hand pressed to the X across his heart.

A THANKS FROM THE AUTHOR

Thank you for joining Echo and Adam in Dark City!

For early access to teasers and trailers of the four books to come in the Berserker Kings series, as well as any special editions and SFW/NSFW artwork that may crop up, sign up to my reader list at www.booksbyelizabeth.com.

You can also follow me on social media :
TikTok @elizabethstephensauthor
Instagram @estephensauthor

And keep reading for an exclusive sneak peek of Shadowlands Omega to meet the Omega who will bring Lord Yaron to his knees…

He's such a good boy.

[Shadowlands Omega temporary cover]

THERE'S A SCREAM FROM UP AHEAD WHERE ORANGE light glows from an opening in the wall. In front of it, an iron gate hangs open. I approach the dungeons, terrified and unable to stop my teeth from clacking. Squeezing a hand over my mouth, I shudder and hiss out every breath, sure that they can hear me. That someone can hear me. That he can.

Cold cuts through the soles of my feet and wraps its hands around my calves like an invisible force, opposite that of the tugging in my chest as this one is trying to slow me down. I falter, but the next scream is one I recognize. Zelie. And then my father's voice, "Hush now, Zelie. It's going to be alright."

"It isn't." Yaron. His voice is unmistakable and I drop into as small a ball as possible just on the outside of the opening, cowering in the shadow of the prison bars.

"But she's…they're just girls," my father yells.

The rattle of chains, the hard whack of something hard against something softer. A grunt of pain… "You're right," comes the low rumble, "just like the sixteen-year-old Alpha girl you murdered."

Murdered? Is that what this is about? The Alpha corpses in the basement? No. No, my father didn't murder them. Yaron's wrong. He must have confused my father with someone else…

But my father says nothing. Hazarding what's sure to be a death sentence, I cross in front of the opening and huddle in front of the gate. No one saw me. There wasn't anyone there. Just a short hallway. My left calf is shaking, the muscle inside jerking with tiny tremors that I don't seem to be able to do anything about. Just as little as I can control the ragged breath tearing in and out of my lungs. It tastes of smoke. *It tastes of shame. Yaron is known to be a good lord. He wouldn't make this up. He must be mistaken. Why doesn't my father say anything?*

"We didn't know. And…and the girls had no…no part in it." It takes me a moment to ideentify my mother's voice, I've never heard it so tortured. Terrified. She's frightened.

Owenna speaks when my mother doesn't, "We were only preparing the bodies for transport. We were promised that they were already dead. We didn't kill anybody."

"Do not make the mistake of thinking that because you are fools, I am equally foolish. The girl had her throat slit, the mother had been gutted and the father had been poisoned. Alphas. In their homes. Neighbors to you, separated by a town's distance. They were merchants. You likely traded your bread with them at a point." Yaron's voice rises to a deadly crescendo, made my terrifying by the fact that he doesn't yell. He booms.

"We swear we didn't know. We didn't know...please, m'Lord. Please..." Another thwack. Owenna screams.

My mother shouts, "Don't hurt my daughter!" Another thwack. Tears spring to my eyes. My hand is shaking against my lips. I don't hear the scream, so I don't know who was hit, but I know that whoever it was, they're my family. I don't know why I wasn't locked in with them. But I do... Omega.

"Baba, say something!" Cyprus yells. "Tell him that he mixed you up with someone else. Tell him that it's not true, that you didn't kill anybody..."

There's a long, weighted pause. Yaron fills it. "Go on. Say the words. We both know that they are meaningless."

"He..." My father sucks in a shaky, broken breath. "He's right. We...I... When the bodies were brought to us, we were told that they died of natural causes, but we...I saw the marks. Their throats had been slashed and I...didn't ask any questions. What Trash City was offering was too good to refuse. I deserve this. I do. But don't punish my family for my crimes, m'Lord. I beg of you."

"Daddy..." Zelie whimpers. I can tell she's crying. I start to cry, too.

"Mom?" comes another broken whisper and my ears flex forward. The voice is Audet's. No. She's here, too? I had hope, albeit a flimsy one, that she might have escaped.

"Please, m'Lord," Mama says.

There's a hush, disrupted only by my family's loud breathing. Mine, too. The tension in the quiet hall feels stifling, the air cold as a crypt, while inside, I feel myself roasting alive. My hands are shaking. I want to will more fire, but I don't know how and I don't know what I'd even intend to do with it? Burn Lord Yaron? Or kill my own kin on accident? I have to do something.

"Bring Trash City forward."

I feel like I'm going to pee myself as I hazard a glance around the edge of the wall, but there's still no one there. I can't see around the bend where, positioned in the corner, sits an empty guard table. I could...I could go to it. I could get closer.

The scraping of chains and the struggle of either a body or bodies spurs me to move, even though it's hard. It's so hard. It's now or never. Use the distraction to get closer. And do what? I don't know. Not even as I scrabble forward, dragging myself and my blanket with me, feeling as clumps of my hair are left behind along with the tattered clumps of my confidence.

A woman screams just as I duck under the ratty rattan tablecloth and slip under the guard's table. The itchy rags stacked beneath it block me from view. They're damp and smell like...no. I don't care to think what they smell like.

"What did you offer them?" Yaron says, voice as emotionless as I imagine an angel of God's to be. Doling out punishments to the wicked with imperious imperviousness. He does not care about us, because he cannot feel.

"Money," a voice answers immediately — it's a voice I don't recognize.

"How much?"

"Fifty pieces of silver."

"Fifty pieces of silver. And this was the value you assigned to three lives?"

Someone chokes on a sob and it isn't the woman who answered before. Her voice was hard and desperate and deep, but it was also stained in an accent I can't place.

Another thwack. My father shrieks, "Yes!"

Though I know I shouldn't, I push the piss and shit and blood-soaked blankets down just enough that I can see past them into the room. The dungeon. I can't see much, not without revealing more of myself than I'm willing to. I can't see my family, who must be on the floor. I can only see Yaron, two members of his guard, and the woman hanging by her wrists from the ceiling.

She has white skin, white-blonde hair that's standing up on end, and the strange outline of a tan on the bottom half of her face, like she must have been wearing goggles or something. Maybe, she's a mechanic. Her clothes would speak to that, all ragged and patchwork as they are. They're also made out of a grey synthetic material not seen in Shadowlands, where we wear mostly linen and sometimes cotton.

Yaron pivots back to face her and I shrink down, afraid for her even though we've never met. "Where did you get fifty silvers?"

"You already know who gave them to me," she sneers. "If you think I'll speak the words out loud and risk their wrath, then you're somethin' else."

He pauses for a long time. I don't like how long he pauses. Clearly the woman doesn't either, because she clenches her jaw and begins to writhe. "Have you seen their labs?"

"Labs?" She balks. "I'm just the messenger. Don't shoot the messenger, Berserker."

"You are no messenger. You're a courier. I want to know where you take the bodies and who picks them up. If you tell me the location, I won't burn you alive."

She laughs — cackles — the sound so full of feeling it makes my bare toes curl into the damp stone beneath me. "I'd rather roast then whatever they got in store for me. I betray them, I'll be turned into one of the undead. Would rather die."

"I admire you." Yaron reaches to the left. One of his guards hands him a torch and he takes it blindly while another begins to move around the blonde, dousing her in foul-smelling fluid. "The doomed rarely rarely realize that they are and almost never so quickly. I should hope that, when faced with a similar circumstance from which I know already there is no other end, I should be smart enough to see it."

She starts to thrash. My blood threatens to burst from my veins. I clamp my hand over my mouth and pray to God that I don't scream. I can't watch this. I can't watch this...but I can't look away, either. Do something. I don't know what. I don't know how. I flex my hands as tension fires through the joints, making it hard to bend my fingers. My knuckle joints all feel swollen. I wipe my forehead with the inside of my wrist and it comes back wet. I'm sweating badly and shaking like I'm made out of marbles.

"Wait...wait! Fuck! Berserker, I said waitgodfuckingdammit!" She's fighting now, trying to kick out at him and the torch in his hand. "I'll tell you! I'm supposed to bring the Alpha bodies to the Golden Delta. Once every month. That's the arrangement."

He tips the flame towards her legs. "In exchange for what?"

"Guns. Money. Food. The good shit you've denied us." Her voice drops in tone and she spits, the bloody wad hitting Yaron in the face. "The chance to fight back and kill you oppressive Alpha fucks."

He pulls a kerchief from his pocket and nods solemnly. "Betas are not oppressed here."

"You're lying to yourself if you think that. All of you Alpha bastards are! And the time of reckoning has come. They're going to kill you. They're going to kill all of you and I'm going to dance on your fucking grave when they're done."

"Your opinion is noted." He thrusts his torch forward and she releases a scream that petrifies me to the marrow. My legs jerk, my head hitting the underside of the table. Her gaze flicks over to me and I'm grateful that hers is the only one. Our eyes meet and my hand snatches at the air without me having to tell it and the fire in Yaron's hand goes out.

She shrieks as hot ash presses to the outside of her tunic, melting it. When Yaron pulls it back, strings of fabric *and flesh* hang strung between the torch and her belly. My hand over my mouth is shaking violently as I watch him lift the torch high up to the light and then cast it aside.

"My Lord, here's another," his guard offers.

He ignores her. "Did you feel that?"

"I felt the breeze."

A low growl peels out of Yaron's throat that causes my lower belly to clench and my thighs to pulse. Lust courses through me, but only because the Omega impulse is meant to respond to strength and cannot apparently see what I see. I rub my extended hand down my face and wipe away sweat and tears. Yaron turns abruptly and I duck beneath the blankets and freeze.

"The Omega is awake. And she is active." Heels slam against stone. "With me. Leave the others. Perhaps, some time weighing the reality of their situation will cause these murderers to consider whether this was all really worth fifty silvers and a pitiable excuse for revenge."

His footsteps pass so close to me, I actually do pee a little. With my blanket pulled up over my back, I sit hunched over into as small a ball as possible and I wait, wait until I hear three, or is it four? Five? Sets of boots retreat and the heavy iron grate creak closed before it's finally shut with a lock.

The footsteps fade and I panic, knowing I don't have much time before they discover I'm gone. I wonder if they'll think I ran out the front door of the castle, wherever that is. I hope it's what they think. They can't possibly assume I'm so stupid as to walk *willingly* into the dungeon where Yaron just tried to burn a woman alive.

"You can come out. They're gone," the woman croaks. I slide out from under the table and stagger forward, tripping over the edge of my blanket a dozen times.

"Kiandah!" My brother and Zelie say at the same time. I go to my brother first, even though the second I veer away from the dangling woman, she starts to whisper-scream at me.

"Get me down from here! You idiot! He's going to kill me!"

I ignore her and drop down in front of my brother's feet. His fingers are moving desperately over the heavy metal ring around his neck. "I think if you can get the bolts hot enough where they go into the rock, I can break them or…or pull them out."

I nod, hands already outstretched, fingertips flaring as I press my palms flat to the metal, not caring that my blanket falls around my waist as I work. The metal bracket goes from black to red in moments.

"Oh…okay. Try now." Cyprus curls up into a crouch, grabs hold of his collar and charges forward. His strength shocks me and I flinch as the bolts explode free of the wall. He staggers as he reaches the middle of the room, dragging the entire length of the chain with him. Landing hard on his shins, he's panting as he rises to stand. His pants are all singed and his tee shirt is hanging off of his right shoulder, decorated in drops of blood. The left side is completely torn, vertical slashes scoring it made by what look like might, just maybe be claws. But he's not bleeding underneath. He's not burned, either. *Alpha.*

"Alright. Alright, let's uh…let's do the others," he says.

I nod and he joins me at Zelie's chain. "One, two," he whispers.

"Three," I manage to say with him. My hands on the wall, his on the chain, one leg braced against the stone. He pulls as I give him the go ahead and, together, we break Zelie free. We do the same for the rest of my family and I don't dare look at them or their injuries as we work. I don't see the blood. I can't see the blood.

By the time we've finished unchaining my dad, Zelie, Owenna, Audet and my mom are already gathered in the middle of the floor. "Here!" Audet says, "come help us with this."

I rush over and see that they've gathered around a trap door. One that's latched and barred shut but that's made of wood, not metal. "Okay. I can do this. Get back," I tell them. They obey and together, we all watch in fascination and wonder as my hands produce sentient flame and I incinerate the door around the metal latches.

I stare down into the darkness, knowing that it's one place I cannot go. "It…it should be enough for you to squeeze through."

"It'll have to be," my father says. He leans further down, but lurches back up just as quickly. His large hand covers his mouth and nose. "Zelie, take this." He takes off his shirt and starts tearing it into strips. "Tie it around your face."

I understand what he's doing the moment I take my next breath — my first breath in minutes. "No." I lurch up, gathering my blanket to my chest and wrapping it firmly around me.

"Zelie, go on."

"You want me to go down there?" She squeaks, staring down into the void. "I think I see dead bodies."

"There aren't bodies floating there. There wouldn't be. The water is rushing. It'll take us out of the castle," Owenna says, shimmying past her into the cubicle of darkness, a wrapped cloth around her nose and mouth. "We have to go now." And then she let's go, plummeting into the below.

A moment of silence, and then a splash, and then Owenna's voice. "I'm fine!"

"Zelie, go!"

Zelie goes next, followed by my mom. My dad looks at me and offers his hand. I shake my head. His brows draw together in cold fury. "We don't have time for your games."

My fear of the dark isn't a game, but I understand that my dad doesn't see it like that. "I need to help her," I say, pointing to the woman who's been screaming at us this whole time. "I'll come right after."

"Kia, we don't have time for this!"

"I can't leave her."

"You must! She's the reason we're in this mess, anyway."

A shiver shakes up my spine. I shake my head. "No. She only offered the silver. You accepted. You and mom and Owenna did this to us." I sniff hard and a look of pure, blistering grief crosses my dad's weathered face.

"Kia… I…" But his voice breaks.

"Go, dad. I'll help her and make sure she comes," Cyprus says, moving past me swiftly and heading to the wall behind the blonde woman's dangling body. "Go!" He rasps when my dad still does nothing.

I turn my back on my father and follow Cyprus to the wall. Halfway through heating the bolts, I hear a splash and I shiver all over again. We manage to free her, but her restraints aren't as easy as the others. Instead, her chain is looped through a metal ring in the ceiling and the long end of her chain where the bolts were plugged in is too large to feed through it.

Cyprus reaches up and pulls, ripping the ring from its post. "Thanks," the woman mutters with what sounds like blood *sarcasm* as she drops to her feet, leaning heavily on my shoulder for support. She ambles towards the drain, looping the chain around her as she walks. It's long. I don't want to bet on her odds, injured and weighted down as she is, once she makes it to the river. But she walks with confidence and doesn't stop. She drops into the hole without looking back.

The moment she disappears Cyprus yanks me to his chest and balls me up into a hug so deep and overwhelming, tears sting my eyes immediately. "Are you sure?" He says.

I nod against his tee shirt. It smells like smoke. It smells like him.

"You can make fire now. You don't need to be scared."

"I can't make fire in a river."

He hugs me harder before pulling back, the gap between us feeling like a chasm more than an arm's length. "Don't die."

"I...Lord Yaron doesn't kill Omegas."

"But he could hurt you. Don't let him hurt you. Fight, if you have to. Never stop fighting."

I nod, wondering how his eyes could appear so green and mine, so black. "Protect the others."

"I will."

"Now, go."

"You, too. Get out of the castle. You have enough friends, you can get through the City. Once you do, head to the forest and meet us where the heart trees grow."

I wince, knowing it won't be easy to get there. Not alone. Not without help. And even if I do make it that deep into Paradise Hole I don't stand a chance against Trolls and blood vines are poisonous to the touch.

I don't say any of that. "I will."

He leans in and sweeps a kiss over my temple in a way he hasn't done in a long time, not since my older sisters locked me in a toy chest and my fear of the dark began. As he pulls back, his full lips cock up into a surprising, yet familiar, smirk. His gaze jerks up and he says, "You look funny bald."

I snort on my next laugh and I'm still smiling as I shove him through the hole and watch my twin, my other half disappear. Strangely, as he vanishes, the tugging in my chest doesn't loosen. If anything, it tugs harder, filling me with a calming, soothing presence that makes it easier for me to move — run — towards the exit.

I'll have to come up with a plan for the gate, but I think I might be able to melt two vertical bars and possibly squeeze through, or under them…

I bump into the guard's table and lurch around the next turn. "Oomph." I crash into something hard and warm and big and I keep crashing as I stagger back because it's coming towards me and *it* has a name and that name is Berserker Yaron and he doesn't look pleased as his hawkish gaze flickers past me and takes in the hole in the floor and the empty spaces along the wall where there once were prisoners in chains.

"What have you done?"

I keep backing away from him, heading towards the wall, fear pounding in my veins as I wonder if it wasn't a better idea to take the plunge. "I…m'Lord," I whisper.

His hand lifts and I watch the back of his palm whip towards me. I try to duck to avoid being struck, but I get caught in my blanket. He strikes my cheek and I land hard against stone, unable to decide what hurts worst, if anything does at all. My fear makes something as inconsequential as pain all but irrelevant.

I look up and see him flexing his hand over and over. He's staring down, tone icy as he speaks to the guards flanking him. "String her up."

PREORDER SHADOWLANDS OMEGA TODAY.

SERIES STARTERS

LORD OF POPULATION (BOOK 1)

Looting the dead alien's corpse seemed like a good idea at the time, until he comes after her — very much alive. When he catches her, Abel's got a choice to make: accept Kane's help or die. But as they cross the hostile post-apocalyptic landscape together, Abel begins to realize that Kane may want more than a temporary alliance, but her body, her blood, and her heart — to keep.

TAKEN TO VORAXIA (BOOK 1)

Every three years, aliens come to hunt the most beautiful women of their small, derelict human colony. Miari's managed to escape notice to now, but this year, the alien king has her in his sight. Raku wants her, and not just once, but for life.

THE HUNTING TOWN (BOOK 1)

Mer is new to town and on a mission — one that does not involve getting involved with local small town boxer, Knox. Knox has never been known to back down from a fight. But getting involved with Mer turns out to be more challenging than saving her battered heart. The nefarious underworld of the city they live in has Mer shackled, and she might also need him to save her life.

ALL BOOKS BY ELIZABETH

BERSERKER KINGS - ENEMIES TO LOVERS. WITH MAGIC.

Dark City Omega, Book 1 (Echo and Adam)

Shadowlands Omega, Book 2 (Kiandah and Yaron)

more to come!

POPULATION - BATTLES AND HEROES THAT BITE.

Lord of Population, Book 1 (Abel and Kane)

Monster in the Oasis, Book 2 (Diego and Pia)

Immortal with Scars, Book 3 (Lahve and Candy)

more to come!

TWISTED FATES - MAFIA. BROTHERHOOD. MURDER.

The Hunting Town, Book 1 (Knox and Mer, Dixon and Sara)

The Hunted Rise, Book 2 (Aiden and Alina, Gavriil and Ify)

more to come!

XIVERI MATES - ALIENS. HEAT. NEW WORLDS.

Taken to Voraxia, Book 1 (Miari and Raku)

Taken to Nobu, Book 2 (Kiki and Va'Raku)

Exiled from Nobu, Book 2.5, a Novella (Lisbel and Jaxal)

Taken to Sasor, Book 3 (Mian and Neheyuu) *standalone

Taken to Heimo, Book 4 (Svera and Krisxox)

Taken to Kor, Book 5 (Deena and Rhork)

Taken to Lemora, Book 6 (Essmira and Raingar)

Taken by the Pikosa Warlord, Book 7 (Halima and Ero) *standalone

Taken to Evernor, Book 8 (Nalia and Herannathon)

Taken to Sky, Book 9 (Ashmara and Jerrock)

Taken to Revatu, Book 10, A Novella (Latanya and Grizz) *standalone

series complete!

⚘ AUDIO

XIVERI MATES - ALIENS. HEAT. NEW WORLDS.

Taken to Voraxia, Book 1 (Miari and Raku)

Taken to Nobu, Book 2 (Kiki and Va'Raku)

Taken to Sasor, Book 3 (Mian and Neheyuu) *standalone

more to come!

⚘ COLLECTIONS

XIVERI MATES - ALIENS. HEAT. NEW WORLDS.

Collection 1: Books 1-3 + Exiled from Nobu

more to come!

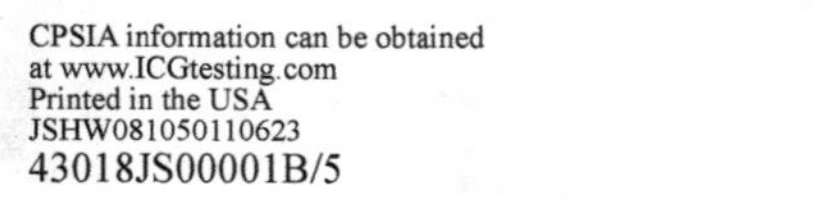

CPSIA information can be obtained
at www.ICGtesting.com
Printed in the USA
JSHW081050110623
43018JS00001B/5

9 781954 244238